All She Wants

A Blazing Collection

VICKI LEWIS THOMPSON

KATE HOFFMANN

KATHLEEN O'REILLY

MILLS & BOON

CONTENTS

Rolling Like Thunder

Vicki Lewis Thompson

A passion for travel has taken *New York Times* bestselling author **Vicki Lewis Thompson** to Europe, Great Britain, the Greek isles, Australia and New Zealand. She's visited most of North America and has her eye on South America's rainforests. Africa, India and China beckon. But her first love is her home state of Arizona, with its deserts, mountains, sunsets and—last but not least—cowboys! The wide-open spaces and heroes on horseback influence everything she writes. Connect with her at vickilewisthompson.com, facebook.com/vickilewisthompson and twitter.com/vickilthompson.

Books by Vicki Lewis Thompson

Sons of Chance

Should've Been a Cowboy
Cowboy Up
Cowboys Like Us
Long Road Home
Lead Me Home
Feels Like Home
I Cross My Heart
Wild at Heart
The Heart Won't Lie
Cowboys & Angels
Riding High
Riding Hard
Riding Home
A Last Chance Christmas

Thunder Mountain Brotherhood

Midnight Thunder
Thunderstruck

All backlist available in ebook format.

Visit the Author Profile page at millsandboon.com.au for more titles.

Dear Reader,

As a card-carrying member of Workaholics Anonymous, I completely identify with Finn O'Roarke. He brews beer for a living and I write stories, but we're from the same tribe. We get a whole lot accomplished, but we can't seem to locate the off switch.

Because of that, I loved hauling Finn from his microbrewery in Seattle to his cowboy roots in Wyoming so he could rediscover the simple joys of ranch life and maybe even allow himself to fall in love. The core values he learned as a foster kid at Thunder Mountain Ranch might be the very things that save him from himself.

And for those of you who loved my Sons of Chance series, I have a treat for you in this book. You'll get to revisit the Last Chance Ranch and catch up with some of your old friends. I promised that the Thunder Mountain Brotherhood series would intersect with the Sons of Chance series here and there, and this is one of those times!

So grab a cool drink and a shady spot because I have plenty to tell you and you won't want to miss a single thing. You especially won't want to miss the moment when Finn realizes it's time to cowboy up!

Your devoted storyteller,

Vicki Lewis Thompson

To Wendy Delaney, fellow author and awesome Seattle friend. If O'Roarke's Brewhouse existed, we'd meet there for a drink!

1

FINN O'ROARKE SCANNED the boarding area for the umpteenth time. First class was already on the plane and still no Chelsea. He would have gladly picked her up instead of meeting her here, but they hadn't been able to agree on timing. He preferred early and she liked to cut it close.

Too damned close. Good thing he didn't fly with her on a regular basis, because this kind of thing would drive him...ah! There she was. He exhaled and promised himself not to say a word. She was doing him a favor by making this trip.

With a roller bag behind her and a laptop case over her shoulder, she walked toward the boarding area with her typical "I have the world by the tail" stride. She wasn't tall but she dressed tall—skinny black jeans, high-heeled sandals and a multicolored tunic belted around her hips. Her light blond hair, recently streaked with lavender, swayed gently with each confident step.

As she came closer, she surveyed the crowd waiting near the Jetway and her brown eyes widened when she spotted him. She hurried over. "Holy smokes, you're dressed like a cowboy! I did not expect that."

At one time Finn would have been annoyed. But after owning a Seattle microbrewery and tavern for nearly five years, he didn't think of himself as a cowboy anymore. He couldn't very well expect her to think of him that way, either.

But they'd be spending time at the Last Chance Ranch in Jackson Hole this weekend. Finn had never seen it, but he'd heard plenty of stories. The Chance family was royalty in Wyoming.

So he'd hauled out his dove-gray Stetson, his yoked Western shirts, his Wranglers and his black boots. He gazed at Chelsea and shrugged. "We're making our presentation to ranch people. It seemed like a good idea."

"Should I have done that, too? If so, I'm screwed. I have these sandals and gym shoes. That's it."

"No worries, Chels. You'll be fine." He thought she looked more than fine. He'd known from the moment they'd met in a coffee shop five years ago that she was too cool and stylish for him.

But meeting her had been a gift. She was a PR and marketing whiz. After listening to his plan for a microbrewery and tavern in downtown Seattle, she'd suggested a Kickstarter crowdfunding campaign to renovate an old building slated for demolition. Then she'd offered to help him for a percentage. He'd saved the building and launched O'Roarke's Brewhouse thanks to Chelsea Trask.

This trip would put him even more in her debt. His foster parents, Herb and Rosie Padgett, were in financial trouble and could lose the ranch where Finn and many other homeless boys had found refuge. A group of them were trying to save it, and because Chelsea knew Finn's background and admired the Padgetts, she'd agreed to help him once again.

Thanks to Chelsea, a Kickstarter campaign had been launched in June for Thunder Mountain Academy, a residential equine education program geared toward teens. But the September 1 deadline for donations was less than two weeks away and they were thousands shy of the goal. Everybody connected with it, including Finn, had begun to panic.

This weekend was make-or-break time. Cade Gallagher, once a foster boy and one of Finn's best friends, had recently discovered he was a Chance cousin. Because of that family tie, Finn and Chelsea had been invited to pitch the concept to potential TMA backers at a gathering hosted by the Chances. Chelsea was the pro, so she'd run the event, but Finn would also talk about the debt he owed Thunder Mountain Ranch.

As the first economy-class group was called to board the plane, Chelsea gave Finn another once-over. "It's probably good that you're all decked out like that."

"I'm glad you approve." He decided not to let the "all decked out" comment bother him, either. Coming from Chelsea, that was a relatively mild dig. When she was wound up, she could really turn on the snark. She'd been irritated with him for months, which made working together on this project somewhat awkward.

Apparently she'd expected them to get together after his divorce from Alison last year, but she, of all people, should have realized that he was married to his business, which was why Alison had left. Yeah, he'd had his share of hot dreams starring Chelsea, but he had no intention of turning them into reality.

Guaranteed if they got together, it'd disrupt his careful routine right when he needed to concentrate all his energy on keeping the microbrewery solvent. The divorce had been expensive. Besides, he'd proved himself incapable of running a business and maintaining a relationship. He'd told her that when he'd turned down her dinner invitation, but she hadn't taken it well.

Because they'd bought their plane tickets late, they'd be in the last group to board, so she had time to study him. "I remember the hat and boots from when we did the photo shoot for the Men of Thunder Mountain calendar, but that was a deliberate beefcake shirtless shot. This is more subtle, but effective."

"Effective for what?" He'd suffered through the photo session last month because some genius had decided Thunder Mountain Academy needed a calendar as a giveaway to backers. Chelsea had volunteered to take his picture rather than having him waste time flying to Wyoming.

"Image." She gave him another assessing glance. "While my PowerPoint presentation is running, you can stand there looking like a guy who can ride and rope with the best of them—all the things they plan to teach students at Thunder Mountain Academy."

Okay, he couldn't let that go. "As it happens, I *can* ride and rope. Maybe not with the best of them anymore because I'm out of practice, but I'd be decent."

"I'm sure you would." Her gaze warmed briefly before she broke eye contact. "Hey, that's us." She waved her boarding pass. "Time to rock and roll."

"Right." She'd captured his attention so completely that he'd missed the announcement. Perfect example of how she distracted him. Adjusting the shoulder strap of his laptop case and grasping the handle of his wheeled bag, he followed her.

Chelsea could sure stir him up. Now he had the adolescent urge to actually do some riding and roping on this trip just to prove to her that he could. Not at the Last Chance, of course, but they'd planned to drive over to Thunder Mountain Ranch for a few days afterward so she could look over the setup for TMA.

After all the work she'd put into nurturing the idea and giving advice—all gratis—she deserved to see the ranch and meet his foster parents. They were eager to meet her, too. He wondered if she rode. He'd never asked.

As they entered the plane a blonde flight attendant smiled at him. "Great hat."

"Thank you, ma'am." He was out of the habit of using *ma'am*, but he'd unconsciously lapsed into it.

"I'd be glad to store it up front for you."

"That would be great." He took it off and handed it to her.

"My pleasure." She gave him another brilliant smile. "I'll take good care of it."

"I surely appreciate that." Yep. He was back to talking like a cowboy.

By the time he caught up with Chelsea, she was struggling to get her roller bag into the overhead compartment, so he helped her. She muttered her thanks and he slid his own in next to it before taking his seat.

The plane was configured with two seats on one side of the aisle and three on the other, and Chelsea had managed to snag the two-seat side when she'd made their reservations. She'd requested the window, which was fine with him because he preferred the aisle.

Once they were buckled in, she turned to him. "'Thank you, ma'am'?"

"I swear it's the hat. I put it on and my words come out different."

"You wore it for the photo shoot and I didn't notice you calling me ma'am."

He laughed. "That's because you were torturing me by making me hold a beer keg on my bare shoulder for hours on end."

"Minutes, O'Roarke. Mere minutes. You were such a baby about that shoot."

"It was embarrassing, posing shirtless and knowing come April I'll be tacked up on someone's wall."

"That reminds me... I brought calendars."

He groaned. "I was afraid you would."

"It's a sales tool. Of course I had to bring them. You haven't seen the final product, have you?" She pulled her laptop case out from under the seat in front of her.

"No, and I don't want to see it now."

"You need to look at it. Don't forget, the Chance brothers volunteered, so this will give you a mental picture of each one before we get there." She unzipped her case and pulled out a calendar.

There was his buddy Cade on the front, manly and shirtless as he leaned against the hitching post with a rope coiled over one shoulder. "I don't need that kind of mental picture of the Chance brothers, thank you very much."

"The pictures aren't all like that." She flipped through the calendar. "See? Here's Jack Chance, fully dressed, sitting on his horse Bandit. He looks part Native American, don't you think?"

"I guess." Finn had to admit that seeing the men in advance would help him remember their names when he met them.

"And here's Nick Chance, Dominique's husband. My picture of you is okay, but I'm glad Dominique was available to take the bulk of the shots because she's such an amazing photographer. And obviously in love with Nick."

Finn looked at the close-up of a smiling cowboy with dark hair and green eyes. His hat was shoved back, which made him seem friendly, as if he'd be a good guy to share a beer with. "You're right. This helps. Where's Gabe?"

"Here." Chelsea flipped to a picture of a sandy-haired man with a mustache. "Dominique said she had to heckle him to get him to unsnap his shirt but he finally did it."

"At least he was allowed to wear a shirt." Finn gazed at the image of Gabe leading a brown-and-white Paint out of the barn. "Some of us weren't so lucky."

"Hey, what have you got there?" The flight attendant paused next to his seat. "Oh, let me see!"

Before Finn could protest, Chelsea handed it to her.

"I love this! Can I hold on to it until after takeoff? I'll bring it back."

"Sure," Chelsea said. "Take your time."

As the flight attendant walked toward the front of the plane, Finn turned to glare at Chelsea. "Now you've done it."

"You were the one charming her with your hat and your 'thank you, ma'am' routine."

"I was just trying to be polite, but now she's—"

"A potential backer for Thunder Mountain Academy. Obviously your cowboy persona will be an asset this weekend. It never occurred to me that you should dress and act the part, although it should have, so props to you. Brilliant PR move."

"I wasn't thinking of it as a PR move." In some ways it had been a protective one. When a guy ended up in a foster home with no relatives to call his own, he tried to put his best foot forward whenever possible. Finn also owned a three-piece suit, but he was Wyoming born and knew that a suit wouldn't impress the Chance family nearly as much as a nice hat and polished boots.

"It's a good look for you, Finn. You should dress like this more often."

He shook his head.

"Why not?"

"Because I refuse to be one of those guys who wears the clothes because he thinks they look cool but who's never sat a horse or mucked out a stall." He wished to hell the flight attendant didn't have that calendar. Knowing they'd be mailed out to people he'd never met and probably never would meet was one thing. This was completely different.

"But you have ridden and...what was that other thing?"

"Mucked out a stall. Cleaned it out, in other words."

She studied him. "I can picture you doing that, especially now that I've seen you in this outfit. But I hope you don't wear that gorgeous gray hat to muck out a stall."

"No, that's my dress hat. Herb keeps some old straw ones for everyday chores."

"Oh, right. You were wearing something like that when all of you were at the ranch in June and you Skyped me about Kickstarter ideas. FYI, the gray felt is a vast improvement over that battered straw thing."

"Thanks."

"What? No 'thank you, ma'am'?"

He decided to lay it on thick. Served her right. He gave her his most winning smile and his deepest drawl. "Thank you, ma'am."

She stared at him for a full three seconds. Then she swallowed and looked away. "You're welcome."

Uh-oh. He'd meant it sarcastically, but apparently it hadn't affected her that way. Unless he was mistaken, he'd just turned her on. And that could present a problem.

Hell, who was he kidding? They'd always had a problem. From that first day in the coffee shop he'd been fascinated by her creativity and zest for life. He loved watching her talk and hearing her laugh. Her mouth was perfect and her skin was impossibly soft, not that he allowed himself to touch it except by accident.

The thought of interacting with her on a personal level as well as a business one scared the crap out of him. If he once gave in and took her to bed, he'd never get a damned thing done. He'd made sure to focus solely on the business angle of their relationship, at least when he was awake. He couldn't control his dreams.

Then he'd met Alison. Quiet and methodical, she'd been the complete opposite of Chelsea. Alison had made it clear that she wanted him and had pushed for a commitment. He'd had some stupid idea that she was the kind of steady, safe woman he needed in his life.

Marrying her, especially so quickly, had been a huge mistake. She hadn't absorbed all his attention, but she hadn't held his interest, either. She'd been understandably upset by his total concentration on his business. He felt damned guilty about that marriage.

And he'd promised himself not to repeat his mistake. These days he only allowed two things to occupy his time: O'Roarke's Brewhouse and his foster parents' financial crisis. Making sure they weren't forced to sell out was his priority this week. As the plane lifted into the air, he renewed his vow that Thunder Mountain Ranch would stay in the family.

CHELSEA GAZED AT white clouds piled up like whipped cream outside the window. And speaking of whipped cream, she wouldn't mind being alone with a naked Finn and a can of the stuff. Their trip was minutes old and she was already in trouble.

His lustrous dark hair and startling blue eyes had caught her attention immediately when they'd met in that coffee shop five years ago. His body was nothing to sneeze at, either. When he'd first arrived in Seattle he'd had a tan, but that had gradually faded. His sex appeal hadn't faded one tiny bit, though. Finn O'Roarke was hot.

Although they'd had chemistry from the beginning, he'd made it clear that he wasn't interested in anything more than friendship and a business relationship. Disappointing, but she'd learned to live with it. At least she'd been able to see him often, and she'd noted with satisfaction that he spent all his time on work and didn't date.

Then the rat had showed up with Alison and in practically no time at all they'd been married. Chelsea had hated that with a purple passion, and when the marriage had predictably broken up, she'd decided enough was enough. She'd waited a decent interval and then she'd asked him out. He'd turned her down.

That was so unfair. Just because Alison had complained about his lack of attention didn't mean she would. She understood the constraints on his time and she had her share of those, too.

But he'd retreated into his anal-retentive shell and wasn't coming out. She longed to give him up as a lost cause, but he sent her checks every month and that guaranteed she couldn't forget him. Then this situation with his foster parents had brought them back together and, once again, she was into him.

Worse yet, he'd added a new level of hotness with his cowboy shtick. She hadn't realized she was susceptible to cowboys. Or maybe it was only Cowboy Finn who made her heart beat faster. She'd find that out after being surrounded by a bunch of them for the next few days.

Last month her first big challenge had presented itself. Logically she'd been the one to handle his calendar shoot and she'd counted on her irritation with his behavior to see her through. It hadn't.

She'd mostly blamed the shirtless part for her overheated state. Finn's hair was the kind a woman itched to run her fingers

through. Turned out he had a sprinkling of that same tantalizing dark hair on his rather impressive chest and it also formed
a narrow path that led to the low-slung waistband of his jeans.

The shoot had taken longer than necessary because she'd
spent far too much time wondering what he kept hidden behind
that denim fly. She suspected he had a package worth bragging
about, but Finn wasn't the bragging type. Of course that made
him all the more tempting. After photographing him posing
shirtless and wearing the Stetson, jeans and boots, she'd hurried home to commune with her vibrator.

Sadly that was the extent of her sex life lately. After his
quickie marriage, she'd indulged in a couple of affairs that had
gone nowhere. The torch still burned for Finn despite all her
efforts. She'd protected herself by being cool and sarcastic in his
presence—until a moment ago when he'd given her that high-
wattage smile and a sensuous "thank you, ma'am."

A man as beautiful as Finn shouldn't be allowed to talk like
that. He also shouldn't wear yoked shirts that made his shoulders seem a mile wide and jeans that cradled the sexiest buns
in Seattle. But he had no idea that he was a walking sexual fantasy. The flight attendant had fallen all over herself sending
"I'm available" signals and he hadn't seemed to notice. Now
that she had the calendar, Finn might discover a phone number
tucked into his hatband.

But he was Chelsea's for the next week, or as close to being
hers as she'd ever experienced. He'd also left his precious business in the hands of his assistant, Brad. With luck he might learn
that he wasn't so damned indispensable, after all.

But she couldn't allow thoughts about sexy Finn to distract
her from her first order of business—wooing TMA backers
during the presentation at the Last Chance Ranch. She'd continued to work on the PowerPoint until after midnight, which
had caused her to oversleep. Now that the plane was at cruis-
ing altitude, she could take another look at it.

Finn, she noticed, was already engrossed in his Excel file.

She'd retrieved her laptop and had balanced it on her fold-down tray when the flight attendant showed up with the calendar.

All her attention was on Finn, who remained engrossed in his spreadsheets. "You're Mr. April, aren't you?"

His head snapped up and he flushed as he stared at her in dismay. "Uh, yeah."

"Gorgeous."

He swallowed. "It was...we needed..."

"What's the deal with Thunder Mountain Academy?"

"It's this...this—"

"A residential equine program for sixteen-to-eighteen-year-olds," Chelsea said. "It'll be a fabulous opportunity for kids who think they might want to build a career around horses. They'll learn horse training and equine health care along with the daily maintenance required. In addition, we have a master saddle maker who'll teach them the basics of that art."

The flight attendant blinked. "Sounds great, but I don't have any kids. Can I just buy the calendar?"

"It's offered as a premium if you pledge a certain amount to the academy's Kickstarter fund." Chelsea pulled out a card with website information on it. "Here's where you can do that. It's all spelled out on the site."

"Thanks." She took the card and reluctantly handed back the calendar. "Maybe some of my girlfriends will want to go together on it." She glanced down at Finn. "I'm a beer drinker, too."

He cleared his throat. "Good."

"Don't forget your hat when you leave the plane."

"I won't."

"'Bye, now." She fluttered her fingers at him and headed back to the front of the plane.

"Good Lord." Finn sank back against the seat and took several deep breaths. "Thanks for telling her about TMA. My mind went blank."

"I noticed."

"Obviously, I'm not prepared for the effect that calendar is liable to have."

"It's not just the calendar." Chelsea gazed at him. "So how long since you've dressed like a cowboy?"

"About five years. Basically since I moved to Seattle. Why?"

"Oh, it's just that some guys get more appealing as the years go by and some get less. You might be in the first category."

He laughed and shook his head. "No. It's the calendar. I just have to brace myself for the reaction to it from now on."

"If you say so." She tucked the calendar back in her laptop case. Then she dug around for her earbuds because she wanted to hear the background music she'd chosen to accompany her PowerPoint, as well as the sound for the accompanying videos. At last she cued it up on the screen and put in the earbuds. "Back to work."

Finn tapped her on the shoulder and she pulled out an earbud. "What?"

"Can I listen, too?"

"Okay." Sharing the earbuds meant leaning close to each other, but she wouldn't mind getting his input even if it meant putting up with the warmth of his body, the delicious scent of his aftershave and the sound of his breathing.

Once they were huddled together, she started the PowerPoint. Focusing on it with him so close wasn't easy, but it was a good test of whether the presentation was any good. She'd opened with stirring music and the TMA logo: a horseshoe with the letters at the top created to resemble snowy mountain peaks. Next was a slide of the snowcapped Big Horn Mountain range with her shout line: Thunder Mountain Academy—Built on a Foundation of Caring.

Rosie had sent her some old photos of the ranch during its years as a foster-care facility and Chelsea had created a montage along with some explanatory text. Finn as a teenager appeared in several of the pictures. She heard his breath catch as he watched.

She'd introduced the next segment with the title "A New Era Dawns" and a brief explanation of the program. Then she'd included videos of Lexi, Cade's girlfriend, giving riding lessons, plus one of Cade schooling a horse. Herb, a retired veterinarian, was shown delivering a foal. Ben Radcliffe would teach saddle making, and he'd sent some beautiful photos of his work. The academic benefits of the program were outlined, and then Rosie appeared in shots of an outdoor feast around a large campfire.

A brief video tour of the ranch house, the barn and the four log cabins where the students would live rounded out the presentation. It ended with a picture of Rosie, Herb, Cade, Lexi and Ben all wearing T-shirts bearing the TMA logo as they stood smiling in front of the ranch house. The last slide was once again set against the Big Horn range and carried the slogan "Thunder Mountain Academy. Fostering respectful stewardship of our equine friends through experience and education."

The music swelled to a crescendo and faded as the image on the screen slowly disappeared. Chelsea thought it was pretty good. Not perfect, but then she was never completely satisfied with her work.

Beside her, Finn took a deep breath as he removed his earbud. "That was spectacular."

"Oh, I'm not so sure it's spectacular, but—"

"No, Chels, it's spectacular." He settled his intense blue gaze on her. "And you're not charging us a dime, either. I don't know how I'll ever be able to thank you."

As she looked into his eyes she could think of several ways, but he wouldn't want to hear them. "Aren't we supposed to meet the Chance family at a saloon called the Spirits and Spurs tonight?"

"That's the plan."

"Then once we get there, you can buy me a drink." It wasn't what she really wanted from him, but for now it would have to do.

2

FINN WOULD HAVE liked to watch the presentation again, but Chelsea wanted to polish it some more. She spent the rest of the trip, including the layover in Salt Lake City, tweaking it. And she accused *him* of being anal.

After they landed in Jackson, they picked up the gray SUV she'd reserved and he drove to the little town of Shoshone while she continued to play with the PowerPoint file.

"You're missing the scenery."

"That's okay." She didn't look up from the screen. "I'll see it on the way back."

"Surely it's done by now."

"Mostly, but every time I look at it I see one more thing I want to fix. The presentation tomorrow is super important."

"I'm well aware of that, but the version I saw on the plane should do the trick."

"It's way better now." Her fingers flew over the keyboard of her laptop. "There. That font pops more than the other one."

"There's such a thing as working a project to death, you know."

She glanced up. "Did you really say that? You, a card-carrying member of Perfectionists Anonymous?"

"I'm beginning to think you founded the club. I don't remember you fiddling this much with the O'Roarke's Brewhouse PowerPoint."

"That's because I worked on it in the middle of the night and you weren't there. How would you feel if something this important was riding on your expertise?"

He contemplated that. "I see what you mean."

"Thank you." There was triumph in her voice. "If you'd been the one responsible for this very important PowerPoint, you would have made me drive while you worked on it."

"Well, you're going to have to stop because there's the Bunk and Grub up ahead. We don't have much time to check in before we head over to meet the Chance family at the saloon."

She turned off her laptop and tucked it into her carrying case. "Looks just like the picture on the website, a cute little Victorian. With a name like the Bunk and Grub, you'd think it would be more rustic."

"The Spirits and Spurs is rustic. We passed it on the way here."

"Is it close?"

"A couple of blocks. We could walk it." Then he thought of her high-heeled sandals. "Or not. I forgot about your shoes."

"If I can take the hills of Seattle in these I can certainly walk a couple of blocks on flat ground." She glanced down at her outfit. "But are you sure I'll be okay wearing this? Not that I have anything more Western and rustic to change into."

"Chels, you'd look great in a feed sack." He wondered if he should have said that. But it was true. She had an instinctive sense of style.

"Unfortunately, I didn't bring a feed sack. I don't even know what they look like, but I'm sure they're rustic. Being a cowboy and all, you probably know all about them."

He laughed. "I do. Listen, whatever you brought will be fine, unless you decide to go riding while we're at Thunder Mountain. Then maybe we should pick up a couple of things in Sheridan.

Or you might be able to borrow a pair of boots from Rosie or Lexi, depending on sizes."

"Could we do that? Go riding?"

"That's up to you. Ever been on a horse?"

"I have, but it's been…jeez, fifteen years. I took some lessons. And I rode English."

"Huh. I didn't know that." He pulled into the parking lot beside the Bunk and Grub and shut off the engine.

"I'll bet there's a lot you don't know about me."

"Probably so." He met her gaze. He'd deliberately avoided finding out too much for fear it would only create more connection between them. Like the riding thing. Although she hadn't kept it up, at one time experiencing the world on horseback had appealed to her.

"If it isn't too much trouble, I'd love to go riding when we get to Thunder Mountain. I'll be rusty, but I think it would be fun to get on a horse again. If the horse is gentle, I should be fine wearing my gym shoes."

"Then I'll take you." He broke eye contact and reached for the door handle. "There's a Forest Service road through the trees. You'll like it." And damned if it didn't sound like a romantic thing to do.

"I'm sure I will." She opened her door and climbed out.

The walkway around to the front door of the B and B was a series of stepping stones set in gravel, so Finn offered to carry both suitcases and Chelsea took their laptop shoulder bags. As he followed her up the steps to a front porch decorated with white wicker furniture and floral cushions, his mind was still on that ride along the Forest Service road.

He hadn't thought much about the second part of this trip, but now that he knew she had some riding experience, he wanted to show her everything—the little clearing where he, Cade and Damon had performed their blood-brother ceremony, the stream where the three of them used to camp when they were older, and the slope they'd cleared of trees so they could use it as a toboggan run in the winter.

She'd like Cade and Damon. Finn was looking forward to seeing them again. So much had changed since he'd been there in June. Cade and Lexi had gotten back together, although still no word on a wedding. Damon had moved back to Sheridan to be with Philomena, the carpenter who'd worked with him on a fourth cabin for TMA last month.

Finn had been back to the ranch a few times since moving to Seattle, but he'd always traveled alone. This would be the first time he'd ever taken someone there. Maybe it was fitting that Chelsea should be the one. She'd helped him make the transition to Seattle and now she'd be able to see where he'd come from. For her, at least, the picture would be complete.

But he had huge gaps in his knowledge of her. He didn't feel good about that. When it came to Chelsea, he'd been a coward. He should be able to get to know the woman's background without forming an inseparable bond. As he walked through the front door of the Bunk and Grub, he decided to use this weekend to learn more about her.

The reception area and an adjacent parlor matched the exterior. Antique furniture and gilt-framed mirrors reminded Finn of the pictures his grandfather had showed him of his great-grandparents' house. Vases of fresh flowers were everywhere.

A middle-aged woman with blond hair rose from behind an antique desk and came forward when they walked in. "You must be Finn and Chelsea."

"We are." Chelsea held out her hand. "And you must be Pam Mulholland. I recognize you from your picture on the website."

"I'm Pam." She took Chelsea's hand in both of hers. "And I'm so excited about Thunder Mountain Academy. I've been talking to everyone I know. You should have a good crowd at the Last Chance tomorrow afternoon."

"My goodness, thank you!"

"The project sounds amazing." She squeezed Chelsea's hand and released it. "And, Finn, I'm delighted to meet you."

"Same here, ma'am." He touched the brim of his hat. "I also want to thank you for getting the word out about tomorrow. Thunder Mountain means a great deal to a lot of people, me included."

"I'm sure it does. When Cade visited last month he kept us all entertained with stories about the days when you boys lived there."

He smiled. "Don't believe everything you hear."

"So you weren't the one who glued the toilet seats shut and put salt in the sugar bowl?"

"Uh, well…" He made a mental note to have a talk with his old buddy Cade.

Pam laughed. "You wouldn't be normal kids if you hadn't pulled a few pranks. According to Sarah, the Chance boys—"

A grandfather clock in the parlor chimed, interrupting her. "Whoops. Time to get moving." She hurried behind the desk and grabbed two sets of keys from a board on the wall. "The bigger one opens the front door when I'm not here and the smaller one's a room key. You can both sign the register later. You two are my only guests this weekend, so we can be more informal."

"That sounds nice," Chelsea said.

"I won't abandon all the protocol, but I've dispensed with our usual happy hour for obvious reasons. You'll be at Spirits and Spurs tonight and at the ranch for dinner tomorrow. We can see about Sunday night's happy hour if you end up hanging around here."

"We might," Finn said. "It's a great house."

"Thank you." Pam looked pleased. "I love it. Oh, and if you should need anything while you're here, dial zero from the phone in your room. It'll connect to me, or if I'm not here, it goes to the housekeeper's room. Yvonne will take care of you. Are you walking over to Spirits and Spurs or driving?"

"Walking," Chelsea said without hesitation.

"Then I'll walk with you. Come on down whenever you're ready and we'll head over. Everyone's so eager to meet you." Pam glanced at Finn. "Josie has the beer you shipped chilling even as we speak. Nice touch."

Chelsea swung around to gaze at him. "You sent beer? What a great idea."

"Testing the market."

"Smart." She glanced at the number attached to her set of keys. "Which way is Room Three?"

"Up the stairs and to your left." She handed Finn the other key. "You're in Four, right next to her. They're my two favorites."

Finn took the key with a smile. "Much obliged, ma'am." From the corner of his eye he caught Chelsea's smirk. But he was in cowboy country now. He'd felt it the minute they'd landed in Jackson, and the Western atmosphere brought back all his cowboy manners. He hefted both suitcases and started toward the stairs.

"Oh, and in case I get caught up in the dancing and forget to mention it," Pam said, "breakfast is at eight. Just follow your nose to the coffee and you'll find the breakfast room."

"Dancing?" Finn paused to glance back at her.

"At the Spirits and Spurs. There's a live band and a dance floor. You and Chelsea will have to try it out."

"Definitely," Chelsea called over her shoulder as she started up the stairs. "Right, Finn?"

"Right." Good Lord, would he really have to do that? He followed her up the stairs and down the carpeted hallway. "I'm not much of a dancer," he said quietly as he set her suitcase by her door.

"Me, either."

"Really? Or are you just saying that to make me feel better?"

"No, really." She unlocked the door and turned to face him. "I hung out with the brainy kids. We considered ourselves too cool to go to dances, so I never really learned how. I sort of regret it now."

"That's surprising. I pictured you being into the whole social thing, maybe even the homecoming queen."

She burst out laughing. "Oh, Finn, you have a lot to learn about me. You can start tonight as you steer me awkwardly around the dance floor."

"We're not actually going to do it, are we?" He stared at her in horror.

"Of course we are. Pam's remark tells me that these folks love their dancing. It's like when you're in a country where you don't speak the language. The locals appreciate it if you at least give it a try. Sitting there like bumps on a log would be a mistake. We should dance, even if we're bad at it. It'll be excellent PR."

"It'll be a disaster."

"No, it won't." She gazed up at him. "It'll do us both good. We've established that we're both perfectionists and we probably carry that to an extreme."

"Speak for yourself."

"I'm speaking for both of us. Let's see if we can tolerate dancing badly."

He groaned.

"Man up, O'Roarke. Have a few beers. Cut loose. I know you have it in you after hearing about the toilet seats and the sugar-to-salt routine."

"Okay, but you'll be sorry. You're wearing sandals, don't forget, and I'm wearing boots. Don't blame me if you're limping by the end of the night."

"I won't blame you, but I might ask you to give me a foot rub."

His breath caught.

"See you in five minutes, cowboy." Grabbing her suitcase, she handed him his laptop, ducked inside her door and closed it in his face.

He stared at the closed door for several seconds. *A foot rub.*

She was taunting him, which wasn't very nice of her, all things considered. But, God, how he loved it.

TWENTY MINUTES LATER when Chelsea walked into the Spirits and Spurs, she recognized immediately that this was the real deal. She'd seen places that gave the appearance of being historic frontier watering holes, but this saloon had earned its ambience the old-fashioned way through years of serving drinks to thirsty cowhands.

The tables were scarred but sturdy, while the polished wooden bar, complete with beveled mirror behind it and plenty of shelves and brass fittings, was a thing to behold. Finn must be wild with envy—it was the kind of bar he'd lusted after but hadn't been able to afford. These beauties, most of them shipped from back East more than a century ago, didn't come cheap.

Chelsea could easily imagine miners, cattlemen and gamblers bellying up to that bar in days gone by. Obviously this saloon had seen it all and then some. The band was tuning up, so the party was about to get started.

A woman wearing jeans and a Western shirt walked toward them. A long blond braid hung down her back and she moved with assurance, as if she owned the place. Chelsea was willing to bet that she did.

She confirmed it immediately. "I'm Josie Chance, and you must be Chelsea and Finn," she said as she shook hands with both of them. "Welcome to Spirits and Spurs. Thanks for escorting them over here, Pam."

"Fortunately they came peacefully." Pam grinned at them. "But if you'll excuse me, I see my darling husband over at the bar and we haven't checked in with each other in a couple of days."

Josie waved her away. "Go for it."

Chelsea noticed Pam heading toward a distinguished-looking cowboy with a gray mustache. "Has her husband been out of town?"

"No, Emmett lives at the Last Chance Ranch. He's the foreman there. They were married Christmas before last, but they maintain separate residences and get together when they can."

"That's fascinating. Don't you think so, Finn?"

"I'm sorry. What?" Apparently he hadn't heard a word because he'd been too absorbed in his surroundings.

"Never mind. Cool bar, huh?"

"It's amazing. I love this whole place, Josie. It has the kind of atmosphere I'm going for at O'Roarke's Brewhouse, but I haven't quite achieved it yet."

Josie smiled. "Give yourself another hundred years."

"That's how old it is?" Finn glanced up into the rafters. "No wonder it feels so authentic."

"And it has ghosts."

Finn's eyes narrowed. "You're kidding."

"I hope she's not." Chelsea shivered with excitement. "I've always wanted to see one."

"Well, I have seen one, right in this room after closing. I knew the saloon was supposed to be haunted by the ghosts of past patrons, so I renamed it Spirits and Spurs, thinking I was being clever. Then I saw my first ghost and realized I was being accurate."

Chelsea sucked in a breath. "That is so cool."

"That is so creepy." Finn didn't seem as happy about the ghost situation.

"Not everyone believes it." Josie shrugged. "Their choice. I know what I saw and I stand by the name. By the way, I've tasted your beer, Finn, and it's excellent. If you can guarantee me a steady supply, I'll put it on the menu."

"I'd be honored, ma'am."

"Aha! Spoken like a Wyoming boy. Nice hat, too."

"We were in coach," Chelsea said, "but the hat rode in first class. Both legs. The flight attendants were very accommodating."

"I understand how that could happen." Josie gave Finn a

speculative glance. "Women appreciate a nice hat. Anyway, I've monopolized you two long enough. The rest of the gang is sitting in the far corner where those two tables are pushed together. Let's get your drinks ordered before we go over. What'll you have?"

"O'Roarke's Pale Ale," Chelsea said, knowing it would please Finn. Besides, she liked it.

"Make that two, please." Finn said.

"Why am I not surprised?" Josie beckoned to a waitress and gave her the order before turning back to them. "Hand-crafted beers are a fun idea. I've always thought owning the saloon was good enough, but lately I've been thinking that a microbrewery would be an interesting challenge."

Finn clutched his chest. "A competitor? Right when I've snagged your business?"

"Relax." She patted him on the arm. "It'll take me ages to get up to speed. By then you'll have the entire West Coast sewed up."

"Just kidding, ma'am. I'd be glad to help any way I can. There's room for both of us."

Chelsea's heart swelled. Finn was turning into a savvy businessman, as evidenced by his decision to expand his territory. But he wasn't cutthroat about it and he was more than willing to lend a hand to a competitor. She'd admired that strength of character from the day they'd met.

Josie ushered them over to the table where the rest of the family sat, and immediately the men all pushed back their chairs and stood. Impressive. Cowboy manners were beginning to grow on her.

As Josie made the introductions, the calendar helped Chelsea identify people. She recognized Jack, Nick and Gabe instantly, and Dominique had to be the short-haired brunette sitting next to Nick. That meant Gabe's wife, Morgan, was the curvy redhead.

"Sarah and Pete will be here any minute," Josie said. "But

they told us to go ahead and order food instead of waiting for them, so have a seat and grab a menu." She laughed. "I refuse to be modest. Everything's good here."

"Well, I'm starving." Chelsea sat next to Jack. That was when she noticed that everyone had a bottle of O'Roarke's Pale Ale in front of them.

Obviously, Finn had noticed it, too. He gestured toward the bottles. "That's right nice of you," he said. "I really didn't expect everyone to be obliged to drink it."

"Why not?" Nick smiled at him. "It was free!"

"Exactly. I love me a free beer." Jack raised his bottle in a subtle salute. "And it's not half-bad. If Josie goes ahead with her microbrewery plan, she'll have to step it up in order to top this. We'll have you beat on the label, though."

"I don't know about that." Finn settled into his chair with a grin. Apparently he was comfortable with this kind of teasing. "You have to admit that an Irish name on a beer bottle just looks natural."

"Maybe so, but you don't have historic information to slap on the back side." Jack turned the bottle around. "In this space here, where you can only brag about the quality of your hops and such, we get to talk about a beer inspired by the friendly spirits of Shoshone, namely, 'Ghost Drinkers in the Bar.'"

Chelsea laughed. "That's good."

"We've worked up a little ditty for the commercial." Gabe smoothed his mustache. "You oughta hear it."

Morgan rolled her eyes. "Hey, they just got here. You don't have to do this now."

"Oh, I think we do." Nick began to hum the tune for "Ghost Riders in the Sky."

Dominique glanced across the table at Chelsea and Finn. "Sorry. When they get like this it's impossible to control them."

"And why would you?" Jack stood and motioned the other two to do the same. As the band started playing the song, the three brothers began singing it, or rather a version of it.

The word *riders* became *drinkers*, who seemed to be riding bar stools instead of horses. They were also the ones with the red eyes, and instead of pounding hooves they had pounding heads. The chorus was YouTube worthy, with the guys throwing their arms around each other's shoulders and belting out the *yippee-yi-yay* part along with *ghost drinkers in the baaaaarrrr.*

Chelsea laughed so hard her sides ached. Through brimming eyes she glanced over at Finn, who was gasping for breath and wiping his eyes. She hadn't seen him have so much fun in... forever.

When the men sat down again, Finn cleared his throat. "I give. With that kind of promo, Spirits and Spurs beer is going to dominate the market."

Jack smiled at him. "I know."

"Don't count yourself out yet, Finn," Chelsea said. "Don't forget your ace in the hole."

He glanced over at her. "What's that?"

"Me."

3

"GOOD POINT." Finn had loved watching Chelsea crack up. Her cheeks glowed pink and her lashes were spiked with tears of laughter. "Gentlemen, I take back what I said. With Chelsea in my corner, I can face any comers."

Jack nodded. "I could tell from the moment I laid eyes on her that she would be a worthy opponent. Never underestimate a woman with purple streaks in her hair."

"Lavender," Chelsea shot back.

"See what I mean?" Jack waved a hand in her direction. "She'll stand up to anyone, even me. So, are we all gonna eat or dance?"

"Both!" called out a male voice.

Finn turned in his chair as a tall, fit man who was probably in his seventies walked toward them with a silver-haired woman who had the bearing of a queen. Finn stood, as did all the men at the table. Sarah Chance was in the building, along with her husband of only a few years, Pete Beckett.

They came over immediately to the newcomers, and Chelsea rose from her chair to greet them. "I can't tell you how excited I am about tomorrow," Chelsea said. "Thank you for hosting this event."

"Yes, thank you, ma'am." Finn looked into blue eyes that shone with intelligence and wisdom. He'd heard that Sarah was a special woman, and after only a minute or so of being in her presence, he understood why people said that. She gave off enough warmth and good humor to envelop everyone at the table, but Finn suspected she was also capable of silencing the entire group with a look.

Pete glanced around the table. "Have you ordered?"

"Not yet." Morgan tossed back her red hair and gave her husband a pointed look. "Some people had to subject us all, including our guests, to 'Ghost Drinkers.'"

"I see." Pete rubbed a hand over his face as if hiding a smile. "Chelsea and Finn, I'd like to say that was an aberration, but I'm afraid things like that go on all the time around here."

"I hope so," Chelsea said.

"But not while you give your presentation." Jack patted her shoulder. "You have my word that we'll behave ourselves tomorrow afternoon."

"But once everyone leaves, all bets are off." Nick winked at her. "I have a feeling you can take it."

"Oh, she can." Finn felt compelled to alert them. "She can also dish it out, so watch yourselves."

"I figured as much," Jack said. "But didn't you say you were starving, Chelsea? We'd better rustle up some grub. Then we can dance while we wait for it." He glanced over at Finn. "I assume you dance?"

"Depends on your definition."

"Hmm." Jack didn't look impressed by the response. "I hope you're not into salsa."

"Only with my chips."

"That's a relief." Jack returned his attention to his menu. "Don't know why I bother looking at this. I know it by heart. Give me your order, everybody. I'll relay it to the cook."

"I can call Heather over," Josie said. "You don't have to play waiter."

"Heather's running herself ragged tonight. I know the menu, probably better than she does. I can do it."

Finn decided that he liked Jack. The guy had a sense of humor, but he also wasn't afraid to pitch in when necessary. Finn had done the same many times at O'Roarke's Brewhouse. Josie was the owner here, but Jack obviously tried to lighten her load.

After he disappeared with their order, Sarah cast a glance at her remaining sons and daughters-in-law. "I checked on the kids before we left and Cassidy seems to have everything under control."

"Good," Josie said.

"Thank God for Cassidy." Morgan looked over at Chelsea and Finn. "My youngest sister. She's the ranch housekeeper and she babysits the grandkids, although now that she has a boyfriend we have to make sure we plan ahead."

Jack returned and pulled his wife out of her chair. "I have a plan. I finally have a night out with the woman of my dreams. Let's hit the floor, lady."

"I like that idea a lot." Gabe offered his hand to Morgan. "Dance with me?"

"As long as you don't sing in my ear." But Morgan looked happy as she joined her husband on the floor.

Nick and Dominique followed, and Pete stood and held Sarah's chair. He paused when Finn and Chelsea didn't immediately leave the table. "How about you two?"

"We'll be out there in a minute," Finn said.

"You're sure?" Sarah hesitated. "We don't want to leave our guests sitting all alone."

"We're right behind you." Finn grabbed his beer bottle and glanced at Chelsea. "I don't know about you, but I need some Dutch courage."

"I'm with you." She took several swallows. "Okay, let's do this thing."

Finn didn't feel ready, but Chelsea was on her feet. He pushed back his chair. "I don't know a lot about dancing, but that looks like what they call country swing. It's fairly popular around here."

"Whatever you say. I'm pretty much clueless." Chelsea studied the participants. "Lots of twirling and fancy footwork. But we might be able to fake it."

"My specialty is standing in one spot and shuffling around."

"That's not going to work, Finn. They'll run you over."

"Should we reconsider? After all, you do have on sandals. If I don't squash your toes I'm liable to place you in serious danger from somebody else. We could sit and drink beer, instead."

"No, we need to try it. Maybe if we spin around a lot nobody will notice we don't know what we're doing."

Finn sucked in a breath. "All right. Let's go." At the edge of the dance floor he grabbed Chelsea and began madly twirling her around the perimeter. He stepped on her a couple of times, but she didn't yell, so it must not have hurt too much.

On his second circuit, Jack showed up beside them and grabbed his shoulder hard enough to stop the twirling. "What the hell is that you're doing?"

Finn decided to brave it out. "The same thing you're doing."

"I think not." He gently set Chelsea aside. "Stay right here, sweetheart. I'll bring him back in a few minutes."

"Hang on." Finn stepped back, both hands raised. "Whatever you have in mind, I'm not doing it."

"Work with me, O'Roarke." Jack grasped his hand.

Finn pulled free. "I'm not dancing with you, Jack."

"You weren't dancing with Chelsea, either. You have two choices. You can continue to look like an idiot out on the floor or you can let me give you a quick lesson."

"Three choices. I can head back to the table and drink."

"You're a quitter? Is that what you're saying? I didn't peg you for a quitter."

Those were the magic words. Finn sighed. "Tell me what to do."

"That's better. Put your hand around my waist. Pretend I'm Chelsea."

"She doesn't have a five o'clock shadow."

"And she has way fancier hair and I'm sure she smells better, too. Just focus on what I'm telling you. The idea is to describe a box with your feet and turn at the same time. Now go."

"You do realize this will look ridiculous."

"It's no worse than the hot mess you were a bit ago. Come on, now, you built your own business. That takes cojones. This is just a little dancing."

Finn could have used more beer, but if Jack was willing to make a fool of himself, then, what the hell? Might as well go along. Good thing nobody he knew was here except Chelsea. Having her watch was bad enough, but at least she'd admitted that she wasn't very good, either.

Then he caught movement on the far side of the dance floor and realized Josie was dancing with Chelsea. "Hey! Your wife is dancing with my..." He trailed off, unable to come up with a proper title for her.

"Your what?" Jack exerted pressure on Finn's shoulder to keep him moving in the right direction. "I'm no expert, but I feel a vibe between you two."

"She's my business associate."

"Yeah, and I'm Elvis. Tell me another one. And lead with your other foot. There. That's better. Good."

"I can't believe I'm doing this."

"Anybody who owns a hat like yours should be able to dance the two-step. I think you have the basics. Josie's coming around again with your *business associate*. We'll trade partners."

And just like that, Jack thrust him into Chelsea's arms and the momentum kept them moving around the floor. Miraculously, they were even doing it in a synchronized fashion. "I'm not sure what just happened."

"I think it was the fastest dancing lesson in history."

"Embarrassing as it is to admit, Jack's a good teacher."

"Josie said he's considered the dancing master at the Last Chance. He's working with the kids now so that they'll grow up knowing how."

"You were right that it's an important skill around here. And believe it or not, we might be actually doing it. More or less. Sort of."

"We might." She smiled as she gazed up at him. "I can't remember the last time I've had so much fun."

"You know what? Me, either." He wanted to tell her that she was the most beautiful woman in the world, but instead he twirled her around one more time and the music ended.

Jack came by and leaned toward them. "Good job. Now let's eat."

The food, as Josie had mentioned, was excellent. Finn noted that the pub fries were better than what he served at O'Roarke's. Humbling, because he was proud of his establishment's pub fries, but this little saloon in Wyoming did them better.

After dinner everyone danced some more. Jack suggested that he partner Chelsea while Josie partnered Finn. Finn improved a lot while dancing with Josie, but he was grateful once Chelsea was back in his arms.

He was comforted knowing that she wasn't any more accomplished than he was, but that wasn't the only reason he liked dancing with her. He'd discovered how much he loved holding her.

She felt so right cradled in his arms. He should have guessed that she would. The warmth in her eyes told him she felt the same way. This trip was designed to deliver a Hail Mary pass that would clinch the Kickstarter project and save the ranch. No small potatoes, there. But already it felt as if even more was at stake.

As the evening progressed, Jack kept bringing over more O'Roarke's Pale Ale. Finn knew his inhibitions were disappearing, and he could tell from the way Chelsea danced with him that hers were, too. He had to stay strong.

She'd made it obvious months ago that she thought they could have a lot of fun together. He completely agreed with her. But starting an affair with her had the potential to make him forget everything else. They had an important mission to accomplish this weekend, and he couldn't let anything distract him from that.

Dancing with her was safe enough, though. They had people all around them and he still had to concentrate on his footwork so he wouldn't step on her or run into other couples. That left him very little time to think about how soft her breasts felt or how perfectly their hips aligned thanks to her high-heeled sandals.

Then they goaded each other into attempting a very fast number. They made a mess of it, but he was proud of them for trying. When the music ended they clung to each other, laughing and gasping for breath.

Gradually he realized he could feel the rapid thump of her heart as she leaned against his chest. His palm, which was flattened against the small of her back, rotated in a slow massage. He hadn't been conscious of doing it at first. He looked down at her and she was looking right back at him, her full lips parted as she sucked in air.

The heat of her body was nothing compared to the heat in her gaze. On cue, his groin tightened. He released her slowly and stepped back as he fought to control his reaction. He hoped she hadn't noticed, but when the corners of her mouth tilted up a fraction, he thought she had. Maybe dancing with her wasn't so safe, after all.

Just his luck, the party broke up after that. Pam came over to tell them she was going back to the Last Chance so she could spend the night with her husband. Breakfast would be served as usual because her housekeeper, Yvonne, was also the cook.

Several people offered Chelsea and Finn a ride back to the Bunk and Grub, but Finn suggested walking and Chelsea quickly agreed. He couldn't speak for her, but he needed a cooling-off period before stepping into a cozy B and B where his room was right next to hers.

At least he hadn't brought condoms. He was grateful for

that as they walked through the cool night air. Fortunately the thought hadn't crossed his mind in connection with this trip, and even if it had, he would have made sure *not* to have any.

"That was fun." Chelsea's heels clicked on the sidewalk, a sharper sound than what his boots made. "I expected to like them and I do."

"Me, too. Great family. I have a good feeling about tomorrow. Their support could put us over the top."

"Yep." She wrapped her arms around herself. "It's kind of nippy out here."

"Yeah." This cooling-off period had turned out to be just plain cold. If he'd had a coat, he would have given it to her, but he didn't, and taking off his shirt would be ridiculous. He felt the chill, too, after all that dancing in a warm room. Her blouse was flimsy compared to his cotton shirt, so she must be freezing.

From the corner of his eye he could see her struggling not to shiver. Aw, hell, he had to do something about that. "Don't take this the wrong way, but I'm going to put my arm around you so you won't be cold."

"That would b-be lovely."

"I didn't think about how the temperature drops at night in late August." He kept his tone nonchalant as he wrapped his arm around her shoulders and matched his stride to hers. "Warm during the day and frosty at night."

"S-so I see." Nestling against him, she slid her arm around his waist. "Thanks."

And he was no longer cold. She fit against his side and synchronized her steps to his as if they'd walked this way hundreds of times. He tightened his grip on her warm, firm shoulder and imagined touching her warm, firm skin.

Oh, God, now he was thinking of what else they could do that would be effortless. Kissing, for example. And then sliding out of their clothes and into a bed, either his or hers. The more turned on he became the faster he walked. He didn't realize it until he heard their labored breathing.

He slowed down. "Sorry. Didn't mean to start race-walking."

"That's okay." There was a hint of laughter in her voice. "Good way to warm up."

He could think of another good way. In fact, that seemed to be the only thing he could think about.

She stopped making conversation and so did he. No telling what would come out of his mouth in his current state.

Her scent teased him with possibilities. Her hair swung as they walked, brushing his shoulder. He wanted to thread his fingers through those silky strands, cup the back of her head and finally taste the lips he'd stared at for years. *Years, damn it!*

Instead of kissing her, he let her go when they reached the B and B's porch steps so he could dig out his keys. As it turned out, she got to hers first and opened the front door.

He followed her into the silent entry. A trace of cinnamon hung in the warm air and a Tiffany-style lamp glowed in the parlor. Etched-crystal sconces along the stairway created an intriguing mix of light and shadow. He remembered they were alone on the second floor of the house. No other guests.

Chelsea started up the carpeted steps and he followed, keeping a safe distance behind her. No, there wasn't such a thing as a safe distance. He watched hungrily as her snug jeans lovingly stretched over her backside as she climbed. Even though he'd slowed his pace, his heart thumped as if they'd run the whole way.

Rational thought drifted away as insanity gripped him. Her hand on the polished railing made him think of her hand on his cock. The lack of condoms was no longer a lucky circumstance that would keep him from doing something stupid. It was a damned inconvenience standing between him and paradise.

Neither of his best friends would have been caught in this situation. Yet here he was, aching for someone who would probably welcome him into her bed if he gave the slightest indication that he wanted to be there, and he was condomless.

Pausing at her door, she inserted the key in the lock. His fevered brain attached a sexual connotation to that, too.

But there would be no inserting anything because he was without those little raincoats.

She glanced at him as he approached her. Her face was in shadow, her expression hidden. "See you in the morning." Twisting the key, she opened her door and started through it. Lamplight from inside the room skimmed her tempting silhouette.

He was pushed beyond reason into a world of primitive needs. Even as unprepared as he was, he couldn't let her go. "Wait."

She turned and peered up at him. "Finn, are you okay?"

"No." His voice rasped in the stillness.

"What's the matter?"

"I..." He stopped to clear the huskiness from his throat. "I want you so much I can't breathe."

"Oh." Her beautiful mouth curved in a smile and she stepped back from the door. "Would you like to come in?"

"God, yes, but I... I didn't anticipate this."

"I'm sure you didn't."

Hope dawned. "Did you?"

"No, of course not."

He groaned. "Then we can't—"

"Maybe not *that*, but there are alternatives."

Alternatives. The word stood out in flashing neon in his frazzled brain.

Curling her fingers into the front of his shirt, she pulled him slowly inside her room. "You haven't dated since Alison. I haven't dated since I asked you out. Do you understand what I'm saying?"

Swallowing, he nodded.

"Good." She took off his hat and laid it on the dresser. "Because I can hardly wait to get my hands on you, Finn O'Roarke."

He had the presence of mind to kick the door shut before his brain shut down completely.

4

CHELSEA HAD TRIED to be good. She really had tried, except for her earlier remark about the foot rub. When they'd had their hot moment on the dance floor, she hadn't teased him about the hard ridge she'd felt pressed against her belly before he'd backed away.

He wanted to keep his distance, and she had vowed to honor that. She would have suffered the cold air on the walk home in silence because it was her own fault for not bringing a jacket. But then he'd wrapped his arm around her. The moment she'd felt his touch and the delicious heat of his body, a fantasy movie had started rolling in her head.

And now—against all odds—fantasy had become reality. Flattening her palms against his chest, she absorbed the wild beating of his heart as he combed his fingers through her hair and tilted her head back. His gaze moved hungrily over her face and settled on her mouth. He groaned. "Chelsea…" And then he was there, his velvet lips covering hers.

At last. Joy surged through her at the urgent pressure of his mouth and the deliberate thrust of his tongue. Oh, yes, this was good, and right, and ahhh…he could kiss better than any man she'd ever known.

He angled his head and went deeper, inspiring shocking thoughts about where else she wanted that talented mouth. He obviously knew what she'd meant when she'd suggested alternatives. They had all night, but that didn't mean they shouldn't get started on that program ASAP.

She wrenched apart the snaps of his shirt, desperate to touch him. When she laid both hands against his muscled chest and stroked him there, he shuddered and lifted his mouth from hers. "I'm going crazy." He gulped for air. "I have zero control."

"That's okay." Pulse hammering, she slid her hand down to his zipper. Oh, my. What she'd felt on the dance floor had been a mere prelude. "I'll just—"

"No, it's not okay." He caught her hand and brought it up to his mouth. His breathing ragged, he kissed her fingertips one by one. "We're changing focus."

"To what?"

His blue eyes glowed with intensity. "You."

She gasped as a fresh wave of lust crashed over her. Her attention shifted to his mouth and her imagination kicked into high gear. She began to tremble. "I could live with that."

His soft laughter gave her goose bumps. "Ah, Chels. You're one of a kind."

"And don't you forget it."

He held her gaze. "I never have." Then he stepped back and looked her up and down, as if evaluating his next move. His attention settled on the belt circling her hips. "How does that come off?"

"Easy." But eagerness made her clumsy and she messed it up somehow. She swore softly and kept working at the clasp.

"Let me see." He knelt in front of her, moved her hands aside and had the belt undone in two seconds. As it slithered to the floor he slipped both hands under the hem of her tunic and before she could take a breath he'd unbuttoned her jeans.

As he started pulling them down, panties and all, her heart beat so fast she grew dizzy. "My...my shoes."

"You get the blouse." His voice rasped in the stillness. "I'll get the shoes." He unbuckled the straps and slipped off one shoe at a time, taking care that she didn't lose her balance. His touch was nimble, practiced and incredibly erotic.

"You're..." She paused to gulp in air. "You're good at that."

"Cowboy stuff."

At first she didn't get it and then she understood. Bridles, halters, harnesses—leather and buckles were no challenge to a man with cowboy skills.

He tenderly divested her of her jeans and panties, too. Still on his knees, he caressed her calves and gradually made his way up her quaking thighs. His questing fingers drew closer to the spot where she ached so fiercely that she barely contained a whimper of longing. She closed her eyes to savor his touch.

Then he paused.

She moaned softly. "Don't stop."

"Your blouse."

"Oh." He'd mesmerized her so completely that she'd forgotten her assignment. Grabbing the hem, she whipped the shirt over her head, then took off her bra and flung it after the blouse. Her breasts ached for his touch, too.

With a sharp intake of breath, he rose and stepped back.

She watched him and was thrilled by his awestruck reaction. Lifting her chin, she looked him in the eye. "See what you've been missing?"

His gaze roved over her. "Yes." His chest heaved. "And I'm a damned fool."

"Not tonight."

"No, not tonight. Thank God for alternatives." And with a swiftness that made her squeal, he swept her up in his arms and laid her on the bed. Then he pulled off his clothes with utter disregard for where they landed. That was so unlike Finn.

Her tidy little Victorian room took on the appearance of a ravishing. She was more than ready to be ravished, even if his options for accomplishing that were limited. But when she had her first unobstructed view of his package, she cursed the lack of condoms.

She'd thought fleetingly about bringing them, but that had seemed like tempting fate. If she'd brought them and then had taken the box home unopened, she would have needed more than a few bottles of O'Roarke's Pale Ale to get over her disappointment.

But, oh, how she yearned for what he had to offer. "O'Roarke, I have one thing to say."

"Only one?"

"Yes." Viewing that kind of male beauty and knowing there were restrictions on enjoying it made her impatient. "Before tomorrow night, we'll obtain a box of condoms."

"It's a small town, don't forget. Word spreads."

"I don't care."

He grinned. "You know what? Neither do I."

If there was ever a more stirring sight than Finn naked and smiling, she'd never seen it. Her fantasies of him paled in comparison to the real man, his erect cock seated in a cloud of dark hair and his impressive balls tight with desire. Better yet, she'd inspired this aroused condition. No matter what happened after tonight, she'd carry that potent image with her.

He walked over to the bed. "Make room. I'm coming in."

"I sort of expected that." She scooted over and patted the spot next to her. "Here you go."

"Thanks." He climbed onto the bed and immediately moved over her, rolling her to her back in the process. "For the next little while, we'll be pretty much occupying the same area."

Somewhere along the way he'd changed his attitude. Outside her door he'd been desperate yet hesitant to fully commit. Now he was all in. This new, more masterful Finn thrilled her to her toes. "You say that as if you're in charge."

"Not necessarily." He leaned down and nibbled at her mouth. "But I think you'd like it if I took over."

Oh, yes, she certainly would. "How did you know?"

"Lucky guess."

And as he captured her mouth and cupped her breast in a

slow, sensuous massage, she abandoned herself to the sensation of letting Finn be in charge. What a heady feeling, turning her body over to a man. She couldn't recall ever doing that. In vulnerable situations, she preferred to be in control.

But it was no mystery why she could surrender so completely to him. His sense of honesty and fair play was bone deep. She'd known that from the moment they'd met. She trusted him more than any man she'd ever been naked with.

And because of that trust, she allowed herself to let go in a way that she never would have with someone else. As he ran his hands over her curves, she arched into his caress with a moan of delight. When he cradled her breasts so that he could use his mouth to drive her crazy, she let herself make all the noise she wanted to.

The pleasure he gave her was more intense because it was Finn. Finn was the man kissing his way down the valley between her breasts and over her quivering stomach. Finn was the man parting her thighs, the man who was about to bestow the most intimate of kisses.

His knowing touch made her gasp as he explored and stroked with clever fingers. His breath was warm against her damp skin and she trembled in silent anticipation. With the first swipe of his tongue, she cried out, electrified by the moist pressure on the most sensitive spot of all.

He did it again, drawing out the motion, and she sucked in a breath. "More."

He obviously knew the meaning of *more*. In seconds she was writhing on the bed thanks to the wonder of Finn's mouth. His hands bracketing her hips, he lifted her up so he could sink deeper, take more. He was definitely ravishing her. And she loved it.

She came in a rush, her breathless cries filling the small room. If she'd expected him to stop there, she'd underestimated him. He teased and taunted her until she spiraled out of control a second time. She forgot where she was as she spun in a whirlpool of sensation.

But she never forgot who was loving her. Finn O'Roarke was in bed with her at last, and the results were more spectacular than she could have imagined. But as he left her quaking center and returned to place a lingering kiss on her mouth, she reminded herself that alternatives included fun for both parties.

Disengaging was no easy task because he seemed to really like kissing her and she really liked him kissing her. But she had other plans for her mouth. Cupping his face in both hands, she pushed upward until he lifted his head. "My turn," she murmured, looking into his passion-glazed eyes. They'd never seemed quite so blue.

"But I love making you come. I'm just taking a short break. You taste so good. I want to—"

"No. *My turn*. I mean it."

He smiled. "I can tell. Your eyes are shooting sparks."

"Fair is fair." She ran her tongue slowly over her lips. "And I think you'll have fun."

As he stared at her mouth, his breathing changed.

"Think about how nice it will feel when I use my tongue on your—"

He groaned. "Lord help me, I want that."

"Of course you do. We're shifting the focus to you, O'Roarke."

Dragging in a breath, he stretched out beside her. "This won't take long."

"Are you sure?" She straddled his thighs, feeling more uninhibited than ever in her life. She embraced showmanship in her job, but she'd never felt motivated to practice it in the bedroom. Two orgasms and a naked Finn stretched beneath her had turned her into a seductress.

"Absolutely sure." His chest rose and fell rapidly and he clenched his jaw. "I've wanted you for five years."

"Ditto." His rigid cock was directly in front of her, magnificently erect with a drop of moisture gathered at the tip. She grasped the base of his penis and squeezed gently. "And now I have you, at least for tonight. If you prop some pillows behind your head you can watch me making you happy."

He gasped. "Dangerous. I already feel as if I could come any second."

"You won't if I keep pressure here." She tightened the circle created by her fingers and the muscles in his jaw gradually relaxed.

"That...helps."

"Good. I want you to be able to savor this. Grab those pillows, Finn."

He reached for a couple and stuffed them behind his head.

She smiled. "Excellent." Leaning down, she kept her fingers in place as she licked the tiny bead of moisture away.

He moaned. "Chelsea. That's..."

Another drop appeared and she licked that, too.

He swore softly.

She glanced up. "Good visual?"

"You have no idea." His voice was strained.

"Just keep watching." She retained her firm grip as she closed her mouth over his cock.

He gasped and fisted his hands in the coverlet. "Go easy."

She'd planned on that. He might not think he could last, but she wanted to draw out the pleasure as long as possible. Predictably, though, the earthy, salty taste of him tightened the coil of desire deep in her belly. Apparently two orgasms weren't enough for her, at least not when she was with Finn.

But she'd declared that this was his turn, so she ignored her own needs and concentrated on his. That wasn't a simple task. As she inched down the hot, tight length of him, her inner muscles clenched in protest. *Tomorrow night*, she vowed.

Tonight she'd love him this way—flattening her tongue to put more pressure along the sensitive vein and hollowing her cheeks as she drew him in. At last the tip of his cock touched the back of her throat.

She moved slowly up and down, and with each swirl of her tongue his breathing grew more labored. He swore again, his words a little more graphic. Despite the restriction she'd created with her fingers, he wouldn't be able to hold back much longer.

Sliding up to the tip, she treated him to some lollipop licks that produced a tortured groan. She followed with easy, deliberate suction. Gradually she became more energetic and he began to pant.

"Chelsea...please..."

She recognized that tone of desperation. Releasing the tight coil created by her fingers, she plunged downward and sucked hard.

He erupted with a deep-throated groan of release. She gloried in that sound, so full of joy and satisfaction. She'd longed to see him break his self-imposed chains, and for this moment, he had.

She swallowed every drop, and when he finally relaxed against the bed, she shimmied up his chest and gave him an open-mouthed kiss. With a soft moan, he embraced her and returned that kiss with an energy that surprised her. She would have expected him to be worn out.

Instead he was using his tongue in ways that reminded her of her own needs and the urges she'd put aside while she made love to him. If she didn't know better, she'd think he was tempting her on purpose. When he thrust his tongue deep into her mouth, she whimpered.

With gentle pressure, he lifted her mouth a fraction away from his. "Slide on up here where I can reach you." His seductive request was delivered in a low, husky voice.

She shivered. Since he could already reach her mouth just fine, that left only one other possibility. Heat sluiced through her as she considered that bold move.

They'd progressed from their first kiss ever to X-rated positions in a very short time. But unexpressed lust had been simmering between them for five years, so maybe their erotic behavior tonight wasn't a surprise, after all.

"Come on, Chels." His voice was like velvet stroking her nerve endings. "Let me taste you again."

"You could make me come just talking that way."

"I'd rather make you come with my mouth and my tongue. You want that, too. I can feel you trembling."

"I do want that." Decision made, she pushed herself up until she was sitting on his chest. Then she leaned over and grasped the brass headboard.

His big hands supporting her hips, he coaxed her into position and...she lost her mind. Lying on the bed in a state of surrender had been incredible, but now she was a more active participant. Holding on to the headboard for support, she could rock forward or back. She could silently ask for anything she wanted from him.

It was like a dance, only she was leading and he was following her every cue. She imagined him as her love slave dedicated to giving her pleasure. And he did...oh, how he did. She moaned, she gasped and at last she cried out as her climax roared through her.

As the quaking finally slowed, he guided her down beside him again. Then he gathered her close and they lay tangled together, unable to move. Eventually a chill in the room convinced them to climb under the covers.

Chelsea had never felt so satisfied and relaxed in her life. With her fingers laced through his, she drifted in a haze of sensual delight. Before she fell asleep, she had one last thought. If loving Finn was like this, she wanted more of it.

5

FINN WOKE UP the next morning with a smile on his face and a song in his heart. That lasted about two seconds and then it occurred to him that he was a complete a-hole. Making sweet love to Chelsea had been the best experience of his life, but it hadn't changed the way he thought about their situation.

If anything, their incredible sexual experience had underscored the problem. His foster parents had a serious situation that deserved all his attention. He certainly hadn't been thinking about it last night.

But even if he rededicated himself to that issue, he'd introduced sex into his relationship with Chelsea, and there was no going back. Now they both knew how great it could be, but he couldn't imagine having an affair, especially with a high-voltage woman like her, and still run his business effectively. So what was he doing in her bed now, when he had his foster parents to think of and no intention of following through with Chelsea once they returned to Seattle?

"That's some frown you're wearing for so early in the morning."

He turned onto his side and discovered she was watching him. "I just figured out what a total jerk I am." And to make matters worse, seeing her lying there facing him with her brown gaze soft and one creamy breast barely covered by the sheet, he wanted to do it all over again. Twice.

Then she smiled, which added one more element of delicious appeal. "I've shared that opinion of you a few times in the past, but right now I'm feeling quite complimentary. You're a wonderful lover, in case no one's ever mentioned that before. You're intuitive, and generous and—"

"And not fit to wipe your boots, let alone climb in to your bed." He'd love to blame the alcohol, but the cold walk home had sobered him up. He'd known exactly what he was doing.

"My goodness!" She propped her head on her hand. "What brought on the self-loathing? You seemed rather pleased with yourself when we went to sleep. As well you should be after—"

"That wasn't right."

"Oh, yes it was. You were absolutely on target every time. You left me wrung out with pleasure." Her brown eyes narrowed. "I can't believe you're the kind of guy who turns prudish in the light of day."

"Nope." If only she knew that under the sheet he was ramrod stiff. "It's taking all my willpower not to reach for you right this minute. But instead I need to apologize for last night."

"What, you should have given me *more* orgasms? You have higher standards than I thought."

"My standards suck. I should never have set foot in this room. I wanted you so much that I made a selfish decision. Because I did, you could logically think I've changed my mind about us, but I haven't."

She met that declaration with silence as if processing what he'd said. Then she took a deep breath. "That doesn't surprise me."

"It doesn't?" He'd expected anger, not this calm acceptance.

"No, not really. I wouldn't have minded waking up to find that you'd seen the light and that you think we should find out where this relationship takes us. I was willing to believe it might happen. Some guys are swayed by damned good sex."

"It was damned good sex. The best ever. But—"

"You still have a business to run." She said it with exactly the same inflection he would have used.

If she wanted to mock him, that was no more than he deserved. "Yeah." He felt like a piece of gum on the bottom of her shoe. "But that's not even all of it. I should be thinking about my foster parents' situation, not giving in to my lust. I'm sorry, Chels. I'll get the hell out of your bed as soon as this erection goes down a little and I can get dressed without maiming myself."

To his amazement she smiled, and the smile turned into a chuckle that became a belly laugh. She flopped to her back and giggled uncontrollably.

"What's so funny?" He'd anticipated she might start throwing things and instead she was laughing hysterically.

"You are!"

"Oh, that's nice. Laugh at the guy with a boner. Actually, though, you're doing me a favor. Yep, I'm much better already. Nothing like having a woman laugh at your willy to make it return to normal." He threw back the covers and got out of bed.

"Wait." She gulped back another giggle and hopped out on the other side. "I wasn't laughing about that. Well, in a way I was, but it was more because you're so adorable."

He barely heard that last part. He was too busy staring at her as the light of early morning caressed her pale skin, giving her a faint glow. Her rosy nipples tightened under his gaze. They seemed to tilt slightly upward, as if inviting him to taste them again.

He longed to span her narrow waist with both hands, to kneel before her and pay homage to that downy blond triangle where he'd spent so much quality time last night. He'd love to revisit that special place now that the sun was rising.

That wasn't the only thing rising, either.

She glanced at his cock and then looked into his eyes. "Finn, I know you think it's unfair to get sexually involved with me on this trip that's supposed to be about your foster parents, especially when you plan to drop me like a hot potato when we get home."

"That's because it *is* unfair. I'm not that kind of guy."

"I know you're not. You're driven and ambitious, but you're not a user."

"That's not true, either. I used Alison and I'll never forgive myself for that."

"Used her? Near as I could tell, she honed in on you like a heat-seeking missile."

"I admit she was determined, but that doesn't excuse my decision to accept her proposal."

"She proposed? I didn't know that, but I'm not too surprised."

"She did, but I could have turned her down." He hated saying it out loud, but she needed to know all the ugly truths about him. "Instead I agreed to marry her because I thought she was a safe alternative to you."

"What?"

"You're the most exciting woman I've ever met. If we started dating, I'd abandon my business so I could spend more time with you."

"You would not! I—"

"Look at how I reacted last night!" He swept a hand toward his stiff cock. "How I'm reacting right now. You turn me on like no one else. I could so easily become obsessed with you. I knew I'd never become obsessed with Alison and I thought…" He rubbed the back of his neck. "This is really hard to say."

"Then don't."

"No, I need to. If you understand how rotten I am, you'll stay away. I knew that something had to change, so I thought if I had a normal, domesticated life with Alison, I'd get over wanting you. It didn't work. She's a nice person, but—"

"She's *not* nice. She walked off with that huge settlement, which was way too much considering she did nothing to build the business. And she took your dog and your cat."

"She deserves the settlement, the two animals and a lot more.

I think she knew in her heart that I used her as a substitute for you, and she was furious. She had every right to be."

Chelsea swallowed. "I knew you were attracted to me, but I had no idea how much."

"Or what lengths I would go to in order to create a barrier between us."

"Finn, I'm not that scary. Honest." She started toward him.

"No, you're wonderful. I'm the one with the issues." He should turn away and get dressed, but he was mesmerized by her lithe body as she slowly approached. "I can't take a chance that I'll ignore my foster parents and their problems. Or somehow lose O'Roarke's because I'm distracted."

"You won't do that." She moved closer. "I know how much you care about Rosie and Herb and I've seen the dedication you bring to your business. You won't allow yourself to be distracted."

"If you're right, then I'd end up shortchanging you. You should have a guy who can give you all the attention you deserve."

"You certainly did last night." She stopped when the blatant evidence of his arousal nudged her belly. "And we have a little time before breakfast."

He groaned. "We have to stop this."

"Look, at the moment there's nothing you can do about either the ranch or your business, so why not give yourself permission to have fun?"

"Because it's not fair to you."

"Let me be the judge of that." She wrapped her fingers around his all-too-willing cock. "Come back to bed with me. Let's play."

He caved. What guy wouldn't? But as he once again explored the wonders of her body, a little voice whispered that this was a prime example. With Chelsea, it was all or nothing. She was his Kryptonite and he indulged himself at his peril.

They ended up missing breakfast entirely. But when Finn

opened her door intending to go to his room to shower and shave, he found a tray with a carafe of hot coffee, two mugs and a basket of pastries. He brought the tray back into the room and they sat on the bed to eat.

Chelsea picked up a croissant. "I could get used to the bed-and-breakfast lifestyle."

"This particular bed-and-breakfast, especially. The cinnamon rolls remind me of my grandfather." The moment he'd said it, he wished he hadn't. He blamed the cozy atmosphere they'd created with sex and breakfast in bed for that unintentional revelation.

She knew about his life at Thunder Mountain Ranch and that he'd landed there when his grandfather had died, leaving him without any living relatives. But he'd never talked about the man who'd raised him from the time Finn was three until he'd died of a heart attack when Finn was thirteen. The memories were so bittersweet—more bitter than sweet, really.

"He liked cinnamon rolls?"

"Loved them. It was our Sunday-morning treat from the bakery down the street."

"Nice memory." She smiled at him.

No it wasn't, because his grandfather had never had quite enough cash to pay for the cinnamon rolls. He'd played on the sympathy of the counter clerk to discount the purchase because of the hungry boy standing beside him. Finn had loved the pastries but he'd hated the serving of pity that had come with them.

Only four people in the world knew about that humiliation as well as the many others that had been part of living with a man who had been terrible with money. Cade Gallagher and Damon Harrison—the other two members of the exclusive group they called the Thunder Mountain Brotherhood—knew. And so did Rosie and Herb.

"You got really quiet all of a sudden." Chelsea gazed at him with an expression that said she wouldn't pry, but she was ready to listen if he wanted to talk.

In the end, it seemed silly not to tell her about his grandpa. After all, he and Chelsea had been business partners for five years, and in the past few hours they'd...oh, yes, they certainly had. They'd torn down some barricades, and he wondered if he'd ever be able to reconstruct them.

"My Grandpa O'Roarke was a failure." He gauged her reaction and could see she was gearing up to refute that. "Yes, he gave me shelter when there was no one else, and I'm grateful. But he barely managed to keep us housed and fed because he was so busy chasing every get-rich scheme he encountered."

Understanding was reflected in her eyes. "That explains a lot."

"I'm sure it does. His favorite dream was to own his own pub. That's probably not unusual for an Irishman, and I so desperately wanted him to succeed. But he didn't have it in him, and I was just a kid. I couldn't see where he was going wrong."

"I'll bet you do now."

"Yep. He won a little money in a lottery. If he'd invested it well, he might have been able to open that pub. But he'd invested it poorly and given the rest to a friend who was about to be evicted."

She sipped her coffee. "So he was generous, like you."

"Generosity is great if you can pay your own rent. If you can't, then you end up asking the landlord to give you a break. You end up talking the baker into letting you have cinnamon rolls for half price because your grandson loves them so."

She regarded him silently for a moment. "And you hated that."

"I did."

"I'm so glad you told me about this. I didn't know what was behind your plan to open O'Roarke's Brewhouse. Now I do."

"Maybe I should have told you sooner."

She shook her head. "We had to get to this point first."

"Meaning that we had to get naked?"

"In a way. But more than being naked, which has been an excellent experience, by the way, I needed to see your disciplined approach to your business. What if you'd confessed all this that first day in the coffee shop?"

He thought about it. "I would have sounded like a nutcase, as if my entire goal was to create a business my grandfather would have loved and make it work the way he couldn't."

She didn't say a word, simply looked at him.

"And that is my goal, pretty much." The realization hummed through his veins. "I've never fully admitted that and certainly haven't said it to anyone else, but that's it. I want to do what he couldn't, both for him and for me."

"And you have."

"Thanks to you." He'd never been more aware of his debt to her than he was now.

"I wouldn't jeopardize what you've accomplished."

"Not knowingly." Even though he should be sexually satisfied, he had only to glance over at her sitting across from him on the bed and his thoughts turned to warm skin and hot kisses. They had an important assignment this weekend, and yet being with her had become a priority.

Her expression was soft with compassion. "Believe it or not, I can be the voice of reason."

"I sure do hope so, because I'm quickly discovering that when sex with you is an option, I'm the voice of what-the-hell."

"You're not used to letting go. To use a horse analogy, you've been keeping yourself penned up. It's logical that when you jump the fence for the first time, you'll go a little crazy."

"Oh, you think so?" He took her mug, put it on the tray and moved everything to the bedside table. "I'll show you how crazy I am, lady." And he tackled her, making her giggle as he pushed her down on the soft sheets.

Then he held her arms above her head while he placed butterfly kisses on her cheeks and her mouth. He didn't dare settle into a real kiss because his beard would scratch like the very devil.

"I've known you could be," she said breathlessly. "I've known it forever."

"Turns out you were right." He moved down her body, nipping at her soft skin but always careful not to rub his prickly chin against her. He licked her navel until she squealed and swatted him away.

Then he settled between her thighs, but before he zeroed in on his target, he carefully laid sections of the top sheet over her creamy skin.

"Now that's crazy." She lifted up to watch what he was doing. "I don't care about a little whisker burn down there."

"But I do. Now lie back and relax because I'm going to make you come again. It's been at least an hour, so you're due."

She flopped back onto the mattress. "I was wondering when you'd check the schedule and realize that."

"Now. Right now." And he returned to his favorite place in the world. To think until last night he'd never visited paradise. He'd never experienced her seashell-pink softness, moist with her arousal. He'd never tasted the tangy aphrodisiac of her.

And he'd never heard her rich moan of pleasure when he used his tongue right *there*. He circled the spot again and she arched off the bed. He raked her gently with his teeth and she cried out. Then he took full control and she exploded against his tongue, bathing it in all things wonderful.

She was right that he'd gone crazy. Licking and nuzzling her heat in the aftermath of her climax, he was already looking forward to the end of the day when they could be alone and he was granted the right to touch her like this again.

He dared any man who'd discovered this kind of paradise to maintain his sanity. He'd tried to drive her away, but she wouldn't go. Instead she'd moved closer and invited him to enjoy her body for as long as he wished.

God help him, he wasn't strong enough to refuse an invitation like that. She knew all the terrible truths about him and she still wanted him in her bed tonight. And when they came together again, they'd have supplies. He'd finally know what it was like to sink deep into her warmth.

He suspected that sensation would make him crazier than ever.

6

CHELSEA HAD ALWAYS imagined she could tell whether a couple was having sex by the way they acted with each other in public. She thought about that as Finn pulled the gray SUV into a circular gravel drive in front of the Last Chance's imposing log ranch house. Not only had she and Finn spent most of the past twelve hours in bed together, but on the way here they'd made a quick detour to the Shoshone General Store. Consequently a box of condoms rested in a small bag at her feet.

Finn thought the purchase would eventually be common knowledge in a town the size of Shoshone, but Chelsea was okay with that. Or so she told herself. Having people know that she was involved with Finn shouldn't matter. Her nerves were probably due to the presentation she was about to give.

No, that wasn't it. Last night when she'd first met the Chance family, she hadn't been sleeping with Finn. Now she was, and despite considering herself a modern, evolved woman, she felt a little self-conscious about that. Stupid, but there it was.

"The Chance family has quite the layout." Finn braked in front of the steps leading up to an elaborately carved wooden door. Rockers lined the long front porch, which stretched on either side of the main entrance.

He glanced at a parking area off to the side of the house that was already crowded with cars and trucks. "Maybe you should get out here. Might be easier on your shoes."

"It would. Thanks." Besides, if she arrived first, that might emphasize the professional nature of her trip here and minimize her connection with Finn. This was a business event, after all, and she was the one giving the presentation. She'd rather not have anyone speculate on her personal life today.

"I'll help you carry your stuff in."

"That's okay." A truck pulled in behind them and she quickly opened her door and grabbed her laptop case. "You should probably vacate the driveway and get a space before they're all gone."

He hesitated.

"Seriously. Much as I appreciate your offer." He was in gallant cowboy mode and certainly looked the part. She'd had trouble keeping her hands to herself when he'd appeared in a dark blue shirt with silver piping and gray Western slacks that matched his hat. "I can handle this."

"Okay." But he didn't look happy about it. "See you in a minute."

"Okay." She stepped down and wobbled a bit as she made her way across the gravel driveway with her laptop slung over her shoulder. She hoped the gravel wouldn't chew up her heels. They weren't expensive, but she liked them and they went great with this dress.

And now they had a hot memory attached. She'd never forget the sensation of Finn gently removing her shoes. The memory sent warmth rushing through her and she paused on the first step to give herself a quick lecture. Thoughts that made her skin flush were exactly why people would suspect she was sexually involved with a certain tall cowboy.

Instead of thinking about Finn, she should concentrate on her immediate surroundings. He'd told her that the Last Chance Ranch was considered a landmark around here, and she could see why. Few people built a two-story log house this immense unless they planned to turn it into a hotel.

Fall flowers in yellow and orange bloomed in carefully tended beds on either side of the steps, softening the overpowering effect of the massive structure. The square center section was flanked by two wings set at an angle resembling open arms. She couldn't imagine how many square feet the house must contain.

As she mounted the steps, the door opened and Jack Chance came out, dressed like Finn except all in black. "I estimated you'd be arriving about now." He flashed a smile. "Let me carry your laptop." He neatly divested her of it before she could open her mouth.

"Thank you, Jack." Cowboys just couldn't help being chivalrous, apparently. If they were hardwired to make these gestures, she might as well relax and enjoy it.

"Lily's inside setting up the projector."

"Lily?" She started toward the door, although he'd probably get his hand on the handle first.

"She's a computer genius, literally." He moved ahead of her and opened the thick wooden door. "When you asked about a projector and screen, I put Lily on the case. She's married to Regan, Nick's partner in the vet clinic, and she also runs an equine rescue operation on the far side of town." He motioned Chelsea inside the house.

"Equine rescue? That sounds fascinating. I wonder if she'd be willing to do some guest lectures at Thunder Mountain Academy."

"You should ask her. She'd probably love it if you took a drive out there tomorrow to see her setup."

"Great idea." The possibility of adding an equine rescue expert to the staff was exciting, both from a humanitarian and a marketing standpoint. She prayed that many generous backers awaited her inside so that all the plans could go forward.

Inside the entryway she took a quick inventory of the living room, which was already full of people. A magnificent curved staircase swept up to the second floor and a wagon-wheel chandelier hung from the beamed ceiling. She figured the usual furniture had been moved elsewhere. Instead, straight-backed chairs and a few folding ones had been lined up in front of the fireplace, which had been draped with a white sheet.

No one was sitting, though. They'd gathered in groups around the perimeter of the room to chat with friends and neighbors. Everyone clutched either a mug or a glass and most held a small plate of cookies, too.

A long table on the left side of the room was the source of the goodies. A coffee urn sat there, along with a clear glass dispenser for lemonade. Platters of cookies were on the far end, along with plates and napkins.

As a PR person, Chelsea was delighted with the welcoming venue. As a staunch supporter of Thunder Mountain Academy, she was touched. Thank goodness she'd spent so much time on her presentation and felt good about how it would be received.

Sarah hurried toward her and held out both hands. "Chelsea!"

"This is such a wonderful thing for you to do, Sarah." Chelsea squeezed her hands. "It sets just the right tone for the presentation. Thank you."

"It was a group effort. I can't wait for you to meet everyone, but I'm sure you'll want to check with Lily first. She's right up front with Jack."

Chelsea turned and discovered Jack had taken her computer case with him. He stood next to a card table while he talked with a woman wearing jeans and a tie-dyed shirt. She also had the reddest hair Chelsea had ever seen. Gabe's wife Morgan had red hair, but this woman's was so bright it practically gave off sparks.

"Come on." Sarah motioned Chelsea to follow her. "You can trust Lily. She'll make sure the technical part of your presentation goes off without a hitch."

"Great." She made her way up the aisle behind Sarah and

was introduced to Lily. Chelsea liked her firm handshake and her steady, intelligent gaze. "I appreciate you being here."

"Of course! I would have showed up anyway, so I'm happy to help."

Sarah squeezed Chelsea's shoulder. "I need to go mingle. When you're finished setting up, come on over to the refreshments table and I'll introduce you to a few people."

"Perfect. Thanks." Chelsea sent her a look of gratitude.

After Sarah left, Jack glanced at Lily and Chelsea. "All set, then?"

Lily smiled at him. "Chelsea and I have everything under control. Thanks for helping me bring in the projector."

"No worries. Sorry Regan couldn't make it."

"Me, too, but that mare needs him right now." After Jack walked away, she turned back to Chelsea. "My husband's a vet."

"Jack told me."

"He wanted to be here, but he got called out to monitor a problem pregnancy. Jack helped me with the projector. God love these cowboys, they can't stand to see a woman carry anything heavier than a purse."

Chelsea laughed. "I've noticed."

"Anyway, let's get you hooked up and test the system."

As they were setting up, Finn arrived and Chelsea made the introductions. "Lily runs an equine rescue operation," she added.

"Oh, yeah?" Finn looked impressed. "What a great thing to do."

"Isn't it?" Chelsea glanced at Lily. "Would you mind if we came out to see it tomorrow?"

"I'd love to have you. Regan should be there, so you can meet him, too. Come for lunch if you want, although I warn you I'm a vegetarian, so you won't get any meat."

"That's no problem for me," Chelsea said.

"Or me," Finn said. "I'm Wyoming born and bred, so I used

to think I had to have steak with every meal, but living in Seattle has changed my mind."

"Then I'll expect you both around one for veggie lasagna." Lily finished hooking up the cables and turned on Chelsea's computer. "Call up your file and let's see if we're ready to rock and roll."

The connection worked perfectly, but Lily insisted on staying to babysit the equipment while Finn and Chelsea went over to join Sarah and be introduced to the guests. Chelsea used her honed memory tricks to keep track of names and faces. That was always good when meeting new people, but it was especially important when asking them for money. She answered questions about Thunder Mountain Academy and explained her involvement in the project.

Finn seemed completely at ease, and she couldn't help contrasting that to five years ago when she'd worked with him on his own Kickstarter campaign. At first he'd balked at the idea of seeking donations from strangers and she'd thought his reluctance stemmed from being a foster boy. But it had been deeper than that. He'd remembered living with a grandfather who'd never had enough money.

But once he'd understood that renovating the old historic building meant giving something valuable back to the community, he'd gradually become more comfortable with the process. Now he was fighting for the couple who'd created a safe haven for him and so many other boys. He obviously had no problem seeking help under those circumstances.

They made a good team as they chatted with people who might possibly mean the difference between success and failure for Thunder Mountain Academy. The meet-and-greet was going along smoothly until Pam Mulholland arrived. She came over to the refreshments table and smiled at Chelsea and Finn. "So how did you both sleep?"

Finn choked on his coffee, which sent several people, mostly women, rushing to his aid. Chelsea stepped back and let them fuss over him while she ducked her head and tried to regain her composure. If Finn hadn't reacted, she might have been able to keep her cool, but her cheeks felt hot.

Apparently, Jack wasn't one of the people making sure Finn didn't choke to death, because he hurried over to her instead. "Are you okay? You're as red as the paint job on my truck!"

"Thank you, but I'm fine. Just…" What? As she gathered her wits and raised her head to meet his gaze, she scrambled for an explanation that had nothing to do with choking, which would be too coincidental. Finally she sacrificed her professional poise to the cause. "Anxiety attack," she murmured. "I'll be fine once I start my presentation."

"You get nervous?" He didn't seem to be buying it.

"A little."

"Must be more than a little. You really were red."

"I know."

"But you're looking better now. You're more the color of bubble gum than tomato juice." He gave her a wink. "That bright red clashed with your purple hair."

"Lavender." She took a deep breath. "Thank you for being concerned."

He nodded, acknowledging her gratitude, but his dark eyes continued to assess her. Then he lowered his voice. "Funny how you and O'Roarke lost your cool at the same time."

"Life is strange."

"Isn't it? Pam comes in and asked how you slept and O'Roarke chokes while you get stage fright. Go figure."

So he'd guessed what it was all about, but she would neither deny nor confirm. "One of those crazy coincidences."

"I knew when you two walked in the Spirits and Spurs last night you had unfinished business with each other."

"Oh?"

"For what it's worth, I'm in favor of taking care of unfinished business." He patted her on the shoulder. "I should probably also mention that the boys are setting up our little homemade dancing platform for the barbecue tonight. We'll have a DJ instead of live music, but he's an excellent DJ. I can say that because he's Josie's brother. I hope to see you and O'Roarke out there."

"We will be. Last night was fun." Then she realized that could be taken more than one way. "I mean, the dancing was—"

"I hope it was *all* fun. Now, what do you say? You're the star of this little show. Shall we get this party started?"

She took another deep breath. "Yes."

"You don't really get stage fright, do you?"

"Not really."

"I didn't think so. You're like me, in control of yourself. I don't get it, either. In fact, I'll be up there introducing you, so if you're ready to go…"

"Bring it on."

"Atta girl." Jack cupped her elbow before turning toward Finn. "Showtime, O'Roarke. Everybody else, find a chair!" Then Jack escorted her to the front of the room.

She recognized that his casual gesture of taking her elbow gave her the seal of approval for the entire crowd. If she was Jack's buddy, then they would listen to her. Finn joined her and they stood together as Jack explained who they were and why they were here.

"And as an added enticement," Jack said, "they've brought these amazing Men of Thunder Mountain calendars, created primarily by our own Dominique Chance, who donated her services." He gestured toward where she sat and the group applauded.

"And," Jack continued, "the calendar happens to feature me as Mr. July. Check it out." He opened it to his picture and walked back and forth, displaying it.

Chelsea worked hard to keep from laughing. He was in his element, and he was going to help bring money to the cause. Jack obviously loved his life as a rancher, but if he ever decided to get into PR, he'd be a natural.

"They brought a limited number of these calendars," Jack

said, "so if you want to take one home, you have to pledge a minimum amount today. If you donate later on, a calendar will be mailed to you, but what we have here is instant gratification until the supply runs out and the added incentive of autographs from four of the calendar boys. Now, let's all silence our cell phones so we can watch the presentation Chelsea's created for us."

Chelsea gave the signal to Lily and the PowerPoint began. It looked almost flawless and drew generous applause at the end. Chelsea added her pitch for Thunder Mountain Academy, one she'd practiced carefully. She discussed the various items being offered to backers in addition to the calendar, such as weekends at the ranch and guided trail rides. The largest contributions would earn a free two-week session for the teen of their choice.

Then Finn said a few words about what Thunder Mountain Ranch had meant to him and why he felt it should continue teaching the values and skills he'd learned there. He told a few stories that made everybody laugh. But the obvious sincerity in his voice affected everyone, including her.

Afterward Chelsea used the card table as a base of operations, setting up her laptop so guests could make an online pledge. Chelsea's pulse rate jumped as the amount grew rapidly.

She wanted to nudge Finn and get him to look, but he was busy autographing the April page of the calendar. Jack, Gabe and Nick sat nearby, signing their pages, too.

Lily had to take off to check on the animals at her place, but she'd glanced at the screen before she'd left and given Chelsea a thumbs-up. The number kept rising, but at the end, when the last guest had gone out the door, they were not quite there.

Oh, but they were so close. So close. Chelsea was jubilant. She motioned to Finn. "Come see!"

"How'd we do?" He glanced at the screen and whistled. "Not bad!"

That brought the rest of the family over. Amid the hugs, back-slapping and high fives, Finn excused himself to go call Rosie.

When he came back in from the porch, Chelsea walked over to him. "What did she say?"

His voice was husky. "Not a whole lot. Mostly she cried."

"Aww." Chelsea's throat tightened.

"She said to give you a big hug, but if I did that, I might not be able to let you go."

"Later."

"Yeah." He glanced over her shoulder. "Hey, there, Jack."

He came up beside her. "Just wondered how your folks reacted to the news."

"I only talked to Rosie, but she's overjoyed and very grateful. And so am I. This was an awesome event."

Jack rubbed his chin. "The thing is, you've almost got it. I was hoping you'd top out. I'm thinking I should just—"

"No, Jack." Chelsea shook her head. "We still have a few days and you've already been so generous."

"She's right," Finn said. "Much as I'd love to hit that magic number today, we're so damn close. That money's bound to come in. You hosted this event and made a sizable pledge already. Someone else will come through for the rest."

"All righty, but if that needle is still sitting there on the last day, you call me, you hear?"

"We will," Finn said. "Don't worry. But I'd say we've got it." His smile was a mile wide as he gazed at Chelsea. "We've got it."

"Well, in that case, let's celebrate!" Jack turned and spread his arms wide. "It's time to party, but first we have us a little mess to deal with." He started folding up chairs.

Chelsea immediately stood and folded up her chair.

"Whoa, not you, Miss Chelsea." Jack came over and took the chair. "You're our honored guest. Only the family has to work around here. And O'Roarke can lend a hand, because I know how much he'd hate being forced to sit and watch us slave away."

She looked him in the eye. "So would I, Jack. Thanks for giving me a pass, but I intend to do my share."

"Oh, well, in that case, here." Grinning, he handed back the chair. "Welcome to the family."

7

FINN COULDN'T BELIEVE the transformation in Chelsea during the past few hours. She'd morphed from a polished professional who made all the right moves, kept track of names and said all the appropriate things, to a goofy lady who joked around and didn't seem the least bit worried about her appearance.

When the air turned cooler during happy hour out on the porch, Sarah took her inside to raid her closet. Chelsea returned looking like a kid in her big sister's clothes. She'd rolled up the legs of the too-long jeans and the sleeves of the oversize sweater. Amazingly, the shoes fit.

As everyone commented approvingly on her outfit, she paraded up and down the porch like a model on a runway. Later on, Josie's brother Alex and his wife, Tyler, arrived with all the grandkids in tow. Nick and Dominique's son Lester, a teenager they'd adopted several years ago, developed an instant crush on Chelsea.

Finn could completely relate to the kid's starry-eyed worship. Chelsea took it in stride and teamed up with Lester to direct the smaller kids in a game of hide-and-seek until it was dinnertime. Naturally all the kids wanted to sit with her, which meant Finn was out of luck.

During the meal served outside, she ate barbecue with her

fingers and then licked them clean. It was cute as hell, but it was also erotic. He finally had to stop watching.

Instead he talked with Alex and Tyler. Alex was blond like his sister Josie while Tyler had dark hair and an olive complexion. Cassidy had a date, so Uncle Alex and Aunt Tyler had volunteered to watch all the kids for the afternoon.

"And I'm not too proud to admit I'm bushed." Alex grinned. "They're great kids, lots of fun, but, oh, my God, are they active."

"Thank heaven Chelsea was willing to take over when we got here," Tyler said. "I love them to death, but I was so ready to turn them over to somebody else. I don't know how Morgan does it with three under the age of five."

"And Morgan's your sister, right?" Finn was still trying to keep everyone straight. He didn't have Chelsea's skill at matching names and faces.

"I know it's confusing," Tyler said. "I took after our Italian mother and Morgan took after our Irish father, so nobody can believe we're sisters, but you can tell immediately that Alex and Josie are related."

"I can." Finn glanced at Alex. "Your sister has a great venue in Shoshone with Spirits and Spurs. I envy her that antique bar with the mirrors and brass fittings. I'd love to have something like that in O'Roarke's, but it wasn't in the budget."

"Josie was smart," Alex said. "She bought it when the market was down and the owners wanted out. Now Spirits and Spurs is a little gold mine." He smiled. "She wants me to help market her beer once she gets going."

"You're in marketing? I thought you were a DJ."

"Only for Chance parties now. I handle the marketing for the Last Chance's horse-breeding program."

"Does Chelsea know that? I'll bet she'd like to trade war stories."

"She might not know." Alex gestured to the table where Chelsea was wiping the barbecue from a toddler's face. "She threw herself into the breach right after we got here and we didn't have a chance to talk. In fact, I wish we could have been here to see the presentation, but babysitting seemed more important."

"Next time Cassidy has a date," Tyler said, "I might have to fly Chelsea in from Seattle."

"I had no idea she was so good with kids." Finn watched the action at the other table with admiration.

"How long have you been together?"

He swung back to Tyler in confusion. "Excuse me?"

Her eyes widened. "Whoops. Sorry. I just assumed…never mind. I shouldn't have leaped to conclusions. Bad habit."

"No need to apologize." Finn took a steadying breath. "We've worked together for five years but never dated. Recently…" *Less than twenty-four hours ago.* "That's changed."

Tyler nodded. "I'm glad my radar isn't totally off. She seems very special."

"She is." He glanced over at the table and noticed that Josie, Morgan and Dominique had descended and were claiming their respective offspring. "And I think she's just been relieved of duty. Excuse me a minute." He moved toward her but hung back as she hugged each tearful child in turn.

Josie passed by first, holding her son Archie by the hand and carrying her daughter Nell. "We're giving the kids a bath and putting them to bed in the ranch house," she said. "I told Chelsea how much we appreciate her effort, but please mention it again. She was a lifesaver."

"I'll tell her."

The five younger ones all left, but Lester seemed reluctant to go. Dominique talked to him, and at last he nodded and trudged back to the house with her.

Chelsea came toward Finn, her smile bright as the stars blinking overhead. "Hi."

"Hi, yourself. When you said I had a lot to learn about you, you weren't kidding."

"I love kids. My cousins all have kids and I'm constantly volunteering to watch them. They're so creative and uninhibited. And the parents seem to love having a break."

"You amaze me." He'd never seen her like this, in clothes that didn't fit and her lipstick worn off. A little girl's flowered barrette was in her hair, probably lovingly placed there by one of the girls. "A few hours ago you were the consummate professional."

She shrugged. "That's one side of me."

"You do realize Lester is smitten."

"He's adorable. Dominique promised him that if he'd help get the other kids in bed, he could come back and have one dance with me."

"Just one?"

"That's all. Dominique explained that I already have a boyfriend, but that you'd allow him to have a dance with me because you're a nice guy."

Finn's pulse rate kicked up a notch. "I suppose she just said that because she needed to keep Lester from getting too attached."

"No, she said that because everyone here assumes we're sleeping together."

That sent his pulse into overdrive. "Why?"

"The way you look at me. The way I look at you. I thought maybe it wouldn't be obvious, but Jack picked up on it this afternoon when we both freaked out about Pam's comment. Judging from things other people have said to me, it's now everybody's assumption that we're together."

"And yet we haven't even had sex yet, not really. Not in the classic sense of the word."

She looked into his eyes. "But we will."

"Oh, yeah." He was suddenly short of breath. "I'm ready to leave now, but we can't."

"Nope. Not after they went all-out for us. We need to stay and celebrate." Her eyes shone. "But I was just thinking that we're close enough to the goal that I could put the rest on my credit card."

"No, that's not a good—"

"I won't do it now. That's only if we get down to the wire. I'm not letting this get away when we're inches from the finish line."

"Let me talk to Damon and Cade. They might have some room on their cards. You shouldn't be putting it on yours when you've already done so much."

"I'm sure none of us will have to worry. The money will come in. But I'm just saying that it's within range and I really don't want to call Jack."

"I know. We're close enough now that we can figure it out among ourselves. And, boy, do I feel like celebrating…in private."

"We will. Be patient."

"I'll do my level best, ma'am." He lowered his voice. "While you were licking barbecue sauce off your fingers, I thought I might have to excuse myself and take a cold shower."

She smiled. "Exactly what I was going for."

"Chels."

"What? Is there some rule that you can't take care of little kids and taunt your lover at the same time?"

"Honest to God, if we didn't have to stay here, I'd haul you back to the B and B and—"

"Hold that thought." She touched her finger to his lips. "Now let's go over and talk to Alex and Tyler. I heard he's in PR and she's the event planner for the town. They might have some suggestions for Thunder Mountain Academy."

His brain still fizzing with thoughts of barbecue sauce and Chelsea's naked body, he followed her back to the table where Alex and Tyler were sitting. If he'd worried that she'd abandon all thoughts of their project now that the presentation was over, he was dead wrong. She might not be dressed to impress, but she obviously wouldn't let that stop her from making important professional contacts.

"We didn't get to talk before." She sat beside Tyler. "But I didn't want to miss a chance to pick your brains. Has Jack filled you in on what we're doing at the academy?"

"He did," Tyler said, "but before we get into that, thank you from the bottom of my heart for taking over entertaining the kids."

"It was fun. I've had lots of practice with my cousins' kids."

"You'd think I'd had lots of practice coming from a family of seven, but I've forgotten what I ever knew about children, apparently."

"And I never knew much in the first place." Alex shook his head. "It's embarrassing to admit I can be intimidated by a five-year-old, but I'm no match for Sarah Bianca."

Chelsea laughed. "Oh, yeah, SB. She informed me that she's going to be a saddle maker when she grows up. I guess she met Ben Radcliffe when he delivered Sarah's birthday saddle last December and she's decided that's the job for her."

"Too bad she's not a little older," Finn said. "She could enroll in the academy."

"It'll still be there when she's sixteen." Chelsea said it with conviction. "That's only eleven years from now. I love thinking of the long-range possibilities of this program."

"That's the strength of it," Alex said. "I've built the Last Chance campaigns on longevity. The academy is new, but the history behind it isn't. I'm sure you used that in your presentation."

"She did." Finn was eager to share the finer points of the video. "She got clips from my foster mom that showed the contribution to the community that Thunder Mountain has made in the past and then she connected that to the potential for continuing that kind of legacy. It was great."

"Send us a copy," Tyler said. "I have a few contacts from my days as a cruise director. If you don't mind, I'll share it with them and see if they might have grandchildren who would be interested in the program, especially if grandma and grandpa were willing to finance it."

Chelsea beamed. "That would be awesome. The more people who know about it, the better."

"Have you considered radio spots for future marketing?" Alex pushed away his empty plate. "People still listen to the radio in their cars. I don't know what your advertising budget will be once you get everything in place, but I could check out some of the major markets and get back to you. If you decide to go that route, I'll record a spot for you."

"Fantastic idea!" Chelsea beamed at him. "I'll look forward to getting the info. Anything else?"

"The calendar's great." Tyler sipped on her wine. "Fun intro. But once you have things rolling, how about doing another one featuring a special student for each month? You'd have to get a release from the parents or guardians, but I think—"

"Yes!" Chelsea bounced in her chair. "Brilliant. Parents would go nuts over that. After today's success, we can start seriously planning for that in the future. I love that idea."

Alex gazed at her. "Anytime you want to brainstorm, just call, email or text."

"I will. I wish I'd known earlier that the Chances had both a marketing guru and an event planner in the family."

"My job's pretty easy," Alex said. "The horses practically sell themselves, plus you've seen Jack in action. He schmoozes like nobody's business. And then we'll have Gabe put on a cutting-horse demonstration, and people can't get their money out fast enough."

Chelsea sat up straighter. "Cutting-horse demonstration?" She glanced at Finn. "Did you know about this?"

"Nope, but I can see where you're going with it."

She turned back to Alex. "Do you think he'd consider teaching a session here and there at the academy? He'd get paid, of course. We don't expect any of the instructors to work for free."

"I can't speak for him, but I think he'd love it." He turned to Tyler. "Don't you?"

"I do. He used to enter competitions all the time, but he doesn't do that as much now that he has three kids. A few teaching gigs might be just the thing—a short trip without the stress, yet he'd have a reason to keep his skills sharp."

"Then I'll ask him."

"Ask who what?" Jack came up to the table.

"Gabe," Tyler said. "Don't you think he'd love teaching cutting-horse sessions at the academy?"

"Hell, yes. Sounds perfect. The competitive circuit was too intense for a family man, but now he's bored and driving Morgan crazy."

Tyler laughed. "I didn't want to say that, but it's the truth." She glanced at Chelsea. "You'd be doing both Gabe and my sister a big favor."

"Yep," Jack said. "I recommend you broach the subject tonight. He'll be here any minute. The kiddos are almost tucked in. We're about ready to start the dancing if our friend Alex here will stir his stumps and spin us some tunes."

"I'm on it." Alex pushed back his chair. "I expect all of you to get out on the dance floor and make this effort worthwhile."

"We will, sweetie." Tyler smiled at him.

Finn experienced a moment of panic when he thought he might be expected to alternately escort Tyler and Chelsea onto the floor. He decided to take defensive action. "I should warn you, Tyler, that I'm not a very good dancer."

"Relax, Finn." She reached over and patted his arm. "The word's out already."

"It is? Who talked?"

"Shoshone's a small town."

He sighed. "I didn't realize it was *that* small."

"Well, it is. Everyone knows everyone else's business. Apparently, Jack gave you enough of the basics last night that you can manage, but Jack, Gabe, Nick and even Pete will make sure I enjoy a few dances. It's not your job."

"Thank you."

She smiled. "You're welcome."

He turned to Chelsea, about to ask her for the first dance, when Lester appeared at her elbow.

His gaze was filled with adoration. "Mom said I could ask you to dance, but only one time. So would you like to?" He shot a furtive glance at Finn. "That's if it's okay with your boyfriend."

Finn regarded him solemnly. "Chelsea makes her own decisions."

"I'd be honored to dance with you, Lester." The music hadn't started, but Chelsea rose from her chair and walked with Lester to the wooden dancing platform. Lester was short for his age, so without her heels, Chelsea was about his size.

Alex's voice came on the mike. "It's a beautiful night in Wyoming. Let's rock and roll!" And the music blasted out, something loud and full of energy.

Lester looked startled, but then he began gyrating to the beat. Chelsea did, too, and in her borrowed clothes, she looked more Lester's age than her own. Considering her lack of dancing experience, she did a fair job of it.

Other couples quickly joined them. Finn spotted Jack and Josie, and they weren't dancing the two-step. Instead they looked like a couple of teenagers wiggling around up there.

"Alex is from Chicago," Tyler said, "so he'll play country songs most of the time, but he's known for throwing in some classic rock to shake things up."

"Looks like everyone's good with that."

"They are. And Lester's having the time of his life."

"Yeah." Finn couldn't help grinning as he watched Chelsea rocking out. "So's Chelsea."

"She's great. I don't know either of you very well yet, but I hope this works out between you two. You seem right for each other."

"Thank you." Finn didn't know what else to say. And suddenly he didn't want to be on the sidelines anymore. "Listen, you don't have to go up there with me, but would you like to dance?"

"Sure. Why not?"

So he escorted Tyler to the dance floor. Turned out she was a woman with rhythm to spare. She coaxed him to let go, and he found himself rotating his hips in ways he'd never tried before. He finished the dance laughing and breathless. When he looked for Chelsea, he found her gazing at him with a knowing smile.

After giving Lester a hug, she walked over and glanced at Tyler. "Can I borrow him for a while?"

"You bet. I got him all warmed up for you."

"Much obliged." Chelsea grabbed him by the shirtfront and tugged him to the center of the platform. "Dance with me, you sexy cowboy."

As a slow country tune started up, he pulled her close and gazed down at her. "You know, if anybody had any doubt..."

"They don't. Do you mind?"

"Nope."

"Good." She slid her arms around his neck. "Without my heels, we don't match up quite as well."

"Sure we do." He nestled her head against his chest and wrapped his arms around her as he swayed to the beat and moved as little as possible.

"Are you doing that shuffle thing?"

"I am." He rested his cheek on the top of her head.

She sighed. "Nice."

"Uh-huh." He'd never felt so warm and alive, or so sure that he belonged right here with Chelsea at this moment in time. Thunder Mountain Ranch was about to be saved. For now, everything was perfect.

8

ALTHOUGH CHELSEA WOULDN'T have minded going straight from the dance floor back to the Bunk and Grub, that wouldn't be a very polite way to end the evening. So she and Finn stayed, and while she desperately wanted to be alone with his adorable self, she had a good time dancing and hanging out with the Chance family.

When they drove away a couple of hours later, after she'd changed back into her clothes and hugged everyone goodbye, she almost hated to leave. Then she glanced at the strong profile of the Stetson-wearing man behind the wheel of the SUV, and she didn't mind leaving at all.

He looked over at her. "I feel like it's been years since I kissed you."

"Same here."

"Hang on. This'll be a fast trip."

"Better not push it. Remember what Alex said."

"About what?" He hit a rut hard and swore under his breath.

"You need to go slower."

"I can see that, but you'd think they'd do something about this damn road."

"I guess you were getting us drinks when Alex and Jack were talking about that. It's bumpy on purpose."

"You're kidding." He hit another rut, but at this speed they only bounced a little.

"Sarah's first husband liked keeping the surface rough. He thought it discouraged trespassers. After he died, Jack declared it would stay that way. They only grade it when it gets *really* bad."

"Then I suggest they get out here with a tractor, because it's *really* bad."

"Alex was trying to convince Jack that it was time, but Jack just laughed. Apparently the debate over the road has been going on for years."

"Well, it's worse at night, that's for sure. When we drove in, I probably avoided the ruts without thinking much about it. But it's black as pitch out here. I'll have to crawl."

"Probably a good idea."

"It's a terrible idea." He eased over to the side of the road and switched off the motor. Then he put his hat on the dash.

"Finn, what are you doing?"

"Something I've been thinking about for hours." He unfastened his seat belt and opened his door. Reaching up, he turned off the overhead light.

That simple gesture told her what he had in mind and her pulse switched into high gear.

Moving with deliberate purpose, he walked around to her side of the SUV and opened her door and the back door. Next he deftly released her seat belt. Last of all he picked up the bag from the floor and put it on her lap. "Hold these." Then he scooped her up in his arms.

"You can't be serious!" Her heart pounded in anticipation. "Someone could come along!" Despite that protest, her skin heated and moisture gathered between her thighs.

"No, they won't. They all decided to stay for poker. Nobody will be on this road for another two hours."

"You're certifiable." The night air did little to cool her off. Finn was taking charge and she was on fire. "Totally insane."

Yet as he leaned down to tuck her inside the backseat of the SUV, she helped him by scooting across the smooth leather.

"We already knew that." He unbuckled his belt, stripped it off and tossed it on the floor. "Now it's just a question of degree." He reached for the button on his jeans.

Her breath caught. He hadn't asked. He hadn't suggested. He'd simply taken command of the situation, and now she was wild for him, so wild that she felt as if she could come at any second. "Stopping alongside the road to have sex when there's a perfectly good bed waiting definitely puts you higher up on the scale." The paper bag rattled when she took out the box. She was trembling just that much.

Nearby, crickets chirped in the tall grass. It was the only sound except for the distinctive buzz of his zipper. "I'll take one of those."

He was only a dim outline in the darkness, but she handed a packet toward him and he plucked it from her fingers. "You'd better take off your panties." His voice was thick with desire. "I might rip them."

She tugged them off over her shoes, not bothering to unbuckle those little straps. He wanted her *now*. God, that was exciting.

Tossing the damp panties to the floor, she hitched up her dress. No time to take that off, either, because he was climbing in.

"Scoot down a little." The words came out tight with strain. "There." Strong hands slid along her thighs, parting them, positioning her, finding her moist entrance. "Ah, Chelsea. You're so wet."

She gulped for air. "Because… I want you."

"I'm here." Braced above her, he slowly guided the blunt tip of his penis into her slick channel. "So good." He gasped. "So damned good."

She had no words. The sensation of him filling her left

her speechless and quivering with pleasure. Instinctively she clutched his beautifully firm ass and urged him forward.

He groaned and plunged deep. She came at once, arching upward with a sharp cry. Breathing hard, he remained rock-solid, firmly tucked inside her as he absorbed her contractions. When they slowed, he began to pump.

Immediately her body tightened again. She would always treasure what they'd shared the night before, but this...*this*. She whimpered with the glory of it, reveled in the sensual feel of his muscles bunching and releasing as he stroked.

At first he moved easily, but soon his thrusts became faster, until at last he drove into her with relentless precision. Her second climax lifted her off the seat. Wailing, she gasped out his name.

Bracing her backside with one large hand, he held her there as he sucked in air and pushed in tight. His powerful orgasm vibrated through her and his full-throated groan of satisfaction shattered the stillness of the night air. Then, slowly, he lowered her to the smooth seat and followed her down. His cock continued a slow, rhythmic pulsing, sending delicious shock waves through her body.

He gulped for air. "My God. I had...no concept."

"No." She panted, unable to catch her breath. "Me, either."

"I feel like someone hit me with a sledgehammer."

"Then don't move."

His soft chuckle seemed to increase the intimacy of the moment. "I can't. Not yet."

As she lay beneath him, waiting for the world to settle down again, she realized that neither of them would ever forget this. Had they driven back to the Bunk and Grub first, the experience certainly would have been memorable. But it wouldn't have been nearly as vivid as coupling in the backseat of a rented SUV under cover of a cool and very dark Wyoming night.

"Are you okay?"

She laughed. "Never better."

"So I didn't mash you against the seat or bang your head against the armrest?"

"No. You just gave me two mega climaxes in a row and probably wrinkled my dress." Then she considered her right shoe, which was currently pressed against his thigh. "Is my high heel hurting you?"

"I can feel it, but it's kind of kinky to think of us doing it while you wore your shoes."

"Finn O'Roarke, I do believe you're a sensualist."

"Takes one to know one. Where's your mouth?" He finally located it with the tips of his fingers. "I need to kiss you."

"Okay." She waited until his lips found hers. Then she cupped his head and kissed him back.

"Mmm." He slipped his tongue into her mouth.

She sucked on it gently and felt his cock twitch.

He lifted his mouth away from hers. "Okay, guess we can't kiss, after all. This has been fun, but I want the next time to be in an actual bed."

"Not up against the wall?"

"How you talk!" He gave her a quick kiss and began slowly easing away from her. "Yeah, maybe up against the wall, now that you mention it. I checked, and Pam is staying with Emmett tonight so we'll have the main part of the house to ourselves again."

"Maybe she's doing that on purpose to give us privacy." She groped around for her panties.

"Maybe." He climbed out of the SUV.

As she found her panties, which were unsurprisingly damp, she could hear the rustle of material as he put himself back together. "I'm not putting my panties back on, FYI."

"Are you telling me you're going to ride back to the Bunk and Grub commando?" He zipped his pants.

"Yes, I'm telling you that."

"You do realize I'll be thinking about it the whole way there." He grabbed his belt and threaded it through the loops.

"Now I do. Bonus."

"You're a wicked lady, Chelsea Trask."

"Apparently you find that appealing."

"I think I just demonstrated how appealing I find that. Okay, scoot over here and I'll carry you back to the front seat."

"I'll scoot over, but you don't have to carry me. I can walk."

"There's high grass and loose dirt. Not the kind of terrain for those sandals. Let me be a hero."

"You already are, but okay." She slid toward the door. "Ready."

He leaned in, but instead of picking her up, he kissed her. Not only that, he slipped his hand under her dress and fondled her until she was squirming. When he backed away she was once again breathing hard.

She swallowed. "No fair."

"Oh, it's very fair." He scooped her into his arms and carried her around the open door before settling her in the front passenger seat. "Girls who announce they're going commando, which makes the guy's cock hard as a gearshift while he's trying to drive, have to expect a little payback. Now buckle up."

He really had her motor running, now, and she loved it. They'd settled into a sexual give-and-take that was exactly how she'd imagined it might be with Finn, only better.

He climbed behind the wheel, closed the door and fastened his seat belt. "What did you do with your panties, by the way?"

"They're on the floor back there along with the box of condoms. Why? Looking for a souvenir?"

"I won't need one." He started the car and pulled back onto the road. Then he reached for her hand. "I'll never forget that episode."

"Neither will I."

He laced his fingers through hers. "Thank you, ma'am. I appreciate you indulging me."

She smiled at his deliberate cowboy-like expression. "Like you gave me a choice."

"I didn't, did I? But somehow I had a feeling you'd go for it."

"Then you're starting to know me better."

"Good. That's very good." He released her hand and took a deep breath. "Now let's talk about something safe so I'm not compelled to pull over again and do you."

And he would, too. Her body grew moist and hot. "Like what?"

"I want to know how you can be totally focused on work one minute and then it's like you flip a switch and you're able to play hide-and-seek with a bunch of kids."

"You mean how do I separate work and play?"

"Yes. Because obviously I can't. I've been able to let go this weekend because I'm far away from O'Roarke's and there's not much I can handle from here."

She hesitated. It was an important question that could impact both of them. "I think it's something you could learn," she said carefully. "If you wanted to."

"I'm not so sure. When I'm in Seattle, I have a constant need to check inventory, taste-test the brews, monitor the cash flow...just *be* there."

"Kind of like the parents of a newborn."

"I know nothing about that, but, yeah, maybe."

"I've watched my cousins, and they were all like that with their first kid."

"And then they got over it?"

"Eventually. It took some longer than others. The second kids are always easier."

"Well, I'm not opening a second brewhouse. That would make me twice as anal." He was quiet for a while. "I don't think it's the same, though. Kids grow up to be self-sufficient, or at least that's the plan. A business never learns to run itself."

"No, but you can delegate some of the work."

"Um, yeah. I'm trying not to imagine how Brad is doing without me there. When I was gone in June I came back to a total mix-up with receipts that took a week to straighten out. It wasn't anything that would sink the ship but, face it, he's not as invested as I am." He took a deep breath. "Let's talk about your family some more."

She could feel the tension radiating from him, so she gladly changed topics. "I have a younger sister, but I felt as if I had more siblings because my aunts and uncles were usually around with their kids."

"In Seattle?"

"No, in Bellingham. That's where my folks live and where I went to high school and college."

"See, I didn't even know where your hometown was. I thought it was Seattle."

"It is now. I think of Seattle as home." She paused. "Do you?"

He hesitated. "I think so. But after the divorce... I haven't felt like my cramped little apartment is home. It still feels temporary."

"It probably is temporary. Where would you live if you could afford any place in Seattle?"

"Somewhere down by the water, within walking distance of Pike Place Market and O'Roarke's. Something like what you have."

She told herself not to put any importance on that. "Then you should focus on what you want. You'll recover from the financial hit of the divorce and eventually you'll be able to live down there. I may be renting now, but I plan to buy when I feel comfortable taking on that kind of obligation."

"And you'll do it. You always accomplish what you set your mind to."

"Not always." She'd been so convinced that his divorce was divine intervention and they were destined to be together. But even now, when they'd had such great sex, she wasn't sure. The explosive nature of that sex might be the very thing that would scare him off. He had a business to run.

They rode in silence for a few minutes and she wondered if he knew what she was thinking. He might.

If so, he obviously didn't want to talk about it. "What do your folks do in Bellingham?"

"Both college professors. Mom's in psychology and Dad's in economics."

"And you didn't want to follow in their footsteps?"

"God, no. My sister, Beth, is getting her graduate degree, but I don't have the patience to teach the same bunch of students for an entire semester. My folks love it, but I would go postal if I had to walk into the same classroom three days a week. I like more variety than that, more control over my schedule. I was born to be self-employed."

Finn laughed, and the tension seemed gone. "I was, too. My grandpa couldn't get it right, but I knew that was the life for me. His bad example taught me a lot about what not to do."

"And in a twisted sort of way, he helped you."

"I suppose. Rosie tried to get me to see that, but at the time I wasn't willing to listen. I was a self-righteous kid who thought I'd never make any big mistakes. Boy, was I wrong."

She reached over and squeezed his thigh. "Give yourself a break, O'Roarke. We all mess up eventually."

"You don't."

"Sure I do." She let her hand rest there because she loved feeling his thigh muscles flex as he worked the gas pedal.

Without warning, he captured her hand and held it against his thigh. Then he slowly moved it to his crotch. "Feel that?"

Did she ever. His fly barely contained what lay beneath. "Yes."

"That's what happens when you put your warm hand on my thigh. All I can think about is finding the nearest flat surface—horizontal or vertical, doesn't matter—and pounding into you until neither of us can see straight."

"Sounds fun." She was being flip but her heart beat like a jackhammer.

"Oh, I'm sure it will be. But you'd better keep your hands to yourself or I'm liable to seduce you in the parking lot of the

Bunk and Grub." He pressed her hand tight against his fly and then gently placed it on the console.

She sat there quivering and wondering if she could last until they reached the parking lot, or if she'd end up begging him to pull over again and take her now, right now. She'd never been this crazed with lust for a man. That made her vulnerable, and she briefly acknowledged that. But with the prospect of having Finn in her bed all night, she couldn't bring herself to care.

9

FINN WAS PLAYING with fire and he knew it. The deeper he allowed himself to sink into this sensual bliss with Chelsea, the more difficulty he'd have extracting himself when the time came. And it would come. On this trip he felt free to carve out large sections of time for this madness, especially now that Thunder Mountain was as good as safe. Back in Seattle it would be a different story.

But he would challenge any man to turn his back on a woman who sashayed up the dimly lit stairs of the bed-and-breakfast in strappy sandals, a dress wrinkled from backseat sex and no panties. The irresistible aroma of sex trailed after her, and his cock swelled with every step leading to the room where he could have her again.

At her suggestion, her laptop had stayed in the locked SUV. He smiled thinking about her terse *"Leave it."* She was as eager for him as he was for her, which almost convinced him to reach for her and take her on the stairs. No one was around and he had a box of condoms in his hand.

He controlled himself. He'd already given in to his impulses once tonight in the backseat of the SUV. Surely he could wait five more minutes before he turned loose the primitive urges raging through him.

He clenched his jaw as she fumbled with her key. Knowing

that she fumbled because she was shaking with anticipation only inflamed him more.

The night before he'd held back, asked questions. All that was gone now. Once she opened the door, they tumbled inside, each of them wrenching at the other's clothes. Maybe because she'd planted the idea, he did take her up against the wall, her legs locked around his hips and her breasts jiggling with every firm thrust.

The rhythm was muted but steady. If anybody had been close by they would have known exactly what was going on in this room. He felt her tighten, felt his own orgasm surge forward and shoved deep. They both came, their cries mingling as their bodies trembled and throbbed.

He sagged against her, gasping, his head spinning as he rested it on her shoulder. He couldn't say how long they stayed like that. After a rocket-ship ride with Chelsea, reentry was a slow process.

"Finn." Her breath tickled his ear.

"I know. We need to move. Give me another minute."

"It's not just that."

He dragged in a breath and raised his head to look into her eyes. "What?"

"We left the door open."

He turned to see, and sure enough, her bedroom door stood wide-open. If anyone had been around and had cared to peek in, they would have enjoyed an eyeful. "Oh."

She snorted with laughter. "Is that all you have to say? *Oh?*"

"Well, yeah." He grinned at her. "I mean, what sort of comment covers a situation like this? We just had wall-banging sex with the door wide-open to the hall of this very lovely bed-and-breakfast. What would the etiquette police say about that?"

"They might suggest that we close the door. Even though we're fairly sure no one is upstairs at this hour of the night, we could be wrong. The housekeeper might have heard strange thumping noises and come up to investigate."

"If she works in a bed-and-breakfast and thinks rhythmic thumping noises at eleven on a Saturday night are strange, then she's lived a very sheltered life."

"I agree, but we should still close the door."

"You're right." He let her down slowly so she wouldn't fall. "I'll leave that to you while I take care of the condom."

"I should be able to manage it."

When he returned, she'd closed the door and climbed into bed. But she'd thrown back the covers so that he was treated to the sight of a naked Chelsea stretched out on soft white sheets. Another woman might have covered herself, but not Chelsea. She apparently liked the no-holds-barred dynamic they had going on.

And so did he. He probably liked it way too much, but now was not the time to question that. All he had to do was to gaze at her lying in bed propped up by several snowy pillows, and he felt desire stir in his groin.

She watched him approach and her glance moved from his face to his slowly rising cock. "Again?"

"That's just my opinion. You may be getting sick of this."

She looked up at him. "Finn, I'm going to tell you something, and maybe it's a mistake, but I'll tell you anyway."

"What's that?"

"From the moment I first saw you in that coffee shop, I've dreamed about having sex with you."

He found that hard to believe. She'd been so sure of herself, and he'd been so clueless about how to survive in the big city. "Why?"

She smiled. "Just asking that question, for example. You're incredibly good-looking but you don't seem to realize it. Women notice you, but you don't seem to see them noticing."

"Sometimes I do."

"You don't act like it."

"If I notice back, then that implies I might want to start something. And I have a business to run." He heard himself and groaned. "God, that sounds sanctimonious. I promise to stop saying that. Even I realize it's becoming obnoxious, like I'm the only person in the world with responsibilities."

"But you're the sole owner of that business," she said gently. "And that's another thing that attracted me. You're very brave. Not too many guys I know would move by themselves to a distant city and plan to open a business on their own."

"And I would have crashed and burned if I hadn't met you."

"I don't think so. It might have taken you longer to succeed, but you were extremely focused."

"Still am."

"I get that. But as you said, the business is far, far away." She patted a spot next to her. "And I'm right here."

He picked up the box of condoms from the floor and tossed them in her direction.

Catching it neatly in one hand, she rolled to her side, facing him as he climbed in beside her. She placed the open box between them on the mattress. "Two down, ten to go."

"Should've bought a bigger box." He took one out and laid it on her pillow. "But first, I'm running low on kisses." Closing the box, he tossed it over his shoulder and it landed...somewhere. He'd find it later.

For the moment his primary target was her rosy, plump mouth. The brief thought that all this kissing might have to end someday made him even more eager to taste often and well. He moved over her and supported himself on his elbows while he gazed into her eyes.

Reaching between them, she wrapped her fingers around his cock. "I want this." Her eyes darkened as she stroked him.

"And you'll get that, but now it's kissing time. Turn me loose so I can concentrate."

"You're getting bossy." But she released him and slid both hands up to his shoulders. "This better be a really good kiss."

"You tell me." He stroked the pad of his finger gently over

her lower lip. Leaning down, he nibbled on it before tracing it with the tip of his tongue.

"That tickles."

"I love touching you here." He outlined the graceful bow of her upper lip with his finger and then with his tongue. "Your mouth is perfect for kissing. Like this." He pressed his lips to hers briefly, lightly, playfully. "And this." Changing angles, he did it again. "And this, and this, and this." He kept it up until she laughed.

"You're silly."

"Mmm." Then he captured her mouth fully, fitting it to his with deliberate intent. He made a leisurely exploration with his tongue, sliding it easily along hers.

Her breath caught.

Shifting the angle, he cupped her jaw and stroked the corner of her mouth with his thumb, urging her to open to him. He kept his thumb there and took the kiss deeper. The thrust of his tongue grew more demanding, more suggestive.

She whimpered and hollowed her cheeks, sucking him in. Her fingertips dug into his shoulders as she lifted into his kiss, her mouth hot and eager. He responded with firm strokes that told her exactly what would happen next.

As she moaned and arched her body toward his, silently begging for that next step, he barely restrained himself from taking it. Ending the kiss, he grabbed the condom, tore open the package with his teeth, and rolled it on.

She lay there gasping. "Hurry."

"Oh, yes, ma'am." He sank into her slick heat with a groan of pleasure. Then he looked into her passion-dark eyes. "This part of you is perfect, too." He pushed deep.

She took a shaky breath. "That was one hell of a kiss."

"You helped make it that way." He eased back and slid in up to the hilt again.

"It was so close to…this." She wound her legs around his, cinching them even closer together.

"My plan." He dipped his head and took her mouth again as he held himself still inside her. Only his tongue moved, yet she tightened around him as if he'd been thrusting steadily.

One spasm became two and then she was coming, sucking hard on his tongue as her climax rippled over his cock.

His climax followed quickly, urgent and strong, making his toes curl and his body flush with heat. He lifted his mouth away and gulped for air. Then he leaned his forehead against hers. Gradually his heartbeat returned to normal.

"Some kiss, O'Roarke." She slowly relaxed and sighed in obvious contentment. Her breathing evened out.

When he roused himself enough to look into her eyes again, they were closed. "Chels?"

She didn't respond, although a smile remained on that beautiful mouth. She'd fallen asleep.

How like her to go until she couldn't anymore. She hadn't wanted to give up these precious moments any more than he had. But finally exhaustion had claimed her.

He gazed at her with a rush of tenderness laced with guilt. She'd been a willing partner the night before and she'd given her all today despite not getting a full night's sleep. After a successful presentation and the triumph of almost reaching their goal, she'd entertained five young children and danced for two hours. Then she'd once again become his enthusiastic lover.

Dropping a light kiss on her forehead, he eased away from her. "Sweet dreams, Chelsea Trask."

SHE WOKE TO golden light streaming in the window and no Finn in bed with her. But he'd left a note on Bunk and Grub stationery propped on the nightstand where she'd see it right away.

Dearest Chels,
I decided to sleep in my own room because if I stayed here,
I might reach for you in the night. Maybe you wanted to
have sex with me from that first day we met, which is still

amazing to me. But I doubt you wanted to have this much
sex. I'll see you down at breakfast.
Yours,
Finn
PS I put the condoms in the nightstand drawer.

She thought back to the last thing she remembered from their
night together. He'd kissed her so thoroughly that he'd created
an intense craving. He'd proceeded to satisfy that craving by
locking them together and kissing her again until they'd both
had an orgasm without moving at all. Incredible.

After that...she had no idea. Apparently she'd fallen asleep
with his cock deep inside her. But he didn't sound insulted in
his note—his words were sweet and considerate, just as he was
when he wasn't being macho and sexy, or adorable and funny,
or...preoccupied and anal.

She showered and dressed while she thought about that last
aspect of Finn O'Roarke. It had the power to cancel out all the
rest. She'd witnessed it first-hand during the painful episode
when she'd asked him out and he'd calmly explained why he
couldn't accept.

He might well be someone who wasn't capable of delegat-
ing because he didn't trust anyone else to do the job. If that was
the case, then he wouldn't have room in his life for her or any
woman. He could build a successful business in Seattle and
expand the territory for his microbrewery. Someday he'd have
the money to buy a place down near the water.

She'd continue to get her checks for a percentage of his boom-
ing business, but she wouldn't be in the picture otherwise. Ironi-
cally, he could make her a lot of money. She'd rather have the
man than the money, but she might not get that choice.

His door was open when she walked into the hall a little
past eight. She checked to see if he was in there, but the room
was empty. He'd pulled up the covers on his bed, although she

wouldn't say he'd actually made it. His laptop was out and his gray hat was brim side up on the dresser.

The signs of his solitary life made her sad, as if he'd already moved on. He hadn't, of course. They were scheduled to spend many more days together, and she couldn't imagine him giving up sex with her unless she was the one who called a halt.

She wouldn't do that. Right now he clung stubbornly to his world view, and maybe he was right. But there was always the chance that he was shortchanging himself. In that case, she'd be there when he figured it out. If he never figured it out, she'd have some beautiful memories of what Finn was like unplugged.

Pam had been right—the smell of coffee led her straight back to the breakfast room. It turned out to be a sunny spot filled with green plants and several tables and chairs that reminded her of outdoor cafes in Paris. She'd never been to Paris, but she'd seen enough pictures to recognize the look.

Finn sat alone at a table drinking coffee and reading a newspaper. He'd turned back the sleeves on his long-sleeved white shirt to reveal his muscled arms sprinkled with dark hair. That alone was enough to tighten the coil of desire in her belly.

He must have heard her footsteps because he glanced up. His smile of welcome told her that he had no intention of pulling back from their interlude. He stood and watched her approach. "You look ready to visit an equine rescue operation."

"It's the best I can do." She'd worn a long-sleeved purple T-shirt, jeans and her running shoes.

"You look great." His gaze moved over her with a trace of hunger.

"Thanks." She cherished that hunger because she wasn't sure whether he'd look at her that way once they were back in Seattle.

"How did you sleep?"

"Like the dead." She lowered her voice. "Missed you, though."

"I didn't trust myself." He motioned to a chair. "Have a seat. I'll get you some coffee. I asked Yvonne to hold off breakfast until you showed up." He walked over to a coffee urn on a side table.

"What if I'd slept until ten?"

He had his back to her as he filled her cup. He shrugged. "We would have made different plans."

"You could have gone ahead and eaten."

"No, ma'am." Turning back to her, he brought her coffee and set it in front of her. "That's not how I operate."

"Meaning what?"

He sat across from her. "Meaning that I want to share breakfast with you."

She looked into the warmth of his blue eyes. "That's nice, Finn. I'm sorry I fell asleep on you last night."

He shook his head. "I'm the one who should apologize. I don't know what I was thinking. I knew you were concerned about the presentation and had stayed up late working on it before the flight. Then I kept you up the next night with..."

"I wanted that as much as you," she said softly.

"I know, but yesterday was intense with the presentation, convincing backers to contribute, and then playing with the kids, and then dancing. I didn't think about you being tired. I just thought about—well, you know what I thought about."

"I thought about it, too. You still don't seem to realize how much I crave your—"

"There she is—the sleeping beauty!" A small, dark-haired woman came into the room. "Are you ready for breakfast, now, Miss Trask?"

"I'm starving," Chelsea said. "Are you Yvonne?"

"I am, indeed."

"And you cook as well as handle the housekeeping chores?"

"That's right." She smiled. "It's a beautiful house to work in."

"It is! And you make wonderful pastries. I can't wait to have some more."

"Coming right up!" The housekeeper turned and headed back to the kitchen.

Finn's attention remained on Chelsea, almost as if they hadn't been interrupted. "I'm flattered that you want me that much, but you know what? Maybe it's time for me to back off a little and let you catch your breath."

She met his gaze. "Don't you dare."

"All right." He chuckled. "But maybe we should at least have some breakfast first. We need to keep up our strength."

"Of course, if you need me to back off so you can catch your breath, then—" She gulped in surprise as he left his chair and pulled her out of hers.

His mouth came down with deadly accuracy. His kiss was short but it delivered a powerful message that left her gasping. Then he settled her back in her chair and returned to his. "Does that answer your question?"

"Yes." She took a shaky breath. "I do believe it does."

10

KISSING CHELSEA MIGHT not have been the wisest course of action. Finn no longer cared about breakfast. He wanted to haul her back upstairs. But he couldn't forget the moment when he'd glanced down and discovered that she was fast asleep. When she was awake, she was a force to be reckoned with, a woman with a sharp wit and a smart mouth.

But with her eyes closed and her mouth curved in a soft smile, she'd looked...vulnerable. She didn't need a man to protect her. He'd never make the mistake of assuming that. She was totally in charge of herself and would resent someone who suggested otherwise. He wouldn't back off, but there was nothing wrong with slowing down, just a little.

So after Yvonne served the food, they ate a leisurely breakfast. They had things to discuss, after all, concerning Thunder Mountain Academy—Gabe's potential classes in training a cutting horse, Alex and Tyler's suggestions, and Lily as a potential guest lecturer on equine rescue efforts.

When they'd finished eating, they lingered over coffee. Now that they'd become lovers, it was a totally different experience from the old days when they'd met in the coffee shop to go over business issues. Without the constant level of sexual frustration that had made all their Seattle discussions edgy and vaguely uncomfortable, they could relax and just be with each other.

"It's so good to know the end is in sight and, one way or another, we'll have the money by the deadline," Finn said.

"No kidding. I'm glad it won't be like that nail-biter we had with yours."

"That was intense." They'd hovered over her computer in the same coffee shop where they'd met and reached the goal a few minutes before midnight. Then they'd gone out for drinks.

She smiled. "That might be the only time I allowed myself to drink too much when I was around you."

"Same here." He met her gaze. "I almost asked you to come home with me."

"I almost asked you to come home with me. But I was afraid you'd say no."

He sighed and leaned back in his chair. "I might have. I don't know. I was pretty happy that night and we'd had several rounds. I might have said yes."

"And then regretted it in the morning?"

He hesitated as he considered the question. "At this point, I can't imagine ever regretting being with you, but, yeah, it's possible. Honestly, Chels, I don't know why you haven't written me off."

"I tried, especially when you married Alison. I worked really hard to find someone who'd take my mind off you."

"I know." Even now his chest tightened when he remembered those agonizing months of his marriage and Chelsea dating other guys.

"No, you don't. You didn't even notice."

"How could I not notice? You brought that first dude, the one with the pretentious beard, into O'Roarke's."

"He did not have a pretentious beard."

"Oh, come on. Trimmed to a little point? Give me an effing break."

"Okay." She seemed to be trying to keep from laughing. "It was pretentious. And scratchy."

"I don't want to hear about that part. All I know is you cuddled in a booth with him for an hour and forty-five minutes."

"You timed us?"

"Damn straight. Watched the whole sickening performance from the kitchen and every minute was torture. Don't tell me you didn't bring him in on purpose so you could wave him in front of my nose."

"Of course I did! But you never said anything so I thought you hadn't seen us and it was a wasted effort. And don't talk to me about torture. You were *married.*"

"Dear God." He scrubbed a hand over his face. "Well, we won't be going through that kind of nonsense anymore. I'd say our cards are finally on the table."

"But the game's not over."

"Yes it is." He reached for her hand. "No more games. I love being with you and wish I could be more like you so that I could neatly compartmentalize my life. I don't know that I can."

She gave his hand a squeeze. "I believe you can, but that doesn't matter. *You* have to believe it."

"I wish I could." Looking into her eyes was a pleasure, one he'd denied himself for years. He hadn't dared let his attention rest there, but now he took every opportunity to bask in the warmth of her gaze. "I'm glad we're going to Thunder Mountain. It seems really important for you to see it."

"I can't wait, Finn. I've been hearing about the ranch ever since we met and I know how much it means to you. I wouldn't miss going there for anything, especially now that we know Rosie and Herb will be able to keep it."

"I'd like to leave first thing in the morning, if that's okay. We can grab breakfast here, but then take off."

"Works for me. Are you willing to drive again?"

"I thought I would. Then you can look at the scenery. You didn't do much of that on the drive from the airport."

"Actually, I could use those hours to work."

"Oh." He shifted his thinking. "Are you getting behind? Here

I've been raving on about taking time away from my job and you've had to do that, too."

"No worries. It's just that right before we left I picked up a new client. He knows I had this trip, but he'd like to have a proposal for his new PR campaign ASAP. He's on a tight deadline and if I can come through, he could be a good source of income for future campaigns."

Her comment provided a much-needed reality check. "Then definitely I'll drive and you can work. I should have asked you before if you had your own stuff to do instead of assuming you were going to be fancy-free once the presentation was over." He released her hand and pulled out his phone. "We don't have to leave for Lily and Regan's until a little before one, so you'd have some time now if you need it."

She shook her head. "It's a beautiful day. I'd rather take a walk through town. Shoshone's so different from what I'm used to and I'd like to check it out. Who knows when we'll be back?"

"Sounds great to me, but I don't want to interfere with whatever you need to do."

"I promise you won't. I wanted to make this trip, both to help out and to be with you. I'll do some work tomorrow, and maybe a little bit while we're at Thunder Mountain. It'll be fine."

Once again, she seemed so comfortable with switching back and forth between work and play, so certain nothing would fall between the cracks. He envied the hell out of that. "Then I'll get my hat. Need anything from upstairs?"

"Just you."

Damn, but that sounded nice. "Be right back."

"I'll wait for you on the front porch."

"Okay." He whistled a catchy little tune as he made a quick trip upstairs. They'd danced to it the night before, although he couldn't remember the lyrics. He hadn't whistled in years... five, to be exact.

What an uptight bastard he'd become. Now that the tension was ebbing away, he'd like it to stay gone. But would it? He knew himself, and once he was back in Seattle, he'd probably have the same compulsion to monitor everything 24/7. Although this trip had given him some breathing room, the fear of failure still lurked in his heart.

After fetching his hat, he went out onto the front porch and found Chelsea sitting in a white wicker chair looking as mellow as he felt. She had a project demanding her attention, but she was putting it aside to spend time with him. He didn't take that lightly.

"You look settled in," he said. "Would you rather stay on the porch and watch the world go by?"

"I'm not sure a lot of the world will go by on this little corner." She stood. "Let's go explore."

"Yes, ma'am." He held out his hand and she linked her fingers through his without hesitation. Walking along the sidewalk holding hands seemed so natural, yet they'd never done it before.

He'd kept any touching to a minimum with Chelsea. Oddly enough, she'd done the same, although she was a hugger with people she knew and liked. He decided to mention it. "I just realized that until this weekend, you've never hugged me."

"That's right."

"So it was intentional, then. Did you think I'd push you away?"

"I wasn't sure what you'd do, but I decided not to risk it, considering the heat we seemed to generate when we were close to each other. I figured a hug could go one of two ways. Either you'd reject it because it was too intense, or we'd end up in the nearest coat closet tearing at each other's clothes."

"Option B is the most likely. I touched you as little as possible because I didn't trust myself. I was worried about that on this trip." He laughed. "Guess we know how that turned out."

"Blame it on the dancing."

"Or I could drop to my knees in gratitude because of the dancing, and the cold walk home, and finding myself in the room next to yours with no other guests in the house."

"So you don't think you'll regret what's happened?"

"I'd be a fool if I did." He hesitated. "How about you?"

"To steal your comment, I'd be a fool if I did."

"No matter what?"

She squeezed his hand. "No matter what. Obviously you believe we won't have the same dynamic in Seattle, and you could be right."

"I probably am. I've known myself a long time."

"True, but we won't find out until we get there. At least we won't have that other thing, that weird Frankenship where we couldn't admit we were in lust."

"'Frankenship'?"

"Sort of a friendship, but with strong sexual overtones that made us act like zombies around each other. A Frankenship. It's a term I made up."

He grinned. "Perfect description. I'm glad we killed it."

"Actually, you killed it. I was headed into my room to sleep alone Friday night until you admitted you were crazy for me."

"But then I was ready to give up for lack of condoms. I say killing our Frankenship was a combined effort. And now it's dead." He took a deep breath. "And I've never felt more alive."

"Good sex can have that effect."

"It's not only the sex, although that's a huge part of why I'm feeling so good. It's—I hate to say this—it's being away from O'Roarke's."

"But weren't you gone for almost a week in June?"

"Yeah, but I was worried sick about Rosie, and then when her condition seemed to be less dire than we'd all thought, we found out that they were about to lose the ranch. Now Rosie's in good health and we have a way to save the ranch." He looked over at her. "But mostly it's the sex."

She laughed. "Thought so. Well, we've walked the length of Main Street."

"So we have."

"Now what?"

He paused to look around. "I got so carried away with what we were talking about I didn't pay attention. Sure is quiet."

"Sure is. Except for the diner, everything's closed up tight. A lot different from Seattle on a Sunday morning."

"That's for certain." He glanced back at the area they'd already covered. While engrossed in their conversation, he'd walked past the general store where they'd bought the condoms, a post office, a hair salon and an ice cream parlor, all closed.

Spirits and Spurs stood at the far end on the opposite side of the street. Beside it was a feed store, and he pointed to a life-size plastic horse on its roof. "You won't see anything like that in Seattle."

"Probably not." She glanced at the building next to it. "No one-story banks, either. But judging from the brick they used, it was probably put up about the same time as the building you renovated for O'Roarke's. In fact, there's mostly brick construction along this street, except for Spirits and Spurs."

"Which might be the oldest structure in town."

"I wouldn't be surprised." She gazed across the road where six pickups were angle-parked in front of the diner. "I'd love to support the local economy, but I'm stuffed from breakfast."

"Me, too. We could go there for dinner."

"Oh, I forgot to tell you. Josie wondered if we'd meet her and Jack for dinner at Spirits and Spurs."

He pictured dancing with Chelsea again and the idea filled him with pleasure. "Sure, that would be great."

"She's really serious about a microbrewery and wants to start ordering equipment. She'd love your advice."

"I'd be happy to talk to her about it, but that might not be so easy if there's a band."

"No band tonight."

"Oh."

She chuckled. "You should see your face. Do you want to dance? Maybe they have a jukebox or a sound system."

"I never thought I'd look forward to dancing, but the minute you mentioned Spirits and Spurs, that was my first thought. I do like it way better than I expected to, and besides, it's a great excuse to hold you."

"Then we'll see if they have music available. Ready to walk back?"

"Guess so." He surveyed the street again. "Let's cross over and walk down the other side."

"Watch out for traffic." Then she laughed. "Kidding."

"It really is a sleepy little town." Other than the pickups in front of the diner, the street was deserted. "I wonder if Josie can make a go of a microbrewery in a place this small."

"If that's all she had to work with, probably not, but she's planning to draw from surrounding areas, and specifically Jackson. Tyler and Alex have all kinds of promotional ideas once Josie gets going."

"And it'll have the Chance name attached. That should help." He decided the joy of holding hands was underestimated. Feeling that connection while walking with Chelsea was turning into one of his favorite things.

"I don't think she intends to trade on the Chance name. The Spirits and Spurs is her baby, not Jack's, and I get the impression she wants the microbrewery to be her project, too."

"But wouldn't the Chance name boost sales? They're so well known around here."

"It might, and naturally some people will know she's married to a Chance, but she doesn't want to emphasize that. The important hook will be the historic saloon, ghost drinkers in the bar and all of that. This family is terrific, but she doesn't want to be totally defined by her association with it."

Finn had a tough time imagining being overwhelmed by family or rejecting a great marketing tool like the Chance name. "I don't really get it, but my buddy Cade might. He was freaked out when he suddenly discovered he was a Chance cousin and instead of having no relatives he had a boatload. But I was a little jealous of the guy."

"Having been here for a few days, I can see how the Chances could be intimidating. We're dealing with a dynasty here, and Josie wants something that she made all by herself. I can understand that."

"Yeah, maybe. I only had one relative, and that didn't feel like enough."

"But he focused all his attention on you. I had a friend who was an only child and I thought that was great. No competition."

"I guess that's true." He felt an unexpected tug of nostalgia. "We did stuff, just the two of us. Simple things like going fishing and camping, sometimes renting movies if it was bargain day. I need to remember that."

She glanced at him. "He sounds like a nice man."

"He was." He didn't say anything for a while. "I'm kind of hard on him, but he was a nice man. He knew I was lonely. He used to say that he'd love to adopt a sister or a brother for me, but he couldn't afford it."

"That's touching."

"It is now. At the time I was mad because I didn't have anybody to play with."

She squeezed his hand. "I get that. Beth and I have had our knock-down, drag-out fights, but I'm glad she's there. If I ever have kids, I'd like to have two."

"Do you want some, then?"

"I do, assuming I find the right person. How about you?"

He sighed. "Honestly, I don't see myself having any."

"How can you be so sure?" Her words had an uncharacteristic edge to them, as if she might be tired of hearing him say things like that.

"I'm just being realistic, Chels."

She sighed. "I know. Sorry. God knows people shouldn't have children unless they really want them."

"Or feel they can give them the time they'll need."

"Right."

"You'd make a wonderful mother, though."

She glanced at him. "Thank you. I think I would, too."

11

THEY WENT BACK in silence. Chelsea resisted the urge to challenge Finn's stubborn belief that he couldn't be a successful businessman and have a personal life. She hadn't walked in his shoes, after all. She hadn't been a kid whose grandfather had begged for half-priced pastries.

His marriage to Alison hadn't helped matters, apparently. Chelsea hadn't gotten to know her very well. She'd been too busy being pea green with envy. But she suspected that Alison had painted an appealing picture of a more relaxed lifestyle. It was a worthy goal, but Alison hadn't been the right woman to carry it off.

Chelsea had done some investigating after Finn and Alison's quickie Las Vegas wedding. Okay, a *lot* of investigating. Alison worked a nine-to-five salaried job for a paper-products company and she'd met Finn because he placed orders through her.

The life of a business owner had nothing in common with a salaried employee. Someone with a regular paycheck was unlikely to relate to things Chelsea felt on a gut level—the uncertainty of monthly or yearly income, the constant threat of some catastrophe wiping out profits and the realization that you were the driving force behind it all.

She understood why Finn was so determined not to let anything interrupt his concentration. She also realized that if he didn't find a way to deal with that kind of pressure and give himself permission to enjoy life outside of work, he could be headed for a lonely life at best and an early grave at worst.

In her PR business, she'd seen it happen. Whether or not Finn ended up with her, she didn't want him to be alone and unhappy. Someone like Alison wasn't likely to be the answer, as he'd found out. Chelsea couldn't guarantee that she'd be any better at helping him balance his priorities, but she felt qualified to make the attempt.

They exchanged only pleasantries as they returned to their respective rooms and got ready for lunch with Lily and Regan. Chelsea decided pleasantries weren't working for her. Leaving her room ten minutes before they were scheduled to start downstairs, she knocked on his open door.

He glanced up from the room's small antique desk where he'd been typing something on his laptop. "Is it time to go? I thought we had—"

"We do. We don't have to leave yet. May I come in?"

"Sure." He shut down the computer and stood. "Something on your mind?"

"You know there is. We started out that walk in a cheerful mood and somehow ended it on a sour note. I want to fix that."

He tunneled his fingers through his glossy, dark hair, mussing it in a very sexy way. "Me, too. What happened?"

His innocent question grabbed her by the heart. He wanted to be happy and carefree, but the poor guy didn't know how. "I think we forgot to live in the here and now."

After a long pause he nodded. "You're right. Instead of walking down Main Street and enjoying the beautiful day and a chance to be together, we got into the subject of having kids."

"Yep. A loaded subject that had nothing to do with our activities today. I can't speak for you, but creating a baby is not a high priority for me today. In fact, I was present when we bought an entire box of supplies to keep that from happening."

"So we did." His frown disappeared and a slow smile touched

his beautiful mouth. "And that's where we should place our focus, on the use of the contents of that box."

"That's my conclusion." She moved in close and slipped her arms around his neck. "Not right this minute, because we have places to go and people to see. We also have a dinner date with Josie and Jack. But after that…" She wiggled against him.

He pulled her in tight. "And we should take advantage of the privacy we have now because I have no idea how things will shake out for us at Thunder Mountain."

"Because they think of us as platonic business associates?"

"Uh, not exactly."

"What do you mean *not exactly*?"

"I mean that Cade, Lexi and Damon, because they all know me so well, might have picked up on a certain…interest I had in you back in June when we asked for your help."

She was delighted to find out that his friends had some advance knowledge of the situation. "What about Rosie and Herb? Do they have any clue that we might be more than friends?"

"Herb doesn't usually get into that kind of issue if he can help it, but Rosie is a matchmaker from the get-go. She'd love to think something was going on between us."

"But we'll have separate sleeping quarters, obviously."

"I'd expect that. They'll probably give you a room in the house and I'll be out in the Thunder Mountain Brotherhood cabin."

"The cabin you shared with Cade and Damon when you all lived at the ranch?"

"That's it. Rosie always assumes any of us who show up will want to sleep out there for old times' sake."

"Then we'll be separated every night, huh?"

He cupped her bottom and his fingers flexed against the denim. "'Fraid so. Unless we get creative."

"Let's do that." She nudged his fly. "Let's definitely do that."

"It makes no sense for me to sneak into the house where

Rosie and Herb would be right down the hall, so you'd have to sneak out and visit me in the cabin."

"How soundly do they sleep?"

"Herb sleeps like the dead. After years of having so many teenage boys to worry about, Rosie keeps one ear open all the time. And she has eyes in the back of her head."

"Maybe that's just as well." Chelsea gazed up at him. "I don't feel right sneaking out of the house when I'm a guest. I'm sure the etiquette police wouldn't approve."

"I figured that would be the case. As it happens, I've given this some thought."

"Have you, now?"

His blue eyes sparkled. "After the past two nights, you think I wouldn't?"

"I'm glad, because I have no clue about this place. I didn't know if we'd have bedrooms right next to each other, like here, but if your foster parents are close by, that's not such a great setup, either."

"That's why I think, all things considered, we should plan on daytime sex."

"Oh, really? Rather than have me sneak out under cover of darkness, you want to do it in broad daylight? Where, pray tell? In the hayloft? In an empty stall? That doesn't sound like a better option to me."

"Cade and Lexi had some hot times in the tack room, but I won't put you through that. Now that I know you can ride, we can pack a lunch, pack our condoms and have us a picnic in some secluded spot."

"Oh." The image of that was erotic enough to dampen her panties. "I've never done it outside."

"It's a whole new experience."

"So you've done it?" She didn't enjoy the image of him enjoying sex in the great outdoors with someone else, but doubtless a guy as cute as Finn hadn't been celibate prior to his arrival in Seattle.

"I have, but it's been a while and I guarantee none of them were as beautiful as you will be lying on a blanket in the sunlight."

"*None* of them? Sounds like you had a high old time in the woods, O'Roarke."

"Hey, weren't you the person who just told me to focus on the here and now? Unless you want me to start asking questions about the guys you've been with…" He lifted his eyebrows.

"No, you're absolutely right. No dwelling on the past or the future. But concerning our present, won't Rosie and Herb suspect what we're doing?"

"Herb won't because I'm sure he feels it's none of his business. Rosie believes everything to do with her boys is her business, but if she likes you, she'll offer to pack the sandwiches and send us on our way."

"*If* she likes me? What if she doesn't?"

"She'll love you. I didn't mean it like that. You're great, and besides, you're the mastermind who helped us create the Kickstarter campaign. Like I said, she'll be trying to play matchmaker."

Chelsea's conscience pricked her. "I don't want to lead her to believe we're headed for the altar, though. That wouldn't be right."

"I'll handle that."

"By telling her what? That I'm a temporary diversion? That's not any better!"

Finn continued to knead her backside, which was making her hot. "I'll tell her that we're exploring our options."

"If she's as sharp as I think she is, she'll recognize that's a load of BS."

"So would you rather swear off sex while we're there?"

"No! I just don't want to fly under false colors. You say she'll know what's going on during these *picnics*. I'm reading between the lines, but Rosie seems like the kind of person—

mother, really—who expects that to lead to something permanent. Am I wrong?"

"No." Finn took a deep breath. "That's what she expects."

"Yet you and I are totally up in the air. We've made no promises. We're just enjoying each other for the time being." She liked the idea of emphasizing that to see if he'd object to the description.

He didn't. "That's right."

"I don't know Rosie yet, but I don't think she's going to like it."

"As I said, we could decide not to have sex while we're there."

"Finn, look me in the eye and tell me you'd be fine with that."

He burst out laughing. "You know I wouldn't, not after the hours we've spent in bed together, not to mention the special episode in the SUV."

"Okay, so what about that? We could take a drive. Would Rosie suspect something then?"

"Rosie will suspect something anytime we make an excuse to go off alone. She spent years raising teenage boys. She's honed her instincts."

Chelsea gazed into his incredibly handsome face. "'Exploring our options'? Is that the line you came up with?"

"It is, but if you can improve on it, please do."

"I can't. Now that you've laid it out for me and I understand we're going into a situation where we want to have no-strings sex and your foster mother would prefer a commitment by the end of the week, then *exploring our options* may be all we can go with. But I can't believe she'll be satisfied with that."

"She won't, but we may be able to hold her off with it, at least for a while. She might not corner either one of us to demand what's really going on."

"She'd do that?"

"Rosie is a force of nature. She would do that and more if she thought it was necessary to secure the happiness of her boys.

I don't know if she would commit murder for any of us, but I wouldn't want to test it."

"Wow." Chelsea smiled. "Now I really want to meet this woman. She didn't just take in foster boys. She gathered them into her tiger den and is ready to challenge anyone who would dare hurt them. That's awesome."

"She is awesome. You two will get along."

"Even if you tell her we're only *exploring our options*?"

"Sure, because she'll blame that on me. She knows what I'm like and she'll decide that I'm the one holding up the works." His voice gentled. "She's right."

"Not necessarily." Pride made her speak up. "You're a complicated man. I'm not sure I could deal with you in a relationship."

"Bullshit." He slid his hands up her back and massaged her shoulders. "You've dealt with me for five years and you haven't cracked yet. She'll take one look at you and know that if anyone can deal with me, you can."

That fascinated her. "And you, Finn O'Roarke? How do you stand on that question?"

He hesitated. "I wouldn't wish my demons on anybody, Chels. Truth be told, I think you'd be better off if you walked away."

"Now?"

Emotion flickered in his blue gaze. "No. I'm selfish enough to hope that you'll stick it out through the week. The idea of giving you up now, when I've just begun to really know you, is…a horrible prospect."

"Then don't even contemplate it. I'll stick it out through the week, and we'll tell Rosie we're exploring our options."

"Speaking of exploring, I wish we could do that right now."

"Wouldn't that be lovely?" She eased out of his arms. "But we've promised to visit Lily and Regan and find out about her horse-rescue operation. I think that's important."

"I know it is." He walked over to the dresser and picked up his hat. "Let's go." He put it on and tugged on the brim so it dipped down, shadowing his eyes and making him look sexier than ever.

Damn. He was one hot cowboy. She sighed softly.

He glanced at her in alarm. "What's wrong?"

"Nothing, except when you tug on the brim of your hat, it's like foreplay."

He grinned. "Every cowboy knows that. It's one of the major reasons to wear a hat." He slung an arm over her shoulder and guided her out of the room. "I'll try to work that gesture into my routine a few more times before we turn in for the night."

"Now see, if I know you're doing it on purpose to get me hot, I probably won't react the same way."

He chuckled softly. "Yeah, you will."

CHELSEA DISCOVERED HE was right about that. He took off his hat during lunch with Lily and Regan, which turned out to be a cheerful meal as they talked about Saturday's wildly successful event. But when he settled that hat back on his head for the tour of the property, he relaxed into full cowboy mode.

Besides tugging on the brim, he often stood with his thumbs in his belt loops. He even seemed to walk differently, more of a casual saunter than the brisk stride she was used to in Seattle. A slight drawl had invaded his speech.

Fortunately, Lily and Regan's place was fascinating, which kept Chelsea from spending the entire afternoon trying not to stare at Finn.

Peaceful Kingdom had plenty of stare-worthy qualities, including the color scheme. When they'd first arrived, Lily had been quick to point out that she'd painted the barn pink with turquoise trim and the ranch house orange with green trim.

"I wouldn't have picked these colors, but they're growing on me," her husband Regan had said, his loyalty obvious.

As they left the house after lunch, Chelsea put on her shades, but even they weren't enough to mute the outrageous color combination. Regan was a tolerant man. She felt as if she'd met him before, but that was probably because he was Tyler's twin brother. He, too, had taken after their Italian mother.

Lily led the way over to one of her favorite sections of the property, a pen containing two potbellied pigs. Chelsea had never seen one before except in movies.

"Meet Harley and Wilbur. Harley's the bigger one." Lily gestured toward the pen.

"But they're both huge!" Chelsea peered at them as she quickly adjusted her mental picture. "Aren't potbellied pigs supposed to be little and cute?"

"Sure, when they're babies," Regan said. "There's lots of misinformation about these guys out there. People who buy them don't seem to realize they're getting baby pigs. When they grow and need more room and a big mud pit to wallow in, their owners bail. We've fostered several we've been able to adopt out, but we've kept these two. We're partial to them."

Finn moved closer, obviously interested in the creatures. "I always wanted a pig, and I would have named him Wilbur, too." He crouched so he was on a level with them. "You are mighty fine-looking animals."

"If you still want a pig," Lily said, "I'm sure another one will show up here. The word is out."

"No place to keep one in Seattle." Finn stood. "But I've always thought they were cool. I tried to get Rosie and Herb to go for the idea of a pet pig, but they weren't enthusiastic, considering we already had six horses, two ranch dogs and three barn cats."

"I'd never been around pigs until I met Lily," Regan said. "Now I'm a fan. They're fun, affectionate and clean except when they've been rolling in the mud. Maybe your foster parents just need a chance to find out more about them. Lily could probably convince them in no time."

"And that's a great lead-in to what we wanted to ask Lily." Chelsea turned to her. "Would you be interested in doing some guest lectures for Thunder Mountain Academy about the horse-rescue movement? You'd be paid, of course."

Lily's freckled face lit up. "I would definitely be interested! What a fabulous idea, to educate teenagers. I'm amazed I didn't suggest it myself."

"Well, good, that's settled." Chelsea smiled at Finn. "We landed another one."

"And I can talk to your foster parents about pigs while I'm there," Lily said to Finn.

"Or not." Finn laughed. "I was the one who wanted them, and I'll only be a casual visitor. I can't in good conscience push the idea."

"But from what I saw on Chelsea's PowerPoint yesterday, it would be a great place for a couple of these guys." Lily obviously was warming to her subject. "I met Cade and Lexi when they were here. I could see them getting into pigs. Now I wish I'd invited them out to meet Harley and Wilbur."

Regan smiled and put an arm around her shoulders. "I hate to break this to you, but not everybody is passionate about pigs. And the academy's supposed to be about horses, right?"

"Right. But what's wrong with adding a pig or two?" Lily glanced at Finn. "It's worth a shot, don't you think?"

He shrugged. "If you can convince someone that a pig would be a welcome addition, then go for it. I'll even lay the groundwork when we go over there this week."

"Great!" Lily beamed at him. "Take some pictures on your phone. I made sure they were all cleaned up before you got here, so they're ready for their close-up."

"Why not?" Finn pulled out his phone and Lily let him into the pen.

Chelsea watched with a lump in her throat as Finn interacted with the pigs. He talked to them the entire time he was in there taking pictures—and he took dozens of pictures.

Lily moved closer to Chelsea and spoke in a low voice. "Does he have any animals at home?"

"Not now. His ex got custody of the cat and dog."

"He might not be able to keep a pig, but he needs some animal to love."

"I can see that." She saw so much more, too—a little boy who'd scraped out a meager life with his grandfather only to have the man die and leave him alone at thirteen. He'd been lucky enough to get taken in by Rosie and Herb, but even their love hadn't filled the gaping hole created by his past.

Now he was trying to fill it by creating a successful business. She understood why he believed that would be enough. But after watching him with Wilbur and Harley, she knew he needed so much more. She hoped he'd figure that out.

12

THE PIGS HAD been an unexpected bonus and Finn had enjoyed the heck out of them. He'd had a good time touring the pink-and-turquoise barn and meeting the rescued horses, but Wilbur and Harley had been the highlight of the trip. There was no way he could imagine having one in Seattle, though, unless he moved to the suburbs and accepted a long commute to work.

By the time he and Chelsea left Peaceful Kingdom, it was almost time to meet Josie and Jack for dinner. He glanced over at Chelsea. "Unless you want to call and say we'll be a little late, we need to drive straight over to Spirits and Spurs instead of stopping back at the Bunk and Grub."

"We can go straight there. That's fine."

"Those pigs were something."

"They were." Chelsea was quiet for a moment. "Taking a wild guess here, but did you get hooked on *Charlotte's Web* when you were a kid?"

"Yep. My grandfather and I watched the movie on bargain day. The next bargain day I begged him to rent it again, so we did. I kept that up until he said that was enough and we needed to get a different movie. So then I found the book in the library. I checked it out so many times that one day I came in and the librarian handed me my own copy to keep. I still have it."

"It was one of my favorites, too."

"My grandfather didn't like it. He said it was too sad. But I loved it. To this day I can't kill a spider." He looked over at her. "Even Cade and Damon don't know that, so I'd appreciate it if you'd keep it to yourself."

"Of course I will. I'm honored that you trust me enough to tell me. Besides, I can't kill them, either. I put them in a jar and take them outside. But being soft on spiders is easier when you're a girl."

"I suppose it is." He turned down the road leading to town. "Herb and Rosie aren't going to want to deal with a pet pig. I have no right to try to convince them they should."

"What about Cade and Damon, or even Lexi? Maybe one of them is a fan of the story and always secretly wanted one."

"If Cade or Damon is, they would have backed me on my campaign when we lived there. Lexi might like the story, although I've never heard her mention it. I need to get over this and not expect someone else to adopt the pig I can't have."

"Or you can find out if there's a potbellied pig rescue group in Seattle. You could have a charity event at O'Roarke's to raise money for it."

"Damn, Chels, that's brilliant. Let's do it."

"You want me to coordinate it for you?"

"Who else? Nobody's better at these things than you are. Name your price."

"No price. I'll do it for the pigs. For Wilbur."

About that time he pulled into the parking lot of Spirits and Spurs. He shut off the engine and unlatched his seat belt. Then he laid his hat on the dashboard. "Lean over here. I have an urgent need to kiss you."

She unfastened her seat belt and turned into his outstretched arms. "We don't have time to stay out here and smooch, you know."

"I know. But I can't last another two or three hours." He cupped the back of her head and felt the silky texture of her hair against his palm. "One kiss. That's all."

"Yes, but how long will it last?"

"As long as it needs to." The console was in the way, but he managed to angle his head so he could fit his mouth over hers. Her sigh of pleasure filled him with joy. This wasn't a kiss of unrestrained passion. Instead he simply wanted to let her know how much he treasured her.

He moved his lips gently against hers and slipped his tongue inside her mouth in one easy, unhurried motion. So sweet. So warm. So…oh, God, he was lost. With a groan he took the kiss deeper.

She pulled back, breathing hard. "Finn, we can't—"

"I know. Sorry." And he went back for more.

If she'd pushed him away, he would have abided by her decision, but she didn't. Instead she grabbed the back of his neck and hung on while he plundered her eager mouth.

He wasn't sure how long the tapping at his window had been going on by the time it finally registered. He lifted his mouth from Chelsea's and gulped for air. "Somebody's…outside."

"Oh!" She scrambled away from him and looked over his shoulder. "It's Jack."

"Of course it is." With a sigh he turned to see Jack giving him a Cheshire-cat smile. The windows were automatic, so he had to switch on the power to roll it down. *What?*

"Hate to interrupt."

"Sure you do."

"Josie sent me out to see if you were here yet. She's made a small batch of what she hopes will be her signature beer and—"

"Already? I thought she was just thinking about it."

"Oh, no. She's been experimenting for a while, just for the hell of it, not sure if she wanted to do this. Then she saw the calendar and realized you were a brewer. She's been extremely focused ever since. Your glass is poured and she doesn't want it to get warm. This means the world to her, and because I love her dearly, I want you to lay off the tonsil hockey and come in and taste her beer." He smiled again. "If you would be so kind."

"We'll be right there," Chelsea said.

"Excellent. I'll tell her." Jack touched the brim of his black Stetson and walked back into the saloon.

Finn glanced over at Chelsea, who seemed to be trying not to giggle. "He violated the cowboy code, you know."

"He did?"

"Well, not the big, superimportant code, but there's a whole list of lesser infractions, and interrupting a hot kiss is right up there at the top."

"Extenuating circumstances." She flipped down the visor and combed her hair with her fingers.

"Like what?"

"The woman he loves is inside on pins and needles, waiting for your evaluation of her signature beer. He needs you to come in and put an end to her suffering."

"Do you realize what an impossible situation this is? What if I hate her signature beer?"

"You'll find a diplomatic way to suggest improvements."

He dragged in a breath and picked up his hat. "Then let's do this thing."

She grabbed his arm before he could get out. "Whatever you do, don't take a sip and make a face."

"I wouldn't do that. I have some sensitivity."

"You're right. You're the guy who won't kill spiders." She patted his cheek. "I know. Imagine Josie as Charlotte. Instead of working on an amazing web, she's been crafting this beer."

"There are so many things wrong with that image that I don't even know where to start. I'll just have to fumble along on my own."

She climbed out before he could round the SUV and escort her, almost beating him to the front door of the saloon. But he got there in time to open that door, at least. The oval glass inserts were similar to what he'd ordered for O'Roarke's, but these were probably original.

The crowd was thin, probably because there was no live

music scheduled. Josie and Jack sat at a far table in the same area where they'd all gathered on Friday night. Probably the designated Chance family corner.

As he and Chelsea approached, Josie gave them a nervous smile and her blue eyes were filled with misgiving. "I thought this would be casual and fun, but I'm rattled." She gestured to the glass of beer sitting in the dead center of the table. "If it's awful, you have to tell me. Don't spare my feelings. This is business."

Finn pulled out a chair for Chelsea before sitting. "I'm sure it's not awful."

"Jack says it's not." She flipped her blond braid behind her back. "But he's required to pump me up. I'm counting on you to tell me the truth."

"I had no idea you'd moved this far into the process."

"I didn't want to say anything because I wasn't sure if I'd have the courage to ask you to taste this. But Jack convinced me that I need to take advantage of you being here. You'll be gone in the morning, so…" She gestured toward the glass. "There it is."

Chelsea spoke up. "Does it have a name?"

"It does if Finn likes it. If he doesn't, then it shall remain nameless and I'll go back to the drawing board."

"No, no, that would be putting too much importance on one person's opinion." Finn prayed the beer would be good. "You shouldn't give my judgment that much weight."

"But you're more of a beer connoisseur than any of us," Josie said. "I'm sure you tasted hundreds of different types before you started brewing your own."

"Yes, ma'am, I did."

"There you go."

"But don't throw out the recipe if I don't like it. We can talk about modifications." Finn decided to lay the groundwork for a potential negative reaction. "Hand-crafted beer is tricky. Some brewers work a year or two perfecting their product, some a lot longer than that."

"I know. I've been reading and trying different things. I finally have something I like, but nobody's tasted it except Jack."

Jack waved a hand in the air. "And she doesn't trust my opinion. Go figure. I may not be a brewer, but I've spent a lot of years drinking the stuff and I think—"

Josie clapped a hand over his mouth. "Don't say anything. I want Finn to go into this without any preconceived ideas."

Finn eyed the glass of beer and thought that taking the first sip wasn't so different from diffusing a bomb. He cautiously reached for the glass.

"Wait." Josie held up both hands. "I forgot to say the most important thing. I don't want you to worry that not liking my beer will somehow jeopardize the Chance family's support of Thunder Mountain Academy. This is completely separate. Right, Jack?"

"Completely separate."

Finn wanted to believe that, but Jack's devotion to Josie was a powerful thing. Anyone who hurt Josie's feelings might not be particularly popular with Jack. Finn was the official representative for TMA, so Jack's good opinion of him seemed pretty damned important.

Once again, he reached for the glass.

"Wait." Josie stopped him again. "I should explain that this beer was crafted with somewhat substandard equipment. That's the other thing I want to talk about tonight. I'm ready to sink some real money into good equipment, so as you taste this, please imagine it being made with whatever you have, because that's what I'm planning to get."

"All right." He had no idea how in the hell he'd make allowances for equipment. The beer either worked or it didn't, but she was a beginner and might not realize that.

He reached for the beer a third time, half expecting that she'd stop him again for another disclaimer. When she didn't, he lifted it to his mouth. He deliberately didn't look at her, but he could feel her tension from across the table.

Closing his eyes, he took a sip. Then another. And one more, just to make sure. Opening his eyes, he smiled at her and put down the glass. "It's great."

With a whoop of joy, she leaped from her chair, overturning it and bumping the table. Jack grabbed the beer before it went over as Finn stood and Josie bear-hugged him. Then she pulled Chelsea out of her chair and hugged her, too. Finally she raced back around the table to give Jack a resounding kiss.

His smile was a mile wide. "We need food," he declared, "and more of this beer, because I happen to know Josie has more of it chilling." He glanced over at Finn with a look of gratitude. "This calls for another celebration."

"I completely agree." Chelsea's face was flushed. "And by the way, is there a jukebox?"

"Sadly, there is not." Josie glanced from Chelsea to Finn. "Are you two turning into dancers, then?"

"Yes, ma'am," Finn said. "And it's all Jack's fault."

"Glad to take the blame."

"You were both a huge help Friday night and now we're excited about dancing." Chelsea settled back in her chair. "But we don't have to have music tonight. I just wondered about the jukebox, because this saloon seems like a natural place for one."

"It is." Josie nodded. "You're not the only one to ask, either. I need to get serious about installing one for the nights we don't have a band."

"Great idea," Jack said. "In the meantime I'll order us up some food. What's everybody ready for?" They gave him their orders and he headed back to the kitchen.

After he left, Josie glanced over at Finn. "So the beer's really okay? You haven't had any more of it."

"I was waiting until everyone had a glass. Sitting here guzzling it all by myself seemed rude."

"But you would have guzzled it?" Josie's expression was endearingly anxious.

"I would. We just need more so we can propose a toast."

Josie's shoulders sagged with relief. "I liked it, and Jack liked it, but I wouldn't let anybody else try it once I knew you'd be here this weekend. Then I lost my nerve and almost didn't ask you. Jack kept pushing me. I'm glad he did."

"Yeah, I'm awesome. Best husband ever." Jack appeared with a tray holding three more glasses.

"Best one I ever had," Josie said with a grin.

"With excellent taste in both women and beer." Jack put down the tray. "Food's coming up soon."

Finn waited until everyone was settled before lifting his glass. "A toast to the Spirits and Spurs signature beer, which is called..." He looked over at Josie.

"Galloping Ghost!" She raised her glass.

"To Galloping Ghost!" they chorused.

Finn touched glasses with everyone, lingering as he clinked with Chelsea's. Funny how he'd thought he couldn't get any closer to her than he had last night. How wrong he'd been.

Sex had knocked down the physical barriers between them, but in spending the day with her, he'd started chipping away at all the mental barriers he'd thrown up to protect himself. And not just from her, either. He'd asked her not to tell his foster brothers that he couldn't kill a spider because of Charlotte.

Why not tell them? They might tease him, but so what? They knew he had that book. He'd kept it on a shelf in the cabin for years. They'd probably figured out that he'd lobbied for a pig because he loved the story of Wilbur and Charlotte.

Watching Josie take this courageous step also made him aware of how self-protective he'd been all his life. She'd let them all know that she was nervous. He would have bluffed his way through the situation by pretending he was totally cool with it. In fact he had done that several times.

Josie put down her beer and reached under her chair. "Before the food comes, I want to ask you about equipment." She pulled out a couple of catalogs he recognized immediately.

Chelsea got up. "Josie, you should switch places with me." She moved over to Josie's seat and Josie sat next to Finn.

From the moment Josie opened the first dog-eared catalog, Finn was rocketed back to the days he used to sit under a large shade tree at Thunder Mountain Ranch, planning his strategy. He'd taken a course on brewing at the community college in Sheridan and he'd worked at a local bar from the moment he was of legal age.

And he'd saved—Lord, how he'd saved, although he'd known in his heart it wasn't near enough. Chelsea had found a way for him to raise the rest. Josie would have more resources than he'd had, but after hearing that she wanted to do this without bringing the Chance family into it, he couldn't assume she had unlimited funds.

So he didn't recommend the top-of-the-line equipment. He didn't have that, after all. Besides, he could honestly give her the pros and cons of what he'd invested in. She'd brought a pen and made notes as they talked.

He lost track of time and even where they were. He did love the process and that was a good thing to remember. Over the years he'd let worry about staying solvent take some of the joy out of doing the work. Josie's excitement brought back what he'd lost.

They'd discussed most of the major items by the time the food arrived.

Josie closed up the catalogs. "That'll get me started."

He pulled out his phone. "Let me send you my email and phone number. You'll have more questions. I sure did."

"I can't thank you enough, Finn." She picked up the catalogs and stood.

"It's been fun."

"For me, too!"

"Hey," Jack said from across the table. "Don't move on our account. Chelsea and me, we've bonded over here. You two can stay put and talk shop. Chelsea's filling me in on the wonders of Seattle. Now I'm hankering to go up in that Space Needle and take me a ferryboat ride."

"You should come and visit," Chelsea said. "It's a beautiful city."

"Then I want to hear about it, too." Josie sat again and tucked the catalogs under her chair. "We've had enough beer talk for the night."

"If you say so. And, oh, will you look at that? Here comes our entertainment, right on time." Jack put his napkin beside his plate and got up to welcome two cowboys who came in carrying guitar cases. "Glad you could make it."

"I'm just sorry our gig in Cheyenne kept us from being here for the barbecue last night." The shorter one, who had a handlebar mustache, shook Jack's hand. "Trey covered himself in glory. I was honored to be on the stage with him."

"Congratulations." Jack grasped the younger man's hand firmly. "That's great to hear. We missed you, but at least now you can both meet Chelsea and Finn."

Finn stood to greet them as Jack explained that the two cowboys, both wranglers at the Last Chance, had become a popular entertainment duo in the area. Trey Wheeler handled the vocals and the older man, who went only by Watkins, played backup.

"And you're here to play for us?" Chelsea looked like a kid on Christmas morning. "That's so generous of you!"

"We love to play, ma'am," Trey said with a winning smile. "When Jack called and said you'd like some dancing music, we were only too happy to oblige. Now if you'll excuse us, we'll go set up. We'll play a few background tunes while you eat, but when you're ready to dance, give us a signal."

Finn glanced at their host after the two men left. "I appreciate this, Jack. It's above and beyond."

"Glad to do it." His dark eyes flashed with amusement. "Can I have the first dance?"

13

THE DEBATE OVER whether Jack would be dancing with Finn continued as they ate dinner and enjoyed some mellow tunes provided by the two guitarists. Finn insisted that he'd learned enough and Jack maintained that he could use another lesson. Chelsea got a kick out of listening to them trade barbs.

Eventually the conversation turned to other topics, specifically Jack's new interest in Seattle. But when they'd all finished eating, Jack's attention swung back to dancing.

"You'll never have a better opportunity to polish your moves than right now with the place practically deserted, O'Roarke. In a little while word will get out that Trey and Watkins are playing and we'll have a crowd." He sounded quite reasonable except for the devilish gleam in his eyes.

Finn finished his beer. "Why do you care if my moves are polished or not?"

"Professional pride. If you go around telling people I taught you and you can't dance worth a lick, that will reflect poorly on me."

"That's the most ridiculous thing I've ever heard. And, besides, I don't need any more lessons. I understand the basics."

"You know just enough to be dangerous, cowboy. I'm sure Chelsea would love for you to become more skilled." He looked to her for support.

"Hey, hey." She made a shooing motion. "Leave me out of this."

"Oh, all right." Finn tucked his napkin beside his plate. "Let's do this thing, Jack." As Trey and Watkins struck up a lively two-step, Finn and Jack took the floor.

"Finn's a good sport." Josie smiled as she watched them. "Jack loves trying to throw guys off balance by insisting on improving their dance skills. He admires the ones who go along with it."

"I think it's great. Finn has a tendency to take things too seriously. Jack's a good influence." She chuckled as Jack went into a twirl in one direction and Finn spun out in the other. Then Jack demonstrated the underarm twirl and hats flew.

Josie rolled her eyes. "Or a bad influence, depending on your perspective." She glanced over at Chelsea. "But Jack went through a serious phase, too."

"Really? It seems so much a part of his personality to joke around."

"It is, but he buried his sense of humor for a while. He had issues. I sense that Finn does, too."

"Yep."

"All you can do is love them and hope they figure it out."

"So true." Chelsea gave a short answer because she didn't want to call attention to that casual remark. At least, it seemed casual, and yet it contained a loaded word.

Chelsea had avoided *love* in connection with Finn. She'd always preferred to think she was in lust with him. But today hadn't been about lust.

Instead it had been about walking hand-in-hand, sharing conversations and discovering facets of each other's personality. She'd seen a different side of him when they'd met Harley and Wilbur. Just now she'd learned that the same man who'd been captivated by a story about a pig saved by a noble little spider could also become completely immersed in the details of a new friend's cherished project.

It seemed as if getting sex out of the way meant that she could view him as a whole person without the static of constant frustration blurring the picture. She liked what she saw. And he was turning into one fine dancer, too.

When he and Jack came back to the table, they were both grinning.

"We're going to be on TV before you know it," Jack said. "O'Roarke can now officially shake his booty."

"All because of you, Jack. All because of you." Finn held out his hand to Chelsea. "May I have this dance, sweet lady?"

"You'd better believe it." She took his hand and walked with him out to the dance floor. The rubber tread on her shoes squeaked, reminding her that she didn't have on the right footwear. "Hang on a minute. I'll be right back."

She met Jack and Josie coming out to the floor. Jack lifted his eyebrows. "I hope you're not going to make that boy dance all by his lonesome."

"Nope. Just handling a slight problem." She sat and quickly took off both socks and shoes. Dancing in sock feet sounded like a recipe for slipping and falling. She'd dance barefoot.

When she returned, Finn looked at her bare toes and shook his head. "I don't trust myself."

"That's okay." She grabbed his hand and pulled him onto the floor. "I trust you completely."

He tugged her into his arms and looked into her eyes. "Foolish woman." But he was smiling, and as he spun her around, he didn't step on her once.

She discovered that she loved dancing barefoot. Josie and Jack were the only other ones on the floor, which gave both couples plenty of room. Jack became something of a showoff, executing complicated steps that involved lots of dips and twirls.

But Finn just...danced with her. Holding her gaze, he used only light pressure to communicate his moves and she wondered if she'd have needed even that. It was as if she could read his mind. They synchronized their footwork effortlessly and she was sorry when the music ended.

She sighed. "That was the best."

Happiness shone in his eyes. "It was. I was so worried I'd step on you, but then somehow I knew I wouldn't."

"We were in the zone."

He laughed. "We were."

"Nice job out there." Jack walked over and clapped Finn on the back. "I knew you had guts, O'Roarke. You wouldn't catch me wearing boots and dancing with a barefoot lady."

"I can't explain why, but I felt like I could do it with my eyes closed."

Jack regarded him silently. Then he gave a short nod. "You'll do." And he went back to Josie as the music started again with a slower tune.

"I haven't known him long," Chelsea said, "but I'm guessing that's high praise."

"Could be." Finn scooped her back into his arms and began an easy circuit around the floor. "But there's only one person in this room I want to impress, and I'm dancing with her."

"For the record, I'm impressed. It's been a terrific day."

He urged her closer and murmured in her ear. "But the sun's going down."

"Mmm-hmm."

"I'm ready for the day to end and the night to begin."

"Me, too." After two nights of making love to him, the desperate, unbearable hunger had been replaced with a steady hum of awareness. After today, tonight would be good. Very good.

Jack had been right that word would spread about the unexpected live entertainment. Customers drifted in, either because a friend had alerted them or they'd heard music spilling into the street. Eventually the once-empty dance floor became crowded.

The four of them agreed it was time to leave. Jack won the fight over the bill by calling it a tax deduction for Josie, and they walked outside together.

"It's been a pleasure." Jack shook hands with Finn and hugged Chelsea.

"That's an understatement." Josie hugged them both. "We'll be thinking of you this week."

"And if that last little bit doesn't show up," Jack said, "you know who to call."

"Thanks." Finn smiled. "We've got this."

"We do," Chelsea said. "And thank you for all you've done."

"Yes, thank you." Finn wrapped an arm around her shoulders.

As they said their last goodbyes, Chelsea stood in the warm circle of Finn's embrace with a cool evening breeze ruffling her hair. A week ago she'd been worried that Thunder Mountain Academy might not happen. A week ago she'd wondered if her crush on Finn was doomed. Now anything was possible.

They rode back to the Bunk and Grub in cozy silence. Nothing needed to be said. They both knew what lay ahead and anticipation vibrated between them.

The lobby was the same as before, with low lamplight and the scent of cinnamon in the air. The scene was familiar yet completely different because she and Finn were different. They climbed the stairs without rushing, yet she felt his solid presence behind her, knew he was as focused on her as she was on him.

She unlocked her door without trembling, but her heart thumped wildly as she walked inside. She'd never made love with someone when her heart was so full. The housekeeper had left a light on and folded back the covers. The door clicked shut and she turned to face him.

Slowly he took off his hat and laid it on the dresser. Then he dragged in a breath and spoke for the first time since they'd left the saloon. "You're everything I've ever wanted, and I'm scared to death."

Her heart ached for him. That couldn't have been easy for him to admit. "I'm scared, too. I've never felt this way."

"Neither have I, and I'm convinced I'll mess it up."

She was fully aware that he might, but she wasn't going to let that keep her from loving him now. "We only get scared when we worry about the future. If we just think about what's happening right now, then we won't be afraid."

He squeezed his eyes shut. "Yeah. We went over that."

She couldn't help smiling. "It's not easy to remember. It should be, but it's not."

Opening his eyes, he moved toward her. "Right now I'm in the bedroom of a beautiful woman who is going to let me make love to her."

"Right now I'm waiting for an outrageously sexy cowboy to kiss me."

He smiled. "Damn. Should've kept on the hat."

"No, it only gets in the way."

"Can't have that." Gathering her close, he covered her mouth with his.

And then everything was okay. There was no past, no future. Only this—his lips moving against hers, his tongue seeking, his breath warm, his hands gently exploring, caressing, arousing her until she molded her body against the steady heat that was Finn.

As they slowly undressed each other, she thought of the effortless way they'd danced. Sliding out of their clothes had the same fluid motion. No rush, no awkwardness. She'd never been so in tune with a lover.

The clothes lay in a glorious heap on the floor. She threw back the covers and he lifted her into his arms so he could lay her in the exact center of the bed. Then he stepped back and gazed at her.

"Finn?" She stretched out her hand toward him.

"I need to look. Let me."

"You've seen me this way before."

"I have. But… I know you better now."

Then she understood. She knew him better, too. She'd explored the many layers of Finn O'Roarke today, and he was more precious to her because of that. Even though they'd seen each other naked before, they'd never truly seen each other.

His intense blue gaze roamed over her, heating her in ways that even his touch did not. She squirmed against the sheets, wanting him to hold her, stroke her, love her. "Finn, please."

With a soft groan he came to her. He kissed her forehead, her eyelids, her cheeks and her mouth. "I can't wait," he murmured. "I need you now."

"Don't wait."

He pulled out the bedside table drawer where he'd stashed the condoms and wasted no time putting one on. Then he moved over her and held her gaze. "Right now I'm sinking deep inside you." And he joined them together with one firm thrust.

She gasped with pleasure. "Right now I'm feeling great joy."

"Is that right?" He pulled back and pushed home again. "This brings you joy?"

"Oh, Finn, you know it does." She wrapped her arms around his muscled back.

"I want to bring you joy."

Her smile trembled as she gazed up at him. "That's very nice to know."

"You deserve buckets of joy." He settled into a steady rhythm.

She focused on those amazing blue eyes. "So do you."

"Right now I'm finding it with you."

Her heart swelled. "Same here, cowboy."

"If only…" He paused to gulp in air. "If only we could stay like this forever."

"But we're here now."

"Yes." He slowed his pace. "We are." His gaze locked with hers. "I'm with you, Chels."

"I'm with you, Finn." They moved together as if they were dancing, his hips keeping perfect time with hers. And because they were so closely attuned, they knew when the energy shifted, when their bodies needed more.

He increased the pace and she responded with a whimper of need. Together they reached for shared glory and found it. She held on tight as they shuddered in each other's arms. Perfection. Was she crazy to want more?

THIS TIME FINN stayed and she woke to find him spooning her, her back tucked against his chest and his arms around her waist. She lay quietly and thought about what their future had in store. The Bunk and Grub had turned out to be a private hideaway, but tonight they'd be separated.

She wanted to visit Thunder Mountain Ranch, but if it meant severing this connection with Finn, that took some of the shine off the prospect. He'd promised they'd go on horseback rides into the boonies so they could have private time. She couldn't imagine how that could be as cozy as snuggling in this bed.

"I can hear you thinking." His breath was warm against the back of her neck.

"I'm getting used to sharing a bed with you."

"I know." He sighed. "I haven't prepared Rosie and Herb for that and I don't want to spring it on them."

"And you shouldn't. Don't mind me. We'll manage."

"But it won't be like this." His arms tightened around her and he nuzzled behind her ear.

"No." She surrendered to his sweet caresses, knowing that soon they'd have to sneak off to do this, and this, and, oh, yes, *this*. He gave her a climax first with his clever fingers and then he ripped open another condom so they could both enjoy the experience.

As they lay flopped on their backs, gasping and sated, she reached over and slipped her hand in his. "Whatever happens is fine," she murmured. "I don't want to be greedy."

"I do." He lifted her hand to his lips. "I'm spoiled rotten after this weekend. I'm not about to take a vow of celibacy."

"Then I'll follow your lead."

"We'll have private time. I promise you." He nibbled on her fingers and then began to suck on them. Before long they'd made use of another condom. It was as if they both realized that the game was about to change.

They left the Bunk and Grub later than planned, but that was mostly because he couldn't seem to stop making love to her. She wasn't about to object. Her room had become a haven where they could explore these new feelings and she was as loath to give it up as he was.

Breakfast was over by the time they headed downstairs, but Yvonne gave them a thermos of coffee and some pastries in a bag. Pam was there to check them out and hug them both good-bye. On the way out to the SUV, Chelsea reminded Finn that he'd been looking forward to the trip to Thunder Mountain Ranch, but that didn't seem to help either one of them. Reluctantly they loaded up and drove away.

Chelsea wasn't in the mood to work, either. But if she expected to have something for her new client's PR campaign by the time she arrived home, she should put in some hours on it now. Feeling less than inspired, she opened her laptop.

Finn glanced over at her. "How about a little music?"

"Sure, why not?"

He flipped on the radio and a country station came on. "Is that okay?"

"That's fine." But the country music reminded her of all the dancing they'd done this past weekend. Would that be the last time she'd get to dance with Finn?

"I feel as if I've been evicted from paradise."

She blew out a breath. "So do I, and that's crazy. We've been looking forward to visiting Thunder Mountain together. You said you wanted to show me all your old haunts."

"Which I do. That'll be fun."

"Plus I'll be able to meet everyone, finally, and see the birth-place of Thunder Mountain Academy. We can all celebrate, knowing the Kickstarter campaign is in the bag. Does it matter so much that we won't be able to sleep in the same bed at night?"

"Yes. Yes, it does."

"We've spent our whole lives not doing that. We've only shared a bed for three nights, and one of those wasn't even the whole night because you left. We should be able to handle this."

"I've been telling myself that ever since I woke up this morning, but the prospect of not having you close by is depressing the hell out of me."

"So what are we going to do?"

"I don't know yet. I'm working on it."

She decided not to point out the obvious, that they'd made no commitment to each other. Once they returned to Seattle, they'd be sleeping miles apart. Had he thought of that?

She had. Because they'd have to separate eventually, worrying about their current situation made no sense. But she must be as bonkers as Finn, because she didn't want to be apart from him, either.

14

WHILE CHELSEA WORKED on her laptop, Finn had plenty of time to think. He *really* didn't want to be apart from her every night they stayed at Thunder Mountain Ranch. When he considered his strong negative reaction to that potential separation he finally admitted that he was falling for her. Or, more likely, had fallen.

If so, he wouldn't magically get over her when they went back to Seattle. He'd want to be with her then, too. Maybe it wouldn't work out because he'd return to his usual anal mode, but maybe he'd changed.

By the time they stopped for lunch in Thermopolis, he'd decided what to do. But he had to run it past Chelsea first. Come to think of it, this conversation could turn out to be pretty damned important. Depending on how she reacted, he'd get a better sense of how she felt about him.

They ordered a couple of burgers and some fries at a cozy little diner that she'd found using TripAdvisor on her phone. The diner would have been right at home in Shoshone, or in Sheridan, for that matter. He was glad she was charmed by small Western towns and downhome eateries, but he wasn't surprised. Her enthusiasm for life in general had endeared her to him from the first day they'd met.

They sipped coffee while they waited for their food. Now

that the moment was here, he had a slight case of nerves. He decided not to leap right into the heart of the matter. "How's the project coming along?"

"Good." She nodded. "I wasn't sure whether I'd be focused enough to get anything done, but I made some progress. I think he'll like what I've come up with."

"Why wouldn't you be focused?"

"Oh, you know. Wondering how things will work out at Thunder Mountain."

Perfect opening. "I have a solution for how to handle our sleeping arrangements, but before I call Rosie, I need your okay."

She blinked. "Call Rosie?"

"I don't like the thought of sneaking around to have sex."

"Neither do I, but I thought we had no choice."

He thumbed back his hat and sighed. "That's because I was thinking like a seventeen-year-old boy instead of a man. I'd like to call Rosie and explain that we're used to sleeping in the same room and we both think it would be fun to stay in the cabin. But there's no bathroom in it. The bathhouse is a short walk away. And it has four bunks, not one bed."

She grinned. "Sounds just like summer camp."

"I know it's a little primitive, but my plan is to push the mattresses together on the floor. I won't kid you, though. It won't be nearly as comfy as the guest bed in the house."

"But you'll be there, which more than makes up for the lack of an innerspring."

"Thank you, ma'am." He reached across the table and took her hand. "So you'd be okay with me announcing that to Rosie?"

"There's a lot to like about your plan, but I thought you said Rosie was a matchmaker. Won't she expect us to have made some kind of commitment? We don't want to mislead her."

His chest tightened. "I don't plan to mislead her."

"So you'll explain that this is temporary? You said she might not like that, either."

"Look, I don't know where this thing with us will end up." He captured her hand between both of his. "But I don't want to stop seeing you when we get back to Seattle."

She went very still and her eyes widened. "You don't?"

"No." He took a shaky breath. "But I might still be the anal control freak I was when I left. I think I might be changing, learning, but it's hard to know when we're in a completely different environment."

"You want…" She swallowed. "You want to do a test run when we get back? Is that what you're suggesting?"

"Yes, ma'am." He stroked her palm with his thumb. "But if you're not willing to try that, I completely understand. You've seen me at my worst and if you—"

"I'm willing to try that." Her voice was breathy and her eyes still reflected shock. "I just never expected you to say this. What…how would we…?"

"I thought maybe…this is just an idea, now, but I thought that you'd let me stay with you for a little while. See how it goes. I'd keep my place just in case, but I'd pay my share of the food and help with utilities. And you could throw me out anytime you wanted to."

"Oh, Finn." She trembled. "It's a big step."

"You don't want to." His heart ached. "I don't blame you. It was just a possibility. We can forget I mentioned it. We could just date. I could live with that. I just don't want everything to go back to the way it was. I want to be with you. Dating would be better than nothing."

"It would be stupid. I don't want to date you. I want to be with you every night. That's what this whole thing with Rosie is about. I hate the thought of sleeping in the house while you're in the cabin."

"So…" He was confused. "What are you saying?"

"I'm saying that it's a big step, but if you're game, I'm game."

His stomach bottomed out. "Chels, are you sure?"

"I'm sure that I want to try. You're right that it might not work, but if we just assume that, then we have nothing. I'd rather try and go through hell if it doesn't work than miss out on a chance at heaven if it does."

"I feel like dragging you out of that chair and kissing you until your toes curl."

Fire flashed in her brown eyes. "Better not start something you can't finish."

He groaned. "I didn't figure this out very well. I need to call Rosie and we should eat. Then we have to make tracks if we're going to get there by dinnertime. That's when she's expecting us and I'm sure she'll cook something special."

"So we postpone our make-out session. Think about this. By calling Rosie, you're setting us up to spend the night together. Short-term sacrifice for long-term gain. You're a business owner. I'm sure you know all about that."

"I've never had to sacrifice kissing you."

She gazed at him. "Yes, you have. You've been sacrificing that for five years."

"Good point. That's why I have so much catching up to do."

"Go make your phone call. I'll be here when you get back."

"Okay." He squeezed her hand and released it. "If the order comes, start eating. Don't wait for me."

"Should we ask them to fix it to go? Then we could leave that much sooner."

He glanced at the time on his phone. "No, we should be fine. Let's stay and enjoy the meal." He smiled at her. "Be right back."

CHELSEA WATCHED HIM head through the door and then she was able to see him through the restaurant's front window as he paced back and forth while he made his call. He still had that cowboy saunter going on, and she noticed more than one woman take a second look as they passed by. *Too late, ladies! He just said he wants to move in with me.*

She still couldn't believe it. After years of frustration, she would get the chance she'd yearned for—to see if they could be a couple. And not just here, where he felt removed from the pressure cooker of his business. He was willing to risk putting it all on the line.

He hadn't mentioned love, but knowing Finn, he wouldn't toss that word into the mix until he thought they had a decent shot at making it together. No point in telling someone you love them and then having to swear off that person for the rest of your life. She felt the same way, although the emotion rolling through her had to be connected to that four-letter word. Either that or she was coming down with the flu.

Right after their food arrived, he came back in wearing a puzzled expression. She'd expected a smile. "Did you talk to her?"

"I did." He put his napkin in his lap. "And she made me promise to relay the message that she's superexcited to meet you."

"Same here. But what about the cabin thing?" Her burger was huge, so she cut it in two before starting to eat. "How did she react to that?" She took a juicy bite.

"Knowing Rosie, I think she's messing with me. I explained the situation, which made her very happy that I'm involved with someone, especially someone she can get to know. She never met Alison." He picked up his entire burger, but then, he had the hands for it. "She and Herb had planned to fly up to see us but we were fighting all the time and I told them not to come." He took a healthy bite.

"I guess I'd better be on my best behavior, then."

He swallowed his bite. "Your behavior is always your best, even when you're being snarky."

"I'm going to start getting that way if you don't tell me what she said about the cabin. Are we sleeping together or not?"

"I'm pretty sure we are, but she said the Brotherhood cabin—that's what we call the one all three of us stayed in—wasn't a good idea and she had a better one."

"She's not giving us a guest room in the house, after all, is she?"

"I doubt it." He put down his burger and grabbed a fry. "I

raved on about how much you would love staying in a real log cabin, that it would be a whole new experience for you."

"No, it won't."

"You've stayed in one before?"

"Sure, at summer camp. That's why I made that remark when you mentioned bunks and a bathhouse that's a short walk away."

"Oh. Well, I didn't know that." He looked a little disappointed as he went back to eating his burger.

She found that adorable. "But I've never stayed in a log cabin with you, so what you told her is true. It will be a whole new experience. And for the record, I loved summer camp, so walking outside to the bathhouse will bring back good memories."

"That's assuming we stay in one of the cabins. I'm not sure what Rosie's up to. All she said was that I'd be pleased."

"She sounds like a pip."

"None of us were a match for her. Herb's pretty easygoing and we could fool him sometimes with our shenanigans. Not Rosie. If she didn't call us on something we'd done, it was only because it was small potatoes and she didn't feel the need to deal with it."

Chelsea started on the second half of her burger. "You've called it the Brotherhood cabin twice now. Does each cabin have a name, like we did at camp?"

"No, just that one. Cade, Damon and I were the first three boys Rosie and Herb took in, and we called ourselves the Thunder Mountain Brotherhood. They started out using guest rooms for the boys, but eventually they built cabins. The three of us got the first one."

"Rank has its privileges."

"Oh, yeah, we lorded it over the others." He ate another fry. "We'd been through a blood brother ceremony and they hadn't, so we were special. It's a wonder any of them still speak to us."

"A ceremony? Really?"

"Actually, I wasn't invited. I was the third boy brought out to the ranch. Cade and Damon had been there for months and were buddies by then. They kind of ignored me."

"Aw."

"It's okay. I was odd man out. Kids are like that." He took another bite of his burger.

"I know, but you'd just lost your grandfather and now nobody wanted to be your friend."

He shrugged as if it hadn't mattered. She knew it had, but if he wanted to pretend otherwise, fine with her.

"To be fair," he said, "I was big on rules, which doesn't tend to make a kid popular."

"Anal, even then."

"Probably worse. Anyway, they snuck out of the house at midnight and I followed them. You weren't supposed to leave the house after lights-out. I hadn't decided whether to tell on them or not, but I scared the hell out of them walking up to their little campfire. When I realized what they were doing, I wanted in."

"And they let you."

"They probably didn't want to, but Cade gave me this look as if he knew it would hurt my feelings if they didn't. So I made a cut in my hand and pressed it against their cuts and we said a pledge Cade had written up. Thirteen-year-olds can be so melodramatic."

"I love this story. I'm so glad you told me before we got there." She hesitated. "Should I let on that I know?"

"Sure. It wasn't exactly a secret, like I said. Apparently Rosie knew we'd gone out there and listened to make certain we came back okay. We all wore bandages the next day, so I'm sure she figured out the whole thing."

"Do you remember where you had that little ceremony?"

"Absolutely. We all do." He munched on another fry, but he still hadn't finished his burger, as if he'd rather talk than eat. "We've joked about putting a plaque in the ground to commemorate it. I'd already planned to take you on a tour of the significant places on the ranch, and that's one of them."

"I'm so excited to go there now."

"Me, too, especially if the sleeping quarters turn out okay." He glanced at the time on his phone. "Speaking of that, we should head out."

"But you haven't finished your lunch."

"No worries. It's been fun telling you about that stuff. I'll get our waitress to box up the rest and I'll eat on the road while you get some more work done."

"Um, right."

"You're planning to work again, aren't you?" He caught the eye of the woman who'd been serving them.

"That was my original idea, but—"

"And it's a good one." He glanced up as the waitress came over. "Ma'am, we have to leave. I wonder if you could please box this up for me and bring the bill?"

"You've got it." She winked at him.

"Thank you, ma'am."

"Anytime." She smiled at him as she whisked away his plate.

He'd made another conquest but didn't seem to notice as he kept talking to Chelsea. "I have so much I want to show you when we get there, so the more you can do on the road, the better."

"True." Maybe she shouldn't admit how excited she was about his plan to move in with her. All through lunch the prospect had hovered in the back of her mind, demanding attention. She needed to think about practical things like making room in her closets and dresser drawers. Maybe she'd buy bath sheets because her towels weren't big enough for him.

But mostly she wanted to sit and contemplate the joy of taking a Sunday morning stroll to Pike Place Market for coffee and croissants, or cuddling on her sofa on a blustery winter's night watching TV—assuming they made it to winter, of course. They liked some of the same shows. She knew that from five years of animated conversation.

So much to think about and so much to anticipate. She doubted that she'd be able to concentrate on work now that he'd dropped his bombshell. But if she told him all that, she might spook him, and that was the last thing in the world she wanted to do.

"You're right," she said. "Using the rest of the trip to work on my client's project makes perfect sense."

"See, that's what I admire about you. You work when you need to work and you play when you want to play."

"Thank you." Okay, she'd definitely better work this afternoon if he was taking her as a role model. Now wouldn't be the time to stare out the car window daydreaming about the future.

"I've been paying attention to how you manage it. If I can learn to unplug instead of constantly thinking about work, you might not toss me out on my ass the first week."

"I won't toss you out the first week, no matter what. We should give ourselves time to adjust."

"You say that now, but you haven't lived with me when I'm in work mode. I made Alison miserable. I might make you miserable."

"No, you won't, because I understand what it's like to have responsibility for the entire operation. I'm not sure she did." She was determined not to rag on his ex, but drawing a few comparisons wouldn't hurt.

"I've thought about that. Her job was nothing like mine and she didn't get it. But I took the whole work thing to extremes, too."

"Sometimes you have to. I burned the midnight oil to finish Saturday's presentation. If you'd been around then, you wouldn't have been able to get my attention." She wasn't positive about that but it sounded good. "When you're self-employed, sometimes you put in long hours and other times you give yourself time off."

"But I've never let myself take time off."

She smiled. "I know. We can work on that." And she had all kinds of ideas about how to coax him to relax and let go for a while. She could hardly wait to put them into practice. She'd been dreading the end of this trip and now...now it could be the beginning of something very wonderful.

15

BACK ON THE ROAD to Sheridan, Finn couldn't remember the last time he'd felt this happy. The weekend at the Bunk and Grub had been great and he'd cherish it forever, but he hadn't had a plan. He always felt better when he had one, and now he did. Or rather, they did.

Chelsea had agreed to give him a shot, and he couldn't ask for more than that. She probably had more faith in him than he had in himself. He was counting on that because his confidence sometimes got a little shaky when it came to a major overhaul of his normal routine.

But she seemed ready and willing to take on the challenge of rehabilitating a confirmed workaholic. From the corner of his eye he could see her typing on her laptop. The soft click of the keys soothed him, letting him know that she was in control of her habits in a way that he wasn't.

He could be, though, given the right motivation. If the promise of being with Chelsea wasn't enough motivation, then he was a hopeless case. He'd dreamed of it for five long years without ever thinking he could be that fortunate. Now a life with her was within his grasp.

Her little apartment wasn't huge, at least what he remembered of it. He'd only been there a couple of times because everything about the place had tempted him to stay. Her furniture had beckoned him to relax into the plump cushions, and the art she'd chosen was so Chelsea—abstract and cheerful.

As he recalled, the apartment had been tidy without being fussy. He had his hang-ups, but extreme neatness wasn't one of them. Living in chaos didn't appeal to him, but he could tolerate a little clutter, even liked it. Chelsea's place had struck that happy medium.

He wondered if her landlord allowed pets. She didn't have any, but that didn't mean there was a restriction. His apartment complex permitted certain pets in exchange for a hefty deposit. Not a pig, of course, but dogs, cats, fish and birds were fine. He'd checked that out before renting.

Then he'd made no move to adopt because his schedule was so insane. Back in June, Lexi had suggested he get two cats because they could keep each other company. But he'd never followed through. He still believed his lifestyle had to change first.

Maybe it was about to. And good thing he hadn't adopted a couple of cats. Asking if he could move in with Chelsea was one thing. Bringing along a couple of cats would be a lot more complicated.

As they drew closer to Sheridan, the landscape began to look familiar. He'd flown in from Seattle in June, but seeing it from the road was better. As he drove, the silhouette of the Big Horn Mountains shifted with the changing angle. Gradually the mountains assumed the burly shape that meant he was almost home.

No, not home, not really. He'd told Chelsea that he'd shifted his allegiance to Seattle and it was true. But these mountains would always tug at his heart.

Unlike the Grand Tetons of Jackson Hole, which thrust skyward in dramatic jagged splendor, the Big Horns were more solid and broad shouldered. He appreciated the beauty of the Tetons and sitting on the porch at the Last Chance had given him a spectacular view of them. But these mountains calmed him in a way that the edgy Tetons never would.

"It's beautiful, isn't it?" Chelsea turned off her laptop and closed the cover. "So different from where we've just been, yet majestic."

"I love these mountains. Sometimes when I was afraid that my grandfather wouldn't be able to take care of me, I imagined that the mountains would." He felt her watching him. "When I was five or six. Not when I was older."

"Why not? It's a lovely thought and they do give you that feeling. They're muscular, in a way."

"That's a good way to describe them, but I don't want you to think I lived in some fantasy world."

"I know you didn't, but there's nothing wrong with a little fantasy now and then if it helps you cope with your problems. I'm glad you had these mountains. I can see why they'd be comforting."

Another knot loosened in his chest. He hadn't realized that he needed her to understand his connection to the mountains, but of course he did. He needed her to understand...everything. "I'm so glad you're here." He glanced over at her. "I should have had sense enough to bring you before without being roped into it."

"Doesn't matter." Her smile was warm. "I'm here now, and I can't wait for you to show me your old stomping grounds."

That made him think of something else. She probably needed him to understand everything about her, too. "We should go to Bellingham when we get back."

Her response was slow in coming. "Yes, I guess we should."

"You sound a little hesitant."

"Maybe because I keep thinking I'm going to wake up and find this was all a dream."

He took a deep breath. "Me, too. But I want it to be real, and that's why we should go to Bellingham. I've known you for five years, but I want to really *know* you. I want to meet your folks. I want to see where you went to school and where you hung out with your friends. You must have gone to the beach a lot."

"We did."

"I want to see what that beach looks like."

She reached over and squeezed his arm. "Thank you. Maybe this is real, after all."

"I'm determined to make it that way." He turned down the familiar road leading to Thunder Mountain Ranch. "We'll be there in about ten minutes. I just wish I knew what sort of arrangement Rosie has come up with."

"She said you'd be pleased."

"Yeah, but whatever it is, she'll milk it for all it's worth. Rosie likes to have her fun. From what I hear, she let Damon think he was going to work on the new cabin project over Fourth of July weekend with a guy named Phil. Turned out to be Philomena. You'll meet her at dinner tonight. They're together, now, which makes Rosie very happy."

"You weren't kidding about her matchmaking, were you?"

"No, ma'am."

"Lexi told me in an email that he was with someone and that he'd moved back to Sheridan, but she didn't mention the Phil-slash-Philomena twist. Why did Rosie let him think she was a guy?"

"Apparently, Damon had some old-fashioned ideas about women in male-oriented jobs and she wanted to give him a wake-up call."

"I see." Chelsea smiled. "I'm getting a better picture of Rosie with every new story. Anything else you should tell me about her?"

"When she was in the hospital last June, she gave everyone strict orders not to bring her flowers as if we thought she was about to croak. So Damon and Cade bought her a case of Bailey's. Needless to say there's still a lot of it left, so if you're a fan, then—"

"I am! I love Bailey's. A little bit in a cup of coffee in the evening is perfect."

"Then you two can bond over that. Nobody else likes the stuff, but it's her favorite." He looked forward to bringing Rosie and Chelsea together. He had a feeling they'd speak the same language. But he wished to hell Rosie had told him her plan. He wasn't big on surprises.

The road was a winding one, and he knew each curve by heart. A few more and he'd reach the turnoff to the ranch.

"We have to take a short dirt road to get there," he said, "but unlike Jack's washboard, this one will be graded."

"I'll admit that's the first time I've heard of someone deliberately keeping a road nearly impassable."

"I guess I understand it. It's such a landmark in the area that they could have tourists driving out for the hell of it. Rosie and Herb don't have to worry about that. Their place isn't anything like the Last Chance. It's a single-story ranch house."

"How big?"

"I'm not sure about the exact square footage, but it's larger than it looks from the front. They have five bedrooms. When they bought it they expected to have kids of their own. That didn't happen."

"I really admire their solution."

"I'm really grateful for their solution. The ranch is perfect for how they used it, especially once they added the cabins. You won't be able to see them when we drive in, but you'll see the barn and a corral off to the left. The front porch is nice, but it's not positioned to give you a mountain view like the one at the Last Chance."

"Not many places are like the Last Chance. So what kind of special meal do you think she's fixed to welcome you home?"

"I have a pretty good idea. All of us loved it when we lived here. When I tell you, you'll probably laugh."

"Lay it on me."

"Tuna casserole." He looked to see her reaction.

She didn't laugh, but she smiled. "With green peas in it and potato chips on top?"

"Yep." He could already taste it. "Nobody makes it like Rosie.

I've tried, but it's never the same. I always ask for it when I visit, but I forgot this time because I wasn't coming straight here."

"I haven't had tuna casserole in years. My mom used to make it when I was a kid, but then she took a cooking class and got into fancy things with exotic ingredients. Tuna casserole disappeared from the menu."

"Too bad."

"I know! I hope Rosie makes it because now I want some."

"If she didn't, there's always tomorrow night. I guarantee she's got the fixings. Okay, here's the turnoff. Wow, somebody's put up a new sign." He pulled onto the dirt road and stopped so they could look at it.

"Very nice."

"No kidding."

Thunder Mountain Ranch was spelled out in elegant brass letters on a slab of polished wood positioned between two sturdy posts. From the bottom hung a second sign. Home of Thunder Mountain Academy was painted in the academy's colors of green and brown.

"I'll bet Damon made the hanging part after I called on Saturday. That would be like him."

"Or he and Phil did it together. You said she worked with him on the cabin."

"Could be. Whoever made it, it's beautiful."

"Let's remember to mention it when we get there. They might have worked hard to finish and hang it before we arrived."

"I'll bet they did." He glanced at Chelsea. "I've always known how much this means, but that sign…"

"It's very special," she said softly. "Now let's go meet your family and eat tuna casserole."

He smiled at her. "I like that you said *my family.*"

"Well, they are, right?"

"They absolutely are." He started down the dirt road and was gratified at how smooth it was. Cade had probably been out here with the tractor recently. They rounded the bend and there stood the house. The eaves had recently been repainted and so had the Adirondack chairs on the front porch. Now the chairs alternated between Academy brown and Academy green.

"I love it, Finn," Chelsea murmured.

"Good. I was hoping you would." As he pulled into the gravel circular drive, one of the few similarities to the Last Chance Ranch, the front door opened and they all came out—Rosie, Herb, Cade, Lexi, Damon and a redhead who must be Philomena. His family. Heart full, he climbed out of the SUV and hurried around to open Chelsea's door.

But she was already out and moving toward the group spilling down the porch steps. "That sign is awesome!"

"I know!" Rosie held out her arms and gathered her in for a hug.

Finn stood transfixed by the sight, because it seemed so natural, as if Chelsea had been here dozens of times before.

Then Cade and Damon swarmed him, punching him on the arm and slapping him on the shoulder.

"I remember this hat!" Cade grabbed Finn's and switched with him, his gray eyes filled with laughter. "I wanted it but you saw it first."

"Yeah, and it looks a lot better on O'Roarke." Damon wore a battered straw cowboy hat over his sun-bleached hair. It would take a while for his surfer-dude image to fade after he'd spent four years in California. He glanced at Cade wearing Finn's hat. "Doesn't look broken in yet. You been hiding it in the closet, O'Roarke?"

"Pretty much."

"See there?" Cade settled it more firmly on his head. "He doesn't deserve such a fine hat. Hats get lonesome if they're not worn."

Finn laughed. "Then keep it, loser. I'm going to see my best girl." He spotted Rosie heading in his direction with a big grin on her face and love shining in her blue eyes.

Chelsea was now talking to Lexi and Phil, so Rosie must

have made sure those three were hooked up before coming to see him. How like her. He pulled her into a bear hug that lifted her off her feet. "I love you, Mom."

"Same here, you big galoot. Now put me down. You're messing with my new outfit."

He set her down and surveyed the red jeans and sparkly top. "Nice job." Her blond hair had recently been styled and her red nails had some kind of glitter on them. But the main thing he noticed was that she looked healthy. Thank God.

"She bought her new duds three weeks ago after we found out you were coming." Herb moved in for his hug. "Good to see you, son."

"Good to see you, too, Dad." Finn could tell the guy had put on some much-needed weight. He'd always been wiry, but when Rosie was sick, he'd worried off some pounds he couldn't afford to lose. Now he felt solid again.

Herb stepped back and glanced over at Rosie. "You were right about the red. It looks good."

"It does, doesn't it? Never had red jeans before, but I decided Finn's arrival warranted something flashy."

"I'm honored."

"You should be." Rosie straightened the hem of her top. "And by the way, she's great." She angled her head toward Chelsea, who was carrying on an animated conversation with Lexi and Phil.

The three women made an interesting group with Lexi's short brown hair that tended to curl and Phil's red hair that reminded him of Lily's. Then of course there was his innovative Chelsea, who was forever adding interesting streaks of color to hers as if not satisfied to be plain blond. He watched as Damon and Cade walked over to be introduced. Chelsea gave each of them a big smile and shook hands. Lexi said something he couldn't hear and they all laughed.

Finn turned back to Rosie. "I'm glad you like her, but that was a really fast evaluation."

"Easy, though. After only a few minutes she's already comfortable here. She didn't wait for you to introduce her to me. She came right over on her own. And she's a good hugger. Not tentative or shy about it."

"She hugged me, too," Herb said. "She told us both that she admired our work with the foster program. That was nice to hear."

Finn glanced at Chelsea, who was listening intently to something Phil was saying. "She was eager to meet you."

"I was eager to meet her," Rosie said. "I went on her website and she normally charges a bundle for her services, but she's not charging us a dime. Of course, I know that's partly because she's in love with you, but still, she's being very generous."

In love? The simple statement caught him off guard. He supposed it was true, just as he supposed he was in love with her, but they hadn't said it to each other.

It wasn't an oversight on his part and he didn't think it was on hers, either. She'd probably come to the same conclusion he had. Using the *L* word should be saved until they'd made it through their trial run of living together. Any sooner than that would be asking for more heartache.

Rosie peered at him. "Are you feeling okay? You suddenly went sort of pale. I know you're paler than you used to be, but this was on top of your usual paleness. Come on inside and I'll get you some water. You're probably dehydrated." She turned toward the house.

"I'm fine, Mom. Don't worry about getting me any water. But I would like to know where you decided to put Chelsea and me tonight."

She turned back to him with a gleam in her eye. "Before we talk about that, you really need to meet Phil. She's been looking forward to you two getting here."

"Well, sure. That would be great." He tamped down his impatience.

"Come on over." She started toward the group gathered by

the front steps. "Phil, you haven't had a chance to meet my boy Finn yet. Finn, this is Philomena Turner."

Phil had an open smile and a friendly blue gaze. She held out her hand. "It's good to finally meet you, Finn! Damon talks about you all the time."

"That must get annoying." Returning her smile, Finn shook hands with her. She had a firm grip, but then, this was a woman who could operate power tools, so no surprise there.

"Not annoying," Damon said. "Entertaining. She especially likes the one where you glued all the toilet seats shut and forgot that you had to use them, too. That gets a laugh every time, particularly the part where—"

"Yes, yes." Rosie rolled her eyes. "We've all heard that story a hundred times."

"I haven't." Chelsea smirked at Finn. "At least not all the way through."

"Well, Finn can tell you later." Rosie slipped an arm around her waist. "Right now let's take a walk so you and Finn can see the new cabin and the foundation for the rec hall."

Good thing Chelsea had worn her running shoes and not her sandals, Finn thought. "You're building a rec hall?" He glanced at Damon. "I haven't heard about that."

"We need one," Damon said as he fell into step beside Finn. "It'll be a combination dining hall, classroom and rec center. We decided the rec room in the house is too small for that many older teens, plus we don't need to have them bothering Rosie and Herb. They're students, not foster kids."

"I get that," Finn said, "but they'll need to be supervised out there."

"That's where I come in. Me and my new hat." Cade tipped it in Finn's direction. "I'll ride herd on 'em."

"Are you putting in a kitchen?" Finn hoped they weren't expecting to ferry food from the house.

Damon nodded. "Yep. You can add your two cents' worth on the choice of appliances if you want."

"I might just do that." He liked the idea of being involved in the nuts and bolts of the operation, and he had some expertise after supervising the remodeling of the space for O'Roarke's Brewhouse. "So did you make the academy sign this weekend?"

Damon grinned. "Like it?"

"I love it."

"Phil thought we should put one up after Rosie relayed your message on Saturday. We got Ben, our saddle maker guy, to help with the lettering. We didn't finish it until around noon. The paint's barely dry."

"Well, it's gorgeous."

"I helped hang it," Cade said.

"What he means is that he stood there and straw-bossed the operation while Phil and I worked our asses off."

Finn nodded. "Yep, I can picture that."

"I knew my supervisory talents weren't properly appreciated." Cade sighed. "Without my discerning eye, that sign would've ended up all cattywampus."

"You were lucky it didn't end up around your neck." Damon made a grab for the hat.

"Hey! Hands off! Get your own." Cade settled it more firmly on his head. "Maybe O'Roarke's got another one tucked away in his closet, gathering dust."

"Nope. That's the only one I kept."

Damon gazed at him. "Not into the cowboy thing anymore?"

"I wasn't, but lately..." Without thinking, he looked over at Chelsea walking with Rosie.

Damon obviously noticed because he chuckled. "I see how it is. Nothing like boots and a hat, right, bro?"

"Let's say this. It doesn't hurt."

They reached the meadow where two months ago only three log cabins had stood. Now there were four, which created a semicircle around the large fire pit where he'd spent so many evenings roasting marshmallows and singing camp songs. The bathhouse looked the same, stretched out behind the group of cabins. Over to the right a foundation had been laid for the rec hall.

"Which one's the Brotherhood cabin?" Chelsea looked around the semicircle.

"The first one." Rosie pointed.

"You'll probably want to take a look at it," Phil said.

"Oh, definitely."

"But first let's show you the new one. Damon and I are really proud of it."

"That's fine. I want to see the results of your hard work. It looks great from the outside."

"Sure." Finn would show Chelsea the Brotherhood cabin later. He had a feeling they wouldn't be sleeping in it, though, which was disappointing. "You did a great job of matching it to the others."

"The main thing we changed was the foundation," Damon said as they all walked past the fire pit on their way to the cabin. "It's cement instead of block."

"You mean the floor won't squeak?" Finn couldn't imagine it.

"'Fraid not."

"I told him that went against tradition," Cade said. "If the floor doesn't squeak, how can you play music on it?"

"My point exactly. I got really good at 'Jingle Bells.'"

Damon looked pained. "Oh, for God's sake. A cement foundation's sturdier. From a construction standpoint it makes sense."

"From a musical standpoint it sucks," Cade said. "But I didn't get a vote. Finn would've voted with me, too."

"I would have."

"Can't please everyone." Phil climbed up two cement steps and opened the cabin door. "We've all seen it, so why don't you two go in and look around?"

"Okay." Chelsea stepped inside and gasped. "Oh, my God."

Finn hurried in after her, afraid she'd found a giant spider or a snake. Instead she stood staring at a queen-size bed made up with sheets, a comforter and extra pillows. There were no bunks, but a couple of end tables had been placed on either side of the bed along with lamps. He whirled around and found Rosie leaning in the doorway.

She looked incredibly smug. "Will this do?"

16

CHELSEA WAS IN LOVE with these people. Rosie had welcomed her with open arms, literally, and because of Finn's earnest request, they would sleep in a real bed inside a brand-new log cabin. Over a celebratory dinner of tuna casserole in the cozy kitchen, Phil explained that they had discussed different configurations for the bunks and desks but hadn't decided yet how they wanted to build them.

"Phil had a great idea," Damon said. "She thinks if we create four loft beds in there with desks and a dresser underneath each one, it'll give each student his or her own territory. Now that the academy's a go, I'm in favor of retrofitting all the cabins that way."

Chelsea remembered her own teen years. "I would have loved it at that age." She glanced over at Rosie. "And in case I forget to say so, this is the best tuna casserole I've ever had in my life. But if you should meet my mother, you can't tell her I said so."

Rosie smiled. "Wouldn't dream of it."

"I believe I'll have some more." Finn picked up a casserole dish, one of two on the table, and began spooning more onto his plate.

"Yeah, me, too." Cade held out his empty plate. "Appreciate it. And a little extra for Ringo." He'd brought his gray tabby up to the house and Ringo was curled in a cat bed in the corner. A scoop of tuna casserole plopped in his food dish brought him running.

"Leave some for me." Damon grabbed the casserole when they were through. "Anybody else? I don't want to be a pig."

"Too late. I believe this is your fourth helping." Cade got up from the table. "Anyone need another one of the beers Finn so generously shipped over?"

"It's great beer," Herb said. "I'll have another one. Besides, we need to drink a few more toasts to the academy."

Chelsea also loved how they all raved about Finn's beer. It was good, but to hear them talk, no beer in the history of brewing had ever been so fine. Their loyalty warmed her heart.

"Speaking of pigs," Finn said, "I met a couple of awesome ones in Shoshone. It got me to thinking."

"No, Finn." Rosie met his gaze over the table. "No pigs. We had this discussion years ago. I love you to death and you brew a great beer, but we don't need pigs at Thunder Mountain."

"You should see his pictures, though," Chelsea found herself saying. "These are amazing pigs. One is named Harley and the other is named Wilbur."

"Wilbur's the name of the pig in *Charlotte's Web*!" Phil sat straighter. "I adored that book. I want to see your pictures, Finn."

The debate about pigs lasted for the rest of the meal with people choosing sides. Chelsea, Finn, Cade and Phil were pro-pig and Lexi, Damon, Rosie and Herb were antipig, at least as far as keeping one on the ranch. Despite Rosie's initial reaction, though, Chelsea thought she could be swayed.

After dinner and a quick cleanup, everyone decided to sit in the newly painted Adirondack chairs on the front porch. Most everyone had another beer, but Chelsea asked Rosie for some coffee laced with Bailey's. Rosie was delighted, and once she'd fixed their drinks, she chose a seat next to Chelsea.

Chelsea sipped her concoction and sighed. "Perfect. And thank you for setting us up in that cabin. It's awesome."

"All I did was come up with the idea. Damon and Cade dismantled one of our guest beds and hauled it down there along with a couple of nightstands and lamps. Lexi and Phil made up the bed. It was a group effort."

"Well, thanks to everyone, then. I can't imagine anything more special."

"You'll still have to trek to the bathhouse. That part couldn't be magically changed."

"I don't mind." She decided not to mention summer camp. Finn had told Rosie that this would be a brand-new experience. Better to keep quiet.

"I can't tell you how happy I am that he's found someone who understands him. He can be a bit of a control freak and a workaholic. I probably don't have to tell you that."

"No, but he's committed to learning when to let go. I'm hopeful he can."

"He can do all kinds of things when he's motivated. And he loves you so much."

She covered her gasp of surprise by taking another sip of her coffee. "Did he say that?"

"Not in so many words, but it's obvious. I know that boy, and I've never seen him look at a woman the way he looks at you. I don't know how he looked at his ex, of course, but he told us not to visit because they were fighting all the time, so it couldn't have been a good match."

"I don't think it was." Rosie's comment continued to swirl in her mind. *He loves you so much.* It gave her the courage to broach another topic. "By the way, I was there when Finn took the pig pictures."

"And I admit they were cute, but we don't need pigs around here."

"Did you know that *Charlotte's Web* was a lifeline for him when he was a kid, before he came here?"

"It was? I knew he had the book on his shelf, but I didn't think much about it. Lots of kids like that book."

"I'm no psychologist, but I think that story of courage and sacrifice helped keep him going when he lived with his grandfather."

"Huh." Rosie took another drink of her coffee. "I didn't realize that. If I had, I might have listened more closely when he asked for a pig."

"He's still asking."

"But he doesn't live here anymore." Rosie glanced at her. "What's the point?"

"He'd see the pig when he visited, and if he successfully changes his attitude, he'll visit more often."

Rosie laughed. "So he can see the pig?"

"*No.* To see all of you, of course. The pig would be a bonus. The thing is, I found out this weekend that lots of potbellied pigs are abandoned once they become adults, so there's a need for people who have some acreage to take them in."

Rosie lifted her coffee mug in tribute. "Chelsea, darlin', I can tell you're in PR. You know exactly what to say to get my attention."

"To be honest, this is more for Finn than the pigs. When I saw him with Harley and Wilbur, it touched my heart."

"So you're saying that if I adopt one of these abandoned pigs, it'll be good for the pig and good for someone I love?"

"That's what I'm saying. And the students would learn something by having that pig around, too. They can spread the word that cute little potbellied pigs get big and need plenty of room and that they're intelligent and trainable, like dogs."

"You are a persuasive young woman, Chelsea Trask." She stood. "More coffee and Bailey's? I'm having another."

"Then I will, too. Thank you, Rosie."

When Rosie went in to refill their mugs, Finn left his chair on the other side of the porch and came over to crouch in front of hers. "How soon can we excuse ourselves?"

"Not real soon. Rosie's getting us a refill and I think I just convinced her to adopt a pig."

He grinned. "You're kidding."

"Would I kid about a thing like that?"

The light on the porch was dim, but it was enough to gauge the flash of emotion in his eyes. "No, you wouldn't." He gave her knee a little squeeze. "When you think we can go, give me a signal."

"I will. And, Finn, I love your family."

He smiled. "So do I."

He loves you so much. She had to believe it was true. He was capable of loving deeply. He felt that way about everyone else on this porch with the exception of Phil, but he'd only just met her. He'd known the rest of them for fifteen years, and he cherished them all. She heard it in his voice, even when he was joking around. Especially then.

Rosie came back and handed Chelsea a mug. "I knew eventually I'd find someone else who likes Bailey's as much as I do. You'll have to visit a lot so you can help me make a dent in that case of it they bought me when I was in the hospital."

"Sounds good." Chelsea cradled the warm mug in both hands. "Finn's business anchors him in Seattle, but I can tell he's left a part of himself here. He needs to come back often and connect with his family."

"I think so, too. I've tried not to be one of those mothers who guilts their children into coming back to visit. That's obnoxious. But in the case of these foster boys, they do need to come back. It may be more important than if I'd given birth to them."

"I agree." She lifted her mug. "Let's drink to that."

That started a whole new string of toasts. She and Rosie lifted their mugs to several things, including the joys of tuna casserole, the appeal of a man in a Stetson and imaginative hair color. Rosie decided that her next salon visit might include lavender.

From there they moved on to movies and TV, where they matched up almost exactly. They turned thumbs down on slasher films and toasted action-adventure flicks with a touch of romance and a gorgeous hero. Rosie reluctantly admitted to following celebrity gossip and Chelsea confessed to having a stash of gossip magazines in her apartment.

When they'd both finished their second mug of coffee, Rosie gazed at her. "I've loved every minute of this, but you need to collect your sweetie pie and head on down to the cabin. We get up early around here."

"How early?"

"I serve breakfast at five-thirty."

Chelsea blinked. "All righty, then." She stood. "I'll just carry this into the kitchen and we'll be on our way."

"Never mind. I'll take your mug." She raised her voice. "Finn, honey, it's time to saddle up your SUV and drive Chelsea over to the cabin."

He was on his feet immediately and a round of hugs followed. It was almost like a bride and groom leaving the reception for the honeymoon, minus the wedding ceremony. Chelsea felt as if they were being given everyone's blessing.

As they took a back road around to the cabins, Chelsea glanced at Finn, who was still wearing Cade's brown Stetson. "Your brothers won't pull any pranks on us tonight, will they?"

He grinned. "Worried?"

"After being around them for a few hours...yeah. And I just realized there are no curtains on any of those windows."

"They won't pull anything. We mostly only do stuff to each other. When a guy's with his girl, he's off-limits unless he's being really obnoxious. Or she is. Damon and Cade think you're terrific, and they're so grateful for your help with this project. They wouldn't do anything that might scare you off."

"I'm the opposite of scared off. I'll probably bug you to come back a lot."

"Works for me. Do you really think Rosie will adopt a pig?"

"I do, but I'd let the subject lie. She obviously likes creating a ta-da moment."

He laughed. "You have her pegged."

"So here's my thought. Don't mention it again, and chances are a pig will be here the next time you visit."

"You could be right."

"Someone will need to contact Lily to set up her guest lectures, so it'll all fall neatly into place."

"Mostly because you backed me up and made that pitch to Rosie after dinner. That kind of support means a lot to me."

"I'm glad." Oh, yeah, he loved her and she loved him right back. They just weren't saying the word. "I wouldn't have thought to do it, though, if you hadn't told me about the book. I'm honored that you trusted me enough to explain how special it is to you."

"It is." He paused. "And so are you."

"Back atcha, cowboy." And that might be as close as they'd come to declaring their love, at least until they'd weathered a few weeks together in Seattle.

She was fine with that. She knew how much he cared for her just by listening to his voice. It had the same richness as when he spoke about his family. Rosie could hear it, too, no doubt. Probably everyone could because they knew him so well.

He parked next to the cabin. Aided by the moon and lamplight shining through the windows, they made their way to the cabin door. Someone must have turned on the lamps earlier.

Finn put himself in charge of both suitcases again and she carried the laptops. She breathed in pine-scented air and the aroma of fresh-cut wood. Heavenly.

She leaned the laptop cases in a corner. The bed and nightstands had been positioned against the back wall, which had no window, and a couple of braided rugs had been placed on either side of the bed. Otherwise the room was empty.

But full of love. She met Finn's gaze. "It's so beautiful."

"No, it's just nice. You're beautiful." He set his hat on top of his suitcase before walking toward her and pulling her gently into his arms. "Inside and out."

"Pretty words." She wound her arms around his neck. "Can I steal them?"

"You can have anything of mine you want."

"How about all of you?" Gazing into his warm blue eyes, she began unsnapping his shirt.

"I'm all yours." He dropped a soft kiss on her mouth. "But first let's turn out the lights." He released her and walked over to one of the nightstands.

"I thought you weren't worried about being disturbed?" She nudged off her running shoes.

"I'm not. I just prefer moonlight." He rounded the bed and turned off the other lamp. Sure enough, the nearly full moon cast a swath of silvery light over the bed.

"Impressive. Did you know that would happen?"

"I guessed it would. I wanted to see if I was right." He drew back the covers to reveal snowy sheets, and she heard the thumps of his boots as they hit the floor.

"I've never made love in the moonlight." Their breathing was the only sound in their darkened, private world. She shivered in anticipation.

"You're going to love it." His bare feet whispering across the wooden floor, he closed the distance between them and pulled her into his arms with the assurance of a man who knew he was wanted.

And, oh, how she wanted him. But the frenzy of those first nights had given way to an urge to tantalize and caress, to savor and explore. They undressed each other more deliberately tonight, each of them taking time to place kisses on the bare skin they uncovered.

Her sense of touch grew sharper in the deep shadows surrounding the bed. The merest brush of his fingertips sent heat spiraling through her veins. The moist pressure of his mouth tightened the coil of desire until she ached for him.

When all their clothes lay discarded on the floor, he swept her up in his arms and carried her to the bed. He laid her gently on the soft sheets and moved aside so his shadow didn't fall on her.

"Look at you," he murmured. "Glowing in the moonlight like a goddess. I could almost convince myself you're not real."

She held out her hand. "Come here and I'll convince you I'm very real."

"And if I touch you, you won't disappear? Or turn me to stone?"

"The only way you'll get in trouble, buster, is by *not* touching me. And I'll bet a part of you has already turned to stone."

Laughing, he climbed into bed with her. "You have a smart mouth, you know that?"

"So I've been told."

He moved over her. "So I guess you're not a goddess."

"Not last time I checked." She wrapped her arms around the solid warmth of his back as he propped himself up on his forearms. "But I think you must be a wizard."

"Why's that?" Bracing himself on one arm, he began a leisurely caress, stroking her throat, her shoulder and the curve of her breast.

He left a trail of sparks in his wake and she smoldered under the light pressure of his palm. "You must be a wizard." She took an unsteady breath. "Because you can turn a rational, intelligent woman into a lusty wench who would do anything—*anything*—to have you between her thighs."

"Good to know." He settled himself there, his rigid cock pressed against her belly. "My boots are dusty from this trip. They sure could use polishing."

"Almost anything. I draw the line at polishing your boots." She was bluffing. When she could feel the hard length of him *right there*, she'd agree to any terms he cared to set.

"Looks like I'm not a wizard, after all."

"Yes, you are." She reached between them. "Look, I found your staff." And holding all that leashed power sent moisture to the very spot where that staff needed to be.

He sucked in air. "Careful. It's hard to control a wizard's staff unless you know the magic word."

"Condom?"

"That would be it." He reached toward the nightstand. "And, presto! One magically appears."

"You can't fool me. You had it there all along."

"Nope. Plucked it out of thin air. That's what wizards do." He brushed it over her nose. "Care to put it on for me, lusty wench?"

"I suppose." She could barely breathe, she wanted him so desperately. She put the condom on him with trembling fingers.

His breathing roughened. "Well done, wench." Lifting his hips, he probed her gently before sliding partway in. "Now how about those boots?"

She gripped his firm buns. "Consider them polished."

"Excellent." He thrust home. Then he held very still as he gazed down at her. "I've been such a fool. Thank God I woke up."

"So I don't have to polish your boots?"

"Just be there for me, Chels." He began a slow, steady rhythm. "That's all I need."

"That's all I need, too." She held on tight as he rocketed them both skyward. She'd warned him to stay in the present. She needed to take her own advice.

17

LIFE DOESN'T GET any better than this. Finn had heard people toss out that statement dozens of times over the years. In his opinion, it had showed a lack of imagination. Life could always get better, right?

Well, no. Nothing could improve on the joy he felt sharing these few days and nights with Chelsea on the beloved ranch he'd called home for ten years, surrounded by the people he considered family. Both Cade and Damon were staying in town with their respective girlfriends, but they spent most of their time at the ranch working on academy projects.

Finn and Chelsea helped wherever they could, but this morning they'd taken a break to ride along the Forest Service Road. Rosie had suggested saddling up Navarre and Isabeau, a chestnut gelding and dark gray mare. Both were beautifully trained and Chelsea turned out to be a fair rider. They even cantered a little.

Then, in a secluded meadow with only the birds and forest creatures around, they'd made sweet love on a blanket in the sunshine. She'd insisted that he had to wear his Stetson to keep the sun out of her eyes. He thought she was just enamored of the hat.

She confirmed that as they returned to the barn and began unsaddling the horses. "I liked the gray hat, but Cade's right.

His brown one is broken in. It looks more authentic and cowboy-ish. You're taking it back to Seattle, I hope."

"I am. Although I'm not sure why." He pulled off the saddle and carried it into the tack room.

"You should wear it at O'Roarke's," she called after him.

"Not happening," he shouted back. He deposited his saddle quickly and hurried back to grab hers before she tried to carry it herself. He arrived just in time. "Let me get that."

She opened her mouth as if to protest.

"Please. I like showing off my cowboy-ish skills."

"Okay." She grinned and stepped away from the horse. "Sure you won't wear the hat at the brewhouse? The customers would love it."

"Not doing it." He piled the cinch and the stirrups on top of the saddle.

"Then will you promise to wear it when we have outdoor sex?"

He picked up the saddle and turned back toward her. "As I suspected, it had nothing to do with keeping the sun out of your eyes, did it?"

"Not really. Sex with you is always great, but when you wear that hat…" She sighed and patted her chest.

"Then I'd better not wear it at O'Roarke's." He carried the saddle into the barn. "I'm liable to be mobbed."

"Good point. Save it for when you're with me."

He came back out with the plastic tote that held the grooming tools and smiled at her. "That I can do." And now he had a reason to take the hat to Seattle.

"Are you going to brush them down?"

"I am."

"Let me help. We used to brush the horses at the stable where I rode."

"By all means."

"Yay!" She picked up a brush and started in on Isabeau.

He watched her for a minute before turning back to Navarre.

Yep, life was perfect right now. Caring for the horses together after going for a ride and making love ranked high on his list of favorite ways to spend a morning. He wondered if he'd have trouble getting back into his regular routine.

Once the horses were turned out into the pasture, Chelsea wanted to go back to the cabin to check the Kickstarter site. A few small donations had come in, so they were inching closer. They only had two days left, but now Damon and Cade could totally cover the rest if necessary.

"I just have a feeling something more has happened," she said.

"Go ahead and check." Finn gave her a quick kiss. "I'll see if Rosie needs any help with lunch." It would only be the four of them today. Damon and Phil were at the lumber yard and planned to stay in town for lunch. Cade was with Lexi looking at a horse she was considering buying.

When Finn walked into the kitchen, Rosie had the refrigerator door open and was pulling sandwich fixings out of the refrigerator.

"Just in time." She handed him a loaf of bread. "Enjoy your ride?"

"We did." He was glad she still had her back to him because she'd surely guessed what had happened during that ride. "Thanks for loaning us Navarre and Isabeau."

"Anytime. Herb and I don't ride them as much as we should." She gave him several packages of lunch meat. "Where's Chelsea?"

"Checking on Kickstarter."

"I looked early this morning and we'd gained another twenty-five bucks. Every little bit helps." She took out mustard and mayonnaise and some lettuce before closing the door with her hip. "Herb's catching up on his email. He'll probably look again before he shuts down the computer."

"Chelsea had a hunch more had happened this morning.

Maybe we're over the top and don't even know it." He washed up at the sink so he could help with the sandwiches.

"Wouldn't that be great?" Rosie took down a large bread-board that hung on the wall. "Cade, Lexi and Damon keep saying they'll cover what's left, but I'd rather they didn't have to."

"I know, but it's not much if they split it three ways, and missing by such a small amount would be stupid." He finished drying his hands and glanced over as Herb walked into the kitchen. "Hey, did you look at Kickstarter?"

Herb didn't say anything. Instead he glanced at Rosie and swallowed.

"Dad?" Herb's expression made Finn's stomach begin to churn.

About that time the front door banged and Chelsea raced into the kitchen, breathing hard. "A backer canceled." She gulped in air. "A really big one."

A chill settled over him as he stared at her, not wanting to believe what he'd heard but knowing it was true. Herb had seen it, too. He just hadn't figured out how to tell Rosie.

Rosie turned from the counter and gazed at Chelsea. "How bad is it?"

"I won't lie to you." Chelsea's face had drained of color. "It's bad. We'll start contacting people right away to see if we can raise more money, but…"

Rosie shook her head. "No. Everyone's been more than generous. All our friends, all our boys, even strangers we don't know. I'm not asking them to give more."

"I'll ask," Chelsea said. "You don't have to. I'll—"

"No. Thank you, but no." Rosie came over and put her hands on Chelsea's shoulders. "Even if you're the one asking, it's still like us asking. We have forty-eight hours left. Maybe something will happen. If not…we tried."

Finn recovered his voice. "Can someone do that? Just back out?"

"They can up until twenty-four hours before the deadline."

Chelsea's gaze was bleak. "This is one of the ranchers who came to the presentation last Saturday. He sent me an email and he's devastated, but his wife had a sudden health crisis and insurance won't cover it. The bills will be enormous. He has no choice."

"Of course he doesn't." Rosie squeezed Chelsea's shoulders. "Here's my philosophy. If something is supposed to work out, it will. Now let's have some lunch."

The meal was a quiet one. Finn ate because it seemed impolite not to after the food had been prepared. He and Chelsea had planned to sand the benches that ringed the fire pit this afternoon. Because he had no better idea for how to fill the time, he suggested to Chelsea they go ahead and she agreed.

"But first I'll call Damon and Cade," he told Rosie as he, Herb and Chelsea helped clean up the lunch dishes.

"Let me call them," Rosie said. "I need to emphasize to them what I just told all of you. We're going to stand pat and see what happens. No heroics."

He recognized the steely determination in her voice and knew there was no arguing with her. "All right."

As he and Chelsea walked back to the cabins, she didn't say anything. He was grateful for her silence. What was there to say?

Damon had designated the second cabin Construction Central, so that's where Finn and Chelsea went for the sandpaper blocks Damon had put together for them to use. The benches were old and he hadn't wanted to use a power sander.

They each picked a bench, straddled it and began to sand. The mindless work was perfect. He was too dazed to be good for much else. They'd worked steadily for almost an hour when his phone chirped. Probably Damon or Cade.

He checked the text ID. So his assistant Brad had decided to check in after being silent all week. Finn had been kind of relieved not to hear from the guy.

Climbing off the bench, he walked away from the fire pit. It had been an instinctive move, but he was aware of Chelsea watching him. He put the phone to his ear and kept his voice down. "Hey, Brad. What's up?"

"We have a situation here."

Of course they did. It figured that everything was turning to shit at once. But he doubted anything could be as bad as the news about Kickstarter. "What's that?"

"Jeff quit last night."

"Why?" Jeff was his most experienced bartender. He trained the new hires and was the steadiest employee Finn had.

"Crisis with his family back in New Jersey. I'm not clear on the details but somebody has cancer and he's needed there."

"Don't let him quit. Give him a leave of absence."

"I tried that. He wouldn't go for it. Said he'd be relocating to Jersey, something about taking care of his little sister. He's not coming back, Finn."

"He's left already?" He felt the first prick of unease. Jeff was the wheelhorse of the waitstaff—bartenders, servers, the whole shebang.

"Yeah, and we need somebody with his level of experience. Roger's not ready to take over."

"No, he's not." Jeff had been training Roger to step in when he was on vacation, but the guy was too young to take over Jeff's position permanently.

"I have somebody in mind who might work out."

"Do I know him?"

"No. He's from Portland. But he has friends in Seattle and has been considering making a change."

Alarm bells went off in Finn's head. He'd done all the hiring from the first day. Sure, he'd made a couple of mistakes with the lower-paying positions, but he'd filled the important jobs with the right people.

Jeff had been one of those people, and now Brad was suggesting that they bring in some unknown from Portland, somebody Finn had never met. A bad hire at this point could have lasting repercussions.

He glanced at Chelsea, who was still watching him, and he wondered if she'd have any words of wisdom. But she didn't have employees. She couldn't understand how critical this was to the future of O'Roarke's. Jeff had a legion of admirers, and whoever took his place would need the same charisma.

It sounded as if this Portland guy might be a friend of Brad's. That wouldn't help Brad make an objective decision. Cronyism might be involved. Finn had to make the call. He hated what that would entail—leaving the ranch today if possible. But, seriously, what could he do here?

Chelsea probably wouldn't want to go and there was no reason she should have to pack up and leave. She could drive the SUV back to Jackson and fly out when they'd planned to.

He didn't like the idea of taking off right now, but Rosie had lectured him about not letting this project screw up his business. She'd been very clear.

"Invite your friend for an interview," he said, "but make it for tomorrow afternoon at the earliest. I want to be there."

"That's why I called you. I thought you might."

"I'll try to get a flight out today. I'll let you know."

"Great. Safe travels."

"Thanks." Finn disconnected. Then he turned to meet Chelsea's gaze. "There's a crisis at work."

"What sort of crisis?"

"Jeff, my most valuable bartender who kept everything running smoothly, has quit."

"Sorry to hear that."

"I have to fly out today."

She leaned on the bench and looked at him, her expression giving nothing away. She used to wear that expression a lot before this trip, but he hadn't seen it recently. "Today?"

"I have to go, Chels. Brad knows a guy from Portland, but this is too important a position to fill based on his friendship with Brad. I need to get a look at the guy. Résumés don't give the whole picture. I need to talk to him."

"You're not willing to take Brad's word that he's right for the job?"

"For any other position, sure. But this is too important to leave to chance. We're replacing a key employee."

"I understand the significance of that."

"Do you? Because you're a company of one. I'm not. Hiring the right people is critical to the success of the operation."

She put down her sandpaper block and got up from the bench. "I may be a company of one, as you phrase it, but I work with clients like you who have many employees. Jeff was an important component. Whenever I went into O'Roarke's and he was there, he lit up the place."

"So you do understand. I'm glad, because—"

"I understand that you feel the need to supervise the hiring of Jeff's replacement."

"Yes, ma'am, I do." He tugged down the brim of Cade's hat to make the point.

She didn't smile. In fact, disappointment dulled the usual sparkle in her brown eyes. "But I don't understand that you're willing to leave Thunder Mountain when the Kickstarter deadline is tomorrow night."

He felt as if he'd been slapped. "Chels, I have to sit in on that interview. I can't take a chance that Brad will hire the wrong person."

"Can't you?" Her voice was a soft plea. "Is that really more important than supporting the people you love while they sweat out this deadline?"

"My presence won't affect the damned contributions!"

"Of course not, but you can lend your moral support! Win or lose, they need you here."

"That makes no sense. Even Rosie said I shouldn't jeopardize my business for Thunder Mountain Academy. Yet you're telling me I should?"

She stared at him for several long, agonizing moments. "No, I'm not. It's your decision to make." And she walked away.

"Don't go. Talk to me, Chels."

She turned back and gazed at him. Her voice shook. "I didn't intend to say this yet, if ever, but I love you, Finn."

He gasped. She'd chosen to tell him now?

"And because I love you, I'm not going to ask you to change a pattern that is so deeply ingrained. You do what you think is best."

"But you don't think it's best, do you?" Now he felt as if someone had poured cement in his veins.

"What I think doesn't matter."

"It does matter." His whole body ached. "Please tell me. I want to know."

She sighed. "Okay. I realize that it's a significant position, but Brad is a capable assistant. You should be able to trust him to make this decision."

"It's not that simple."

"It's exactly that simple. If you can't trust your assistant to act in your absence on matters large and small, then you're locked into a situation where you'll have to supervise every detail forever. I love you, but I'm not willing to deal with that mindset. Your decision to leave now tells me that your thinking hasn't changed at all." She gazed at him. "We'd have no chance, Finn. We'd crash and burn." Tossing down the sanding block, she walked away.

And instead of going toward the cabin they'd shared, she headed up to the ranch house, as if making it clear that her loyalty was to Thunder Mountain Ranch and not him.

She really didn't get it, probably because her operation was so different from his. She couldn't see how a bad decision now had the potential for a domino effect. If the wrong person took over Jeff's position, gradually Finn's customer base would disappear. His revenues would drop off and he'd begin a slow slide into bankruptcy.

Good thing she hadn't gone back to the cabin, because he

needed to boot up his laptop and make plane reservations. God, he felt stiff. He rolled his shoulders as he walked.

The minute he opened the door, he decided he'd have to take his laptop somewhere else. Chelsea wasn't physically there, but her presence could be felt as strongly as if she had been. There was her gray suitcase on the floor, and by now he knew every item in it.

They'd made the bed together this morning, just as they had every morning. He could see her plain as day, her hair mussed from sleep and good lovemaking as she dutifully helped him tug the covers into place, all the while complaining about having to get up before the chickens so they'd make it to breakfast on time.

This morning she'd started a pillow fight. He'd wanted to make love afterward, but they would have missed Rosie's breakfast. Being there had become a point of honor for both of them.

So he'd told himself it didn't matter because they'd be back in this bed tonight and eventually they'd be living together. They'd have plenty of pillow fights followed by great sex.

Apparently not.

He massaged the back of his neck where he'd developed a really bad crick. And he had the beginnings of a charley horse in his left calf. When he leaned down to pick up his laptop from the floor beside his suitcase, he felt a twinge in his lower back.

Damn it, now was not the time to be falling apart. He needed to be 100 percent to deal with the situation at O'Roarke's. He left his hat inside and walked out to sit on the stoop with his laptop. Time to stop playing cowboy.

For some reason his fingers were clumsy on the keys and he blamed it on the sanding. That probably explained the pain in his shoulders and the crick in his neck, maybe even the charley horse. He'd been hunched over in an unnatural position for too long.

His stomach didn't feel all that great, either. He shouldn't have forced down that sandwich. And now the damned site was slow loading. He finally got something to come up, but all the flights he looked at for today, even the red-eye tonight, were booked. Sheridan didn't tend to have as many choices as a bigger city.

He decided to check other locations and found a red-eye leaving tonight out of Cheyenne. That wasn't optimal, but he might have to go with it. His neck really hurt. Straightening, he rubbed it some more as he looked around at the meadow and the three other cabins.

Except for the birds chirping in the nearby pine trees and the rustle of a slight breeze, the meadow was quiet. Peaceful. *Precious*. And not just to him. It was precious to his foster parents and all the boys who'd sat around the fire pit roasting marshmallows and singing silly camp songs.

This meadow had the potential to become precious to a whole new group of kids who would learn a lot about caring for horses and even more about how to live. They might even learn about potbellied pigs.

Hard to imagine that the fate of this meadow hung in the balance and would be decided tomorrow at midnight. He tried to convince himself to book his flight, but it wasn't a good option. Maybe he should take a break and try again in a few minutes. Things could change.

Shutting down the laptop, he left it on the stoop and got to his feet. Slowly he walked around the fire pit until he came to the Brotherhood cabin. It was unlocked, so he walked inside, leaving the door open so he could hear the birds and the wind in the trees.

After all these years it still smelled the same. He closed his eyes and imagined being here at fifteen, before he'd kissed a girl, before he'd had a driver's license. He pictured what it had looked like with posters tacked on the walls. A radio was usually on because they'd all loved their music.

Cade's junk would be strewed around, but his and Damon's areas would be neat. Unless he was studying, his books, including *Charlotte's Web*, were always lined up on the shelf. He knew that book by heart, all the text and the illustrations.

Charlotte had stuck by that pig. When it looked as if nothing would save Wilbur, she'd stepped in. She'd been a true friend, a loyal friend. She hadn't abandoned him at the zero hour.

Opening his eyes, he rubbed a hand over his face. It came away wet. Slowly he turned around, reached up and traced the TMB initials he and his brothers had carved into the beam over the doorway. He thought of the pledge they'd recited during the blood brother ceremony. *Loyalty above all.*

When he heard footsteps in the grass, he immediately knew whose they were. He recognized them now.

Chelsea walked over and peered up at him. "Rosie sent me to ask if you need a ride to the airport. And, don't worry. I explained how important this is to you and she's fine with it."

"I'm not." His throat was clogged and the words came out sounding weird.

She came up the steps and stood just outside the door. "Can't you get a flight? I figured it wouldn't be easy, but I was hoping, for your sake, that—"

"I'm not going."

Her stoic expression softened and emotion flickered in her gaze. "Why?"

"Because if it weren't for Rosie and Herb, and Cade and Damon, I wouldn't have a business. I might not even have a life. I owe them…" He paused, struggling to keep from breaking down.

"Oh, Finn." She came to him, wrapped him in her arms and buried her face against his chest. She was trembling.

He closed her in a tight embrace and laid his cheek against her soft hair. In that moment he regained his soul.

"I was so scared I'd lost you." Her voice was muffled against his shirt.

"Me, too. Literally petrified. All my muscles started locking up." He kissed the top of her head and stroked her hair.

"Wow." She lifted her head and her brown eyes were shining. "Epic."

"Yeah." He took his time looking into her eyes, because he would never again take that privilege for granted. "I love you, Chels, and not just because you're funny and sexy and beautiful and creative, even though you're all those things. I love you because you had the courage to tell me the truth, even when I didn't want to hear it."

She swallowed. "It wasn't easy."

"I know, and I hope to God I never again get that close to betraying everything and everyone I care about. But if I do..."

"I'll kick your butt." Her smile was filled with tenderness. "But I have a feeling you don't have to worry."

"I have a feeling you're right." When he kissed her, he swore he'd never take that privilege for granted, either. He'd come so close to ruining everything. But thanks to the inspiration of a tiny spider, a blood oath in the forest and the woman in his arms, he'd gained the world.

Epilogue

FINN'S DECISION TO STAY changed everything in Chelsea's mind. She was no longer worried about having him move in, and she was convinced that a miracle would happen and the Kickstarter campaign would be funded by the deadline. Logically his presence shouldn't have any effect, but she had a superstitious streak.

She could tell everyone else appreciated him being there, too, although she and Rosie were the only ones who knew how close he'd come to leaving. They'd both decided that talking about it after the fact would serve no purpose.

But despite Chelsea's firm belief that the money would appear, at one hour before the midnight deadline they were still short the amount that had dropped out yesterday, too much even for them all to cover.

Everyone had gathered in the kitchen where they had three different laptops on. Rosie plied everyone with snacks and free-flowing beer, all except for Chelsea and Rosie, who drank coffee and Bailey's.

At eleven-thirty, Ty Slater, a former foster kid and their legal consultant who lived in Cheyenne, showed up at the front door. When he walked into the kitchen, Chelsea recognized him immediately from the calendar. Because it was a sixteen-month calendar, Ty had volunteered to be the cowboy on the page for September through December. Not even Cade had wanted to be hanging on someone's wall for that long.

But Ty apparently was willing to do anything he could to help the cause, including donating his legal services. "I was watching on my computer at home," he said, "and finally I couldn't stand it. I knew you'd all be sitting around hyperventilating, so I'm here to hyperventilate with you."

"And drink Finn's beer." Cade handed him a chilled bottle. "We planned to save some for when we reached the goal, but we decided to drink it now because we need to fortify ourselves."

"I understand. Tense times always call for a good beer." Ty pushed his brown Stetson to the back of his head and smiled at Chelsea. "Here's to you, lady. That was another reason to drive up, so I could meet our Kickstarter guru. You're amazing."

"She is amazing." Finn stepped up quietly behind her chair and put a hand on her shoulder. "I'm a lucky guy."

"I'd say so." Chelsea noticed Ty and Finn share a look, and the subtle flirting stopped immediately. "When are you two heading back to Seattle?"

"Tomorrow," Chelsea said. "It'll be tough to leave, though. I've loved being here."

"I'll bet. What kind of stuff did you do?"

"Helped Cade and Damon," Finn said, "but I had some time to show her around the place. One night we went dancing in town."

Ty blinked. "You? Dancing?"

"You'd be flabbergasted." Damon wandered over to join the conversation. "Old Finn, the guy with two left feet, has found his rhythm. Now he puts me to shame."

"That I'd like to see." Ty peered at Finn. "What'd you do, take lessons?"

Finn laughed. "You might say that. Actually, I—"

"Oh, my God!" Chelsea had been keeping an eye on the screen off and on while she tried not to panic. Then she looked and...

"We're over!" Lexi jumped up from the table and grabbed

Cade around the neck. "Somebody just donated a whole bunch, and we're over!"

The room erupted into cheers, shouts and a few quiet tears from Rosie. Chelsea thought she might have been the only one to see that because Rosie quickly wiped them away and began hugging everyone. Chelsea almost didn't hear her phone when it rang, even though it was right in her pocket.

"Who was the donor?" Ty asked.

"You check." Chelsea pulled out her phone and hurried into the living room where she could hear. "Lily? Did you see that we made it?"

"Duh. I just donated. I thought you guys were solid when you left here, but then I looked just now and you were seriously under, so I gave you the rest."

"What? But you already gave us a donation, Lily. I hate for you to go into debt. I'm grateful, but that's a chunk of money. And now you're stuck."

Finn had followed her into the living room and stood listening to her end of the conversation.

"I have plenty of money," Lily said. "Didn't anyone tell you? I made a killing on a video game a few years ago and I'm living off the royalties. I didn't want to be obnoxious and just throw money at you before. Then it would have been all about me."

"You could never be obnoxious, and thank God this didn't put you in the hole."

"Not even close to the hole."

"That's great to hear. Whew."

"Congratulations! Thunder Mountain Academy is a go!"

Chelsea took another deep breath and let the tension flow out of her body. "Yes, because of people like you."

"Hey, it took everybody to make this happen."

Chelsea paused to catch her breath. "And FYI, I may have Rosie talked into getting a pig. We're going to slow-play it, but be ready if the subject comes up."

"I will! Now go on back to the party. I'm sure there is one."

"There is. Good night, Lily." Chelsea disconnected the call and stared at Finn. "I think she's a millionaire or something. Who knew?"

"I don't think she wants the whole world to know." He pulled her into his arms. "Congratulations, Chels. This is mostly your victory, and I want you to go back in there and claim it, but—"

"Come here, cowboy." She pulled him by his shirtfront the way she had their first night in the Bunk and Grub.

"I love it when you do that."

"I'm glad, because I intend to be doing it for a long, long time."

"Then it looks like I'll be doing this for a long, long time." His mouth came down on hers.

Not surprisingly, his kiss was ended soon after it began. Cade and Damon broke it up and hauled them both back into the kitchen for a loud and jubilant toast.

But that was okay. Toasting the future of Thunder Mountain Academy was important. She'd have plenty of time for kissing once they returned to Seattle. And now, because Finn had seen the light, so would he.

* * * * *

The Mighty Quinns: Logan

Kate Hoffmann

Books by Kate Hoffmann

ABOUT THE AUTHOR

Kate Hoffmann has written more than seventy books for Harlequin, most of them for the Temptation and Blaze lines. She spent time as a music teacher, a retail assistant buyer and an advertising exec before she settled into a career as a full-time writer. She continues to pursue her interests in music, theater and musical theater, working with local schools in various productions. She lives in southeastern Wisconsin with her cat, Chloe.

Prologue

DROPLETS OF RAIN spattered against the wavy glass in the manor-house windows. Aileen Quinn stared out into the lush green of her garden, her gaze fixed on a niche in the tall stone wall. A small statue of an angel was nestled into the ivy, the rain dripping off the outspread wings as if it wept.

"Are you certain?" she asked.

"I know this is a lot to handle, Miss Quinn. Perhaps we should continue later?"

She gripped the head of her cane and turned back to the genealogist. "No," she said. "I'm ninety-six years old. There will be no more secrets in my life. That's why I chose to write my autobiography. I want it all out there so I can leave this world in peace."

"You realize the chances that your older siblings are still alive are virtually zero."

Aileen moved to a wing chair near the fireplace and sat down, turning toward the warmth. "Of course. But I would like to know if they had children and grandchildren. I have a family and I'd like to know at least a little bit about them before I die."

She stared into the flickering flames, her thoughts carrying her back to her childhood. She only had the thinnest of details, facts that the nuns at the orphanage had relinquished after years of persistent questions. Her father had died in the Easter Rising of 1916, shot through the heart by a British soldier. Her mother, left pregnant and desperate to provide for her newborn daughter, grew sick with consumption and brought Aileen to the orphanage a few weeks before she died.

The story had been told so many times in the media, the rags-to-riches tale of an Irish orphan girl who became one of the world's most popular novelists. Aileen's stories had been a reflection of her life, tales of struggle and triumph, of heartache and great happiness, and all set in the land of her birth, her beautiful Ireland.

"Tell me again," she said. "Their names. What were my brothers' names?"

"The eldest was Diarmuid. He was twelve when he was sent off to work as an apprentice to a shipbuilder in Belfast in 1917. Then there was Conal. He was nine and Lochlan was six when you were born. And Tomas was five. There were three other children who didn't survive. A baby girl between Diarmuid and Conal who died at birth. And a daughter named Mary and a son named Orin between Tomas and you. They both died of scarlet fever the year before you were born."

"So there were seven, not four."

The young man nodded. "Yes."

"I need to know where they went," Aileen said, leaning forward in her chair. "How they lived. You need to find everything you can about them."

"Yes, ma'am," he said. He riffled through his papers. "I was able to learn that the youngest, Tomas, was sent to Australia. He traveled with a missionary and his wife on a ship called the *Cambria,* which sailed from Cork and landed in Sydney in December of 1916."

"Then that's where you'll begin," Aileen said. "In Australia. I don't care how many people you need to hire to help you or how much it costs. I'm giving you unlimited funds to do whatever is needed, Mr. Stephens. And I want a weekly report of any progress you've made, no matter how inconsequential."

"Yes, Miss Quinn."

"That's all for now," she said.

He nodded and walked out of the solarium, his research tucked under his arm. Aileen watched him leave, then drew a deep breath. She'd spent her whole life believing she was alone in the world, a victim of circumstances beyond her control. But now, in a single instant, she had a family, siblings who had once held her and kissed her...and loved her.

The housekeeper walked into the room, her footsteps silent on the ornate rug. Sally set the tray down on the tea table. "I've baked some lovely scones," she said. "Will you not have one?"

Aileen shook her head. "Just the tea, Sally."

"Did your Mr. Stephens have anything interesting to share?"

"Not at the present," she replied. The news about her family was so startling that she wanted to keep it a secret just a bit longer. It wasn't a good thing to hope. She'd learned that as a child, every Sunday, when visiting day at Our Lady of Mercy orphanage arrived. Just over a hundred girls, dressed in their very best, would stand in proper rows, hoping that someone would come, would choose to take one of them home.

But she'd been a sickly child, smaller than the others and plagued with respiratory infections, and often pushed into the background. After a time, she'd decided to stop trying. She was safe with the nuns and had dreams of joining the Sisters of St. Clare herself.

The orphanage provided a harsh type of life. Punishments were meted out regularly for the girls who refused to conform. Those that were considered chronically impure—the illegitimate, the criminal, the intractable—bore the brunt of the nuns' disdain. But Aileen was pious and penitent for even the slightest sin.

When Sister Mary gave her a coveted job in the school library, shelving books and reading to the younger girls, she'd quietly been marked as a favorite and was spared the worst of chores.

By the time she was eleven, she'd run out of books to read

in the school library and was allowed to accompany the lively young teacher, Sister Bernadette, to the Kinsale library, where she'd been handed a copy of *Jane Eyre* and told to hide it from the older nuns.

The book had opened a whole new world for her. The story of the plain orphan girl, snatched from her cruel fate and whisked into a life as a governess, had been a revelation. How was it possible to put words in such an order that they could create a truth in her mind?

From that moment on, Aileen had begun to write her own stories, at first just weak copies of what she read. But as her methodical march through the town library shelves continued, she learned more about how to craft a plot and develop a character.

In the evenings, she'd offered to empty the rubbish bins at school, just for the chance to gather spare paper for her work. And then, when she was in the seventh form, Sister Bernadette became her teacher. The sweet-tempered nun recognized Aileen's talent for writing. From that moment on, Aileen always had pencils and tablets to spare, and someone to read her stories.

Though the girls at the orphanage were trained toward industrial employment, Aileen had been encouraged in her plans to devote her life to God and join the order as a novitiate. But the closer she got to the decision, the more Aileen knew that the life she wanted, and the stories swimming around in her head, couldn't be contained within the walls of the convent. She'd have to go out in the world and make her own way, to live the life that she so desperately wanted to write about.

And so she did what Jane Eyre had done. She became a governess for a wealthy family in Dublin, moving from the orphanage into a grand home situated on a posh street. She cared for three boys by the name of Riley while their father ran a bank and their mother busied herself with charitable works.

And at night, after the boys had been tucked into bed, she wrote. And wrote and wrote and wrote. She saved her meager salary and bought a secondhand typewriter for her twenty-first birthday, then spent what she had left on paper and inked ribbon.

At night, she'd sneak up to a far corner of the attic, lantern in hand, so that the family wouldn't hear the tap-tap-tap of the keys. She sold her first novel five years later, the story of an orphaned Irish girl who falls in love with the son of her employer, only to be cast aside and left to rebuild a life for herself. Set between the two world wars, the novel sold well enough for her to leave the Rileys and rent a tiny flat in a run-down section of Dublin.

Now, seventy years later, Aileen Quinn had become the grande dame of Irish women writers, the one they all referenced when they talked of their greatest influences. She'd won every award and accolade available to her and had enjoyed her life and her success.

Her only regret had been that the love her characters always struggled to find had never found her. She'd always thought there would be time for a husband and a family. But the years between thirty and fifty had seemed to fly by in a blur. Then, she'd still hoped a man might come into her life. And then another blur between fifty and seventy. By then it was too late for hope. Too late to have a family of her own.

But all that had changed now. She did have a family, people who were related to her by blood. And she was going to find every last one of them.

1

LOGAN QUINN STARED down the long, tree-lined driveway. He'd expected Willimston Farm would be upmarket, but he hadn't expected a feckin' estate. He turned the campervan off the main road and felt a sense of unease come over him.

When he'd made plans to stop along his weeklong route to Perth, all Logan had wanted was a spare stable, fresh water and a place to park. His old mate Ed Perkins had been working as a stable manager at Willimston for the past few years and had offered a place to overnight. Logan wondered how Ed's boss man might feel about the raggedy campervan and trailer ruining the perfectly groomed landscape.

If the sprawling house didn't give visitors a clue to the wealth of the owners, the outbuildings did. The low-slung buildings were painted white with green doors and shingles, a clear indication of the bottomless bank account that funded the place. Logan couldn't help but think of his own ranch on the fringes of the outback, the ramshackle house, the rough stables.

He'd worked for years to put together the cash needed to buy his own operation, sometimes juggling his job as an investment banker with one or two other jobs. And though the ranch was far from perfect, it was the first home he'd ever known.

After a childhood spent watching his father bounce from place to place, sheep station to cattle ranch, all the family's belongings contained in the back of a pickup truck, Logan needed a place to put down roots.

Every time he drove up the dusty road and saw the weathered stable and tiny house, he felt a measure of pride. He was building something for the future. And maybe someday, he'd have a family and they'd know a real home, a place where they could feel safe and secure.

A kid couldn't help but feel that way on Willimston Farm, he thought to himself. "Someday, my place will look like this," he murmured. Logan chuckled to himself. "Yeah, right. And someday, pigs will fly."

He slowly pulled the campervan to a stop and turned off the ignition. They'd been on the road for eight hours. It was time for the both of them to stretch their legs. He watched as a tall, lanky figure approached, then recognized his old friend Ed beneath the brim of the faded hat.

Logan stepped out of the camper and pulled off his sunglasses. "Ed! Hey, mate. Good to see you."

Ed yanked off his leather gloves and shook Logan's hand. "Logan Quinn. How was your drive?"

"Long. It feels good to stand instead of sit." He glanced around. "This is quite the place. You landed yourself a nice spot."

"It's good. The owner isn't around much. He has a mansion in Brisbane, too. But when he is here, he's a decent chap. Simon Grant. He's big in energy. Appreciates fine horses, too. So, who's watching your place while you're on the road?"

"I've got Billy Brantley working for me. Remember him? He worked with us that summer out on the Weaver ranch."

"He's a good guy. Hard worker." Ed nodded in the direction of the trailer. "Enough of this chatter. Are you going to show me?"

"Sure. Let's get her out." Logan walked to the back of the trailer, dropped the ramp and opened the doors. He smoothed his hand over the flank of the filly as he moved to take her halter.

"Come on, darlin'," he murmured. "Let's get you out of this trailer and into a paddock. You need some exercise." The filly slowly backed down the ramp and, when all four hooves were on firm ground, Logan circled her around Ed, letting him observe the horse.

He'd never been more proud of something that he'd accomplished as he had been of breeding and raising Tally. And though he knew not to get too attached to one of his horses, Logan was forced to admit that he loved everything about the pretty filly.

"Jaysus, Logan, she's a beauty." Ed stepped forward and examined the filly with a keen eye. He ran his palms over her, peered into her eyes and patted her neck. "You say she's sold?"

"Why? Do you want to buy her?"

"Hell, I'd be crazy not to show her to my boss. He's always looking for new stock."

Logan shrugged. "Yeah, she's sold. To a guy over in Perth. He's got a nice breeding operation."

"No. How much?"

Logan told him the price and Ed shrugged. "It's a fair price. I probably could have gotten you more. I would have liked to breed her with a stallion we have. They would have made some beautiful babies together." He paused. "Why didn't you keep her for yourself?"

A sliver of regret shot through him at the question. "I would have loved to. But I need the money."

"Things are tough?"

Logan chuckled. "Define *tough*."

"Why didn't you give me a call? I could have helped you out."

"You're helping me out now. Letting me stay here for the night. Now, do you have a paddock for my lady? I think she could use a good run."

"Come on, then. I saved the best for you."

They walked toward one of the low barns and when they reached the paddock, Ed opened the gate. Logan rubbed the filly's neck then sent her inside. She trotted around the perimeter, her ears up, her nostrils sniffing the air.

"What's her name?"

"I call her Tally," he said. "Her official name is Quinn's Tally-Ho Wallaroo. But maybe the new owners will give her a different name."

"She is a beauty."

Logan nodded. "Yeah. She's the first colt born on the farm, the first I raised from a baby. Hell, I feel like she's my kid and I'm sending her off into the world."

Ed patted him on the shoulder. "I expect letting the first one go is always the hardest. I've set up a stall in this barn here," he said, pointing over his shoulder. "You can pull your campervan around to the back. Just inside the door there's a loo and a shower."

"Thanks," he said.

"Have you had dinner yet?"

"Yeah. I picked up something along the way. Once I have Tally bedded down, I'm going to turn in, too. I'm knackered."

"Well, I'm up at sunrise. I'll bring you some breakfast before you leave."

Logan nodded. "Thanks. For everything. I really appreciate it."

"No worries," Ed said.

As Ed walked back to the stable, Logan turned his gaze out to the chestnut filly in the paddock. He'd always thought that Tally would be the center of his breeding program at the farm. He'd never imagined that he'd have to give her up. Just the thought of turning her over into someone else's care caused an ache deep in his gut. But horse breeding was like roulette. Sometimes you hit the jackpot and other times you walked away with nothing.

He braced his arms on the top of the gate and rested his chin on his hands. He'd had a choice. Keep the horse or keep the ranch. Without the filly, the ranch would survive. Without the ranch, he had no place to keep his horses.

Hell, maybe another filly like Tally would come along. Though her sire and dam had produced two males in the past two years, the odds were good that he was due a filly. But what were the chances that she'd be as perfect as Tally? He'd hate to think that his one-in-a-million horse had come at a time when he couldn't keep her for himself.

A quiet curse slipped from his lips. This trip wouldn't be any easier if he continued to drown in sentimentality.

"Nice horse."

The sound of her voice startled him. Logan turned to find a woman standing beside him on the lowest rail of the gate. The sun was behind her and he had a hard time making out her features, so he stepped back from the gate and pulled down his sunglasses.

The beauty of her profile, outlined by the setting sun, hit him like a ton of bricks. Flaxen hair gleamed in the golden light, the strands falling around her face in delicate curls. She looked as if she'd just crawled out of bed.

Her eyes were hidden behind dark sunglasses. She wore a loose-fitting T-shirt and the bottoms to a hot-pink bikini that barely covered her backside. The soft curves of her breasts were outlined by the thin cotton, and he could almost imagine the body beneath the shirt. His gaze drifted back up to her face and he took in her lush lips.

A tiny smile twitched at the corners of that sensuous mouth. "What's next? Are you going to want to check my teeth? Maybe run your hands over my withers? I can take a turn around the paddock if you like."

He hadn't realized his stare was so obvious. He turned away and fixed his gaze on Tally. "You—you startled me."

"Good," she said. "I always like making a memorable first impression."

He laughed softly. She was teasing him and wasn't trying to hide it. But to what end? "Well done, then," he said. "I'm impressed." Logan glanced over at her. "Who are you?"

She held out her hand. "Lucinda Grant. My father owns this place."

He took her hand and gave it a quick shake. Her fingers were long and slender and tipped with shiny red polish. His mind flashed an image of those hands, skimming over his naked body, touching him in places he hadn't been touched for a while. Logan swallowed hard. Yeah, right. No chance a pretty little rich girl was going to waste her time on guy without a penny in his pocket.

"Nice to meet you, Miss Grant," Logan said.

"Oh, please. You stared at my arse. I think we're beyond Miss Grant. You can call me Sunny."

"I thought your name was Lucinda."

"It is, but everyone calls me Sunny. With a *u*. Actually, it really should be an *o*. My father always wanted a boy so he called me Sonny with an *o* until I was five. My mother changed it to Sunny with a *u*."

"It's nice to meet you, Sunny with a *u*."

She pushed her sunglasses onto the top of her head and turned her green-eyed gaze his way. "It's usually customary for you to tell me your name. You really do have the worst manners."

"Are you always such a smart-ass?" he asked, starting to enjoy the little game they were playing.

That brought a laugh. "I developed the talent in my teenage years and have perfected it since then. It's one of my best qualities."

He saw the glint in her gaze and Logan shook his head. He'd known girls like her, girls who weren't afraid to push the boundaries, girls who would say anything that came into their heads just to get a reaction. He usually made it a point to stay away from that type. They were impossible to figure out.

But there was something about Sunny, something more than just a quick wit and a sharp tongue. He saw something more… vulnerable behind that bold facade. He could see it in those eyes, those incredibly beautiful green eyes.

Logan rubbed his hand on his faded jeans before holding it out to her. "Logan Quinn."

She stared down at his hand for a long moment and Logan wondered if she didn't want to touch him. But then, she reached out and ran her finger along the length of his forearm. The feel of her nail scraping his skin sent a shiver through his body. She glanced up at him and smiled coyly. "You have nice hands, Logan Quinn." Her gaze turned toward the filly, who was now watching them both with a suspicious eye. "Is she yours?"

"For now," Logan said.

With that, she crawled over the gate and dropped down on the other side, her bare feet causing a soft thud in the dirt. As she walked toward Tally, Sunny turned back to him. "Come on," she said. "I want to hear what you have to say about her."

Logan followed her over the gate and hurried to catch up. As he walked beside her, he risked a glance at her face again. God, she was the prettiest thing he'd ever seen. And the oddest, as well. She didn't seem to be bothered by the fact that she was wandering around in a T-shirt that was just thin enough to reveal what was underneath. Maybe she'd spent the day sunbathing...topless.... He swallowed hard as a vivid image flashed in his mind.

When they got within ten feet of the filly, Sunny stopped and held out her hand. "What's her name?"

"Tally," he said.

"Hey, there, Tally," she murmured.

Logan reached in his jacket pocket and pulled out a biscuit, then handed it to her. "She likes these."

"Anzac biscuits? Me, too." She took a bite from the biscuit, then held the treat out to Tally. The horse immediately walked over and snatched the biscuit from Sunny's fingers.

Gently, she grabbed her halter and led the horse in a wide circle. Logan watched Sunny, his attention completely captivated by her long, slender legs and her lithe body. He felt a current of desire skitter through him and he drew a long breath.

Sunny carefully examined the horse, smoothing her palms over Tally, slowly taking in her conformation. And when she was finished, she motioned him over.

"Give me a knee up," she said.

"You're going to ride her?"

"Why not?"

Logan linked his fingers together and she slipped her knee into the cradle. He boosted her up and Sunny gracefully straddled the horse. Tangling her fingers in Tally's mane, she gave the filly a gentle nudge, and Tally moved forward.

The sight of them both, a beautiful woman and an equally beautiful horse, was enough to take Logan's breath away. His pulse quickened and he found himself searching for his next breath. As she urged Tally into a gallop, he groaned, trying to keep his mind off the images running around in his head.

It had been months since he'd enjoyed the company of a woman in his bed. Hell, in any bed. Life on the ranch was filled with plenty of time for self-reflection. When it came to women, he didn't have much of anything to offer besides a really good time in the sack. After buying feed for his horses, he usually didn't have much left for himself, so even a dinner out or a movie would be out of the question. But the sale of Tally would keep him solvent for another year and perhaps available for dating.

He fixed his attention on Sunny. There was no way a woman like her would want a bloke like him. No way. But that wouldn't stop him from using her as fantasy material. His fingers clenched as he thought about touching her—her hair, her face, her beautiful body.

Sunny brought the horse to a stop in front of him and slid off. "Whatever Daddy offers you, ask for 50 percent more. And don't back down. He admires a man who sticks to his principles." She started toward the gate. "I'll see you later, Logan Quinn."

"Wait!" he called. He took off after her and caught up with

Sunny after she'd crawled over the gate. "She's not for sale. Tally isn't for sale—at least, not to you—or your father."

Sunny gave him an odd look, her forehead furrowed. "Then what are you doing here?"

He drew a deep breath. "Just...passing through."

Silence spun out around them, and his gaze drifted to her lips. He wanted to kiss her, just once, just to see how her mouth felt on his, how she tasted and how she reacted. It took every ounce of his willpower to stop himself from pulling her into his arms. But the gate stood between them, as great a barrier as anything else that separated them.

She sucked in a sharp breath and, suddenly, the silence was broken, along with the spell that had overcome them both. "She's still a beautiful horse," Sunny murmured.

Logan watched her walk away, her hips swaying provocatively. He'd never met a woman quite like her. So tantalizing, so sexy. "Forget it, mate," he muttered to himself. "That's the first and last time a woman like that is ever giving you a second look."

SUNNY STARED UP at the ceiling above her bed. She measured her breathing, trying to fight back the surge of tears that had been threatening for the past hour. Grabbing her pillow, she hugged it to her body, but nothing seemed to ease the emptiness inside of her.

Her thoughts wandered back to the argument she'd had with her father earlier that evening. He'd phoned from Sydney to check up on her plans to participate in an equestrian event that weekend in Brisbane. When she told him she had no intention of riding, the call escalated into a cold recitation of all of her flaws as both a daughter and a human being.

She pinched her eyes shut, cutting off the source of her tears. Nighttime was the worst. Her mind just wouldn't shut down. The same things replayed over and over in her head, and though she tried to make sense of it all, she couldn't.

She'd worked for years to get to London, to be a part of the Olympics and to show her father that she could be just as good as the son he'd always wanted. All the training, all the travel, competing in equestrian events all over Australia.

Three years ago, she'd stepped up to international competition, all with an eye to the Olympics and her crowning achievement, a gold medal in show jumping. When she made the world team two years ago, her father had been delighted but reserved. When she made the Olympic team, her father had been proud, ecstatic even. And that's all she'd ever wanted from him. Just a simple recognition that she was someone worth loving.

But what had come next had been so unexpected. She'd landed in London with a strange sense of foreboding, a dark cloud hanging over her. The pressure to succeed just seemed overwhelming at times and she found herself fighting off panic attacks.

One stumble in the qualifying rounds had led to another and by the time the preliminary competition was over, Sunny's confidence was in shreds and her hopes for a medal were gone. She had hesitated when she should have been aggressive; she had tried to make up for her mistakes by taking silly risks. And her sweet horse, Padma, didn't understand what she was supposed to do, the unfamiliar signals causing the mare to react nervously and refuse gates that she'd always nimbly jumped over.

A tear streaked down Sunny's cheek and she brushed it away. Who was she if she wasn't an equestrian? Where was she supposed to go from here? She wasn't prepared to do anything but ride. Her life was a total car wreck with no one there to help her fix it.

With a long sigh, she closed her eyes. The image of Logan Quinn drifted through her thoughts and she groaned softly. She'd been thinking about him all night long. If he knew who she was, he didn't mention it. And if he didn't, then he must have been living on another continent for the past six months.

The media had been brutal right after the games, with all sorts of rumors about partying and drugs and men.

None of it had been true, but that didn't make it any less painful. She smiled to herself. It had felt good to talk to Logan, to tease and laugh again, as if nothing had happened. Part of the attraction was his body, lean and muscled, hidden beneath faded, comfortable clothes. And he had that rugged, self-assured look about him, as though he could survive for a month in the outback with just a paper clip and a piece of string. He had a quiet confidence that was reassuring.

For the first time in months, Sunny found herself interested in something other than her own troubles. And though seducing a handsome stranger probably wouldn't change her situation all that much, it would be nice to feel close to someone. It would give her something else to think about at night other than all her failures.

Sunny rolled onto her stomach and pressed her face into the pillow. What if he wasn't interested? What if he didn't want anything to do with her? Leave it to Sunny Grant to fail on both a worldwide and a personal scale.

Sunny sat up in bed and tossed the pillow aside. She had to stop doing this to herself. It was time to move on. She'd made mistakes and hadn't been prepared to handle the pressure, but there was no going back and fixing it. If she ever expected to be happy again, she needed to—

"I need to get out of this house," she muttered, raking her hair away from her face.

Scrambling out of bed, Sunny grabbed a robe and shrugged into it. Silently, she slipped out of her room and hurried down the hall. The house was dark and only the dogs, Wendy and Whip, noticed her passing, their heads rising as she opened the kitchen door.

She drew a deep breath of the warm night air, then ran across the damp lawn to the stables. A yellow bulb on each end of the building offered a faint light and she hurried to Padma's stall and pulled open the door.

The horse turned and looked at her with her big brown eyes. Sunny hadn't ridden her in the three months since she'd returned from London, knowing how she'd failed. "I'm sorry," she murmured, tears filling her eyes. "I'm so sorry. You're the only one who has ever loved me, unconditionally and without any expectations. And I let you down. I embarrassed us both."

Her father had talked about selling Padma after Sunny had vowed never to ride again. The horse was well trained, an experienced competitor in the prime of her jumping career. But she was still here, in her usual stable. Though her father could be cold, he wasn't entirely heartless.

"You're going to be just fine," she murmured, stroking the white blaze on Padma's forehead. "I need to take a little more time away and then I'll be back and we'll start all over again. I promise. We'll get back to the top and get our gold medal." She pressed her face against the soft muzzle of the horse, then gave her a kiss. "And this time, I won't mess it up. You'll be proud of me."

She stepped out of the stall and pulled the door closed. When she turned, she saw a figure standing in the shadows. A gasp slipped from her throat, but when he stepped into the light, she recognized Logan Quinn.

"You scared me," she said.

"Sorry. I didn't mean to. I was just checking on Tally and heard you talking."

He was dressed in just his jeans, the top button undone. Like her, his feet were bare. He'd shoved his hands in his front pockets and he watched her warily. "It's late," she murmured.

"I couldn't sleep. It was too stuffy in the campervan."

"Me, too," she said.

"It is kind of warm tonight. I thought maybe we'd get some rain."

She smiled to herself. He looked so sweet standing there, his dark hair rumpled, his chest bare. Though he looked as if he were in his late twenties, he had a boyish quality she found undeniably attractive. "Are we really talking about the weather?"

"No," he said.

Sunny held out her hand. "Come with me."

He tucked his hand into hers and walked with her toward the house. "Where are we going?"

"You'll see," she said.

There was a formal garden in the rear of the house, surrounded by a tall iron fence. She unlatched the gate and then stepped aside, motioning for him to enter. They walked along a narrow brick path and, suddenly, the lush greenery disappeared and he found himself staring at a huge swimming pool.

"Oh, hell. Now, that's a nice-looking pool."

"Come on. Take your jeans off and jump in."

"Ah, I don't have anything underneath," he said.

She reached for the tie of her silk robe. "You don't have anything I haven't seen before." Sunny spun around in front of him. "And I don't have anything you haven't seen before."

With a laugh, she dove into the pool, slicing neatly into the water and swimming beneath the surface to the other end. When she came up for air, he was no longer standing on the deck. She glanced around and then, a moment later, he popped up in front of her.

"What are your parents going to say if they catch us out here?" he asked.

"My father is in Sydney, visiting his mistress and their two children. My mother went to the Paris fashion shows last year and never came back." She reached out and brushed the wet hair out of his eyes. "Except for the housekeeper, we're alone."

"Okay, then."

"You don't talk very much, do you?"

He grinned. "Actually, I do. You just leave me a little speechless."

She bobbed in front of him, her gaze taking in the details of his face. Droplets clung to his dark lashes, and when he blinked, they tumbled onto his cheeks. He was a beautiful man, the kind of man who didn't realize the effect his looks had on a woman. She liked that. Sunny didn't know very many regular guys.

His body was finely muscled, long limbed and lean, and made that way by hard work. The attraction was undeniable, but could she act on it? She'd felt so alone for such a long time, trapped in a life that had no direction or purpose. Touching him, kissing him, was all she could think about.

And what harm could it do? She'd enjoyed one-night stands in the past. The man was leaving in the morning and she'd never see him again. Why not take advantage? The thought of losing herself for just a short time with this beautiful man was more than she could resist.

Sunny placed her hands on his shoulders, her gaze fixed on his lips. She leaned forward ever so slightly and he took the cue, slipping his fingers through the wet hair at her nape and pulling her into his kiss. A wave of desire coursed through her body, and the intensity of her reaction startled her.

He knew how to kiss, that much was clear. And Sunny had kissed enough men to make a valid comparison. He began softly, his lips teasing at hers until they were both ready to taste. And then, he used his tongue to test her further, to tempt her into surrender. She parted her lips and they were suddenly lost in a whirlwind of sensation.

Had there ever been a kiss that affected her so completely? She felt her limbs go weak and her mind begin to falter. When his hands moved to her face, she moaned softly and wrapped her arms around his neck. Logan reached down for her legs, pulling them around his waist until their bodies were locked together in an unbreakable embrace.

He was already hard, and she moved against him, resisting the urge to simply sink down on top of him. She knew they ought to find a condom before they went any further, but if she brought up the realities of protection, he might have a chance to reconsider what they were about to do.

Drawing a deep breath, she unlocked her legs and pushed away, swimming to the far end of the pool. "I could get in a lot of trouble with a boy like you," she said, sinking down until her chin touched the surface.

She'd always maintained control in her casual encounters. There was never anything beyond the physical satisfaction of being with a beautiful man. But she felt something different with Logan, something that made her want him even more. It was as if they already knew each other, and yet she knew nothing about him.

Sunny brushed the water out of her face. She wanted to be with him, to experience the sensation of his body moving inside of her. "Do you want me?" she asked softly.

Logan nodded. "I'd be a fool not to."

"It's only about the sex," she said. "Nothing else. Are you all right with that?"

He nodded again as he slowly approached. "Here?"

She shook her head. "We need protection."

"I have some in the campervan."

Sunny swam over to the ladder and then slowly climbed it to the pool deck. She grabbed a towel from a nearby bin and wrapped it around her body, then handed one to Logan. He hurried after her, and when he reached her side, he took her hand. They walked back to the stable, Logan picking up his jeans and her robe along the way.

A cool breeze rustled the trees, and goose pimples prickled Sunny's damp skin. For the first time since London, she knew exactly what she wanted. And there was no shame in it. The need to feel close to another person was a basic part of human nature, wasn't it? And since Logan was just passing through, it made the choice even easier. There would be no messy entanglements after the fact.

Raindrops were beginning to fall by the time they reached

the campervan. Logan opened the door and helped her up the steps. All the windows were open, and the sound of the rain on the roof provided a relaxing soundtrack. A tiny light near the sink provided the only illumination, casting the interior in a soft glow.

When he closed the door behind him, Sunny turned and stepped into his embrace. There was no hesitation between them, no doubt of what they both wanted, no time wasted. The towels were tossed aside, and his hands moved over her body, his touch gentle yet assured. Sunny closed her eyes and tipped her head back, letting the wonderful sensations wash over her.

When his lips finally found hers, Sunny opened to the determined assault. He was warm and his mouth tasted sweet and when he pulled her body against his, she surrendered completely. It had been months since she'd felt any kind of connection to a man. But now that he had dropped into her life, Sunny felt desperate to experience the power and the passion, the complete and utter satisfaction.

Though there was no reason to rush, Sunny had never been one to deny herself anything she wanted. And she wanted to experience the ultimate intimacy with this man. She pulled him over to the bed that spanned the back end of the campervan.

Logan sat down on the edge and smoothed his hands around her waist. "Are you certain about this?" he murmured, pressing a kiss to her belly.

Sunny ran her fingers through his sun-streaked hair and turned his face up until his gaze met hers. "I wouldn't be here if I didn't know what I wanted," she murmured.

He smiled and she reached down and ran her thumb across his lower lip. He was so beautiful, his hair damp from their swim, his skin smooth and deeply tanned. Falling back onto the bed, he reached into a nearby cubby and pulled out a box of condoms, setting them beside a pillow.

Sunny held out her hand, wiggling her fingers, and he pulled a package from the box and handed it to her. He held his breath as she slowly stroked his hard shaft. A low groan slipped from his throat, and he leaned back and braced himself on his elbows, his gaze fixed on her caress.

With a deft touch, she smoothed the latex over him, then crawled onto the bed, her legs straddling his hips. She couldn't wait any longer, she craved that exquisite sensation of a man moving inside her.

Sunny closed her eyes as she slowly lowered herself on top of him. When he filled her completely, she let out a soft breath. There was nothing more perfect than this, she thought to herself. As his fingers splayed over her hips, she began to move. When Logan cupped her face in his hand, she turned into his touch and looked at him.

Their gazes locked, and Sunny watched as every reaction was reflected in his eyes. A smile curled the corners of his mouth, and she felt a tremor course through her, setting every nerve on edge. There was something about him, something sweet and warm and slightly vulnerable, that made it impossible to separate herself from the emotion bubbling up inside of her.

Another tremor assailed her body, but this time it wasn't pleasure but fear. This connection wasn't normal. She'd always been able to maintain a careful distance with the men she took as lovers. But for the first time in her life, she wanted to surrender everything, to let the walls fall and experience this man as if there were something more than just desire between them.

Logan pushed up from the bed and wrapped his arms around her waist, pressing his lips to a spot just above her breast. Sunny could feel her heart pounding, and the sudden shift in position bought a fresh rush of desire.

She pulled him closer, her fingers tangled in his hair. The rhythm became like a pulse between them, driving them on, pushing them both closer and closer to the edge. It was nothing she'd ever experienced before, and she fought the instinct to stop and regain her composure.

Sunny didn't realize it until she was teetering on the brink between pleasure and release. It usually didn't happen this way, but when the first spasm hit her, she cried out. Logan held her close as he drove into her one last time. And then they both dissolved into their climaxes, the shudders and sighs blending until she felt as if they were one body and one mind.

When they were both completely spent, Logan pulled her down beside him, wrapping his arms around her shoulders. They didn't speak, just looked into each other's eyes for a long time. There was something about this man that was different, something about him that touched her soul.

"I should go," she murmured.

"You don't have to. Stay. I'm not tired."

She always left, she never stayed. And yet, the rules she'd set down for herself so long ago didn't really matter now. It felt good to lie here with this man and to share something beyond the physical.

"Are you really going to sell your horse?"

Logan nodded. "Yeah. I'm taking her to Perth."

"That's a long drive. At least a week on the road. Why not put her on a plane?"

Logan was silent for a long time. "I guess I needed the time to get used to the fact I have to sell her. Plus, I'm saving some money."

"Maybe you should stay here for a few days and let me try to change your mind," she said. "I'd take good care of her."

He chuckled softly. "That's an interesting proposition."

"Is it one you'd consider?"

Logan reached out and smoothed a strand of hair from her eyes. "I can't. I'm kind of pressed for time. And I've already spent the down payment. The sooner I get this over with, the better."

"I can give you the down payment," she said. "You can give it back to him. I have money, or my father does. And Ed can buy anything he likes. Anything I like."

He shook his head. "That's a lovely offer, but I made a deal.

I can't go back on it. And I really need to be on my way." He paused. "I could always stop by on the return trip."

She smiled and snuggled closer. "I suppose that will have to do." Sunny closed her eyes and let her body relax. For the first time in weeks, she felt content. And for now, that was enough. As for what would happen in the morning, she'd deal with that when the sun came up.

2

WHEN LOGAN WOKE UP the next morning, she was gone. At first, he wondered if it had all been part of some crazy dream. But when he found the two damp towels, he knew it hadn't been.

He pulled on his jeans and ran his fingers through his hair as memories of their night together flooded his brain. A sudden rush of adrenaline washed away the remaining effects of sleep, and he felt energized. Alive. He hated to admit it, but he had needed a night of really great sex.

Logan bent down and picked up the towels, then carefully folded them. It had been great, hadn't it? It was pretty obvious she'd enjoyed herself, and he'd certainly found the experience memorable. He wasn't sure what the protocol was after a night like last night. Should he find her and say goodbye? Or maybe thank her? Or would that be assuming too much?

She'd left his bed, so she must have decided their night together had come to an end. A rap on the campervan door startled him out of his thoughts, and he hurried over and opened it, hoping he'd find Sunny standing on the other side. Ed was waiting with a plate heaped with food.

"Hey," Logan said, rubbing his eyes against the rising sun.

"Morning," Ed replied. "Come on out. I brought you a proper breakfast. I stopped by earlier, but you didn't answer my knock."

Logan crawled down the stairs and sat on the top step, then

took the plate from Ed. It was loaded with eggs and sausage and two slices of toast. He dug in, and a few seconds later, Ed handed him a mug of coffee.

"Thanks. I really need this."

"Didn't sleep well?"

He glanced up and forced a smile. "No, just fine. Like the dead."

"I had one of the stable boys feed and groom Tally. She's all ready to go as soon as you are. I won't bother you with another offer, but if this falls through, make sure I'm the next guy you call, all right?"

"Thanks," Logan said. "Thanks for everything."

Ed held out a piece of paper. "And I called a few breeders and vets that we do business with. You're welcome to stop at any of them if the drive works out right. They'll take good care of you and the filly."

Logan took a deep breath, then grabbed the paper and scanned the five names. "I don't know what to say."

"Why don't you just finish your breakfast? I'll get one of the boys to load Tally, and you can get on the road. And on your way back, make sure you stop. We'll go out for a pint or two."

He thought about the promise he'd made to Sunny. "That would be great. I'll do that." Logan paused. "And if you see Sunny, can you tell her I'm sorry I wasn't able to sell her my horse?"

Ed's brow shot up. "You met Sunny?"

"Yesterday. She came out and rode Tally in the paddock. She offered to buy her and I told her I'd already made a deal."

Ed chuckled. "If that woman didn't have horse sense, she'd have no sense at all. She's right about the filly. I'll give her that."

"Is she always like that? I mean, a little…?"

"We don't call her crazy. She's high-spirited. But I guess I don't blame her. She kind of raised herself, from what I hear. Not much input from the parentals. But she's a helluva rider. She went to the Olympics in London. Show jumping."

"Really? Oh, my God, she's that Sunny Grant. I didn't make the connection."

"She fell apart, knocked out in the early rounds. She's been hiding out here since then. The media has been brutal."

"That's too bad," Logan said, his mind occupied with thoughts of Sunny and that tiny glimmer of vulnerability he'd seen in her eyes. He knew her intimately, yet he really knew nothing about her life at all. Now that he had a few more pieces, Logan wished he could have had more time with her. Who knows what else he might have discovered?

He finished his breakfast as one of Ed's grooms loaded Tally into the trailer. Logan checked her before he closed the trailer doors, then grabbed his shirt and boots and finished dressing. He'd dragged his departure out as long as he could, hoping he'd see Sunny again. But in the end, Logan had to accept that there would be no goodbye between them.

He got behind the wheel and steered the campervan around the stable and past the house. He glanced over, wondering what she was doing, imagining her lying in bed, her naked body tangled in the sheets. He smiled to himself and headed for the highway.

The next hour was spent rerunning the previous night in his head. It had been a long time since he'd been with a woman. He lived a quiet life on the farm, just him and his right-hand man, Billy. Occasionally, he'd spend a weekend in town, and when he got lucky, there'd be a woman willing to give him a second look.

Since he'd left his job as a banker five years ago, women just didn't find him as attractive. Funny how a nice guy looked a lot nicer when he had big money. He'd used all his savings, liquidated all his investments to buy the ranch and good breeding stock.

The dream was worth the risk, he'd told himself. And when he'd walked away from the bank on his last day of work, he'd pulled off his tie and unbuttoned his shirt and realized that he was a free man, a man who would determine his own destiny.

Now was not the time to start doubting himself. He had never assumed it would be easy. But the one thing he never realized was how lonely it would be. Logan reached over and slid a CD into the player, then turned up the volume on an old AC/DC tune. He sang along with the song, keeping time with his fist on the steering wheel.

"What time is it?"

The sound of her voice over the song caused him to swerve, and Logan cursed as he brought the campervan and horse trailer back under control. He glanced over his shoulder to see Sunny leaning off the edge of the upper bunk, her pale hair tumbled around her face.

He turned down the music. "What the hell— What are you doing?"

"I was sleeping," she said. She stretched her arms above her head, the sheet dropping away to reveal her naked breasts. "What time is it?"

"What the hell are you—" He turned his attention back to the road and carefully pulled off onto the edge of the highway. Logan turned off the ignition, then stood up. "What the hell are you doing here?"

She frowned. "I decided to come with you. I packed my things and came back, but you were spread across the bed. So I crawled up here and fell asleep." She dragged the sheet around her bare body.

"No, you left. Sometime in the middle of the night."

"Yes, but I came back."

Logan raked his hand through his hair, shaking his head. "Oh, bloody hell. We're two hours gone from your place. I'm going to have to take you back now."

She swung her legs over the edge of the bunk and shrugged. "No. I'm not going back. Nobody cares whether I'm there or not. My father decided to extend his stay in Sydney and won't be home for another month. So I'm going with you. I don't have anything better to do." She jumped down from the bunk and moved toward him, smoothing her palm against his cheek as she passed. She paused and brushed a kiss across his mouth. "Morning," she murmured with a coy smile.

Logan groaned. "This is just what I need right now."

"No reason to get narky," she said, putting on a pout. "I decided I needed more time to convince you to sell me the filly."

"Oh, really. That's why you're running away from home?"

She stared at him for a long moment. "Well, not entirely. But I don't want to talk about that right now. Besides, we'll have fun. I make a very agreeable traveling companion."

The night's activities flashed through his mind and, with a soft curse, Logan slipped his arm around her waist and pulled her against him. Their lips met in a long, deep kiss, and he felt her warm body melt into his. He couldn't say that he was angry or even surprised. He'd known Sunny Grant for less than a day and he already knew she was the most unpredictable woman he'd ever met.

"Won't someone notice you're gone?" he murmured.

"They won't care." She stepped back and ran her fingers through her hair. "I need coffee." She glanced down at the sheet wrapped around her body. "Can we stop somewhere?"

"I think you should get dressed," he said. "Did you bring clothes?"

"Yes," she said. "And money." She reached up and dug through her bag, pulling out her purse. But after rummaging through it, she looked up. "Oh, no."

"What?"

"I don't have money. I must have taken my wallet out of my purse and I was half-asleep when I packed and—"

"Don't worry, I have money."

"I'll pay you back. I can call Lily, our housekeeper, and she can send me some. I'm a really cheap date."

"I find that very hard to believe," he muttered.

She smiled at him, then crawled into the passenger seat, tucking her feet beneath the sheet. "I like this. It'll be a little adventure. God knows I needed to get out of that house."

"A little adventure," he repeated. With Sunny Grant in tow, that was the understatement of the day.

Logan slipped behind the wheel and started the campervan, then carefully pulled back out onto the highway. He stole a glance over at her and found her watching him. "What?"

"Nothing," she said. "I'm just glad you didn't put me out on the highway."

"I wouldn't have done that," Logan said. "Maybe if you had shoes and clothes on I might have considered it. But dressed in just a sheet, you would have been at a disadvantage."

"Well, thank you for that," she said.

"Am I going to be sorry I let you stay?"

She grinned. "I don't know." Her smiled faded and she drew in a deep breath. "But if you really don't want me here, I can find my way home."

For a moment, she looked so sad, and he wondered what would bring such sorrow to that beautiful face. Logan groaned inwardly. He would have plenty of time to figure her all out. From here to Perth was a long drive. "No," he said. "I think we'll be fine."

SUNNY STOOD IN FRONT of the refrigerated section in the supermarket. Logan had given her thirty dollars and a half hour to buy whatever snacks and drinks she needed. She'd never done much shopping for food. That was usually left up to their housekeeper. But there were certain things that she liked.

She glanced down at the money she held in her hand. Though he didn't come right out and say it, it was clear to Sunny that Logan didn't have a lot of extra cash, especially to spend on food for her. As she wandered the store, she'd been trying to figure out a way to get some money of her own, but she wasn't really sure where they'd be stopping or when they'd get there.

It felt strange to be living in the real world, where money

dominated almost every decision. Throughout her life, she'd never had to worry about how to pay the bills. Her father had handed her a bank card when she'd turned thirteen and there were never any questions asked about what she used it for.

"Are you almost done?"

She saw Logan's reflection in the glass door then spun around. "Sorry." She pulled out a couple of bottles of orange juice and put them in the shopping basket.

"Is that all?" he asked.

"Yes."

He reached inside and grabbed a few more, then took some bottled water, as well. "We're not going to find a lot of places to stop once we head west. I'm going to get some ice. Pick out some snacks. Maybe something for sandwiches."

Sunny found some packaged ham and sliced cheese, then searched the store for bread. Along the way she grabbed a few packages of crisps and then decided a bottle of wine might come in handy. By the time Logan returned with the ice, she'd spent her thirty dollars.

As they walked to the checkout, he examined her purchases, then pointed to the wine. "Maybe you should have gotten another bottle," he said.

"One is enough for now," she said with a smile.

"I'm not used to traveling with women. Is there anything else that you need? Lipstick? Nail polish?"

"I remembered my toothbrush," she said. "But I forgot shampoo. I can use yours, I guess."

He stopped. "I'll get some for you and meet you in the queue."

When he returned, he set the shampoo down next to her purchases. "I'd rather not smell my shampoo in your hair. This smells like grapefruit."

Sunny opened the bottle and took a sniff. "Mmm. That's nice."

The checkout operator was watching them closely, and she

turned to Logan, awaiting his next comment. He cursed beneath his breath, then nodded. "We're done. Add it up."

"Are you sure?" the checkout operator asked.

"Add it up," Sunny said. She grabbed a package of Tim Tams from a rack and put it next to the shampoo. "Women need chocolate, too."

They walked back to the campervan, and Logan opened the passenger door for her. Sunny jumped in and settled herself into the now familiar spot. A few seconds later, Logan got behind the wheel.

"Thank you," she murmured. "I do intend to pay you back."

"No worries," he murmured.

"I'm wondering if I might arrange to have some money sent to me. If we pick a town down the road, I can have it sent there. But I'm not sure where we're going next."

"We're not going to have a lot of time for shopping. I know you're used to luxuries—"

"No," she murmured. "I just don't want to be a burden. In fact, from now on, I'm not going to eat at all. Unless you let me arrange for my own money, I'm going to fast for the rest of the trip."

"Don't be ridiculous. You have to eat."

"I don't have to do anything I don't want to do," she said. "I'll eat my Tim Tams. I can make those last at least three days."

"Oh, Jaysus," he said, leaning over the steering wheel and bumping his head against the top edge. "I should probably kill myself now." He drew a deep breath, then reached down and grabbed his mobile phone from one of the cup holders. "Have at it."

"Where?"

He pulled out the map and traced their route. From Brisbane they'd head west, into the interior of New South Wales on A2, then southwest to the coast again. He pointed to Adelaide. "There. We'll be there day after tomorrow. Have it sent to a local bank."

"Cool," she said. Sunny dialed her home number and when Lily answered, she quickly explained her dilemma. In the end, the housekeeper agreed to express her wallet and credit cards to her father's business office in Adelaide. After spending a few days on the road in the campervan, she'd treat Logan to a comfortable bed and a hot shower.

"All right," she said to Lily as she scribbled down the office address. "And if it's not too much trouble, can you just gather a few nice things for me to wear? Some summer dresses. And my lavender-scented lotion? And—" Sunny paused. She'd learned to do without the creature comforts. She could certainly last a little longer. "That's all." She hung up and handed the phone to Logan, who was watching her suspiciously. "What?"

"Lavender-scented lotion? Is that what you were wearing last night?"

She nodded. "It's my favorite. And it's really hard to find. It's French."

"I like the way you smell," he said.

Sunny crawled out of her seat and settled herself on top of him, her backside wedged against the steering wheel. Wrapping her arms around his neck, she bent close and gave him a long, deep kiss. " We're going to have fun. I promise."

He smoothed his hands beneath her shirt, sliding his palm along her torso until he cupped her breast. She wasn't wearing a bra. "Maybe we should have bought you some underwear."

"I brought underwear," she said. "I just don't like to wear it. It gets in the way."

"Of what?"

"Of your hands on my body," she whispered. Sunny bent close and brushed her lips across his, teasing with the tip of her tongue. A tiny smile curled the corners of his mouth. Though she was just getting to know him, she'd already decided he was the sweetest guy she'd ever met.

He was so humble and genuine and he didn't try to be anything but himself. She'd known far too many men who spent their energy trying to impress. He had a quiet confidence that she found incredibly attractive.

For a long moment, they lost themselves in the kiss, Sunny wriggling against him until he groaned in protest. But then a loud bang interrupted them and they turned to see a security guard standing outside the driver's-side door.

"Move along now, folks," he said.

Sunny giggled as she crawled back to her own seat. Logan started the ignition and slowly pulled out of the parking lot. She opened the box of biscuits and slowly munched on one as she watched the traffic.

"Are you going to offer me one of those or are you going to eat them all yourself?" Logan asked.

"I was thinking about eating them all by myself. Why, do you want one?"

"I could eat one," he said.

"I'll give you one if you answer a question," she said.

"What kind of question?"

"A personal question. Before last night, when was the last time you were with a woman?"

"Tim Tam first," he said, holding out his hand. Sunny gave him one of the biscuits. "I had a beer at the local pub the night before I left and I believe Becky Pelson was the barkeep."

"You slept with the barkeep?"

"No, you asked when I was last with a woman. As I recall, she was the last until I met you."

"Oh! Waste of a Tim Tam! You cheat."

"I can't be held accountable for your poor phrasing," he said with a grin. "If you give me another biscuit, I'll answer the question."

She handed him a Tim Tam. "Honest answer."

"It's been a while," he said. "Probably about six months. I'm not sure, exactly."

"You don't have a woman in your life, then?"

He glanced over at her. "No. I wouldn't have spent the night with you if I had. I'm not that kind of bloke."

"I know," Sunny said. "I can tell that about you. You're one of the good ones." She handed him another biscuit.

"Will you answer a question from me?"

Sunny nodded. She knew what he'd probably ask, but for some reason she wasn't afraid to reveal anything to this man. They had a lot of kilometers in front of them and plenty of time to get to know each other. She wasn't sure what would happen at the end of the trip, but there was no reason to play games. "All right."

"Was it me that you wanted last night or were you just looking for a warm body?"

"It was you. When we were standing by the fence watching Tally, you were nice and you didn't judge me. I was just really tired of people judging me."

"Why would they judge you?"

"Because of what happened in London?"

She didn't see any change in his expression. "Ed told me about it. Everyone has bad days, Sunny."

"Well, I picked a very bad day to have a bad day. Washed out of the qualifying round in show jumping. I was supposed to win a gold medal. Instead, I embarrassed myself, my horse, my father, all my coaches and the entire country."

"You're human," Logan said.

"Yeah. I keep telling myself that, but it doesn't make me feel any better."

He pointed to the package of biscuits. "You want to ask more questions? I'm still hungry."

As they headed west, they traded questions, learning more about each other with each kilometer that passed. And with their lighthearted conversation, Sunny was able to put her troubles behind her and just relax. There were no expectations between them beyond an enjoyment of the scenery that passed and the company they kept.

THEY STOPPED FOR the night near Moree, a small town in the heart of the black soil plains. Ed had given him the name of a local veterinarian who'd worked at one of the equestrian centers in Brisbane before starting a practice of his own. He had a spare stable for Tally, and once she was fed and bedded down, Logan unhitched the trailer, and he and Sunny headed into town.

They bought dinner from a Thai restaurant, then found a small park along the river, sitting at a picnic table near the water. They opened the bottle of wine Sunny had purchased and shared the prawns and noodles, eating with the single fork that he had in the campervan.

She'd changed into a pretty cotton dress, her arms bare and her body beneath the same. He couldn't help but think about how simple it would be to pull the dress over her head to reveal her silken skin.

He'd tried not to let himself become infatuated, but there was just something about her he found irresistible. It was so easy to forget that they'd just met. Already, there was an ease between them, as if they'd been friends for years.

Though he'd known a lot of women, he'd never really been able to figure them out. But Sunny was like an open book to him. He could look at her and tell exactly what she was thinking. Not that she really kept her thoughts to herself. She had an opinion about everything, from his driving to his taste in Thai food to the way he wore his hat.

Logan stretched his legs out in front of him and took a long sip of his wine. He reached over and slipped his fingers through the hair at her nape, then pulled her into a quick kiss. "I'm glad you fell asleep in that bunk. I'm having a lot more fun than I ever thought I'd have on this trip."

"I thought I annoyed you," she said.

"No. You don't annoy me."

Sunny took a bite of the noodles and stared out at the river. "Do you really want to sell her?" she asked.

Logan took a deep breath and shook his head. How many

times were they going to talk about this? "No, but I really don't have a choice. Sometimes you're forced to make the hard decisions. If I want to keep my ranch, I have to sell her. And that's what my business is, Sunny. Raising and selling horses. If I get attached to every horse I raise, I'm not going to make any money."

"She should be ridden. And trained for the ring. She's big and beautiful, too beautiful to use just for breeding. I could make something of her. I could train her."

"I assume she will be ridden," he said, forcing a smile. "It's fine. She's going to a good place. And I'm glad you decided to come along. If you weren't here to distract me, I'd probably be a basket case by the time I got to Perth."

"How long have you had your ranch?"

"Five years. I used to make big money as an investment banker. I worked real hard for four years and saved all my money to buy the ranch. It isn't much, but it's mine. And the bank's."

"I can't imagine you in a suit and tie," she said. Her brow furrowed into a frown. "Wait. Give me a second. All right, yes I can. I bet you were quite the handsome man."

"I am quite the man now," he said. "Even without the suit and tie."

She handed him the carton of noodles and took a sip from her own wine. "You know what I'd like to do? I'd like to find a spot where we could park and build a campfire. I saw a sign for a caravan park. We could get a spot and maybe they'd have a shower?"

"I think we can do that," he said. He'd been wondering about finding them a motel room for the night, but camping sounded like much more fun. "Grab the wine. Let's find a spot."

When they got back out to the street, they found the sign and followed it to a large caravan park on the south side of the town. The park featured a special attraction in the town of Moree— hot mineral springs and thermal baths.

"Oh, that sounds wonderful," Sunny said. "Now I wish I had my bikini. I wonder if Lily has sent my things yet."

"I'm sure they probably have a spare that you could borrow," Logan said.

They paid the fee for the site and got things set up, hooking up to the power and opening all the windows to the late-evening breeze.

It was almost nine when they strolled over to the thermal pools. The park was quiet. It was still early in the season and the middle of the week, so the campground was nearly empty. Sunny sat down on the edge of one of the smaller pools and pulled off her shoes, then let her legs dangle in the hot water.

She looked up at him with a smile. "I feel healthier already. I think I'm going to have to go in."

"Do you have anything on under that dress?"

She shook her head. "Nope. But no one will see. It's dark and there's no one around."

"Did you bring anything you could swim in?"

"I suppose I could just wear my underwear." Sunny grinned at him. "Would you go get my underwear? I put it in the drawer next to the bed."

He pointed at her, giving her a warning glare. "Leave that dress on until I get back."

Logan strode back to the campervan. Once inside, he picked through the skimpy bits of lingerie that Sunny had bothered to bring with her. There was nothing even remotely close to a bikini amongst the lace and silk panties and bras.

It felt odd picking through her underthings. He barely knew her. In truth, he wasn't even sure what she was to him. His girlfriend? His lover? If he were forced to suddenly define their relationship, he had no idea what he'd say.

Logan picked out a black bra and a pair of red undies that looked as if they'd at least cover part of her bum. When he got back to the thermal pool, he noticed her dress, tossed into a heap beside the water. "I thought I told you to wait," he said.

She turned and folded her arms on the edge of the deck. "I couldn't. The water looked so nice. And we're all alone here."

Logan's gaze drifted along her naked body, the sweet curves of her backside, her slender legs barely hidden by the rippling water. He'd been in a heightened state of desire all afternoon and evening, just barely able to contain himself whenever he touched her or even looked at her. But now, seeing her body, so incredibly beautiful and distracting, he felt his desire bubble over into a very distinct reaction.

"Put these on," he said, holding out the bra and undies.

"Don't be a prude, no one can see me."

"I can see you," he said.

A wicked grin curled the corners of her mouth. "I want you to see me. I'm actually trying to seduce you."

"Yeah? Well, I'd have to be an idiot not to realize that."

"Come in," she said. "The water feels wonderful." She held out her hand and he caught a glimpse of her naked breasts. "Wear your underdaks if you don't want to get naked."

He held out the lingerie then dropped them into the water. "I'll come in when you put those on."

Reluctantly, she pulled the undies on, then struggled with the bra. "I could use some help."

He squatted down next to the pool and, with fumbling fingers, he hooked the back of the bra. Touching her sent a current through his body, setting every nerve buzzing. Smoothing his hands over her shoulders, he leaned close and pressed his lips to the curve of her neck.

She spun around and floated away from him, watching him from the far side of the small, round pool. "Come on," she said.

Logan glanced around. What the hell...the place was practically empty. He tugged his T-shirt over his head, skimmed his cargo shorts over his hips, kicked off his trainers and stepped down into the warm water. Her gaze fixed on his crotch, on the growing erection that pressed against the soft fabric of his underdaks.

"You're trouble," he murmured, sinking down into the pool.

She came over to him and slipped her arms around his neck. "Isn't that exactly what you're looking for?" she asked. Sunny wrapped her legs around his waist, then kissed him, her lips lush and ripe, the taste of her like the most exotic fruit.

He'd never put much thought into kissing. It was a great way to lure a girl into bed, but beyond that, it was nothing more than foreplay. But now Logan realized that he'd just never been kissed by Sunny Grant. Like everything she did, she kissed with reckless abandon, holding nothing back.

"Isn't this where we started?" he murmured.

"No," she responded. "We started in the paddock with that beautiful horse."

"We did?"

She nodded. "From the first moment I saw you, I was... interested."

"When did you decide to seduce me?"

"When I saw you staring at my ass," she teased. "I knew you were seducible."

"And now? You better have something planned for me now, Sunny."

She boosted herself up on the edge of the pool and motioned him over. "Turn around and sit." When he did, Sunny began to massage his shoulders. "You really should let me do some of the driving. You wouldn't get so tense."

"Hauling a trailer is a lot harder than it seems," he said, tipping his head. "Oh, now, that feels fine. Right there."

Sunny continued to work at the knots in his neck and shoulders, and he lost himself in the feel of her hands on his body. When he was completely relaxed, she slipped back into the water and sank down in front of him.

She reached down to touch his shaft. Logan sucked in a sharp breath and watched her. Her touch was like a powerful narcotic, making him forget all truth and reason, bringing him to the point of complete surrender.

"I'm not sure that the managers are going to appreciate what we're doing in their pool," he whispered.

"I'm sure people have done worse," she said, grinning. A moment later, she submerged and ran her tongue along the length of him, before bobbing back to the surface and sending him a wicked smile. Then, she floated away from him and stepped out of the pool. "Are you going to come?"

"I think I'm just going to sit here for a spell. I don't want to embarrass myself if we run into any other campers."

"Suit yourself," she murmured. Grabbing her dress, she turned and walked toward their site, the water from her hair running down her body, her skin gleaming. Logan groaned softly when she reached back to unhook her bra.

Wincing, he got out of the water and snatched up his clothes, holding them in front of him. When he got back to the campervan, he noticed that the lights inside had been turned off. He opened the door and stepped inside, and in an instant, she pinned him against the wall.

Grabbing his clothes from his hands, Sunny tossed them aside, then twisted her fingers in the waistband of his underdaks and pulled them down over his hips. He barely had time to take a breath before he felt her warm mouth on his rigid shaft.

A gasp slipped from his lips and he braced his hands on the back of the passenger seat, stunned by the wash of sensation that nearly overwhelmed him. Logan closed his eyes, his body dancing on the edge of sublime surrender.

Holding his breath, he tried to regain control, to focus on something other than what her lips and tongue were doing to him. His heart slammed in his chest and the world seemed to blur all around him. The need to surrender could only be denied for so long. And when he finally felt that he'd reached his limit, she slowly stood, then pulled him over to the bed.

He quickly stripped off the lacy undies, tossing them to the floor. When they fell onto the bed, their bodies met, skin against skin, limbs tangling. It was as if she were made just for him, every perfect part of her designed for his touch alone.

And when she sheathed him and he buried himself deep inside her, Logan knew that there was something extraordinary happening between them. The most improbable emotions surged up inside of him as he looked down into her beautiful face. He'd known her for a day, yet he was already hopelessly infatuated with her. And to his complete and utter surprise, he wasn't afraid to admit it to himself.

Though all of this would come to an end in a few weeks, for now, Logan was going to enjoy Sunny while he could.

3

SUNNY SAT DOWN on the edge of the bed, then leaned over and pressed a kiss to Logan's shoulder. She loved to watch him while he slept. There was a perfect peace about him, so different from the simmering energy he gave off when he was awake.

She wondered if she'd ever really know what went on inside his head. Usually, she had a man figured out by the time he took her to bed. Most of the men she knew had been a simple mix of ego and desire, satisfied to have one need stroked, ecstatic to have both tended to.

But Logan kept his ego in check. And she was just beginning to understand the depths of his desire. For him, it wasn't just about physical pleasure. When they were in the midst of making love, theirs was a deeper connection, a bond that grew stronger with every minute they spent together.

She stared down into his face, carefully taking in each perfect feature. He was a virtual stranger, and yet she felt as if she'd known him her whole life. If she weren't so cynical about love, she might actually believe that was what she was feeling. But after watching her parents' marriage fall apart, she'd vowed never to indulge in that particular emotion. This was just an infatuation, a wonderful, playful crush that would probably end the moment their trip did.

Sunny sighed. As romantic as this little getaway was, she'd

do well to keep it all in perspective. Sure, he made her feel good about herself—he made her believe there was at least one person in the world who really cared about her.

But she'd been with other men. And she'd always found a way to destroy whatever affections they'd had for her when she grew bored or frustrated with the relationship. Though she couldn't imagine that happening with Logan, her own history told her the time would come just as sure as night followed day.

Sunny held the cup of coffee near his nose and softly called his name. "Wake up," she said. "Time to get up."

He opened one eye, then the other, and pushed up on his arm. "You got coffee?"

"I took some money out of your wallet. I hope you don't mind."

He raked his hand through his rumpled hair. "No. Well done, you." Taking the covered paper cup from her hand, he leaned over and dropped a kiss on her lips. "Morning."

"Good morning. You slept well."

"I did," he said. "Thanks to you and that massage you gave me. I was knackered after all our activities."

Sunny reached out and brushed a strand of hair from his eyes. "You needed the exercise. After sitting on your arse all day."

"I do appreciate that you're watching out for me."

The coffee was strong, and Sunny sipped at it as she glanced around the interior of the campervan. "You know, this wouldn't be such a bad place to live. I mean, if you got it all fitted out and bought some supplies. You could just travel all around, see things you never saw."

"I'm not sure a girl like you would be comfortable living out of a campervan."

She frowned. "Why not?"

He paused. "I'd think you'd want the comforts of home. Running water, hot showers? A big soft bed."

"Those kinds of things don't make you happy."

"What does make you happy, Sunny?" he asked.

She wanted to admit that it was him, but her feelings were still too new to believe in them. "Good coffee," she said. "And a hot man. Or is it hot coffee and a good man?"

He sat up and crossed his legs in front of him, pulling the sheet over his lap. "I used to live in this campervan. When I first bought the ranch, the house was a wreck. The roof leaked, there were birds living in the kitchen. It took me quite a while to make it habitable."

"I'd like to see your place sometime," she said.

He smiled tightly. "Sure. Sometime."

"I mean it."

"It's nothing like your place, Sunny. You live in a castle, I live in a cardboard box."

"Are you really that preoccupied with money?"

"I'm practical. And realistic. Money makes everything easier. It buys access, it smooths the way, it provides comfort and security. You can't deny that, can you?"

She shook her head. He was right. She'd always taken her father's wealth for granted. Having every little need catered to had turned her into a vapid and self-centered child. When she looked in the mirror lately, she didn't really like what she saw—a woman with nothing to call her own.

Sunny stood up. "All right, then. Perhaps later we can talk about religion or politics."

He grabbed her hand and pulled her back down on the bed, capturing her mouth in a long, sweet kiss. Maybe she wasn't sure who she was. But she knew who Logan thought she was, and seeing herself through his eyes made her feel better about herself. He wanted her, he needed her, and she got the sense that he might just be falling for her.

"We should probably get on the road," he said. "We still have to pick up Tally from the vet's place. And we've got a long day ahead. I want to get to Cobar tonight, and with a long drive tomorrow, we'll be able to reach Adelaide. Ed gave me the name of a horse breeder about an hour outside Adelaide. I'm thinking we might stay a few days and give Tally a chance to recover a bit."

"All right, let's get going," Sunny murmured, her lips soft against his mouth.

"Or maybe we could go back to bed for a bit."

"Are you saying I wasn't enough for you last night?" she asked.

"I'm saying I'm never going to get enough of you, no matter how much time we spend in bed."

She set her coffee cup down and flopped back on the bed with him, turning to face him and look into his eyes. "Tell me the truth," she said, nerves twisting and tightening deep inside her.

"The truth," he said.

"Do you think less of me because we...because I seduced you without even knowing you?"

"No," he said, cupping her face in his hands. He brushed a kiss across her lips. "No, not at all. I wanted to be with you. But I'm not sure I would have had the courage to make the first move."

"You don't think I'm...you know...the village bike?"

He chuckled. "No. I thought you were a woman who knew what she wanted and wasn't afraid to go after it. And I still think that about you. You're not afraid to live life, Sunny. And when I'm around you, I'm not afraid, either."

"You're a very kind man, Logan Quinn."

"And you're a very beautiful woman, Sunny Grant."

They came together for a long, sweet kiss, Logan dragging her body against his, his hands searching for bare skin beneath her T-shirt. When he found her breast, he teased at her nipple with his thumb, drawing to a hard peak. Sunny closed her eyes and moaned softly.

What was it about this man that made him so irresistible? He was real and true, possessed of an inner resolve that she found so admirable, the kind of man a woman could depend upon.

When she was a teenager, she'd dreamed about her own personal Prince Charming, a man who would rescue her from all of her fears and insecurities. But as she grew older, the cynicism began to set in. She saw the worst that love could become in her parents' horrible marriage and she stopped believing in fairy-tale endings.

But maybe she'd given up too soon. She was only twenty-six. That was far too early to harden her heart. "Come on," she said. "The sooner we leave, the sooner we get where we're going."

"Maybe I don't want this trip to end," he said.

Sunny crawled off the bunk and grabbed her coffee, then slipped into her spot in the passenger seat. She pulled out the map. "How long is this trip?"

He followed her off the bed, standing in the middle of the campervan completely naked. The sight of his perfect body sent a delicious shiver through her. "From here? About four thousand kilometers. When we get to Adelaide, we'll be about halfway there, give or take a few hundred kilometers." He reached down to pick up his shorts.

"Stop," she said.

He glanced up. "Stop?"

"Just let me look before you put your clothes on. It's going to be a while before you take them off again."

He chuckled. "Once we get out of town, I could strip down and drive starkers if that would please you."

"Oh, yes," she said. "That would be lovely."

With a laugh, he pulled on his shorts and a T-shirt, and found a pair of trainers for his feet. Then he slipped behind the wheel.

"What, no underdaks?" she asked.

"If you refuse to wear knickers, then so can I."

Sunny leaned over and kissed his cheek, then pointed out the windscreen. "Once more into the breach, dear friend," she cried.

"Shakespeare. *Henry the Fifth,* isn't it?"

"Yes." Sunny paused. "'There's nothing so becomes a man as modest stillness and humility.'" It was the perfect description of him, she mused.

"All right," he said, glancing over at her. "Prepare to be schooled. I happen to be a Shakespeare expert. I've got his complete works somewhere in this campervan."

"We had to memorize all kinds of quotes in high school," she said.

"The benefits of a posh private school?"

"Hey, I learned how to kiss boys and smoke cigarettes in private school."

He grinned. "All right then. I'll want to be hearing about that a bit later."

THE DAY'S DRIVE HAD been long, the past two hours south of Bourke spent on a narrow strip of sealed road that cut a straight line through the Aussie outback.

They pulled into Cobar at seven in the evening and found another caravan park. But this time, they kept Tally with them. Once they had their site, Sunny helped Logan take her out of the trailer. He attached a long lead to the filly and Sunny patiently exercised the filly on an expanse of grass, softly speaking to her as the horse made a wide circle around her.

It was easy to forget that they shared a love of horses, but now, watching her work with Tally, he had to admire how she focused on the task at hand. He was seeing a whole different side of her, not the brazen sex goddess that he'd come to know from their nights together, but a professional, with a depth of knowledge much greater than his own.

He was sorry he hadn't called Ed first when he'd decided he'd have to sell the filly. He could have almost handled parting with her if he knew the horse was going to someone like Sunny. She would love and appreciate Tally as much as he did.

"Look how beautiful she is," Sunny called. "It's like she's got feathers for feet. I'd love to see her jump. Have you trained her at all?"

He shook his head. "No."

"She just looks so graceful. I hope your buyer appreciates what he's getting."

He watched them silently. Why not just sell her the horse? His loss would at least be tempered by the knowledge that the filly was in the best possible hands. But he wasn't even sure how to back out of the deal. Papers had been signed, money had been exchanged.

He'd taken a third, eight thousand dollars, as a down payment, but that had already gone to paying bills at the ranch. He had nothing to return to the buyer. Logan shook his head. Never mind the fact that he was driving across Australia to deliver her.

"I saw a restaurant just down the road," Logan said. "I'm going to walk over and grab us something for supper. Is there anything special you'd like?"

"A cheeseburger," she said. "And a chocolate malt. And see if they have pie. Or cake. Something yummy for dessert. And a bag of crisps would be good, too. I think we finished the crisps this afternoon."

"That all?"

"Biscuits for my horse," she said.

"Your horse?"

She glanced over her shoulder. "I can dream, can't I?"

"I have biscuits in the trailer," he said.

"That's all, then," she said, shooting him a smile. "Hurry back."

The street was quiet as he walked over to the restaurant, a slight chill in the air. He drew a deep breath and looked up at the first stars twinkling in the midnight-blue sky.

Of all the things he'd expected on this trip, Sunny hadn't even been a glimmer in his mind. And here she was, the best traveling companion he could have hoped for. He felt content, completely satisfied by life. And one of the hardest things he'd have to do—selling Tally—would be made easier by her presence.

The roadside restaurant was nearly empty when Logan entered. He sat down at the counter and grabbed a menu, then recited the order for the waitress. He had a cup of coffee while he waited, taking the time to think back over the events of the day.

He'd never been on a family holiday. His parents had never had the extra money to waste on a special trip. Occasionally, his mother would take Logan and his younger brother somewhere exciting. Once they spent the day at the zoo and another day on the beach. He imagined that his road trip with Sunny might be something like the typical family holiday.

They'd sung songs to each other and played trivia games, they'd told silly childhood stories, and she'd quoted Shakespeare from the book she found in campervan. And then, there were times when they were just quiet, watching the scenery pass by, lost in their own thoughts.

The waitress delivered their dinner, packed in two paper sacks. They still had cold drinks in the cooler, purchased along the route that day. He got to the door, then remembered Sunny's request for dessert and returned to the counter. "How much for the rest of that chocolate cake?" he asked.

"You want a half a cake?" the waitress asked, eyebrows raised.

Logan nodded. "My girlfriend loves chocolate."

"I don't know. There's probably six pieces there. I'd say twelve dollars?"

He laid out the cash and waited as she packed the cake into a box, then tied it with a string. It wasn't much, but he knew it would please her. And for some reason, he felt the need to do that more often. Wasn't that part of romance, making those tiny gestures?

When he got back to the caravan park, Tally was grazing on a clump of hay out of the rack on the side of the trailer. Sunny had filled a bucket of water and clipped it next to the hay. The horse looked up at him as he passed, blinking silently. "You're a pretty girl," he said.

The lights were on inside the campervan, and music drifted out from the CD player. He looked through the door to see

Sunny straightening up the small galley kitchen. He knocked on the door and she turned and smiled.

"Honey, I'm home."

A tiny giggle slipped from her lips and she opened the door for him and stepped aside. "Hello, honey, how was your day?"

"Oh, honey, it was wonderful. How was your day?"

"Just lovely," she said. "Now give me my cheeseburger. I'm famished."

They sat down at the table and spread the food out in front of them, sharing the chocolate malt between them. When that was gone, Logan fetched a couple of beers, removing the caps before setting the bottles on the table.

"I talked to the park manager. They don't treat the grass here, so we can let Tally graze."

"Great," he said.

"I noticed there was an old saddle in the trailer. I was thinking I might get up early tomorrow, before we have to leave, and put her through her paces. Would that be all right with you?"

Logan nodded. "Just don't get too attached to her."

"I won't," Sunny said. "I know she's meant for someone else."

In a different life, he might have been able to make a gift of the horse. What would it be like to have that kind of financial freedom? He'd already had doubts that he could make the ranch work. There were times when all the scrimping and saving just wore him out.

"How many horses to do you have on your ranch?"

"I started with six mares and I have twenty-six now. I breed them artificially."

"We do, too. Although we own the three stallions that we use for that. It's sad that the mares never get to enjoy that particular pleasure."

"Pleasure?"

Sunny grinned. "Yeah, I know, it isn't a pretty sight when they do it the natural way." She took a bite of her cheeseburger. "Thank goodness, humans know how to do it better."

He chuckled softly. "Thank goodness."

They lingered over the meal, chatting about Logan's ranch and his theories about horse breeding. He imagined this was what it would be like to have a woman in his life full-time. Meals together, companionship, mind-blowing sex and someone there to back him up, to make him feel as if life wasn't as bad as it sometimes looked.

When they were finished, he helped Sunny clean up the table then watched her from the sofa as she sorted through her clothes and neatly folded them. "What time do we have to leave tomorrow?"

"Early. I'd like to get to the breeder's place before dark. And then, I was thinking we could find a place to stay for the night. Maybe near a beach?"

"So, we don't have to go to bed right now," Sunny said. "We can have a little fun?"

"What kind of fun can we have in Cobar?"

She held out her hand, then pulled him to his feet. "It's not what you do, it's who you're with."

The moment he touched her, he couldn't help but draw her into his arms and kiss her. It had become such a natural part of their life together. Kissing and touching. He couldn't imagine how he'd go on without having her beside him.

Logan knew the realities of their relationship already. They'd have a beginning and a very definite ending. When their trip was over, he'd go back to his life and she'd return to hers. No matter how he looked at it, they couldn't exist in the same world. Sunny wasn't cut out to live in the middle of nowhere and he wasn't going to settle into her life, living among the tall poppies.

"What are we doing?" he asked as she leaned over to turn up the music.

"We're dancing," she said.

He gasped. "You might be dancing, but don't include me in this. I'm not going to let you turn me into a fool for your own amusement."

"No, I'm not going to make fun. Dancing can be very sexy. It's public foreplay. Everyone should know how to dance." She listened to the music, then shook her head. "This won't do."

She searched the CDs but finally settled on a radio station. A soft instrumental tune came through the speakers and she glanced over her shoulder at him. "There. See?"

Sunny stood in front of him and took his hands. "Now, we'll just sway a little bit, until you get the rhythm of the music."

He drew a deep breath. "Really? I'm not going to be good at this."

"Any man who is as good in bed as you are has to have some kind of rhythm. Now slip your right hand around my waist and pull me a little closer."

"All right, I can get behind that." But when he did, he forgot to keep swaying and he stumbled a bit before getting back into the song.

"Now, hold your left hand out and I'm going to just let my hand rest there."

They continued to move around the cramped interior of the campervan, their bodies coming closer and closer with each verse of the music. To Logan's amazement, he was doing quite well.

"It's like sex," she murmured, her lips brushing against his ear. "You just have to let go and enjoy it."

"What's next?"

"Now we keep doing this. And you whisper sweet things to me and kiss me and imagine what it would be like to take me to bed."

"I don't have to imagine that."

"But you do," she said. "Because dancing is all about anticipation and patience. Letting the feel of your body against mine play with your senses." She drew back to look into his eyes. "Do you feel it?"

Logan had danced before, but never like this. It was exactly as she said—slow, delicious foreplay. And yet, nothing they were doing was overtly sexual. It was all happening in his imagination. "I do," he said.

They continued to dance, their bodies moving together, a slow burn growing between them. He bent close and captured her mouth with his, and yet the rhythm went on, as if the seduction had a life of its own. And when they finally stumbled to the bed, Logan wasn't sure he'd be able to maintain any control at all.

His mouth covered hers in a deep, almost desperate kiss as they quickly undressed each other. She arched against him as they tumbled onto the bed. Pinning her hands above her head, he slowly entered her, and when he drew back, Logan looked into her eyes, as if reading her response to every move he made.

He knew he ought to get protection, but when he reached for the box of condoms, she shook her head. "I'm all right," she said softly. "If you are..."

They'd been together such a short time, yet he knew he wanted to feel her completely. And it was perfect, a sensation so intense that his body trembled as he tried to maintain control. He knew how to move, exactly how to dictate her responses, how to bring her close and then draw her back from the edge. It was as if their bodies had been meant for each other, designed to give each other pleasure.

He braced himself on his arms, slowing his pace until she could feel every inch of him as he plunged into her moist heat.

Sunny's breathing grew quicker, and he felt her body tensing ever so slightly. And when he was certain that she was as close as he was, he let himself feel it all. A delicious heat spread through him, his body slowly coiling tighter with each stroke. It was a tantalizing ascent, spinning up and up until every nerve in his body was humming.

"Look at me," he whispered.

She moaned, her voice sounding like an echo in his head. He gently bit her lower lip and she opened her eyes. Sunny's breath caught in her throat and, suddenly, she was there, tumbling over the edge.

A cry of surprise tore from her throat as her body dissolved into deep spasms. Their gazes never faltered and he drove into her one more time before joining her in his own powerful orgasm.

The pleasure seemed to go on forever, only abating when they were both completely spent and gasping for breath. Though his arms felt boneless, Logan braced above her and bent closer to kiss her. "Do you know how incredible that feels? To do that together?"

"Mmm," she murmured with a sleepy smile. "We are becoming quite good at it."

He chuckled softly and rolled off her. "You know what they say about practice?"

"What?"

He stretched out beside her, lying on his stomach and toying with a strand of her hair. "It should be done enthusiastically and often."

"I'll remember that," she said with a laugh.

Logan stared at her beautiful face. He wanted to tell her how much she meant to him, how he was falling completely under her spell, but he knew it was too soon. Sunny wasn't the type to want undying proclamations of love and affection. She seemed to be happy when everything was light and carefree.

He ran his fingers over her brow, then dropped a kiss on her lips. For now, he'd play the game by her rules. "I'm going to go put Tally into the trailer for the night."

"I'll come and help you," she said.

"No, you stay here. It'll only take me a minute."

She watched him from the bed as he pulled on a pair of shorts and slipped into his trainers. He noticed the box with the chocolate cake sitting on the counter. "We forgot dessert," he said.

"What?"

Logan grabbed the box and set it down beside her on the

bed, then retrieved the single fork they had. "Why don't you get started on that and I'll be back in a few?"

He walked outside into the cool night, quietly closing the screen door behind him. A moment later, he heard a tiny scream and smiled to himself. Sunny was pleased.

Tally gave him a curious look as he approached, the light from the campervan reflected in her eyes. "Don't worry," he murmured. "You're still my best girl."

He rubbed the horse's neck and she nuzzled his shoulder, her soft nose nudging him for a biscuit. He unclipped her from the lead, then walked her back to the trailer. He opened the upper sections of the trailer doors and turned Tally around so she could enjoy the scents on the night air. Then he grabbed a biscuit from the tin and held out his hand.

"One more day on the road," he said as the horse took the biscuit from his palm. "Then I'm going to give you a few days' rest." He fetched her water and put the rest of the hay in the rack, then closed the trailer door. The filly hung her head out and he gave her another biscuit. "Good night, baby."

He walked back to the campervan, and when he got inside, he found Sunny sitting cross-legged in the center of the bed. She pointed the fork at him. "You are the most amazing man I've ever met."

Logan sat down next to her. She fed him a bite of cake and he smiled. "Are you saying that because of the sex or the cake?"

"The cake," she said. "And the sex. The cake wouldn't taste nearly as good without the sex. Although, the sex might have been even better had I known there was cake at the end." She bumped against his shoulder then gave him a quick kiss. "Is Tally put to bed?"

Logan nodded and took another bite of the cake. "If it's all right with you, I think we should take a couple days in Adelaide. Tally could use the break and so could we."

"I don't need to be anywhere," she said. "I'm enjoying this trip."

"We've got a long stretch of outback to get through tomorrow." He reached out and took her hand, then pressed a kiss to the spot below her wrist. "I'm glad you're going to be there when I have to give her up. It will make it a lot easier."

"You are going to miss her," she said softly.

Logan nodded. "Yeah. I've raised her, I've seen her almost every day in the last three years. She has this personality and it's like we know each other so well."

Sunny set the box down beside her and wrapped her arms around his neck, giving him a fierce hug. "I understand," she murmured. "Really, I do."

"I know," he said. And she did. She was maybe the only person who truly would know how hard it was for him to give Tally away. Logan flopped back onto the bed and Sunny curled up beside him, throwing her leg over his hips.

They lay quietly, Logan listening to the rhythm of his own breathing. He was starting to come to grips with losing Tally. But at the same time, he was wondering how he'd ever let Sunny go.

Before they slept, he pulled her into his arms and made love to her once more, this time slowly, savoring every single moment between them. It was all right to dream about the life he wanted someday. But it wasn't very practical to wish for things that he couldn't possibly possess.

Sunny was one of those impossible dreams. Though he could see a future in his mind's eye, he didn't really want to believe it could happen for him. It was best to keep his hopes and dreams based in reality and not pure fantasy.

4

"GOOD MORNING, DARLING. Did you have a good night?"

Sunny ran her hand over the filly's nose, and the horse nodded her head. Tally had such a sweet disposition that Sunny had already fallen in love with her. Though she felt a bit guilty about her feelings, she knew Padma would understand. There was enough room in her heart for two favorite horses.

"We girls have to stick together," she murmured.

Her father had tried for years to get her to ride a gelding, but Sunny had stubbornly insisted that her mare could jump just as well as any male—or formerly male—mount. It wasn't accepted wisdom in the equestrian world. Very few show jumpers rode mares. But she felt a duty to at least promote the idea that female horses were good for more than just breeding.

She clipped a lead onto Tally's halter and slowly led her down the ramp. The horse seemed grateful to be out of the confines of her traveling coach and pranced along beside her. Sunny attached her to the secure line and Tally bent down and began to nibble at the damp morning grass.

The sun was just above the horizon. Glancing over her shoulder, Sunny wondered how much time she'd have before Logan woke up. They had a long drive ahead of them, most of it a straight line through the desolate outback, but she found herself looking forward to the time on the road. She and Logan made good traveling companions.

She'd never thought much about the kind of man she wanted in her life. She'd pretty much enjoyed whatever sort wandered through. But spending time with Logan, Sunny realized there were certain qualities she needed to find in a long-term prospect.

A tiny smile curved her lips and she shook her head. She'd never been the kind of girl who thought about forever, especially when it came to men. But now, she realized she'd just never met a man who was so perfectly suited to her personality as Logan was.

He had a calming effect on her, a way of making her slow down and think before she reacted. And he didn't tell her what she wanted to hear—he told her the truth. If she was acting like a brat, he called her a brat. He wouldn't allow her to goad him into an argument, thus making it impossible to have the tempestuous type of relationship that she'd always sought in the past.

It was strange how her whole attitude had changed since she'd met him. After London, she was like a ship without a rudder, just circling aimlessly with no destination in mind. But now, she felt focused, completely aware of who she was and what she was doing. And she wanted to ride again.

Not just ride, she thought. Really train. Get her mind and her body into the right place to win. Immerse herself in the sport. She was never more comfortable than when she was in the saddle. But now, she realized she could be comfortable off the horse as well—with Logan.

She leaned against the wall of the trailer and closed her eyes. Though she was twenty-six years old, Sunny had never really felt like a woman. And now she did. Now she knew what she wanted from her life, and it wasn't just cute boys and expensive things. She wanted a man who fed her soul, who made her laugh. A man who expected her to be a better person.

She drew a deep breath and shook her head. Though life on

the road seemed to pass at a slow pace, Sunny felt as if she were on board a runaway train. Everything about her was changing inside and she couldn't keep up. The problem was she didn't want to keep up. She just wanted to let it all happen.

Opening her eyes, Sunny glanced around the interior of the trailer. Her gaze fell on the wire racks in the front that held feed and straw. Above that, she'd noticed an old saddle and bridle, and she grabbed them both, then searched for a saddle pad.

The pad was buried under a moldy duffel bag. She shook the straw off it, then walked out of the trailer into the new morning. "Look what I found," she said, calling to the filly.

Tally perked her head up and slowly walked toward her. When Sunny reached her side, she set the saddle down and examined it carefully. The leather was dry and cracked and the fittings tarnished, but the cinch was still strong.

"You wanna go for a ride?" she asked. She smoothed the pad over the filly's back then lifted the English saddle over the pad. "We're going to have some fun, you and I."

The bridle was in better condition than the saddle, but it needed adjustments before it fit the filly properly. Sunny worked at the buckles and snaps, and when she was satisfied, she unclipped Tally from the rope line and jumped up into the saddle.

Gathering the reins between her fingers, she softly clucked her tongue and touched her heels to the horse's flanks. Tally immediately sprang into action with a quick walk.

Sunny had a very precise warm-up and she took her new mount through the paces, learning to read the horse's reactions and adjusting her commands along the way. When they were both warmed up, she nudged the horse into a slow gallop and made a big circle around the campground lawn.

Tally was grateful for the freedom, and Sunny wished that she had an open field or a dirt track so she could give the filly her head and let her fly.

When they'd made two circles around the grassy area, she let the reins go slack, and Tally continued in the wide arc. Sunny let her hands drop to her side, then closed her eyes and tipped her head back.

The connection between them was so perfect. They moved together, like one being. Sunny held her arms out and smiled. She was a horse, running through an open field, the sun growing warm on her back, the air crisp in her nose, her mane flying out behind her.

She heard a whistle and felt the horse shift beneath her. Opening her eyes, she saw Logan standing in the doorway of the campervan. He watched her with a smile on his face and he waved to her.

She grabbed the reins and steered Tally toward the campervan, drawing her to a stop in front of Logan. "She's wonderful."

"You look wonderful on her," he said.

She bent over the horse's neck and hugged her. "Then sell her to me. I promise, I'll take good care of her."

Sunny saw the change in his expression, the shadow of regret that colored his reaction. "I can't," he said. "The deal is made. There's nothing I can do."

"I'll make you a better deal," she said. She could see how much Logan loved the filly. It just didn't seem fair that he had been forced to sell her, especially to someone he didn't know.

"I bet you will."

She met his gaze, staring at him with a stubborn tilt to her head. "I'm not going to give up. By the time we get to Perth, she's going to be mine. You won't be able to say no." With that, Sunny pulled the horse around and continued her circle of the lawn. "Can she jump?" she called.

"I never tried," he said.

"Go inside and get a blanket, the white one."

He did as she asked and she explained how to lay it out on the ground in a long, narrow rectangle.

"What are you going to do?"

"See if she'll jump over it."

"She'll just run over it," he said with a smile.

"Maybe, maybe not. Go grab a few of the cushions and put them on top of the blanket." When the impromptu jump was constructed, Sunny brought the horse to a slow gallop again and, carefully controlling her speed, turned her toward the jump.

To her surprise, the filly didn't rush or balk. She neatly leaped over the obstacle as if she'd been doing it her entire life. Sunny glanced over at Logan. "See."

"That was beautiful."

"She wants to jump. She's meant to jump."

"I'm going to walk over to the restaurant and get us some breakfast." He turned to walk back inside.

"I'm not going to give up," she called after him.

Sunny continued to ride until Logan left, then cooled the filly down and got her fed. The ride had left her sweaty, so she grabbed a towel and her cotton dress and headed for the showers.

It was going to be a long day on the road, and it felt good to work off a little excess energy before heading out. She ran her fingers through her hair then lathered it up with the shampoo that Logan had bought her.

When they got to Adelaide, they'd need to pick up the package that Lily had sent her. After that, she and Logan would be free to enjoy themselves, with an unlimited budget available for hotel rooms and decent meals. But Sunny knew she'd need to proceed carefully. Logan had his pride and he could be stubborn. He wasn't going to appreciate her throwing her wealth around as if she thought nothing of it.

She stepped out of the shower and wrapped the towel around her wet hair, then pulled the dress over her damp skin. The thin fabric clung to her curves but she didn't care. After brushing her teeth, she gathered her riding clothes and slipped into her shoes.

The few campers in the campground were still asleep as she headed back to the campervan. Tally walked up to her and nudged her hand, looking for a treat, but she gave the filly a pat on the nose and continued on.

The breakfast bags were sitting on the table when she stepped inside. But Logan was nowhere to be found. She opened a carton and grabbed a piece of bacon, nibbling on it as she went back to the door. She saw him coming across the lawn, his hair damp from the showers. He was bare chested, a towel draped around his neck.

She felt a warm rush of desire at the sight of him. He was such a beautiful man, long limbed and slender hipped, his broad chest burnished by the sun. He stopped to rub Tally's nose, then continued toward her.

"I am ready to eat," he announced.

"Me, too," she said.

As he stepped into the campervan, he grabbed her waist and pulled her into a long, deep, electrifying kiss. Sunny moaned as she dropped her things on the floor and wrapped her arms around his neck. Logan gently tugged the towel from her hair and tossed it aside. His fingers tangled in the damp strands and he molded her mouth to his.

When he finally drew away, she was breathless, her heart beating at a frantic rate. Logan kissed the tip of her nose and then dropped one more kiss on her lips. "I think we better eat our breakfast and get on the road."

She smoothed her palm down his chest and then lower, to the front of his jeans. She could feel the stiff ridge beneath the denim. "What are we going to do with this?" she asked.

"I'm sure that will go away on its own. Don't worry. There are more where that came from."

Sunny giggled then kissed him again. "Good. I'll be counting on that."

As Sunny finished unpacking the breakfast and spread it on the table, he wrapped his arms around her waist and rested his chin on her shoulder. This was what it was between them, these easy, sweet mornings followed by wild, passionate nights. She could survive forever living a life like this, Sunny mused. Anywhere, as long as Logan was with her.

She drew a deep breath and closed her eyes for a moment. It seemed like a dream. But then, sometimes dreams did come true.

THEY'D SPENT ALMOST the entire day driving southwest on the narrow sealed road, a straight and seemingly endless line through the outback.

The towns were few and far between, sometimes more than a hundred kilometers between anything remotely civilized. Logan couldn't imagine what the endless stretch would have been like without Sunny's company. But between the music and the sound of her voice, the drive was bearable. No, it was actually enjoyable.

She made everything so much more fun. And he hadn't had this much fun in his life for a long time. He hadn't really thought it was important to laugh and be silly. From the time he was a child, he'd taken a serious approach to life. His father had moved from job to job, mostly finding work on sheep stations or cattle ranches in desolate areas of the outback.

All of this emptiness brought back old memories, those days that they'd travel, looking for work, wondering where the next meal would come from. His younger brother had suffered most. They'd both overheard the conversations, his father's angry outbursts, his mother's sobbing pleas. But Sam hadn't been able to deal with the fear and uncertainty as Logan had.

"New game," Sunny said, reaching over to touch his arm.

"No more memory games," he said. "You beat me every time."

"No. This is called What Were You Thinking?"

"Are we going to talk about selling Tally again?"

"No, I want to know what you were just thinking. And you have to answer me honestly. Complete and total honesty."

Logan shook his head. He'd told her stories about his childhood and his family, but they'd been shined up and all the sad and pathetic details had been omitted. He shouldn't have lied, but he'd never thought there'd be a time he'd want to tell the truth.

"I was just thinking about when me and my family would travel through the outback. Just recalling all those old feelings I had."

"What kind of feelings?"

He paused, considering how to explain to her. "Dread," he finally said. "Fear. Frustration." He glanced over at her. Her expression had changed from lighthearted curiosity to concern. "It just wasn't a good time in my life."

"Tell me," she said softly. "I really want to know."

"My dad never had a good job. We moved from place to place while he looked for work, usually on sheep stations or cattle ranches. Sometimes they had a house for us. Usually it was more like a shack. And sometimes we lived in a tent." He shook his head. "School was always a spotty thing. If we lived near a town, my little brother and I would go, usually dressed in the same clothes every day. But if we were out in the bush, my mom would teach us. I always liked that."

"How did you learn about horses?"

"I worked a horse farm during my summers off from high school. I got a scholarship to a private boys' school, but I couldn't stay there in the summer and my folks didn't need me around, so I worked. Learned everything I could about horses. Then I worked my way through university and took a job at a bank and started saving to buy my own place." He chuckled softly. "And here I am with you."

"What is your brother doing now?"

Logan drew a deep breath. It was still difficult to talk about. "He died when I was at university. He got mixed up with drugs and he died. He was never really into school, so he stayed with my parents until he was sixteen and then took off on his own. I tried to help him out, but he was pretty mad at me for leaving him."

She reached out and smoothed her hand over his cheek. "I'm so sorry," she murmured.

Logan grabbed her fingers and placed a kiss in the middle of her palm. It felt good to tell her, as if a weight had been lifted from him. "Now you have to tell me one of your sad stories. If you have any."

"Oh, I have plenty," she said. "But I will tell you one. I think if I had to pick one thing that defined my life, it would be the time that I realized my mother and father didn't have a marriage."

"How did that happen?"

"My parents were fighting, but this time it was really big. My mother had shut herself in her room and she wasn't coming out and I was supposed to go get new riding boots for a competition, so my father took me to his office and we were supposed to be there for just a few minutes so he could make a phone call. But then, this woman showed up and they were arguing and whispering and she was touching him and trying to kiss him and I knew something was up. I was nine years old and I could feel it."

She sighed. "They sent me out of the office and they stayed in there a long, long time. And when the woman came out, she smiled at me, but it wasn't a nice smile. I could tell she hated me."

"I'm sorry," he said.

"For what?"

"That you had to go through that."

Sunny shrugged. "I guess, in the end, it was better to know. It explained a lot of what was going on in our house. Why my mother was so angry and why my father paid more attention to my riding career than he did to her." She forced a smile. "It did kind of screw me up as far as men went. I guess you could say I have trust issues."

"Do you trust me?" he asked.

A smile broke across her face and she nodded. "I do. That's the really strange thing. The minute I met you, I just felt it. That's why I slept with you that night. Because I knew I could trust you. It's why I didn't want you to take me back home."

"We make quite a pair," he said.

Sunny nodded. "Yes, we do."

As they got nearer and nearer to the coast, the landscape gradually changed. Barren land gave way to ranches, then farms; the towns came in closer succession, and the endless horizon was broken by the dark outline of Mount Remarkable in the distance.

Ed had given Logan the name of a horse breeder with a farm about forty-five minutes outside of Adelaide, and he was glad to see a tiptop operation as they rolled up the driveway. The stable manager met them outside the barn and was happy to board and exercise Tally for the next two nights.

When Logan offered to pay him, he refused, saying there might come a day when Logan could be of assistance to him. Logan suspected that it was Ed who would be of assistance and not a second-rate horse breeder from the middle of nowhere.

While Logan got Tally settled in a stall and brought out her feed and grooming supplies, Sunny wandered around the stables, looking at the horses. He saw her chatting with one of the grooms and before long, she had a small group gathered around her.

She glanced over at him and he sent her a quizzical look, wondering if she needed to be rescued. A small shrug told him that for the moment, she was fine, so he continued his work.

Logan smiled to himself as he rubbed Tally's nose. He and Sunny had spent so much time together over the past few days that they were now able to communicate without even talking. But then, that shouldn't surprise him.

He leaned back against the plank wall and remembered their encounter last night. They hadn't needed words then, either. A shiver ran through him and he sucked in a sharp breath. Logan knew he ought to just be happy with what he had at the moment—a beautiful, sexy woman in his bed. But it was human nature to want more.

He'd had plenty of time to work it all out in his head, but no matter which way he turned it, he couldn't see anything more than an occasional weekend together. Once she got back to riding again, she'd be busy. And his ranch was an eight-hour drive from her parents' place.

A groan rumbled in his chest and he ran his hands through his hair. Why even think about this now? He should just enjoy his good fortune while he had it. Who knew when he might get so lucky again?

"Are you all right?"

He glanced up to see Sunny standing at the stall door. Strange how just looking at her made him feel better. "Yeah, I'm good."

"Can I help you with anything?"

Logan shook his head. "Naw, you just stand there looking pretty."

"I called Lily and she told me that my package is waiting at my father's Adelaide office."

"What does your father do?"

"He's into energy," she said. "Oil, petrol, electricity. I really don't know all the details."

"My power bill is overdue," Logan joked. "You think he could help me out with that?"

"Next time I see him, I'll ask."

She stepped inside the stall and wrapped her arms around his neck, then gave him a kiss, her tongue teasing at his until he was forced to drop the pitchfork and wrap his hands around her waist.

"I'm never going to be finished if you keep interrupting me," he murmured, pressing his lips to her neck.

"Stop complaining," she replied.

"Oh, I'm not complaining. I'm just looking forward to the rest of the night."

By the time Sunny and Logan got to Adelaide, it was nearly seven o'clock. Sunny had thought about stopping at her father's office the next morning, but when she called, she was surprised that the receptionist was still waiting for her arrival.

Logan stayed in the campervan while she went inside the glass-and-steel building in the downtown business district. A pretty girl sat behind a wide desk, the Grant Energies logo on a wall behind her.

"Are you Sunny?"

Sunny smiled and nodded. "I'm so sorry to make you wait."

"Oh, no worries. I was happy to do it." She picked up a large box and set it on the counter. "Your father's assistant took the liberty of preparing our beach villa and you're welcome to stay there while you're in the area. It's just fifteen minutes from here." She handed Sunny another envelope. "It's a lovely place on the water."

She stared down at the envelope. Her father had a beach villa? "Thank you," Sunny murmured. "And thank my father's assistant. I'll be sure to mention her kindness. And yours."

The receptionist smiled. "There's a map in the envelope. And the combination for the lockbox with the key. Have a lovely time."

"We will," she said.

A man suddenly appeared, picked up the box and nodded at her. Sunny glanced back and forth between the receptionist and him. "This is Darrell. He'll help you with your box."

Sunny turned and walked to the door, smiling to herself. She knew her father was a very successful businessman. When they traveled to equestrian events or went on holiday, the accommodations were always first-rate. But she never knew that he employed so many people just to take care of the details of his life. Too bad he couldn't find someone to bring her mother back from Paris.

Sunny held the door open for Darrell, and when they reached the street, Logan was standing next to the campervan. Darrell took in the battered state of their vehicle and gave her an odd look.

"I can take that," Logan offered.

"Where do you want it?" Darrell asked.

He quickly opened the side door to the campervan and Darrell set it inside. Then Darrell turned to Sunny and nodded. "You have a fine evening, Miss Grant. Drive safely."

"Thank you," Sunny said.

Logan stepped to her side as she watched Darrell walk back inside. "Should we have tipped him?"

She shook her head. "No, he works for my father. I'm sure he's well paid." She turned to him. "We have to talk."

"What?"

She saw concern cross his features and she reached out and took his hand. "You know how I said we could rent a room tonight and maybe sleep in a real bed. And have a real shower?"

He nodded. "We don't have to do that. There are plenty of nice campgrounds in—"

"I know a place where we can stay for free," she said. "My father's assistant set it up."

"I'm all for that," Logan said. "No need to spend money when we don't have to."

"All right, then. Let's go."

The got back into the campervan and Sunny pulled the map out of the envelope. Her father's assistant had drawn a line from the office to the Henley Beach villa.

"Where are we going?"

"Just turn left and then forward until the next signal."

They found the beach villa without any trouble, and when Sunny hopped out of the campervan, she smiled. Though the villa blocked the view of the water, she could smell the sea in the air and could hear the waves over the traffic on the street.

She grabbed Logan's hand and pulled him along to the front door. As promised, there was a lockbox. She punched in the code and it opened, revealing a set of keys. Sunny unlocked the door and they walked inside.

The interior was airy and spacious. Through a wide wall of windows on the beach side of the villa, Sunny could see the sunset, a blaze of orange and pink.

Logan slowly walked over to the windows and stared out. "Holy shit," he murmured.

She ran over to him and threw her arms around his neck. "Is it all right? Can we stay? It is free."

He slipped his arms around her waist and pulled her close. "Yeah, I think we can stay. Hell, maybe we should just move in."

She unlocked the door to the terrace and walked outside. A narrow path through the scrub led to a beautiful white-sand beach. She looked up and down the beach and in the distance saw a high jetty jutting out into the water. This was the perfect spot to relax for the next few days. "Thank you, Daddy," she shouted.

She turned around and walked back inside to find Logan standing in the kitchen, the refrigerator door held open. "You should see what's inside here," he said. He pulled out a bottle of champagne and held it up. "Do they think we're on our honeymoon?"

"They're just making us comfortable."

"Well, I would have been happy with a beer and some crisps."

"So what should we do? There's a pier not far from here. Maybe we could walk down and see what's happening." She paused. "Or we could check out the bed. See if it's comfortable." Sunny slowly approached him, unbuttoning the front of her dress. "Or we could always take a shower."

He chuckled softly. "Why don't I go get that big box of yours and we'll change and take a walk. I need to stretch my legs before you put me through my paces in the bedroom."

"Giddy up," she said with a teasing glint in her eye.

They hurried outside to the campervan and gathered up all their things, then carried them inside. Sunny tore open the box and was thrilled to find that Lily had packed some of her favorite things.

She dumped everything out on the bed then hung the clothes up in the closet. She slipped out of her dress and put on her hot-pink bikini, pulling a comfortable cotton dress over the top. She found a pair of thongs in the bottom of the box and slipped them on her bare feet, then went to find Logan.

He was sitting on the terrace, his long legs stretched out in front of him, a beer in his hand. His sunglasses shielded his eyes against the sunset, and when she stepped outside, he held out his hand.

Sunny placed her fingers in his and he pulled her hand to his lips. "It's a whole different world," he said.

She knew how he must feel, especially after all the things he had told her about his family. To him, money meant comfort and security. But what he didn't understand was that sometimes all the money in the world couldn't make a person feel as safe as she did with him.

Sunny wanted to find the words to tell him that, to tell him how wonderful he was and how perfect he made her feel and how she didn't think of their differences when they were together. But she'd never completely understand what he'd gone through.

"It's a perfect summer night," she said. "Let's enjoy ourselves while we're here."

"I can do that," he said.

They walked down to the water and dipped their bare feet in, letting the waves wash up as they stared out over the Indian Ocean at the setting sun. From a distance, Sunny could hear music, and they picked up their shoes and started down the beach.

Logan draped his arm around her shoulders as they walked, and they chatted about simple things, riding and horses, Sunny's competitions and Logan's ranch. They never seemed to run out of topics. One question always led to another. And when there was silence between them, it was because they just wanted to enjoy being together and not because they didn't have anything to say.

When they reached the jetty, they walked up toward the street and found a huge square. A band played on one end and people had gathered with food and drinks, to watch. Logan grabbed them each a beer from the bar and they found a place to sit.

As they watched the band, Logan seemed to lose himself in his thoughts. When he finished his beer, he got another. Sunny watched him, worried that she'd done or said something wrong.

When the band took a break, they walked out to the end of the jetty. He leaned over the rail, resting his arms as he stared out at the sea. Slipping her arms around his, she rested her head on his shoulder. "If this is too much, we can find somewhere else to stay."

"No, this isn't too much," he said. "It's just…perfect. Really, it is."

"It's not who I am," Sunny said. "Maybe it used to be, but not anymore. It's not important."

"That's easy to say. Especially when you have everything you could possibly want."

"I don't," she said. "I have nothing that I really want."

He laughed and glanced over at her. "I find that hard to believe."

"It's true."

"What do you want that you don't have?"

"A life of my own. A future. Someone who'll love me forever. I want to get up in the morning and have something important to do."

"You have your riding."

"Is that really important?" she asked. "If I stop riding tomorrow, no one would care. No one would miss me. I want to be an important part of someone else's life. I want someone to need me and to miss me if I'm not there."

"And I want to wake up someday and not have to worry

about where the next dollar is going to come from," he said. "I want to stop worrying about what I might lose and just enjoy what I have."

She gave his arm a squeeze, wishing she could just wipe away the doubts in his mind. They were from two different worlds, but some strange twist of fate had put them together, and Sunny sensed that, sooner or later, the reason would be revealed.

She had always believed in destiny, in the idea that there were forces at work in her life that would determine her future. But she was coming to understand that she could have a hand in her fate, that she could even control it if she wanted.

What would it take to become a permanent part of Logan's world? How would she convince him to be part of hers? Were they so different that it would be impossible to find a place where they could exist together?

"You are the most wonderful man I've ever known," she said. "You're kind and patient and funny and romantic, and all of those things mean so much more than what's in your bank account."

"Pretty words," he murmured.

"Just because they're pretty doesn't mean they're not true." She pulled him away from the railing. "Come on. Let's go back."

He reluctantly straightened, then took her hand. "I'm hungry."

"I'll make you something," Sunny said.

"You can cook?"

"Yes, I can cook. I used to spend a lot of time hanging out with the help."

"Well, this should be interesting," he said with a grin. "I never would have guessed you could cook."

"There's a lot you don't know about me," she said.

Logan nodded. "I'm beginning to realize that."

5

LOGAN STOOD ON THE TERRACE, staring out at the black horizon, the sound of the waves lulling him into a sense of comfort.

He and Sunny had a late dinner and then decided to curl up on the sofa and watch a movie. But she'd fallen asleep after just ten minutes. He glanced over his shoulder and smiled.

He liked the way she looked when she slept. It was a different, more relaxed Sunny. When she was awake, she was always bubbling with energy. Even in their quiet moments, he could sense her mind running at high speed. But when she slept, she was still, her body relaxed and her mind at peace.

She was so different from the woman he'd first thought she was. When she had climbed up on that fence, dressed in nothing but her T-shirt and pink bikini bottoms, his first impression had not been all good. She'd seemed prickly and difficult, like a girl with a chip on her shoulder. But then she'd smiled and everything changed.

He knew the first time he looked into her eyes that all that bravado was hiding some very deep hurt. He'd always thought that money was the only thing that could buy happiness, but now he knew the truth. Sunny had all the advantages anyone could want, yet she didn't have what she really needed—unconditional love.

Logan cursed beneath his breath. Was he prepared to give

that to her? The longer they spent together, the more he found himself imagining a life with Sunny. Part of that fantasy required him forgetting about the objections her family might have, and ignoring the money issue and the fact that she probably wouldn't want to live in the outback. But once he factored out all those things, it did make a lovely little dream.

"Jaysus," he muttered. There was delusion and then there was just outright batty. If he were thinking with his head, instead of his libido, he'd send her home tomorrow. Or leave her to her daddy's luxury apartment while he drove off into the distance.

There were plenty of other women in the world who'd find life on a dusty old horse ranch to be an adventure or a challenge. He just couldn't see Sunny among that group.

"Let her go," he murmured to himself. "Make a clean break and walk away."

It made perfect sense. He wasn't at a point in his life when he could afford to fall in love. Life was hard enough looking after himself and the ranch. He didn't need another responsibility. So he'd spend the next few days with Sunny, enjoying her company, and then, in the middle of the night, he'd leave.

She'd understand, Logan rationalized. She knew as well as he did that any future between them was doomed. So why not just enjoy their attraction for a bit longer and call an end to it, sensibly, without any regrets?

Or why not just leave now? Sunny was safe here. She had a place to stay until she went back home. It would be simple enough for her to get a flight to Brisbane. Now would be the best time, he told himself.

But was it the coward's way out? Would he leave to make things easier for her—or for him? Falling in love with Sunny was the last thing in the world he wanted to do. It would only cause more complications in a relationship that was complicated already.

"Just go," he murmured. Turning away from the railing, he walked back into the villa. Sunny didn't stir as he passed on his way to the bedroom. Logan silently began to gather his things, stowing them in his rucksack.

When he was finished, he stood beside the empty bed, considering what he was about to do. There'd be no going back. Any future that he might have dreamed about with Sunny would evaporate.

Gathering his resolve, Logan walked back through the villa and paused as he passed the sofa. Scanning Sunny's profile, he tried to commit the last details to memory. It would be a long time before he forgot her—and the time they spent together.

He turned and walked to the door, then opened it slowly. She'd be fine. This was all going to come to an end anyway. Better sooner than later.

The night air was chilly as Logan walked out to the campervan. He opened the door and sat down behind the wheel, tossing his rucksack onto the passenger seat. But when he pulled his keys out of his pocket, he couldn't bring himself to go any further.

His gaze fell on the volume of Shakespeare sitting on the console between the seats. They were in the middle of *As You Like It,* a play made much better by Sunny's narration. He picked the book up and opened it, then pulled out a bubblegum wrapper she was using as a bookmark. She'd bought a handful of bubblegum a few days ago and they'd spent a hundred-kilometer stretch outside of Bourke in a bubble-blowing contest.

As he looked around the campervan, there were reminders of her everywhere. Cursing softly, he flipped on the overhead light and moved into the back, picking up Sunny's things along the way. She'd made herself at home, that much was clear.

Logan stopped short and tossed the items onto the sofa. This was crazy. Just because he rid himself of her things it wouldn't stop the memories from coming. He got back behind the wheel and reached for the ignition. But a knock on the window startled him.

He glanced to his left and saw Sunny standing outside,

wrapped in a blanket, her hair tumbled down around her face. Logan rolled down the window.

"What are you doing out here?" she asked. "I woke up and I couldn't find you."

He scrambled for an answer. He couldn't tell her the truth—it would only hurt her. "I—I thought I left a light on and I just wanted to check to see if it drained the battery." He turned the ignition and the campervan started. "It's all right. Go inside. I'm just going to let it run for a while. I'll be in in a few minutes."

She gave him a puzzled look then nodded. "All right. But hurry up."

Logan watched as she walked back to the villa. Groaning, he bent his head over the steering wheel, resting it against his clasped hands. What the hell was he doing? It might very well be the noble thing to do, to break things off cleanly now. But the only one he was really protecting was himself.

Sunny was a big girl. She knew the pitfalls of love, probably better than he did. When things didn't work out in the end, she'd go on with her life. She'd find a nice guy, maybe settle into a good relationship and eventually get married.

He'd be the one left regretting what could have been, wondering if he'd had more to offer he might have convinced her there was a future between them. She was right here, standing in front of him, offering him fantasies that would last a lifetime and he was too afraid to reach out and grab them.

With another curse, Logan turned off the ignition and jumped out of the campervan. He wasn't going to be the one to end it. He would leave that up to her. And when it happened, he'd be grateful for the time they'd had and go on with his life.

When he got back inside, he dropped his rucksack on the floor beside the sofa and walked into the bedroom. Sunny was already in bed, curled up beneath a down duvet. He stripped off his clothes and crawled between the crisp bed linens, snuggling up against her naked body.

A soft sigh slipped from her lips, and she reached back and

tangled her fingers in his hair, pulling him closer. Logan pressed a kiss to the curve of her neck, his lips finding her pulse point.

She gently guided him inside her, and for a long time they didn't move. He thought that she might have fallen asleep, but when he smoothed his palm down her belly to the juncture between her legs, she moaned softly. Logan touched her, gently rubbing his fingers over the core of her desire.

He felt her grow damp around him, and then a delicious heat that he found irresistible. Every instinct told him to move, but he stayed still, enjoying the changes in Sunny's body as she came closer and closer to her release.

When it finally came, it was quiet yet incredibly powerful. He felt every spasm of her body as he held her close. She melted against him, boneless and relaxed. Then, in two quick thrusts, he was there himself, tumbling over the edge and losing control deep inside her.

They didn't speak, both of them completely sated. Logan listened as her breathing grew slow and deep and before long, he knew she was asleep again.

"What the hell am I going to do about you, Sunny Grant?" he whispered. It was so easy to say he wouldn't fall for her, but harder to admit that he already was—deeply and madly in love with Sunny.

SUNNY RAKED HER HANDS through her hair as she sat up in bed. She glanced over at the clock and saw it was nearly nine. She wasn't even sure when they'd finally gotten to sleep last night, but she'd slept so soundly she felt refreshed.

Glancing over at Logan, Sunny could tell he was still a few hours from getting up. In normal life, between the two of them, he was the early riser, but since they'd been spending their nights in carnal pursuits, he usually slept until she woke him up.

Sunny carefully crawled out of bed and searched the floor for something to wear. She pulled a T-shirt from her bag and tugged it over her head, then headed to the kitchen. But as she passed the sofa, she noticed Logan's rucksack sitting on the floor.

She picked it up, wondering why he'd left it where he had. Curious, Sunny opened it up and rummaged through his belongings, a strange realization setting in. Everything was inside. His clothes, his shaving kit, everything that he'd—

Sucking in a sharp breath, Sunny dropped the rucksack on the floor. It all made sense now. Last night. The campervan. He was going to leave. If she hadn't found him gone and searched him out, she'd be alone right now.

Sunny wasn't sure how to feel. Should she be hurt or angry? Should she confront him and get to the truth of the matter? What other explanation could there be? Slowly she sat down on the end of the sofa, then buried her face in her hands.

Maybe she'd just been fooling herself. They'd been getting along so well, enjoying their trip. But she had to wonder if the attraction was all one-sided. Yes, they had a fantastic sexual relationship, but the men she'd known had always been able to separate affection from sexual desire.

Was that all it was? Was he afraid that her feelings were deeper than what he was prepared to handle? Sunny thought back over the past few days, wondering if she had said or done something to scare him off. God, how did she always manage to pick men who were emotionally unavailable?

So what was she supposed to do now? Was this just a momentary crisis or did he still have plans to desert her along the way? She'd never asked for any type of commitment from him, so why was he so afraid that he wanted to leave her? She leaned back into the suede sofa and stared up at the ceiling.

Maybe he was worried she'd be the one to leave. Could she really blame him? He saw her life as perfect and only because she'd never had to worry about money. But he refused to see that her happiness didn't come from financial security, it came from feeling loved and wanted.

Sunny pushed to her feet and walked to the kitchen. She'd

just pretend she never saw it. That was the only thing she could do. That...and wait. She pulled open the refrigerator door and peered inside. Breakfast. That would take her mind off the rucksack sitting beside the sofa.

Her father's assistant had provided them with a wide variety of food for any meal they might want to prepare. Sunny pulled out a grapefruit, a carton of eggs, a package of bacon and some English muffins. She even found a jug of fresh orange juice.

A tin of coffee came next, and Sunny scooped enough into a filter to make a strong brew. She filled the coffeemaker and flipped it on, then started the rest of the preparations.

They had a whole day here in Adelaide and until this morning, she'd been looking forward to it. Tomorrow, they'd be back on the road, driving the last few days to Perth. She couldn't spend that whole time wondering what he was thinking and feeling. And she certainly couldn't sleep with him, knowing what she knew.

"Oh, that will be easy," she muttered as she put the bacon in the microwave. She'd never been able to hold her tongue. Usually, when she was upset by something, she couldn't stop talking about it. And Sunny had always been able to hold a grudge much longer than anyone she knew.

She dumped the eggs into a sauté pan and stirred them. It would probably be best if she just let it go. Maybe her suspicions were wrong. Maybe he was just keeping his things tidy, or maybe he expected a fire or an earthquake or—

For the next five minutes, she concentrated on the breakfast preparations. When everything was ready, she set it all on a tray and carried it into the bedroom. Logan was still in exactly the same position he'd been in when she'd left. She sank down on the bed and he stirred.

"Are you awake?" Sunny asked.

"Mmm. Is that bacon I smell?"

"I made breakfast."

He slowly rolled over to face her, then sat up, bracing himself on his outstretched arm. Raking his fingers through his tousled hair, he sent her a sleepy smile. "You made this?"

"Yeah. I thought it would be easier than going out." She pointed to the tray. "There's coffee, too. I forgot that."

She moved to get off the bed, but he caught her hand and pulled her close. "Good morning," he murmured, brushing a kiss across her lips.

"Morning," she said, her gaze meeting his.

Sunny quickly crawled off the bed. "I'll just get the coffee." She hurried to the kitchen and poured mugs for them both, adding sugar and cream to hers and just sugar to Logan's. She knew how he took his coffee. That was more than she'd ever bothered to learn about any of her other lovers. "What does that even mean?" she murmured.

As she walked back to the room, she grabbed the leather portfolio sitting on the coffee table and tucked it under her arm. The contents would provide something to talk about while Logan ate breakfast.

Sunny handed him the coffee, then took her place on the other side of the bed. "There's all sorts of information in here," she said, patting the front of the portfolio. "Things for us to do today." She opened it up and flipped through the pamphlets. She noticed a note printed on Grant Energies letterhead and pulled it out.

"'Use of the car,'" she read. "We have a car?"

"We do?"

Sunny crawled off the bed and ran back to the kitchen, then walked out the front door. She found the keypad to the left of the garage door and punched in the security code written on the paper. The garage door opened, revealing a Volkswagen convertible and a Range Rover. "Wow, Daddy, that's a nice surprise."

After she'd closed the garage door, she wandered back inside and headed for the bedroom. "We have a car," she said as she strolled back to the bed. "Two, actually. A cute little convertible and a Range Rover. So, I guess we can go anywhere we want today. My father is paying for the petrol."

"Where would you like to go?"

Sunny began to pick through their options. She felt his gaze on her and drew a deep breath, trying to maintain her composure. It took every ounce of her resolve to keep from asking him about the packed rucksack. But she'd promised herself that she'd let it go—for now.

She bit her bottom lip, fighting back a flood of emotion. How could he even think of doing that to her? She'd been deserted by every single person she'd ever trusted in her life. First her mother, then her father. Then every lover she'd ever taken. Had she made a mistake in trusting him, too?

"Wineries," she said. "Just south of here. That might be fun."

"Are you going to have any breakfast?" he asked, holding out a toasted English muffin.

She shook her head. "No, I'm not hungry right now."

"Are you feeling all right?"

Sunny glanced over her shoulder. "I'm fine."

"You're not fine. You never turn down breakfast."

"All right. Put some jam on that muffin. I'll have that." Sunny continued leafing through the pamphlets. She pulled out another. "Here. Sunset penguin tour on Granite Island. I want to do that, too."

"Penguins. That would be kind of cool."

"Good," she said, getting up from the bed. "While you're finishing your breakfast, I'm going to take a shower."

"Would you like me to join you?" he asked teasingly.

"I think I'll be fine on my own. There's more coffee in the kitchen."

With that, she walked through the bedroom into the bathroom and shut the door. Turning, she leaned back against it and closed her eyes. She could have walked right past that rucksack without even noticing it. If she had, she'd probably be happily sharing her shower with Logan, not putting doors between them.

She crossed to the sink and stared at her reflection in the mirror. Why did it even make a difference? So what if he'd been planning to abandon her? He wasn't any different than any other man she'd known in her life. Sooner or later, the affair ended and they disappeared.

It was no big deal. She just wouldn't allow herself to love him.

THEY LEFT THE VILLA after breakfast, driving the Volkswagen convertible out of the city. The morning was warm and the sky filled with fluffy white clouds. And for Logan, it was wonderful to be free of the lumbering campervan.

They stopped at a couple of wineries and enjoyed a tasting at each, but by the time they were headed to the third winery, Sunny was feeling the effects of the wine and Logan was feeling the effects of her mood.

"Where are we headed next?" Logan asked.

"I have no idea," she said, grinning. "Just keep driving until we see a sign with grapes on it. We'll figure it out then."

The views along the way were spectacular. When they weren't driving parallel along the water and beautiful white-sand beaches, they were winding through pretty little inland towns or speeding through wide meadows and low-lying hills.

He reached over and slipped his hand through the hair at Sunny's nape. "Are you sure we shouldn't just stop and get some lunch?"

"No, I'm having fun. I'm seeing the countryside. I never really got to do that when I traveled for riding events. I always thought it would be fun to just take off and spend an entire summer traveling around the country. Maybe I'll get myself a campervan and do that."

Logan chuckled. "Just avoid the wineries."

Sunny unfolded the map she'd brought along and pointed to a sign up ahead. "Turn right at this next crossroads. There's another winery about a kilometer down the road."

Logan did as she asked, turning his attention back to the

drive. Sunny hadn't been herself since they'd gotten up that morning. She was usually so full of energy that he had to constantly engage her in witty conversation or mind-numbing sex. But she'd been lost in her own thoughts and he couldn't help but wonder what was going on in her head.

Maybe another glass of wine would finally loosen her up a little bit. He'd stopped drinking after the first two samples, but she'd been enthusiastic about anything they offered.

They drove up a winding road shaded with trees, and stopped at a low stone building. The carved sign across the front was decorated with grapevines. Carney Creek Winery.

Logan parked the car and got out, jogging around to open Sunny's door. But she'd already done that for herself. She stumbled slightly and he grabbed her hand as they walked to the front entrance, but before he opened it, Logan pulled them to a stop.

"Wait," he murmured.

"What?"

"Is everything all right?"

She gave him an impatient look. "Why do you keep asking me that?"

"Because you're acting...odd. You've been quiet. You've been drinking wine like you don't want to stop. Like maybe you're angry at me for something."

"Can we just go?"

Logan grabbed the heavy wooden door and pulled it open. They walked into a spacious room with timbered beams and stained-glass windows. A few other couples were wandering around the displays and chatting softly as relaxing music filled the interior.

The next tour was due to start in a half hour, but they were shown into the tasting room, where a young woman stood behind a counter, pouring wine into large crystal goblets.

They started out with white wines, and Sunny chatted with the young woman, the enologist, and listened to her describe the qualities of each sample. Logan sat next to her for a time then decided to leave her to her mood.

He walked back out to the shop and found a table, then flipped through a magazine about wine. There were things he'd never understand about women. If she was angry at him, why not just tell him? Why torture him for an entire morning?

Sunny had always been so open and honest with him and, suddenly, she wasn't interested in talking. His questions were answered with a single word or with a shrug. There was a storm brewing and he could feel it. He just wasn't sure when it would strike or why he was the target.

After the tasting, Sunny bought several bottles of wine and then found him outside. "I bought lunch," she said with a giggle. "I think we need to go to one more winery. I'm becoming an expert on wine."

"You're also a little drunk," he said.

"We're on holiday. I'm allowed to have fun, aren't I?"

Her tone was defensive, as if she was looking for an argument. But Logan wasn't going to rise to the bait. Sunny wasn't one to keep her feelings to herself. Given time, she'd say what was on her mind. He loved that they were so honest with each other. But maybe that time was over. Once they starting having expectations, there was much more opportunity for hurt feelings. Why couldn't things remain simple, he mused. The last thing he wanted to do was fight with her.

They walked back to the car park and Sunny climbed in the car and pulled out the map. When Logan got behind the wheel, he paused before reaching for the key in the ignition. "Do you want to tell me what's wrong or do you need a little more wine before that happens? We can just do it here in the car park."

"You want to do it here?" she said with a laugh.

"I want to discuss why you're cheesed off. And don't tell me that it's nothing. I've been living with you for the past five days. I know when something is bothering you."

"All right," she said, throwing her arms out and nearly hitting him in the face. "Let's just do that. And let's start with your rucksack."

"My rucksack?"

"Yes. I found it this morning, completely packed with everything you own, sitting on the floor near the sofa. So, either you were preparing for some type of natural disaster or you were going to leave last night. And," she added, her finger punching at his chest, "I found you out in the campervan. Care to explain?"

Logan winced. He hadn't realized until that morning that he'd left the rucksack where he had. He'd just assumed she hadn't noticed. "I was going to leave, but I changed my mind."

"Why? Why would you do that to me? I thought we were friends." She shoved the car door open and started off down the driveway, a bottle of wine still clutched in her hand.

"Sunny, stop." He went after her, but she turned and threw the bottle at him. Logan dodged it and it fell into the long grass at the side of the road.

"I thought I could trust you. Why would you do that?"

"I was... I was scared. That if we stayed together any longer I'd fall in love with you."

She opened her mouth to shout at him then snapped it shut. Wiping a tear from her cheek, Sunny shook her head. "Well, what's so bad about that? Am I unlovable?" Tears filled her eyes. "That's why no one wants to stick around. Everyone leaves me. Except my horses. And they only stay because they're locked in the stables at night. They'd probably run away, too."

With a groan, she sat down in the middle of the road, burying her face in her hands. Logan ran over to her and grabbed her arms, pulling her to her feet. "Stop it, now," he said. "There's no reason to cry."

"Don't tell me what to do. I hate when people tell me what to do."

All that wine on an empty stomach was making Sunny

slightly irrational, but Logan was determined to smooth things over. "I'm sorry. I was stupid."

"You're a coward."

"Yes," Logan said, ready to agree with anything she said. "I am."

She looked up at him. "I'm not going to fall in love with you. Don't you know that? I—I just can't let that happen." Tipping her chin up, she met his gaze. "We're just friends. Friends with benefits. That's all."

"That sounds just grand to me," Logan said. He motioned to her. "Come on. If we're going to go see the damn penguins, we need to leave now."

"The penguin tour is at dusk," Sunny pointed out.

"By dusk, you'll probably be sound asleep. If we can't see the penguins this afternoon, we won't be seeing the penguins."

Logan walked back to the car and Sunny reluctantly followed. Well, at least he got a chance to see a side of Sunny that wasn't normally visible. He couldn't blame her for acting like a brat. He knew she had issues with her parents abandoning her and what had he almost done? The same thing.

He held the car door open for her and she got inside, a dark expression on her face. When he was settled in the driver's seat, he turned to her. "I'm sorry. I never, ever meant to hurt you. I just thought it would be easier if we didn't let it go on too long. I thought we might develop feelings that complicated things. I was wrong. Now that I know exactly how you feel, I think we'll be all right."

Sunny glanced over at him. Her defiant expression dissolved and she leaned over and pressed her face into his shoulder. Logan slipped his arm around her and pulled her close. "I'm sorry," she murmured. "Sometimes I can be a real bitch."

"No," he said. "You aren't. It was all my fault."

"Maybe we could see the penguins another time. I think I'd really like to go back to the villa and spend the day sleeping on the beach."

"I think that would be a wonderful idea. Maybe we could drink that other bottle of wine you bought?"

She drew back then laughed. "If I wasn't getting a bloody headache, I might agree."

Logan started the car and they drove away from the winery. They'd had their first major argument and, looking back, it hadn't gone too badly.

"The penguins can wait," she murmured. "We'll see them another time. We could make a holiday of it, maybe next summer."

Next summer, Logan mused. So there was going to be a next summer between them? And he'd spent so much time worrying about next week.

6

SUNNY STRETCHED OUT in the wide chaise, stifling a yawn. They'd come back to the villa to spend the afternoon on the beach. The weather was warm and the skies were clear and after so much wine, Sunny was relaxed and sleepy.

She shaded her eyes and watched as Logan stood knee-deep in the water. Since her temper tantrum earlier that morning, he'd been quiet, his thoughts occupied with matters that he wasn't interested in sharing with her.

It didn't surprise her how the argument started. She'd been simmering since early that morning and the wine just made it easier to say what she was thinking. But after her fears and insecurities had been laid bare, Sunny felt a bit guilty. After all, she and Logan had known each other less than a week. It wasn't fair to have any expectations this early on, was it?

And yet, she felt closer to Logan than she had to any other man she'd known. He was solid and honest, and he didn't get lost in his own ego. And even though she insisted he was just a friend, Sunny knew that wasn't true. She also knew that hiding her true feelings was the only way to keep him around. And that was her primary goal—to keep Logan in her life until he realized she was more important to him than any other person in his life.

It wasn't difficult to imagine what stood between them. They existed in totally different worlds. Hers was comfortable and his was a constant struggle. But she wasn't going to apologize for something she had no control over. Her father's money didn't define her.

She hadn't made her father wealthy, he did that on his own. And it wasn't her money. She was almost as poor as a church mouse. Her total wealth amounted to the credit limit on her bank card, and she wasn't even sure what that was.

Why couldn't they just be two people who shared an overwhelming passion for each other? Why did they have to live in the real world, where wealth seemed so important?

Logan ran back across the beach and plopped down next to her on the chaise. He shook his wet head, cold droplets falling over her warm skin. Sunny screamed and tried to scoot out of the way, but he grabbed her and pulled her back. His lips met hers in a long, lazy kiss.

"I think that we should do this every year," she murmured, running her fingers through his hair.

"What?" Logan said. "Kiss on the beach?"

"Travel. Go somewhere interesting. You have to admit, we make a good pair. We've only had one fight in five days and that was due to your stupidity and my overconsumption of wine."

"That's true," he admitted.

"And we don't have to rent separate rooms, so that saves money."

"Also true."

"So, I thought I could plan the trip and you'll come with me. For a week or two. It will be fun. Sex and travel. Doesn't that sound nice? And you could get away for a week or two, couldn't you?"

"I could," he said. "Where would you want to go?"

"Fiji. I've always wanted to go to Fiji. New Zealand. Bali. Iceland. There are so many interesting places. My mother lives in Paris. Paris is meant for lovers. Where would you like to go?"

"I've always wanted to go to Ireland," he said.

"Right. Quinn. That's Irish."

He nodded. "I probably have some relatives there, although I don't know for sure."

"That's where we'll go first then," she said. "It's a date."

"We'll see," he murmured.

"But, you have to say yes. I don't want to go with anyone else."

He slipped his arms around her waist and pulled her close. "Sunny, I don't know what I'll be doing next month, never mind two or three months from now. I don't make plans more than a week or two in advance."

"So what then? How am I supposed to think about you in the future?"

He stared at her for a long moment. "I don't know. I don't know what you want or what you expect. I just know that I can't offer you what you need."

"You don't have any idea what I need," Sunny said, her anger bubbling up inside her. God, there were times when she just wanted to shake him. He was so careful, so predictable. Why couldn't he just loosen up a little and live?

"Let's not argue," he said.

"No, let's. We've been telling each other the truth for the past five days, why stop now?"

He glanced around, as if worried that someone might overhear. "I'm not going to argue with you here. I don't even know what this is about."

"Don't just dismiss me," she said.

"Sunny, I'm not dismissing you. You want to talk about holidays, fine. Go ahead, I'm listening."

"Now you're pacifying me."

"Jaysus, I'm glad you know what I'm doing, because I sure don't."

"Well, let me give you some time to figure it out," she muttered, getting to her feet.

"Sunny, you know this is the wine talking."

"No, I'm fine. I just need some space." Sunny threw her towel around her neck and walked back to the villa. She shouldn't be surprised. They couldn't possibly agree on everything. But she thought at least he'd be interested in making some plans for the future.

She knew there wasn't much chance they'd have a real relationship. He lived in the outback and she was a city girl. And there was the money thing that always seemed to get in the way. But she'd be satisfied with an occasional getaway in some exotic location. What could be more fun?

Logan Quinn had no imagination. After their trip was over, he'd drop her at home and just drive away. How long would it take him to forget her? A month, maybe two? Well, she never had any intention of remembering him anyway.

She cursed softly, trudging through the sand. But as she climbed the steps to the villa, she looked up to find a figure standing in the open doorway. Her breath caught in her throat and she froze for a moment.

Then, gathering her wits, she continued up the stairs to face her father, Simon Grant. "Hello, Daddy," she said, stopping in front of him.

"Hello, Lucinda," her father murmured.

He was dressed in a suit and tie, his shirt still impeccably pressed even at this late hour of the day. He never really looked human to her when he was in a business suit. She found him much more pliable when he was dressed for riding.

Sunny cleared her throat. "Lucinda? Is that how it's going to be? You only call me Lucinda when you're angry with me. What have I done wrong now?"

"Do you even have to ask?"

"I'm sure you can't wait to tell me."

"You take off with some…some stranger and you don't think you've done anything wrong? No one had any idea where you were or who you were with."

"I called Lily. She knew. I didn't think you cared. I haven't seen you in over a month."

He cursed softly. "Don't be ridiculous."

"Don't call me ridiculous," Sunny said. She wasn't going to let her father bait her into an argument. It always happened this way. He'd goad her into a fight and then he'd spend the following half hour making her feel like an ungrateful child. She drew a deep breath. "Why don't you come inside? I'll get you something to drink."

She walked past him and, to her relief, he followed her inside. Tossing her towel onto the granite countertop, she headed to the refrigerator. "We have beer, orange juice."

"A vodka martini," he said.

"I'm not sure if we—"

"The vodka is in the cabinet above the sink. There should be—" He sighed. "Never mind, I'll make it."

Her father joined her in the kitchen and Sunny pulled out a stool at the breakfast bar and sat down, cupping her chin in her hand. "I didn't realize you had a place here in Adelaide, too, until your assistant offered to let us stay here."

"Us?"

"His name is Logan. Logan Quinn. He's a horse breeder and he has a horse I want."

"And that's why you've decided to run away with him?" Her father tossed some ice in a glass and filled it full of vodka, then threw in a couple of olives.

"I didn't run away. I just needed to...get away. I needed out of that house and he was going somewhere, so I decided to hitch a ride. I figured I could convince him to sell the horse."

"What do you need another horse for? You're not riding the one you have." He took a sip of his vodka and watched her over the rim of his glass.

"Tally is a beautiful horse. And I'd like to train her. Ed has seen her. He agrees." In truth, she wasn't sure that Ed did agree, but he'd be stupid not to.

"That's all this is, then? Some crazy scheme to get a horse you want?"

"Yes," she lied. But as soon as she answered, Sunny felt the guilt set in. She wasn't just lying to her father, she was betraying herself—and Logan. There was more to this than just Tally. So much more. But how was she supposed to explain that to her father?

"Sunny? Is everything all right?"

She spun around on the stool and saw Logan standing in the middle of the room. He slowly approached, his expression curious but guarded.

Sunny drew a deep breath. "Logan Quinn, this is my father, Simon Grant. Daddy, this is Logan."

Logan quickly stepped forward and held out his hand. "Sir, it's a pleasure to meet you."

Reluctantly, her father returned the gesture. "You're the man with the horse? How much is it going to take?"

"Take?" Logan frowned. "Oh, you mean to buy her? She's not for sale. Actually, she's already been sold."

Her father scowled, turning back to Sunny. "The horse is not for sale. You've been running around the countryside with this guy and he has no intention of selling you his horse." He slammed the glass down on the countertop, causing Sunny to jump. "Get your things. We're leaving."

"I'm not," Sunny said sharply.

"Do not try my patience. I can cut you off in a heartbeat."

"Do it," Sunny said. "Go ahead. I don't care. I'll take Padma and I'll leave."

"Padma doesn't belong to you," he said.

"You gave her to me for my twenty-first birthday, don't you remember?"

He strode to the door. "Maybe you need time to think about what you're giving up. I'll expect you in my office first thing in the morning. If you don't show up, you know what will happen."

"Oh, Daddy, please. You threaten me all the time with that. It's getting old."

He turned to Logan. "If you think you're going to benefit from my bank account, you might as well move on to your next target. Sunny doesn't get anything unless it comes through me. I won't have her associating with the likes of you."

With that, her father strode to the door. He slammed it shut behind him, leaving the interior of the villa silent and Sunny stunned. "I—I'm so sorry. He should never have said that. He doesn't know you and he—"

"He's right," Logan said. Crossing the kitchen, he opened the fridge and grabbed a beer, then twisted off the cap. "He's right."

"No, he isn't. He doesn't know anything about you."

"I'm sure he took one look at the campervan and could see everything he needed to know." He shrugged. "It's all right. I understand completely. Hell, if I were him, I wouldn't want my daughter hanging around with a guy like me, either."

"Don't say that," Sunny murmured.

Logan took a long drink of his beer. "It's the truth."

With that, he silently strode back through the villa and out the door to the beach. Sunny watched him leave, knowing that her father's objections were not going to go down well with a man like Logan. If he was anything, he was proud.

She sat down on the stool and grabbed her father's glass of vodka, taking a swallow. "Well, if I'm going to be disowned, I'm going to have to make some plans."

LOGAN STOOD IN KNEE-DEEP water, staring out at the horizon. Every now and then he could spot dolphins in the gulf, breaking the surface. He felt as if he'd been punched in the stomach and he couldn't catch his breath.

He shouldn't have expected a warm reception from Sunny's father, but he certainly didn't anticipate such a hostile reaction. The fact that he assumed Logan was only after her money was a bit hard to reconcile, but it was probably a logical conclusion.

He heard the water splashing behind him and a moment later, Sunny's hand slipped into his. They stood silently for a long time. Logan saw a pair of dolphins and pointed. "See them?"

"What?"

"Dolphins. Just out there. To the right of that big boat."

Sunny held her hand over her eyes and then smiled. "I see them. They look like they're having fun." She laughed softly. "They probably don't have an awful dolphin father telling them what to do every moment of every day."

"He's not awful, Sunny. He's just trying to protect you."

"From what? From you?"

"Yeah. Me and a million other men who might have ulterior motives."

"I'm twenty-six years old," Sunny said. "When do I get to make decisions for myself?"

"I reckon that's up to you," he replied.

"And what if I decided I didn't want to obey my father? What if I decided I didn't want to go home?"

He turned to her, slipping his arms around her waist. "What are you saying?"

"I don't have anywhere to go," she said. "If I left, would you take me in?"

Logan gasped. "What?"

"You heard me. Can I stay with you? Just until I figure out what I want to do with my life. I can help you work the ranch. You know I'm good with horses."

"Sunny, this is not a decision you make lightly. This is your family. What about your riding? I thought you were going to start that again."

"Well, I figured we could steal Padma on our way back through and take her to your ranch. The two of us could live there."

"You're going to steal a horse from your father?"

Sunny sighed in frustration. "She's my horse. He gave her to me for my twenty-first birthday. There was a huge party. Everyone was there. I have witnesses."

"All right. Let's say we get your horse and we take it to my ranch. How are you going to afford to pay for the travel and the entry fees and everything else that comes with competing on a world-class level?" He fixed his gaze on hers as he waited for her answer. But Logan could tell that there wouldn't be one coming. "You can't ride without your father's help, Sunny. So it seems that you have no choice in the matter."

She spun away from him and trudged through the water, cursing angrily. Logan knew the feeling, being trapped in a life she couldn't seem to escape. But he certainly wasn't going to encourage her any further. He'd been running away from poverty and uncertainty. She was running away from a comfortable life, a life she wouldn't find with him.

"What do you want, Sunny?"

She turned to face him. "I just want to be happy. I want to wake up in the morning and know that I'm going to spend the day doing something I love."

"Isn't that riding?"

Their gazes met and locked for a long moment, then she shook her head and started down the beach, dragging her feet through the shallow water. Logan watched her retreat and wondered if he ought to go after her.

The thought of her living with him at the ranch was like a dream come true. Every day, waking up beside her. Every night, making love until they fell asleep from exhaustion. Having her with him would make his life complete. But it would only fracture hers. And he couldn't do that to her.

Maybe it was best to let her sort this all out on her own. She knew what she needed to do. She was just angry with her father and looking for a way to punish him.

Logan walked back to the villa and climbed the steps to the terrace. The doors were thrown open, the salty evening breeze thick in the air. He glanced around the interior, taking in the luxurious surroundings. This was the life, Logan mused. Comfortable, relaxed, not a care in the world. Why would anyone give it up voluntarily?

Maybe he should take the easy way out and just leave. It would make Sunny's decision much easier. And they had a long stretch of road ahead of them—the desolate Eyre Highway, a seemingly endless road that connected Southern Australia and Western Australia.

But Logan was too selfish. He wanted her company for this final part of the trip. He needed her there when he finally had to give up Tally to her new owner. He wasn't willing to relinquish a single day of their time together.

He grabbed a beer from the fridge and walked back out on the terrace. The sun was beginning to sink toward the horizon, and he wondered how long she'd be. Logan tried to still the impulse to go find her. He imagined all sorts of trouble she might find along the beach. But his instinct to protect her was tempered with the knowledge that sometimes Sunny just needed to be alone.

He walked back inside the villa and ran his hands through his damp hair. A shower would keep his mind off things, at least until she got back home. He took another sip of his beer and walked into the bedroom, kicking off his shorts along the way.

The shower was just as luxurious as the rest of the villa, lined with pale green glass tile. It was large enough for two, with double showerheads hanging from the ceiling. Logan adjusted the water temperature and stepped inside, his beer still clutched in his hand.

The rush of warm water felt good on his salt-caked skin. Running his hand through his hair, Logan turned his face up to the spray. Unlike the shower at his ranch, this one didn't run out of hot water after five minutes

When he felt arms slip around his waist, he realized that he'd been indulging in the luxury far longer than normal. She pressed her lips to the center of his back, and he slowly turned to face her, capturing her lips in a deep, delicious kiss.

No matter what was said between them, however harsh it might be, they could always come back to this—this sweet and powerful attraction. A kiss, a touch, a simple sigh was all it took to communicate more than an entire conversation.

Logan set the beer on the marble bench in the shower, then smoothed his hands over her naked body. He'd become so familiar with every curve, every perfect feature. There wasn't a spot on her body that his lips hadn't grazed or his fingers hadn't explored. She'd taken her own time learning his body, as well.

Now, when she wrapped her fingers around his hard shaft, Logan knew her touch would set every nerve in his body on fire. She sensed when to caress softly and slowly and when to be more aggressive. And when he reached between her legs and ran his fingers along her damp slit, he knew exactly what would make her writhe and gasp.

There would come a time, in the near future, when he wouldn't have her close, when her kisses and her touch would only be a memory. As she brought him closer to completion, Logan tried to enjoy every sensation, knowing he'd want to recall it all later.

"I love the way you touch me," he whispered, the warm water still falling down over them.

Logan slipped a finger inside her and Sunny moaned as he increased the pressure. Her forehead was pressed against his chest, her hair hiding her face. But as she came closer, she looked up at him, their gazes meeting through the rush of the shower.

She whispered his name once and then dissolved into a series of powerful spasms, her body crumpling against his. Watching her surrender was all he needed to tumble over the edge, and he followed her, her hand growing slick with his seed.

When it was over, Logan pressed her back against the wall of the shower and kissed her, his tongue teasing at her lips, nipping and sucking. "I have to get a shower like this," Logan said. "It never runs out of hot water."

"Oh, I thought it was the naked girl in the shower that you liked."

"Well, I can find one of those anywhere," Logan teased.

She tightened her grip on his shaft. "Really."

"No," he said in a high-pitched voice.

"Good. Because you may find me in your shower occasionally."

"I can live with that," Logan murmured, kissing her again.

So she hadn't changed her mind about moving in with him. He wanted to talk about her plans, to understand why she'd make such a rash decision. They hadn't made any kind of commitment to each other. They'd talked about the future only in very vague terms. But it seemed, for now, that they actually had a future together.

LOGAN PULLED THE campervan up in front of the Adelaide headquarters for Grant Energies. It was still early in the morning but the street parking had all been taken. Sunny knew her father was inside, probably waiting impatiently for a daughter he never seemed to have time for in the first place. "I'll find a spot," Logan said. "Maybe you better go in. You don't want to keep your father waiting."

Sunny turned to Logan, trying to calm her nerves. "Promise you'll wait for me," she said, ignoring a flutter in her stomach.

"I will. I'm not going anywhere."

"Ten minutes. That's all it will take. I just want to explain to him what I'm doing and try to smooth things out."

Logan nodded. "And if you don't come out?"

"I'll be back," she said. "I promise. Ten minutes. Don't leave." She leaned over and gave him a quick kiss, pressing her palm to his cheek. "Wish me luck."

"Luck," he said.

Sunny forced a smile. "All right. This is going to go well."

She reached for the door, then thought better of it and gave him another kiss, this one longer and more intimate. The contact seemed to give her strength. A moment later, she hopped out of the passenger door and hurried to the entrance of the building. She glanced back over her shoulder and gave Logan a wave, then walked inside.

She stopped at the security desk and announced herself, but the guard recognized her from two nights before. As she strode through the spacious lobby, Sunny carefully went through all she planned to say.

The receptionist was waiting behind the desk as she had been that first day, and Sunny wondered whether she ever left—or if she ever stopped smiling.

"Good morning, Miss Grant. Your father is waiting for you in his office. Jennifer is coming up to take you there."

Sunny sat down in one of the chairs, twisting her fingers together in an attempt to still her nerves. A minute ticked by and then another before Jennifer appeared in the lobby. Though she didn't know much about her father's business, it was clear that he enjoyed surrounding himself with attractive employees. His mistress had started off her "career" as his assistant.

"Follow me, Miss Grant. Can I get you anything to drink? Coffee, juice?"

"A large bottle of vodka would be good," Sunny murmured.

"I'm sorry?"

"Never mind. Just a little gallows humor." Sunny pasted a smile on her face. "Thank you for making the arrangements for the villa. I appreciate everything you did."

"Not a problem," she said. "We were happy to host you." Reaching for the knob on a huge wooden door, she opened it and then stepped aside. "It was a pleasure to finally meet you, Miss Grant."

Sunny slowly walked into the office. Her father was sitting at a sleek, modern desk, his gaze fixed on his laptop computer. "Sit," he said.

"I'll stand. I'm not staying long."

Simon Grant glanced up. "I've called a driver. He'll take you to the airport." Her father retrieved an envelope from his pocket and pushed it across his desk. "There's a ticket inside. And some spending money. I'm glad you've seen the error of your ways."

Sunny approached his desk. "What error, Daddy? I had the wonderful luck to find a kind and understanding man. He hasn't had a lot of breaks in his life, but he's hardworking and honest. And I decided I wanted to spend more time with him. And now, I think I'm falling in love with him. I can't, for the life of me, see how that could possibly be an error."

"What do you even know about this man?"

"I know enough. When you decided to cut me off, he told me I could stay with him. He cares about me, without any conditions or expectations." She drew a ragged breath. "We make each other happy."

"You can be so naive, Sunny," her father said, shaking his head.

"I'm not naive, Daddy. I'm optimistic. You taught me to dream big and that's what I'm doing. I believe that I can find a man who'll make me happy for the rest of my life. And I believe we could be deliriously happy. Do you know how amazing that feels? I've watched you and Mom tear each other apart, and yet, I still believe in love. Somewhere, deep inside my heart, that hope didn't really die."

"You're going home," he ordered.

"I'm not. I'm going with Logan. And after that, we're going to drive back to the farm and we're going to pick up my things and Padma and I'm going to live with him."

"You're just going to give it all up? I don't think you will." He opened a drawer in his desk and pulled out a leather-bound book. When he opened it, Sunny knew what was coming next. *Money.* Whenever her father couldn't bend her into submission, he always dangled money in front of her. Well, this time it wasn't going to work.

"How much?" he asked.

"You can't buy me off."

"You wanted that horse. The one he's selling. How much will it take to get it?"

Sunny stifled a gasp. Was he really offering her a chance to buy Tally? Emotion welled up inside her at the thought that she might be able to save Tally for Logan, to save the filly for both of them.

It seemed as if their entire relationship was tied up around Tally, and the moment they let her go, what they shared together might suddenly dissolve.

"Well? What will it take?"

"I—I don't know." Sunny held her breath. If she took the money, she'd have the horse. But would she be expected to give up Logan in return? Or was there a way to have them both? "I'd have to talk to the owner." She drew a deep breath. "Would she be mine then?"

"As long as you give up this Logan person and rededicate yourself to your riding, you can do whatever you want with the horse." Her father signed the check and handed it to her. "It's blank. Fill in whatever you need. I'll expect you back home by the end of the week and ready to focus. If I don't find you there, I'll stop payment on the check or I'll sell the horse. Do we have an understanding?"

"We do," she murmured. Sunny met his gaze. "Are you happy now?"

"You need to get your life back on track, Sunny. World championships are in two years and Rio is in four. Equestrians can ride for years. You still have a chance to make your dream come true."

"I do," she said. It wasn't a lie. The only problem was, the dream her father spoke of wasn't her dream anymore. At least, not the one that occupied all her thoughts and desires. "Is there anything else?"

He tapped his finger to his temple. "Back on track," he said. "Think like a winner."

"Back on track," she replied.

Sunny glanced over at the clock, then realized she'd been in the office nearly ten minutes. Logan would be waiting downstairs, wondering if she was ever coming back. "I have to go. I'll see you at home."

"We'll go riding," he offered.

Sunny nodded. "Goodbye, Daddy. And thank you. For the money. You won't be disappointed." She walked calmly out the door, tucking the check into her jeans pocket. It took forever to get back to the lobby, weaving through a maze of cubicles and hallways. When she finally reached the receptionist, she was running.

"I'm late," Sunny called, racing out of the office. She was breathless by the time she got to the street and gazed around, looking frantically for the campervan.

"Logan?" She ran up the block, but there was no sight of him. She should have known he'd leave. He wasn't willing to stand between her and her father and he'd taken the only way out. Sunny stopped and ran her fingers through her hair, tears pushing at the corners of her eyes.

It felt like every bit of energy had just been sapped from her body. Her knees were weak and all she wanted to do was sit down on the sidewalk and have a good cry.

"Sunny?"

The sound of his voice startled her and she spun around to see him walking toward her. With a tiny cry, she ran to him and threw herself into his arms. "I thought you'd gone."

"I couldn't find a place to park. The campervan takes two spots. The last time we were here it was after work hours."

He drew back to look down into her face. "Why are you crying?" With his thumb, he wiped away a tear from her cheek. "I'm not going anywhere."

"Let's go get our horse and get on the road." She drew a

ragged breath. "I'm done with this city. We seem to have a better time of it when we're headed somewhere."

When they finally reached the campervan, parked a few blocks away, Logan opened the passenger door for her and helped her inside. "Your carriage awaits," he teased.

As she settled into her seat, Sunny couldn't help but feel a sense of optimism. She had the money to buy back Logan's horse. For now, that was enough. And once Tally was hers, the rest of it would sort itself out.

"Where are we headed today?" Sunny asked as Logan got behind the wheel.

"I don't know. Let's just drive west and see where the road takes us."

Sunny smiled to herself. After a few rocky moments, things were back to normal now. She and Logan were together in a place that had always been comfortable for them both. All was right with the world.

7

THE LAST THIRD of the trip was the most difficult, spent crossing the Nullarbor Plain, a swath of land that was nothing more than a giant slab of limestone, unable to support any vegetation beyond scrub brush. It was the epitome of Australian outback, desolate and remote.

At times, looking out to the horizon, it seemed as if they were on another planet. There were no houses, no towns, nothing but the straight strip of sealed road in front of them, a thousand kilometers long.

Every two or three hundred kilometers, they'd come upon a roadhouse where they could buy food and get petrol and spend the night if they chose. But Logan had wanted to put that part of the trip behind them as quickly as possible so they did the crossing in two very long days of driving, spending their only night on the border between the two states in Eucla.

Since the road was so straight and virtually void of traffic, Sunny finally got her chance to drive the campervan. Though Logan was reluctant to relinquish control to her, she turned out to be a very good driver, patient while she learned and very careful once she felt comfortable.

After pulling into the Eucla caravan park at almost midnight, they took Tally for a short ride and then got her fed and bedded down for the night. They were back on the road again early the next morning, this time hugging the coast and spending the night near Albany.

It was their last night with Tally, and Logan had decided that the final four-hour drive to Perth could wait until the afternoon. He was determined to spend the morning riding and taking his last chance to say goodbye to his favorite filly.

They found a caravan park near a small beach and left the campervan and trailer, leading Tally to the long stretch of white sand. She seemed to sense that something was wrong and, as they walked, continued to nudge at Logan's shoulder.

"I think she knows," Sunny said, looking up at him.

He held her hand, clasped in his, and gave it a squeeze. "I think she does, too," he said. "But I have to believe she'll be fine."

"Of course she will," Sunny said.

"I hope they'll appreciate what they have. I mean, she was the most beautiful horse in my stable. I always liked walking in every morning and seeing her head peeking over the stall door, looking for her morning biscuit."

"And she'll be the most beautiful horse in their stable."

When they reached the beach, Logan gave Sunny a knee up and then jumped up behind her, settling Sunny against him. They rode without a saddle, the two of them as comfortable riding together as they were riding alone.

After two long days on the road, Tally was full of energy and ready to run. Logan urged her into a gallop and they ran along the edge of the surf, the horse's hooves sending spray up all around them.

They rode until they were both exhausted, then walked along the beach as Tally cooled down. There was nothing to say, and Logan was grateful that Sunny hadn't tried to brighten his mood. In truth, she seemed almost as sad as he was.

He always thought he might take the option of selling the horse to Sunny. It was a last-minute escape clause in case he couldn't go through with the sale. But now that she'd cut off ties with her father, that was impossible. The sale would go as originally planned.

"So, are we ready to turn around and go home?" Sunny asked.

Logan nodded. "Yeah. I think we can get back a lot faster. We can put in longer days, maybe just pull off the road when we need sleep. If I can keep this trip to two weeks, it would probably be a good idea."

"We'll have to stop and get Padma," Sunny said. "And pick up my things."

"Sunny, are you sure you want to do this? Maybe you should go home and try to smooth things over with your dad. We'll just keep to our plan of taking a holiday every now and then."

She stopped walking and turned to face him. "Don't you want me to live with you?"

"Of course I do. That's not the point. The point is, are you going to want to live with me? I don't have anywhere for you to train. And it takes hours to get to the closest equestrian park. I don't even know where the closest one is."

"We can build some fences. It's not that difficult."

"Sunny, come on. I just want you to understand what you'd be giving up. If you're really serious about riding at Worlds in a couple years, you're not going to get there living on my ranch."

She stared at him for a long moment, then sighed softly. "I know." Sunny pushed up on her toes and kissed his cheek. "But thank you for offering to take me in. If I ever feel like running away, I might show up on your doorstep."

"I could handle that," he said.

"We will see each other after this is over," she said. "I'm not even sure I'm going to be able to sleep all alone again. I've gotten used to having you there."

Logan chuckled, wrapping his arm around her shoulders and pulling her close. "You have managed to wiggle your way into my life. I don't think there's any getting rid of you now."

"Absolutely not," she said.

He handed her the reins. "Here. Take her for one last ride. I want to watch you."

"Should I take off all my clothes like Lady Godiva?" Sunny asked, looking up and down the beach. "We're all alone here."

"Only if you're determined to make me cry," Logan teased. He held his linked hands out and gave her a boost and Sunny gathered the reins in her fingers.

"Are you sure you don't want to come along?" she asked.

"No, I just want to look at my two favorite girls for a little bit longer."

Sunny clucked her tongue as she gave the horse a gentle nudge with her heels. Logan stepped back and sat down in the sand, resting his arms across his knees.

He wished he'd had a camera with him so he could keep a memory of this moment in time. He reached into his pocket and looked at his mobile phone, then realized that he did have a camera.

He pointed it at Sunny and Tally and snapped a picture, then squinted to see it on the phone's display. After he saved it, Logan noticed that he'd had a call from Billy at the ranch. Logan had promised that he was going to contact him when he got to Perth, but there was obviously something Billy needed and wasn't willing to wait.

Logan punched in the number for the ranch, then listened as the phone rang six times before the voice mail kicked in. "Hey, Billy. I noticed that you called. I'm in mobile range right now, so ring me back. I hope everything is all right. I just got to Perth and will be dropping Tally off this afternoon. All right, then. Get back to me when you can."

With a frown, he hung up and stared at his mobile, wondering what Billy wanted. He'd worked for Logan for three years and had always been trustworthy and responsible. Logan also had a couple of local boys who were working the place in return for using a couple of horses for amateur camp drafting competitions.

Sunny approached him, Tally at a brisk walk. "Hey, I thought you were going to watch me. You're playing with your mobile."

Logan held it up and snapped another photo of her. "That was a nice one," he said.

"Take one of us together," she said.

Logan got to his feet and Sunny bent over Tally's neck. He held out his arm and snapped the picture, then showed it to her. "I like that one," she said. "You'll have to send me that so I have a copy."

"I will," he said.

"What is it? You look worried."

"No. Billy called and I guess I must have turned off my phone, because I didn't hear him ring. He wouldn't call unless there was some type of emergency."

"Did you ring him back?"

Logan nodded. "Yeah. He didn't answer. I'm thinking I should try one of the other boys, but they only come by after they're done with school. They might not know what's going on."

He frowned. "He's got a mobile. Maybe I should text him. I'll just tell him to call me." Logan typed in a quick text then waited, hoping that he'd ring right back. But as they stood there, staring at the phone, he realized, even if there was an emergency, he was at least five days away from being able to help.

"Maybe we should get going," he said. "If there's something wrong, I'm going to have to head back right away."

"All right," she said. "But hop up on Tally. I want to take a photo of you."

Logan did as she asked and Sunny stood back and snapped the picture. "There," she murmured. "That's perfect."

She turned the phone to him and Logan nodded. "That is nice. I think I might have to frame that one and put it up in my stable."

"I'll frame it for you," Sunny said. "And the one of us together. It will be a good memory of our trip."

"I don't think I'm going to be forgetting this trip anytime soon."

Sunny grinned as he slipped off Tally's back and drew her into a slow heated kiss. "Good. I don't want you to forget a single moment."

THOUGH SUNNY HAD BEEN happy to delay the inevitable, she knew they were due to deliver the filly to the equine vet by three that afternoon. The new owner would be waiting to pick her up and the sale would be finalized.

Since her fight with her father, she'd stopped trying to convince Logan that she'd be a better owner. The closer they got to Perth, the gloomier his mood seemed to become. So she'd dropped the subject and, instead, Sunny had decided to bide her time, the blank check from her father tucked securely in her pocket. If Logan was so determined to go through with the sale, then she'd have to work around him.

Years of getting her way with her father had trained her to look for every available option, and she still had plenty. In the worst case, her blank check would be turned down. Then she'd go home, have Ed call and make another offer for Tally and keep negotiating until they finally said yes. Tally wasn't going anywhere, and Sunny had enough money to keep tempting them with better offers.

They found the equine vet without any trouble. His practice was located about thirty kilometers outside of Perth, not far off the coast highway.

Logan slowed to pull into the car park. "I feel like I should just keep driving. Make a big circle around Oz and end up back at home."

"We could do that," she said. "Just keep going, I won't talk you out of it."

Logan shook his head. "Nope. I breed horses. And I sell horses. I'm all right with that."

They followed a driveway around to the back of the equine clinic and found a small barn with a white-fenced paddock attached to it. Logan pulled the campervan to a stop and turned off the ignition, then reached down for the envelope that contained the horse's medical information and breeding papers.

"Do you want me to come with you?" she asked.

He opened his mouth to answer, then sighed softly and closed it. His hand rested on the steering wheel, and Sunny watched as his fingers clenched and unclenched. "You take her in," Logan finally said.

"Me?"

He nodded. "I can't do it. Once the vet has looked her over, you'll get the check and then we'll be on our way. I don't need to be there."

"Are you sure?" she asked.

He drew another deep breath. "I've never been surer of anything in my life. I want my last memory of Tally to be on that beach, watching the two of you ride through the surf. I'd be happy with that."

Sunny leaned over and gently kissed him. "You'll be all right. I promise."

He gave her a weak smile. "I know. I'm going to have to get used to this." Logan handed her the envelope. "Say goodbye for me, will you?"

"I will," she murmured. She gave him another long, sweet kiss before she hopped out of the campervan. She walked around to the back of the trailer and lowered the ramp, then unlatched the door.

"Hey, sweetheart," she crooned as she moved beside the horse, stroking her back. "Come on, you and I have some business to take care of." The horse looked at her with a quizzical gaze. "I know. It's been a long trip. But if you're willing to travel just a little bit farther, then you and I are both going to get exactly what we want."

Gripping the halter, she slowly nudged Tally back, guiding

her out of the trailer onto firm ground. After over a week on the road, the horse seemed to take the travel in stride. Her ears perked up and she sniffed the air, getting her bearings again before walking beside Sunny to the gate.

She rang a bell on the gatepost, and a few minutes later, the equine vet came out, tugging his hat on his head against the afternoon sun. He was followed by an older man, dressed in jeans and a cotton shirt.

"Hello," the vet said. "Is this Tally?"

Sunny nodded. "It is. I understand you're going to look her over and I'm supposed to give these to the new owner and collect a check."

"I'm here for Mr. Morton," the man in the plaid shirt said. "Beck Crenshaw. I'm his stable manager."

"Then you're the man I need to talk to," Sunny said, grabbing his arm. "Will you excuse us?"

The vet nodded and started his examination, running his hands over the horse's front legs.

"Is there something wrong?" Crenshaw asked.

"There is. I want to buy the horse," Sunny said.

"That horse?"

She nodded. "Yep. I know what you're paying for the horse. I'll give you that and twenty thousand more to buy her back."

Crenshaw laughed. "You have to be joking. You just drove that horse across country and now you want to turn around and take her right back?"

"No, I'm going to board her on your farm for a week and then we're going to put her on a plane and send her back to Brisbane."

"And you're going to pay me almost twice as much as she's worth." Crenshaw stared at her for a long moment, shaking his head. "Wait a second. You're Sunny Grant, aren't you?"

"I am. But don't hold that against me."

"And you want to buy *this* horse?"

"I do. I think I'm offering you a very fair price. Can we come to an agreement?"

He chuckled. "Hell, yeah, I think we can make a deal," he said. "I'm in the business of buying and selling horses. If there's a profit to be made, I'll take it."

"All right, then," Sunny said. "It's a deal. Forty-four thousand plus boarding for a week. Now, do you have a mobile? I left mine at home."

He handed her his phone and she punched in the number for the stable office at Willimston Farm. When Ed answered, she drew a deep breath. "Ed, this is Sunny. I'm going to put you on the phone with a Mr. Crenshaw. I want you to make some travel arrangements to bring Logan's filly back to Willimston. I've offered him forty-four thousand, which is probably more than we'd normally pay, but I don't care. I'm going to give him another five thousand for board and airfare. Can you do that for me?"

"Sunny, what the hell are you—"

"Just do this for me. I've worked out all the details with my father. You know I'm right about this horse. I know you know."

"All right. Let me talk to the man."

Sunny smiled at Beck. "You have a check for me, right?"

He reached in his pocket and withdrew an envelope. "This is the easiest money I've ever made selling a horse."

Sunny filled out her father's check and exchanged it with him. "It was a pleasure doing business with you." She handed him the phone. "Ed Perkins is our stable manager. He'll help you make travel arrangements for Tally."

"Are you going to train her to jump?" Crenshaw asked, nodding at the filly.

"I'm not sure. I haven't decided what I'm going to do."

Sunny shook his hand and then turned and walked back to the campervan. She closed the trailer doors and stowed the ramp, then walked around to the passenger side. Logan was inside, still sitting behind the wheel, his hat pulled down low over his eyes. He looked over at her and she could see him fighting back tears.

"We're done," she said. She handed him the check. "Make sure it's right before we leave."

He opened the envelope and peered inside. "It's right."

"Then let's go," she said. "I'll buy you dinner and we'll rent a pricey hotel room. And then maybe, you and I will get a little bit stonkered."

"All right," he said. "That sounds perfect. I'm a rich man now. I can afford a few extra luxuries."

"Oh, no, this is my treat," she said. "We're going to find a place that has room service, we're going to take a nice long shower and then we're going to order dinner. I'm going to spend my money before my daddy puts a stop on my bank card. And after dinner, we're going to curl up in bed and I'm going to seduce you very, very slowly."

He drew a ragged breath. "I really am glad you're here with me, Sonny," he said.

"Are you happy you didn't desert me in Adelaide?"

He chuckled softly. "Yes. That was not my finest moment. I was just feeling a little...overwhelmed."

"And what about now?" Sunny asked. "Does all this still scare you?"

Logan leaned back and closed his eyes. "Yeah, it does," he said. "Right now, I'm the saddest I've been in a long time, but I'm happier than I can ever remember. Does that make sense?"

"No, but I'm sure you'll figure it all out. Come on, let's go."

Logan started up the campervan and they drove out of the car park and onto the highway. Sunny held out her hand and he placed his palm against hers, weaving their fingers together. "It feels different," he said. "Driving with the empty trailer."

"Maybe you'll let me drive again on the way home?"

"I think that can be arranged."

Sunny tried to keep the conversation light as they drove into Perth and searched for a place to stay. He might feel sad now, but there would come a day when she'd give him everything he ever wanted and needed. For now, she'd look forward to that moment and not worry about anything else.

SUNNY SLIPPED THE KEY CARD into the lock and waited for the light as Logan looked over her shoulder. His hands spanned her waist as she opened the door to the room and he gently pushed her inside, dropping their bags on the floor along the way.

He'd been waiting for this since the moment they'd left the vet's, and he stumbled with her toward the bed, his mouth searching for hers. Caught in a long, desperate kiss, they tore at each other's clothes.

There was nothing to say that they couldn't say with a touch or a sigh. He needed to be close to her, to possess her. It would reassure him that everything was still all right, because it suddenly felt as if the world was out of balance.

She worked at the button on the front of his jeans and when it was finally undone, Sunny smoothed her hand beneath the waistband of his underdaks. Wrapping her fingers around his shaft, she began to stroke him.

It was all Logan needed. There was a comfort in the intimacy, the way she knew his body and what made him ache with desire. This was what he had to keep, this feeling, this woman who had captured his heart. Horses would come and go, but he couldn't afford to lose Sunny.

He cupped her face in his hands, molding her mouth to his, tasting deeply of her sweet lips. The need was overwhelming, and he wanted that perfect moment, when he buried himself deep inside her heat. That had become home to him.

Together, they stripped away the last of their clothes. When she stood naked in front of him, he drew her leg up along his hip, the tip of his shaft teasing at her entrance. He was already on the edge and Logan had to focus on the feel of her hair between his fingers, the sound of her sighs as he kissed her.

Everything he'd ever wanted was here in front of him. He'd always felt like home was a place, a house, a piece of property. But he now knew the truth of love. Home was wherever that one person was. That's what had kept his parents together, through all the troubles.

He could be happy with her anywhere, even living out of the campervan. But he wanted to give her a life she could depend upon. He needed to know she'd be safe with him—forever.

Sunny wriggled against him, the warm flesh of her breasts pressed against his chest. When she slipped her arms around his neck, Logan grabbed her waist and pulled her up against him. With her legs wrapped around him, he pressed her back against the wall.

"Tell me what you want," he murmured.

"You," she breathed, gasping as he entered her. "It will always be you."

She moaned as she sank down on top of him, burying him deep inside her. Logan held on to her hips, his self-control wavering. But this time, he didn't want it to end. He needed this wave of sensation to continue on, an endless surge that could last a lifetime.

He'd never known passion like this, never known it was even possible to feel so deeply for a woman. Grabbing her hand, he kissed it then clasped it behind her as he began to move.

At first, the rhythm was slow and deep, but as he saw her dancing closer to her release, he knew she needed more. He drew away, nearly breaking the intimate contact, and then brought her down on him quickly.

Sunny gasped as he thrust again, his pace increasing until she writhed against him, her cries of pleasure echoing in his ears. And then, her body tensed and it was all over. Sunny dissolved into deep and powerful spasms, spasms that sent fresh waves of pleasure coursing through his body.

When she was sated, she opened her eyes and looked at him. And that was all it took for Logan to reach his own orgasm. He drove into her one last time and then let himself go, his body shuddering, his legs barely strong enough to keep them both upright.

"I think I might fall down," he murmured.

"I don't want to move right now."

He slipped his hands beneath her backside, and he carried her over to the bed then gently set her down, stretching out beside her. Logan reached up and brushed a strand of flaxen hair from her eyes, tucking it behind her ear.

"Remember when you told me that we were just friends— friends with benefits?"

"Vaguely," Sunny said. She smiled. "I don't remember it all that clearly since I'd had a little too much wine, but I do recall throwing that wine bottle at you. Why do you bring it up?"

"What does that mean?"

"Friends with benefits?"

"I know what that means. What does it mean for us? Do we see each other when we can and then see other people on the side? Or are we kind of...together?"

"Why do we need to define it?" Sunny asked.

"Maybe I'm feeling insecure," he said.

"You? I thought you were a rock."

He pressed his forehead to hers, closing his eyes. "Don't tease about this. I'm about to get serious here."

"All right," she said.

He heard a tremor in her voice and he opened his eyes. "I used to think that this would end after a few weeks and we'd both go on with our lives. But now, I realize that maybe this is a beginning for us."

"You do?"

"I don't have a lot to offer you, Sunny. And I'd like you to seriously consider the consequences of leaving your father's house and taking up with me. Not that I wouldn't love having you. In fact, having you with me would be like a dream come true. But living at the ranch would limit your chances to make your dreams come true." He paused. "If you decide to stay at home, I'll understand. It won't change the way I feel. Ever."

"How would it work?"

"We could see each other every now and then. I don't expect

any type of commitment and I'd understand if you didn't want to, but if you did, I—"

"Yes," she said.

"Yes? Yes to what?"

"Yes, to whatever you want."

"Just like that?"

Sunny sighed. "Yes. I don't want this to be over, either. You can come and visit, I can come and visit. Maybe we can think about the holiday idea again."

"I'd like that," he said.

She leaned into him and touched her lips to his. "Me, too."

"What's the first thing you're going to do when you get home?" he asked.

"I'm going to ride Padma," she said. "I haven't ridden her since London. I just couldn't bring myself to do it. I want to start training, but this time I'm going to really focus. And I'm thinking that I might want to start eventing. I used to do dressage, but I wasn't patient enough to be good at it. But I've changed. I have more perspective now. And I feel I need to challenge myself more. The World championships are in France in two years and then the Olympics in four years in Rio. I could be ready. I could be better than I ever was."

"I know you could," Logan said.

"Do you?"

"Sunny, I think you could do just about anything you set your mind to. You got me to—" He stopped suddenly. He was about to tell her that he'd fallen hopelessly in love with her. How was it possible that those words had come so naturally that he could say them without even thinking?

Was he in love with Sunny? Yes. Did he want to spend the rest of his life with her? Yes. Was he going to tell her that now? Logan drew a deep breath. Probably not the best time.

"What?" she asked.

Logan dropped a quick kiss on her lips. "You got me to haul

you across the country just so you could get away for a week or two."

Sunny laughed. "I did. And you almost threw me out on the road that first day. Aren't you glad you kept me?"

"Yeah," he conceded. "We've done all right together."

She grew silent for a long moment, her fingers tracing lazy patterns on his chest. "I want you to know that you'll be the only one."

"The only one for what?" Logan asked.

"My only one. As long as you want, it's just going to be you. In my bed." She drew a deep breath. "There won't be other men."

Logan stared down at her face but she continued to trace patterns on his chest. "Are you—is that—practical?"

Her shoulders rose in a tiny shrug. "It's the way I want it. What about you?" She risked a glance up. "Are you sure you want it that way?"

Her eyes were wide and questioning and he knew that this was probably the most important moment in their relationship so far. They were making a commitment to each other, vague as it might be. "Yes, that's what I want, too."

"Good," Sunny said. "Then I guess we're kind of...going together."

"Going together," he repeated. He wasn't exactly sure what that meant, only that they'd just promised that they wouldn't have sex with anyone else. As far as he was concerned, Logan wouldn't have any trouble keeping that promise, since he hadn't had much of a sex life since he moved to the ranch.

But Sunny was a different story. She'd have more opportunities. Men noticed women as beautiful as she was, and that kind of attention could turn to attraction...which could easily lead to seduction. After all, she'd seduced him, hadn't she?

"There is one thing," Logan said.

"What is that?"

"If you change your mind, I want you to tell me. Don't avoid me if I ring you up. Don't pretend that everything is all right. Just be straight with me and let me know you've moved on. Can you do that?"

"Don't you trust me?" she asked.

"Of course I do. It's not you I'm worried about. It's all the other men in the world who will see you the way I do. As a beautiful, sexy, irresistible woman."

"All right, I promise," she said.

It was the best he could hope for, Logan mused. Until he had more to offer Sunny, he'd have to be satisfied. But he wasn't going to fool himself. She'd move on, to someone more geographically available, someone with a bigger bank account, maybe even someone her father approved of. And that was all right by him.

Logan was lucky to have her at all. And he'd enjoy the time they had together for as long as it lasted.

8

SUNNY OPENED HER EYES slowly, snuggling deeper into the expensive linens on the hotel bed. She loved waking up next to Logan. They'd been together just over a week and it already seemed like the most natural thing in the world to lie naked beside him. She moved to the middle of the bed, searching for the warmth of his body, but when she couldn't find it, Sunny sat up and looked around the room.

He was standing at the window, looking down on the view of the river as the sun rose, his expression pensive. She studied him in silence, taking in his naked form, the long limbs muscled by hard work, the wide back and shoulders and narrow waist, so masculine, so perfect.

"Are you up already?" she asked softly.

He turned to look at her. "I wanted to call the ranch and make sure everything was all right. And to let Billy know we'd be on our way back today."

"And everything isn't all right?" she asked, watching him intently.

Logan shook his head. "Billy said there was a guy who stopped by the ranch who insisted on speaking with me. Something about official business. And when Billy said he could call me, the man said that he had to speak to me in person. He had to verify my identity. He said he had very important news about my family and an inheritance. He refused to tell him any more details." Logan cursed softly. "I'm afraid that— No, I don't even want to go there."

"How long has it been since you've heard from your parents?"

"I don't know. Maybe a year. I haven't seen them since right after I bought the ranch. I tried to get them to come and stay with me, but they refused. I can't keep track of them, it's all but impossible. So instead, I just wait until they decide to contact me."

"Do you think something has happened?"

He closed his eyes and drew a deep breath, then let it out. "Yeah, I do."

Sunny crawled out of bed and joined him at the window, slipping her arms around his waist and pressing her body against his. "Then you need to get home," she said. "You need to get on a plane and go. You can fly back to Brisbane and take a bush plane the rest of the way. Do you have a landing strip near the ranch?"

"There's one in town. Billy can come and pick me up."

"Then that's what you'll do," she said.

"Yeah. First, I have to find a place to cash this check. I don't have enough on the bank card for a ticket and a bush plane. And then I'd need to fly back here to pick up the trailer and campervan. Unless I just sell them both."

"No, you don't have to do that. I'll drive them back."

He turned to face her, his fingers toying with a strand of hair that hung over her eyes. "You? Sunny, the drive was difficult for me. I can't ask you to do that. Especially not alone."

"I want to. I'm not ready to go home yet and I'd like to see a little bit more of the country. I might just continue on around and make one big circle. Hey, it could be an adventure."

He chuckled softly. "I think you've had enough adventure."

"I can do this, Logan. Trust me. I promise I'll take my time. And I'll be very careful."

He considered her offer for a long moment and at first, she was certain he'd refuse. But Logan finally shrugged. "All right. But I want you to go home the way we came. You know the route and where to stop along the way. And I don't like you pulling that trailer. I'm thinking you can leave it here and we can figure out a way to get it back. Or I'll just sell it."

Sunny hugged him tight, happy that he was allowing her to help him. He was a proud man, but not too proud to appear vulnerable to her. He trusted her and that meant more than anything to her. "Why don't I call and get a ticket, and then you can take me out for some driving lessons before you leave."

"I don't like this," Logan warned. "You should just fly home with me."

"I don't want to go home yet."

"Then I should stay and we'll drive back together," he countered.

Sunny rolled her eyes. "Are you saying I'm not capable of taking care of myself?" she asked, feeling her temper rise.

Logan paused. "No?"

"Good answer," she said. "Now, bring me your mobile and let's make some travel arrangements. Then, we'll have breakfast and I'll drive you to the airport."

Sunny spent the next half hour making arrangements for Logan to catch a Qantas flight that morning. She gave the agent her bank card info and carefully wrote down the itinerary on a hotel notepad. When she'd confirmed it all, she handed him back his mobile.

"You leave at ten. It's a direct flight from Perth to Brisbane."

"How will I get home from there?"

"I'm going to call my father's pilot. He's usually at my disposal, so he'll fly you. You should be home before dark."

He shook his head. "Thank you. I don't know what to say. I'll pay you back as soon as I get home."

"You don't have to say anything. You can pay me back when I see you the next time," she said. "It's not like I don't know where to find you." She paused. "Actually, I don't really know where to find you."

"I'll draw you a map before I leave." He reached up and smoothed his hand over her cheek. "You're an amazing woman, Sunny Grant."

"Watch me try to convince my father's pilot to fly you out of Brisbane. Then you can tell me I'm amazing."

Sunny sat cross-legged on the bed as she called the number for the small hangar at Brisbane. She usually flew on the company plane to her equestrian events, so she had the number memorized. Once the last leg of his trip was confirmed, she held out the mobile to Logan. He crawled onto the bed and pulled her down beside him.

Sunny leaned over and smoothed her fingers over his furrowed brow. "Don't worry. It might not be anything. You don't know."

"I can feel it," he said. "It's like when my brother died. I got a phone call and my roommate answered. They wouldn't say anything to him. They'd only talk to me."

She drew his body close to hers. It was hard to know what to say. She'd never really lost anyone close to her. Though her parents were estranged, they were both still alive. And her grandparents were all gone before she turned five.

Running her hands through his hair, she placed a kiss on his lips. "I want you to ring me when you get home tonight," she said.

"How?"

"I'll keep your mobile."

He nodded. "All right. And if you have any trouble along the way, you ring me."

"All right."

"I don't want to leave you, Sunny. I don't like the thought of you driving back through the Nullarbor all by yourself."

"I've learned so much on this trip, but I think I need a little more time to myself. It will be good for me. I have the mobile and plenty of music to listen to. And I'll be back before you know it."

He drew another deep breath and then let it out slowly. "I thought we'd have another week together. I didn't think it would end so quickly."

Sunny stared into his pale blue eyes. She saw fear there, but she wasn't sure what had caused it. Was it what awaited him at home or was it leaving her? "It's not over," she said. "We'll see each other next week. I have to bring back your campervan and trailer. And I can see your ranch and check out your horses. And maybe hang about for a few days."

"That makes me feel better," he murmured.

"Now, we can either go out and get some breakfast or we can spend the next hour in bed. Which would you prefer?" Sunny asked.

"I'd rather lie here looking at you. Memorizing the color of your eyes and the way your nose wrinkles when you smile."

Sunny kissed him and, gradually, their passion overwhelmed them. This time, when he entered her, it was a sweet, slow experience. It was as if he were savoring every moment, trying to commit it to memory.

She'd never expected to fall in love. When she'd driven off with Logan Quinn, it had been on a lark, just something to do with a few wasted weeks. But now, looking back on their time together, she realized that this trip had been a turning point for her.

She suddenly knew what she wanted out of life and she was ready to make it happen. Though she wasn't sure how she planned to go about it, at least she knew. And though Sunny couldn't figure out all the details right now, she had complete confidence that her life had changed for the better.

After they'd both found their release, they stayed in bed, talking softly about the experiences they'd shared on their road trip. It had become so easy between them and, though they'd had a few ups and downs, Sunny had never felt their disagreements threatened the bond that had formed between them.

It was odd to think that she had a boyfriend now. She'd never had an official boyfriend. There had been men in her life, but never any commitment on her part. But this time it was different. This time, she was determined to make it work.

THE PICKUP TRUCK SENT a plume of dust into the air behind them as they bumped along the narrow road to the ranch house. Billy had come to pick him up from the airstrip near town, and they'd passed the half-hour drive in a detailed interrogation, Logan asking the questions and Billy doing his best to answer them.

"I told him you'd be back late, but he said he'd hang around and wait," Billy said. "When I left he was just sitting in his car reading a book."

"And you're sure he said it was about an inheritance?"

"I—I think so. I really can't remember. He kind of scares the piss out of me. I think he might be from the government."

"And he didn't want to ring me? You're sure of that?"

"Yes, that's one thing I do remember. He said he had to talk to you in person."

"Tell me again exactly what he asked," Logan prodded.

"Mostly things about your family. He knew your dad's name is Daniel and your mom's Lizbeth. And he knew about your brother."

A stab of fear shot through him, and Logan had to remind himself to breathe. What else could this be? It had to be some news about his parents. And the fact that the visitor was unwilling to tell him over the phone didn't bode well.

Logan had always wondered how it would feel to be completely alone in the world. He knew the day would come when his parents weren't around anymore, but he hadn't expected it to happen so soon. If it were his father, then his choice would be obvious. He'd bring his mother to live here at the ranch.

But if it was his mother, he knew his father would never want to settle down in one place for more than a few months.

"Maybe it's not bad news," Billy said. "Maybe…maybe some uncle you didn't know has died and he's leaving you a million dollars."

"I don't have an uncle," he said. "My da was an only child."

"Maybe you won the lotto and don't know it," Billy suggested.

Logan shook his head. Billy had always been an optimistic chap, always looking for the silver lining in every dark cloud. But this dark cloud refused to go away. "Do you think he's still waiting?"

"I'd expect so," Billy said. "This guy is really a bit of a pest. He's not giving up easily."

He'd spent the flight back thinking about Sunny. It had taken every ounce of his determination to leave her at the airport. But she hadn't seemed sad to see him go. In truth, Logan sensed that she was looking forward to the last leg of her adventure. They'd stocked the campervan with food and supplies, she'd recharged the mobile and tested it out, and he'd filled the tank with petrol, warning her not to let it get down below a quarter tank.

Hell, he already missed her. He'd started missing her the moment he walked through the entrance doors at the airport. But it wasn't just a sense of loss that he felt. It was more an emptiness inside of him, as if her presence in his life had become part of who he was.

Where was she right now? he wondered. If she'd left Perth directly after dropping him at the airport, she was probably close to her planned destination in Esperance on the southern coastline. Logan glanced at his watch. She'd promised to call once she stopped for the evening. He needed to hear the sound of her voice now more than ever.

"Did you have a good time?" Billy asked.

His words startled Logan out of his contemplation. "What?"

"A good time? Did you at least have a good time? You haven't been on holiday in…well, since I've come to work here on the ranch. Did you—"

"Yeah," Logan said. "I had a very nice time. The best."

As they came into view of the house, Billy pointed in the direction of a dark sedan. "There it is. I told you he was persistent. That's his car. And that's him, there, sitting on the porch."

Logan stopped the pickup truck and slowly got out. Billy followed close behind him. "You want me to back you up here?" he murmured.

"No, I think I'll be good," Logan said.

As he walked closer, the stranger stood and pasted a smile on his face. "Are you Logan Quinn?" he asked.

Logan stopped, crossing his arms over his chest. He didn't like the look of this guy. Though he was trying to appear friendly, it was obvious he was nervous. "Billy said you wanted to talk to me."

"I do," he said. "I've been waiting around for a couple days now. That Billy. He's a very loyal employee."

"Can I help you with something, Mr.…."

"Winthrop. Arthur Winthrop of the firm of Capley and Drummond in Brisbane. I'm representing Ian Stephens, who represents your great-aunt Aileen Quinn." He paused. "The author."

Logan frowned, the man's words making no sense to him at all. "You're not here about my parents?"

"Do you know where they are? I've been trying to locate them, as well. They're also in line to receive a portion of Miss Quinn's estate."

"Then they're all right?" Logan asked in relief. "My parents are all right? Nothing has happened?"

Arthur blinked. "Not that I know of. As I said, I haven't been able to find them—"

Logan stepped back, shaking his head. "I don't understand. I don't have a great-aunt."

"You do. She's your grandfather's sister and she lives in Ireland. The family was split apart many years ago. She's quite a famous author and now that she's aware of you, she'd like to meet you and to leave you part of her estate. She wants to bequeath you a million dollars, half of which you'll get right now, the other half upon her passing."

The words hit Logan like a punch to the stomach. He gasped, then realized how ridiculous it sounded. "Right. This is some kind of joke." He glanced around. "Where are the cameras? You guys should be ashamed of yourselves. I mean, how low—"

"Mr. Quinn, I'm quite serious. Your great-aunt is extremely wealthy and doesn't have children of her own. She wants to make sure her family benefits from her good fortune. When we find your father, he will also receive a share, and any other surviving heirs of Tomas Quinn. I've confirmed that you are an heir." He reached in his jacket pocket. "This is half of your inheritance. There is only one condition. Miss Quinn wants you to visit Ireland to meet her. Of course, we'll make all the arrangements for you."

Logan closed his eyes. Was he really supposed to believe this? He looked down at the check. It appeared to be real. He recognized the name of the bank and it was written out to him. "What does she want me to do with this?"

"Whatever you want." He glanced around. "It looks like this place could use some improvements. I'm sure this will go a long way. Now, if you'll just sign here."

He held out a paper and Logan added his name to the bottom. "That's it? You're handing me a half-million dollars and that's it?"

"If you don't mind, Mr. Stephens has asked that I take a photo?" He withdrew a digital camera from his pocket. "May I?"

Logan glanced over at Billy then shrugged. "For a half-million dollars? Snap away."

When Winthrop was finished, he handed Logan a business card. "Just ring my number when you're interested in visiting your great-aunt. I'd suggest you do it soon as she is ninety-six years old. Good day, Mr. Quinn, and good luck."

With that, he turned and walked back to his car. A few moments later, he disappeared down the driveway in a plume of dust. Logan stared down at the check, then flipped it over and examined the back. It looked real. But things like this didn't happen to Logan Quinn. He'd had to fight for every single thing he'd ever been given in life.

"Holy dooley, Logan," Billy muttered. "If I'd have known that's what he wanted, I would have called you a lot sooner."

"I can't believe this." Logan laughed. "It's like my future just fell out of the sky and landed at my feet. Do you know what this means?"

"We can afford to fix up the stables?"

"We can afford to sell this place and buy something that's closer to civilization. We can buy a farm with a stable that isn't falling to pieces and a house that doesn't have a leaky roof. A place we can be proud of."

"I'm proud of this place," Billy said, frowning. "We've worked hard here."

Logan nodded. "We have. And someone else who's just starting out will love this place. But, Billy, it's time to move on."

"Are you firing me?"

"No, I'm saying you and I are going to start looking at real estate first thing tomorrow morning." He paused. "And once we get settled, I'm going to buy Tally back. I can offer them whatever they want. She'll be back with us, back on our place."

As he smoothed his fingers over the check, he realized there were other things that wealth could afford him.

Billy grinned. "You think maybe we could get one of those big-screen televisions? Then I wouldn't have to watch football on that thing you call a television."

"I'll put a television in the barn if you want," Logan said. "You can watch football while you're mucking out the stalls."

"Really?"

Logan grinned. "I think we're going to need to spend carefully," he said. "I have to make a few phone calls and then tomorrow, we're going to the bank to deposit this check, before someone changes their mind."

Logan grabbed his rucksack from the pickup and turned toward the house. As he approached the place that he'd called home for the past five years, he stopped to examine the ramshackle house. He'd grown attached to this place. But now he realized that his home wasn't a spot on a map or a structure made of lumber and nails.

His home was anywhere Sunny Grant was. For the first time, he could imagine a future, a real future, with her. With the money he'd been given, he could buy a nice place, closer to Brisbane, maybe near Willimston Farm. She wouldn't have to make the choice between a life with him or a life pursuing her Olympic dreams.

They could be together. And maybe, when the time was right, he'd ask her if she'd want to spend the rest of her life with him. He jogged up the porch steps and opened the screen door. For now, he'd keep his plans to himself. And maybe, when Sunny arrived at the ranch next week, he'd be ready to share them.

He walked to the phone and dialed the number to his mobile. It rang six times before the voice mail picked up. It had been almost nine hours since he'd last heard her voice, and he craved the comfort that talking to her gave him.

Logan left a message, frowning as he hung up the phone. He wasn't going to be right again until she was here, safe and sound. Even now, he regretted leaving her to drive back on her own. But then, Sunny usually got her own way.

That was one thing he was going to have to get used to if Sunny was going to be a part of his life. But it wasn't the worst thing in the world—to spend the rest of his life making her happy.

IT FELT GOOD TO BE BACK in her own bed. Sunny rolled over on her stomach and looked at the clock. She'd arrived back at Willimston a few days before and had planned to stay just a night before driving the extra day to Logan's ranch. But he'd insisted that he didn't need the campervan or trailer immediately and urged her to relax and enjoy some time at home.

Sunny sighed. It was nearly eight, at least four hours earlier than she'd been accustomed to rising at home. But her time on the road with Logan had changed a lot of her bad habits. And since Tally had arrived on the farm the day before yesterday, she'd been out of bed at first light, anxious to get the filly settled in her new surroundings.

Reaching over, she smoothed her hand along the empty side of the bed. There wasn't a moment during the day when she didn't miss having Logan near her. They talked a lot on the phone, but it wasn't the same. And though they missed each other, he'd been reluctant to set a time when they could get together again.

Sunny wasn't sure what had happened since they parted, but she suspected it had to do with his hasty departure from Perth. All he would say was that he was working on some serious business matters and that he'd tell her all about it when he saw her next. The problem was, Sunny didn't know when that would happen.

For now, she'd wait. She was learning to be patient, and Logan was a man who was worth waiting for. Even with a day's distance between them, she was certain of the depth of her feelings. They'd be together soon and there would be time to talk about all the challenges they were both facing and the future they'd have together.

Still, the physical distance did take its toll. It was impossible not to miss the intimacy they'd shared. The hours before she fell asleep were filled with thoughts of the pleasure they'd given each other in bed and out. They had barely scratched the surface of their desire and now they had to put it on hold.

She crawled out of bed. So she'd do what she'd been doing since she got home. She'd put on her riding clothes and spend the day in the paddock working with Padma and training Tally. After that, she'd groom them both and muck out their stalls and then, hopefully, she'd fall into bed that evening, completely exhausted.

Sunny got dressed in her breeches and boots, then pulled on a freshly washed shirt. Her helmet was sitting on the chair near the window where she'd tossed it the previous afternoon. She put it on her head and jogged down the stairs.

"Coffee, please," she said to Lily as she passed through the kitchen.

The housekeeper poured her a mug, and Sunny grabbed it, along with a croissant, as she passed by. "Thank you, Lily," she said with a smile. "You always take such good care of me."

As she walked back to the stables, she noticed an old campervan parked next to Logan's camper. She stopped and looked it over, her mind flashing back to that day she first met Logan. That day had completely changed her life. She couldn't help but wonder what the driver of this vehicle was doing at the farm.

As she rounded the corner of the stable and walked toward the paddock, she pulled on her gloves. Now that she'd bought Tally, she was anxious to find out how quickly the horse could learn. Though Padma had already been trained to jump when she arrived at the farm, it would be a challenge for Sunny to train a horse herself. The bond between them was already becoming strong and, hopefully, it would take them both to an Olympic championship in four years.

Sunny stopped short when she saw a girl standing on the gate, petting Tally's nose. She looked to be about ten or eleven years old, her skinny legs revealed by baggy shorts and her pale blond hair swept up in a ponytail.

"She likes Anzac biscuits," Sunny called out.

The little girl turned around, then quickly jumped off the

fence, shoving her hands in her pockets as if she'd been caught doing something wrong.

"Sorry," she mumbled, her face turning scarlet. "My dad said I wasn't supposed to get out of the campervan."

"Oh, you don't have to be sorry."

"I just really wanted to see the horses. I love horses."

"Tally can be a pest when it comes to getting her biscuits. Go ahead, you can pet her." Sunny joined the girl at the gate. "What's your name?"

"Anna. Anna Fleming."

Sunny held out her hand. "I'm Sunny Grant."

The girl shook her hand, staring up at Sunny with wide eyes. "My dad said you lived here. I saw you on television. At the Olympics. We watched at the pub."

"Oh, dear," Sunny replied. "I was not very good, was I?"

"Your horse was pretty," she said.

"Do you ride?"

The girl shook her head. "I don't have a horse. We don't have a place. My dad and I, we live in our campervan."

Sunny tried to hide her surprise. "Your mom, too?"

Anna shook her head. "My mom left when I was three. It's just me and my dad."

Sunny smiled. "I lived in a campervan for a while, too. I really liked it. It was very cozy."

Her shoulders rose and fell in a weak shrug. "I'd like to live in a house. And maybe have a puppy. And sleep in a real bed."

"Maybe you will someday." Sunny paused. "Why have you come to the farm?"

"My dad is looking for work. He's really good with horses. He's worked on horse farms all over Australia."

Sunny drew a deep breath. "I'm going to go get some biscuits for Tally. Why don't you stay here and I'll be right back?"

She left Anna standing at the gate and headed to the stable office in search of Ed. She found him there, deep in conversation with a wiry man who looked a few years older than Logan.

Sunny poked her head in the door. "Ed, I need to speak with you. Can you spare just a few seconds?"

"I'm in the middle of something," he said.

"This won't wait." She stood outside, and when he joined her, Sunny grabbed Ed's arm and pulled him along to the far end of the stable. "I want you to hire that guy. Fleming. I want you to hire him."

"Now, Sunny, I don't mind you getting yourself involved in the occasional purchase of a horse, but the hiring and firing of the stable staff on this farm is up to me. I make those decisions."

"I don't care. I want you to hire him."

"You don't even know him," Ed pointed out.

"He has a daughter, about ten years old. They're living out of that campervan. She's got no mother. And I think it might be important that she has a real home for a while. I think that home should be here." Sunny stared up into his eyes. "Please?"

He studied her for a long moment, then nodded. "All right," Ed muttered.

"Really?" Sunny asked. She threw her arms around him and gave him a fierce hug. "You're a nice guy, Ed."

"Hell, I was planning on hiring him anyway. He's got great experience, comes with fine references and knows as much about horses as I do."

Sunny stepped back. "Can we give him the house near the grove? It needs to be fixed up, but Lily and I could do that. It would be perfect for them. The girl could have her own bedroom, and it has a nice little garden."

"Fine with me. Now can I get back to my interview?"

"No worries," she said with a wide grin.

He strode back inside the stable, then stopped and turned to her. "Since when do you care about strange kids?"

"She needs a home, Ed. We've got something to offer her. And she wants to learn how to ride. I figure, I can help her with that."

"*You?* Teach a kid how to ride?" He chuckled softly and shook his head. "Now, there's something I never expected to hear." He ran his hand through his hair. "Miss Grant, I do believe that you grew up when I wasn't looking."

"It's about time, no?" she said with a grin. "I'm twenty-six years old."

"Yeah," he said. "It is about time." Ed paused. "Does this have anything to do with the trip you and Logan took?"

"It might," she said. "I'm not sure yet." Sunny gave him a wave. "Offer him a decent salary. He might be raising a budding equestrian."

Ed chuckled. "All right. But next time you see the Sunny Grant I used to know, tell her I like the new Sunny Grant a lot better."

"I'll do that. But I'm pretty sure we won't be seeing her around this place anymore."

Sunny found Anna waiting where she'd left her.

The girl turned and hopped off the gate as soon as she noticed her approach. "Did you get the biscuits?"

Sunny groaned. "I forgot. But that can wait. You're going to come with me and we're going to find you a proper riding habit."

Her eyes went wide. "But—I don't think my— Why?"

"Because you're going to be staying at the farm for a while. Ed is going to give your daddy a job. And if you're going to live here you're going to need to learn to ride. And I just happen to be a very, very good teacher—I think."

"You think?"

"I've never taught anyone before, but I think I'll be grand. What do you think?"

A wide smile broke across her serious expression. "You will be grand," Anna said, nodding.

Sunny slipped her arm around the girl's shoulders. "I think I have some old breeches in my closet. And I know I have a pair of boots that will fit you."

They started off toward the house and, as they walked, Sunny couldn't help but smile. Maybe Logan had changed her for good.

Maybe he'd taught her to see people for what they were, to know them for the lives they led and not for what she saw on the surface.

She couldn't help but think about the child he'd been and the troubles he'd seen. If she could spare another child from that kind of insecurity, then she would. Anna Fleming would get a home for as long as she wanted one.

And maybe Sunny would get something, too. She had always thought that teaching children how to ride was something she might be good at. Riding had given her an incredible sense of power and purpose in her own crazy childhood. Perhaps, it might do the same for someone like Anna.

Sunny drew a deep breath and smiled. So many things had changed for her in the past few weeks. She sometimes didn't even recognize herself anymore. And maybe that was a good thing. The Sunny Grant that she once knew wasn't worthy of a man like Logan Quinn.

Now maybe she was.

IT HAD BEEN NEARLY four weeks since he'd last seen Sunny, and Logan was just a little more than nervous. There had been so many things that required his attention at the ranch that a day's drive into Brisbane had been an impossibility. A half-million dollars had just dropped into his lap and that wasn't something he took lightly, never mind the other half million waiting for him in Ireland.

It still hadn't really sunk in. It was as if fate had stepped in to make all his dreams come true. Only, fate had come in the form of an elderly Irish novelist with money to spare. Though he hadn't scheduled his trip to Ireland, he was anxious to go. Logan needed to explain to his great-aunt how much her help had meant to him.

He'd kept his news a secret from Sunny, choosing to get all his plans in order before he told her. All she knew was that his parents were fine and he was working on some financial issues with the farm. He could hear the worry in her voice when they spoke on the phone. But she hadn't pressed him for details, and for that he was glad. No matter what happened, Sunny always seemed to know exactly what to say and how to act. But he also knew that she would be there for him, in the bad times and the good.

He'd planned their future in his head, working out all the little details. As a former investment banker he knew the risks of putting all his money into property. He'd decided to look for a small place, something within his conservative budget. After that, he'd invest the remainder of his inheritance for their future.

There had been so many things to consider. Was it better to spend money and fix up the ranch and then sell it? Or should he sell it as is, keeping the price low so that someone with limited resources might buy it? How much closer could he afford to be to Willimston without significantly reducing the amount of land he wanted? How far away should he stay just in case things didn't work out?

Everything had required careful consideration. Decisions were made after deliberate thought. But in the end, he had decided to look at a farm thirty kilometers west of Willimston, a beautiful place that had everything he'd ever need to raise his horses. And a place that Sunny might, one day, want to call home.

It was all falling into place. He'd get the farm. Then, he'd get the girl. And after that, they'd get the horse. He'd already set aside money to buy Tally back from the breeder in Perth and, though he wasn't even sure they were interested in selling, for the first time in his life, he had the power and the money to make it happen.

Logan frowned. "One step at a time," he murmured. *First the farm, then the girl, then the horse.* He clutched the steering wheel of the new pickup. Impatience would be the end of him.

He'd always been cool under pressure, but the stakes had never been so high. His future happiness was at risk. But they'd never really talked about a commitment. They'd discussed holidays together a few times a year. They'd discussed the option of being "friends with benefits." They'd even discussed, for a short time, Sunny living with him instead of returning to her home and family. Never once had they come close to mentioning the C word—commitment.

And now, he was prepared to ask her for that. He was ready to move his entire life to be closer to her. Though he wanted to believe Sunny would say yes to his proposal, he couldn't be sure. Hell, he hadn't even decided what his proposal was.

The options ranged from dating to marriage and everything in between. Should they spend more time together, getting to know each other better? Or should he just jump in and risk it all with a proposal of marriage? Maybe they ought to live together first and make the serious decisions later.

He groaned softly. There was always the chance that she'd say no to everything. That their time apart had weakened the bond they shared. A curse slipped from his lips. Maybe he should have gotten the horse first and then gone after the girl. At least with Tally, he'd have something significant to offer her besides promises and an engagement ring.

The sign for Willimston Farm appeared, and Logan turned into the driveway, taking the same route he had on the very day he'd first met Sunny. All that seemed so long ago, though it was barely six weeks. So much had changed in that time that it was hard to remember his life without her.

He pulled the truck to a stop in front of the house, a nervous knot growing in his stomach. Grabbing the bouquet of flowers he'd picked up in town, Logan drew a deep breath. He jumped out of the truck and smoothed his hand over his shirt. Eight hours on the road had left him a little rumpled, but dressed in khakis and a pale blue shirt, he wanted to impress. He'd even managed a haircut before leaving. Raking his fingers through his hair, Logan stood at the front door of the house and pushed the button for the doorbell.

A few moments later, the door swung open. He expected to see Sunny, but instead, he saw an older woman. "I—I'm here for Sunny?"

She smiled. "Well, there you are," she said. "I'm Lily, the housekeeper. Sunny's back in the stables. She said you're to go on back and meet her there. I believe you know the way?"

Logan nodded and started down the steps. But then he turned back to Lily. "Do I look all right?"

"Oh, you look grand," she said with a warm smile.

"And the flowers?"

"Sunny loves flowers. Daisies are her favorite, but I expect you know that."

"No," he said. "I didn't. It was just a lucky guess. But it is good to know. I need to know things like that."

In truth, there were still huge gaps in what they knew of each other's lives. They'd talked about many subjects on their way to Perth, but some things, like her favorite flowers, had gone untouched. But that was what the future was for. There would be fun in the discovery.

As he approached the stables, he heard a shout from the paddock nearby. Logan strode around the corner of the building and looked over the fence to find Sunny sprawled in the soft dirt next to a rail jump. With a quiet curse, he hopped over the gate and ran to her.

"Are you all right?"

"I'm fine," she said breathlessly. "She just refused. She doesn't like the white rails."

Sunny sat up, wincing, then looked into his eyes. Her expression brightened and she laughed, throwing her arms around his neck. "You're here," she exclaimed. "And you brought me flowers."

Logan chuckled, reaching out to straighten her riding helmet. "I am. It took me a while." He handed her the bouquet.

"It took you too long." Sunny hugged him again and pulled

him down into the dirt with her, rolling on top of him as they kissed.

At that moment, Logan didn't care about his new shirt or his clean khakis. He just wanted to lose himself in the taste of her mouth and the feel of her body. This is exactly what he'd needed all these weeks, the perfect antidote for his loneliness. His fingers tangled in her hair as he molded his mouth to hers.

He pulled her beneath him, his body already responding to the kiss in ways he couldn't control. But as he looked down into her beautiful face, he felt a nudge on his shoulder. Logan glanced back to find a horse—

With a soft curse, Logan scrambled to his feet. Startled by his sudden movement, Tally shied away, but Logan held out his hand to calm her. Sunny stood up and wrapped her arm around his waist. "Look who's here," she said.

"Jaysus, Sunny, what did you do?" He looked over at her. "Please tell me you didn't steal her."

"Of course not," she said, giggling at the thought. "I bought her. She's mine. Actually, she's yours if you want her. We can work out a nice deal. Or we could share her. I'm teaching Tally to jump. She'd been doing well until she refused this fence. I think she wanted to toss me into the dirt."

He stared at the horse, unable to believe what he was seeing. A lump of emotion blocked his ability to speak, and he pulled Sunny into his arms and pressed a kiss to the top of her head. "I can't believe you did this. Thank you."

"I couldn't let her go," Sunny said. She smoothed her hand over his cheek. "The same way I could never let you go. I love Tally as much as you do, Logan. And I love you even more." She turned her face up to his. "You're part of my life now. Not just for today or for tomorrow, but forever. And it wouldn't have been complete without the horse that brought us together."

Logan closed his eyes and hugged her tight. "I've been thinking the same thing, Sunny. We belong together. All three of us."

She kissed him, her lips soft and sweet against his. "You

changed me, Logan," she murmured. "You made me want more for myself. And you made me want you. I can't be happy without you."

"I love you, too," he murmured, drawing her into another kiss, this one deep and delicious. When he finally pulled back, there were tears glittering in her eyes. "Are you going to tell me how you managed this?"

"I made him an offer he couldn't refuse," Sunny teased.

"And you drove her back yourself?"

Sunny sucked in a sharp breath. "Actually, no. I drove back, Tally flew. I didn't want to risk her safety. And she's a lot to take care of on the road. Tally arrived here the day before I got back, and she's been settling in just fine."

"You're an amazing woman," he murmured, bending close.

"Yes, I am. Are you only noticing that now?"

"No. I've known that all along."

His kissed her again and, suddenly, he couldn't seem to get enough of her. She was intoxicating, the scent of her hair, the taste of her lips, the feel of her curves. He ached to touch her the way he used to, skin to skin, his fingers exploring her naked body.

"Maybe we should find someplace private," she murmured. "You could take off your pretty new clothes. I don't want you to get them any dirtier."

"That sounds like a wonderful idea. But there's something else we need to discuss first."

"There's something more important than getting naked and making love to me?"

"Well, yes. For the moment, there is." He grabbed her hand then pulled her along toward the gate. "We're going for a drive. It's not far, but I really need to get your opinion."

"A drive? Now?"

Logan nodded. "I promise, it's about twenty minutes west of here."

"But I have to take care of Tally. She's still got her bridle and saddle on."

She turned to hurry back to the horse, but Logan scooped her up in his arms and tossed her over his shoulder. "That can wait."

"No!"

As they passed the stable, Ed walked out, a bemused expression on his face. "Well, I can see where this is going already. Do you need any help?"

Sunny pushed up and reached out her hand. "Can you—"

"I was talking to Logan," Ed said.

"Yeah, take care of Tally, will you? Sunny and I have some important business to take care of."

He didn't set her down until they reached the side of a shiny new red pickup truck. He opened the passenger side door. "Get in."

"This is yours?"

"Like it?"

"It's very...very new," she said, frowning.

Logan opened the door and she got inside. When he slipped in behind the wheel she was staring at him. "When did you get this truck? And where are we going?"

"I'll explain when we get there," he said.

"And where is there?"

"A real pretty horse farm about twenty minutes west of here. I'm thinking about buying it—if you like it."

Sunny reached out and grabbed the truck keys from his hand. "Wait a second. Where is all this money coming from? You bought a new truck and, now, you're buying a new farm? Is there something you're not telling me?"

"Did I tell you that I loved you?"

Sunny nodded.

"And did I tell you that someday, I'm going to marry you?"

Her jaw dropped and she blinked. "No."

"I'm getting ahead of myself. We'll talk about that later. Can

I have my keys now?" She held them away from him and Logan leaned close and captured her lips in a very persuasive kiss.

"No! Did you just propose marriage to me?"

Logan reached into his pants pocket and pulled out the small velvet box, holding it out. "The keys for the box," he teased. "I know that I can't give you everything, Sunny. But I can give you myself, my heart and soul. My life. And my promise that I'll do my best to make you happy forever."

He opened the box and removed the simple diamond ring. "This doesn't have to mean we're getting married tomorrow. Or even next month or next year. But I want to spend the rest of my life with you, Sunny. And I want that life to start now. Is that something you would want, too?"

The next few seconds seemed like an eternity. Sunny stared at the ring then glanced up into Logan's eyes. A tear trickled from the corner of her eye and she brushed it away. "Yes," she finally said. "Yes, it's something I want. I think I've wanted it since the moment I met you."

He slipped the ring on her finger and found it a little too large. "That's one more thing I need to learn about you. Your ring size."

She stared down at her hand. "It doesn't matter. It's perfect just the way it is."

He leaned forward and pressed his forehead to hers. "I guess it's you and me now," he whispered.

She kissed him softly. "I guess it is. I wouldn't want it any other way." Sunny looked down at the ring again. "So you bought a new truck and you bought me a diamond ring. And you're buying a new farm. How many horses did you have to sell?"

"Not one," Logan said.

"But—"

He caught her lips in a kiss, his tongue tracing the crease until she opened for him. "It's a really interesting story. Oh, and there's one more surprise."

"Another surprise? I'm not sure I can take any more surprises."

"You and I have to go to Ireland next month."

Sunny sat back in her seat. "All right, start the truck. You can explain the whole story to me on the way to your new place."

"*Our* new place," he corrected. Logan grinned. "It's a really, really good story. You're going to like it."

"I already do," she said with a smile that said so much more. "I already do."

Epilogue

"MISS QUINN?"

Aileen Quinn looked up from her computer, her reading glasses perched on the end of her nose. She took off the glasses and laid them on the desk, then motioned Ian Stephens in. It had been weeks since she'd first sent him to search for her family and, though he'd sent her progress reports, she knew he was coming to report on some important news.

"Sit, sit," she said, motioning to a chair. "So, you have found my great-nephew."

"I have. And he's been given a share of his inheritance as you instructed. I understand he's very anxious to meet you. He's asked that we arrange a visit at your earliest convenience."

Ian handed her a folder and she opened it to find photographs inside. She picked one up of a handsome young man with dark hair and a sweet smile. "This is him?"

"That is," he said. "His name is Logan Quinn. Your brother Tomas married late in life. He was nearly fifty and his bride was thirty. They had just one son, Daniel, who also married. He had two sons. Only one is still living and that's Logan. He runs a horse ranch in Queensland."

"What of Tomas?"

"He passed away in 1973 and his wife a few years later. He made some rather bad investments and the family lived a penniless existence for the most part. Tomas's son, Daniel, seems to have followed in his father's footsteps when it came to financial matters."

"You found him? He would know about his father. He'd be able to tell me about my brother."

"Unfortunately, the son, Logan, isn't sure where his father is right now. According to my man, Winthrop, Daniel moves around from job to job, mostly working at cattle and sheep stations in remote areas of the country. But Logan expects that his parents will be in contact at some point in the future."

"And tell me. How is this horse ranch doing?"

Ian forced a smile. "It's a rather rough affair as you can see from the next photo," he said. "I suspect Logan Quinn has been living on a shoestring and that the shoestring was been very badly frayed. I believe that the inheritance may have saved him from ruin."

"Good," Aileen said. "I've spent my life collecting wealth and now it's time I start giving it away. Who better than my family? Tell me more."

Ian smiled. "Of course, he's very anxious to meet you," he said. "I hope I haven't overstepped, but he's going to be arriving week after next."

She smiled and pressed her hand to her heart. "It's so soon. I'm not sure I—"

"I could always ring him and have him delay his trip, Miss Quinn. I just thought since he was anxious to meet you that—"

"No, no," she said, waving her hand. "It's just...well, I've lived my whole life thinking I was all alone in the world. And now, I have family. I have a great-nephew and he wants to meet me. I'm afraid we shouldn't delay."

"He's a very nice young man according to the report. Very grateful."

Aileen slowly stood. "I'd like you to continue to search for his parents. And what news have you regarding my other siblings?"

"Good news on your brother Diarmuid. We've tracked him to the States. He found a job on a passenger liner when he was sixteen and worked until he could buy his own passage. He landed in New York City in 1923, but we haven't been able to trace him further. There are some very hopeful leads, though, and I'm certain we're going to have a breakthrough very soon."

Aileen circled the huge mahogany desk and sat down on the chair next to Ian. "You've done wonderful work, Mr. Stephens, and in such a short time. But I'm sure you'll understand when I tell you that you must work even faster."

"Yes, ma'am, I understand. I will hire more investigators. And I'm certain that I'll have much more at our next meeting."

She reached out and took his hand, patting it as she spoke. "I'm sure you'll understand why time is of the essence. I've lived without a family all these years. I'd like to know them before I leave this mortal coil."

As she walked him to the door, Aileen slipped her hands around his arm. Their footsteps were soft on the old Chinese carpet. She walked outside and waved goodbye as he drove off in his little sports car.

There was nothing like family, she thought to herself. And now, she'd meet this young man, this Logan Quinn. Would she recognize something of herself in him? In the way he spoke or the way he laughed? Or was their connection so distant that there would be nothing that bound them together except blood?

"A horse rancher," she said to herself. "My, he sounds like he'd be an interesting young man." She hurried back into the house. "Sally? Sally?"

The housekeeper came running out into the entry hall, her hand pressed to her chest. "Yes. Yes, I'm here. What is it? Oh, sweet Jesus, I thought you'd fallen. You sounded so panicked."

"Just excited," Aileen said. "We're going to have a house-guest in a few weeks. My great-nephew will be visiting from Australia. I think we need to freshen up the guest rooms. Maybe do a bit of redecorating. I want to make sure my family feels comfortable here."

"Yes, ma'am. Why don't the two of us sit down and have some lunch and we'll go over all the details?"

"Details," she said. "I have so many details. Mr. Stephens put them all in his report. Did I tell you his name was Logan? That sounds like such a lovely name. I wonder what he likes to eat?"

"I don't know. Maybe we should start planning some menus."

Aileen took the housekeeper's arm as they slowly walked back inside the house. "Family is a wonderful thing, isn't it?"

* * * * *

Just Give In...

Kathleen O'Reilly

Dear Reader,

I come from a very frugal family. As a kid, I never realized this because we had the world's greatest toys. A mismatched swing set, a yellow rickshaw, and this great brass bell that you had to hand-crank to bong (and yes, it did not ring, it *bonged)*. I still own a chair made out of a tractor seat, and in our den sits a lamp made out of an old water pump.

Eventually, it dawned on me that it was not little elves that were making these toys for us, but my dad. After I was married, the husband and I bought ten acres of land in the Texas Hill Country. And I saw the same enterprising tendencies there.

In Texas, there are a lot of hands-on folks who know how to fix a car, how to saw down a tree, and can do all their own electrical work without missing a beat. I love that pioneer spirit in the Lone Star State, and I took full advantage of it when creating Jason Kincaid.

It's always hard to say goodbye to all the characters in a series, and this one was no exception. I hope you have loved the Harts of Texas as much as I do.

Best,

Kathleen O'Reilly

To the big-hearted people from the big-hearted state.
Texas, forever.

1

EVERY FAMILY STARTED with a house, a mother, a father and a passel of squabbling siblings. Brooke Hart had no father, two unsociable brothers who seemed deathly afraid of her and a 1987 Chevy Impala.

As far as families went, it wasn't much, but it was a thousand times better than before. Then there was the mysterious message from an estate lawyer in Tin Cup. They needed to "talk" was all that he said, and apparently lawyers in Texas didn't believe in answering machines and voicemail, because every time she tried to call, no one answered. In her head she had created all sorts of exciting possibilities, and journeyed cross country to see the lawyer, bond with her brothers and find a place to call home, all of which was exciting and expensive, which meant that right now, she was in desperate need of a job. Money was not as necessary as say, love, home and a fat, fluffy cat, but there were times when money was required. One, when you needed to eat, and two, when your three-year-old Shearling boots weren't cutting it anymore.

In New York, the boots had been cute and ordinary and seventy-five percent off at a thrift store. In the smoldering September heat of Texas, she looked like a freak. An au courant freak, but a freak nonetheless.

As she peered into the grocery store window, she studied

an older couple who were the stuff of her dreams. In Brooke Hart's completely sentimental opinion, the spry old codger behind the cash register could have been Every Grandpa Man. A woman shuffled back and forth between the front counter and the storeroom in back. Her cottony-gray hair was rolled up in a bun, just like in the movies. The cash register was a relic with clunky keys that Brooke's hands itched to touch. The wooden floor of the grocery was neat, but not neat enough, which was the prime reason she was currently here.

They looked warm, hospitable and in desperate need of young, able-bodied assistance.

The one advantage to living with Brooke's mother, Charlene Hart, was that Brooke knew the three things to absolutely never do when searching for a job.

One. Do not show up drunk, or even a more socially acceptable tipsy. Future employers frowned on blowing .2 in a Breathalyzer.

Two. Do not show up late for an appointment. As Brooke had no appointment, this wasn't a problem.

And the last, but most important rule in job-hunting was to actually show up. Although Brooke believed that deep down her mother was a beautiful spirit with a generous nature and a joyous laugh, Charlene Hart was about as present in life as she was in death, which was to say, not a lot.

Frankly, being family-less sucked, which was why she had been so excited to track down her two brothers. Twenty-six years ago, a then-pregnant Charlene Hart had walked out on Frank Hart and their two young sons, Tyler and Austen. Seven months later, Brooke had been born in a homeless shelter in Oak Brook, Illinois. Charlene never spoke of Frank, or her sons. Charlene had rarely spoken of anything grounded in reality, and it wasn't until after she died that Brooke found an article about Tyler Hart on the internet. After feeling so alone for all her life, she had stared at the picture of her brother, with the same faraway look in his dark eyes, and the world felt a little less gray.

She knew then. Over and over she had repeated her brother's name, and Brooke realized she wasn't family-less after all.

To better appeal to her brothers, she'd concocted the perfect life. Storybook mother, devoted stepfather, idyllic suburban residence, and a rented fiancée (two hundred bucks an hour, not cheap). But her brothers had clearly never read the Handbook on Quality Family Reunions, and although they'd been polite enough, their shields were up the entire time. If they found out the truth of Brooke's less than storybook existence? A disaster of cataclysmic proportions. Relatives never reacted well when poor relations with no place to call home showed up on their doorstep. They weren't inclined to "like you" or "respect you" or even "want to be around you." Oh, certainly, they might act polite and sympathetic, but homelessness was a definite black mark, so right now, she wasn't going to let them find out.

And then, when the time was right, Brooke would spring the truth on the boys, and work her way into her new family's good graces.

Her first step involved getting a job, paying her way, shouldering her own financial burdens. Second, find out what the lawyer wanted.

Slowly she sucked in a breath, bunching her sweater to hide the green patch beneath the right elbow. In New York, the mismatched patch looked artsy, chic-chic, but to two elderly citizens, it might seem—frivolous. Finally satisfied that she looked respectable, Brooke walked through the rickety screen door, catching it before it slammed shut.

The friendly old proprietor gave her a small-town-America smile, and Brooke responded in kind.

"I'm here about the job. I think I'm your girl. I'm energetic, motivated. I have an excellent memory, and my math skills are off the charts."

The man's jovial mouth dwindled. "We didn't advertise for help."

"Maybe not, but when opportunity knocks, I say, open the door and use a doorstop so that it can't close behind you."

Behind her, she heard the door creak open, as if the very fates were on her side. Her spirits rose because she knew that this small grocery story in Tin Cup, Texas, was fate. Emboldened, Brooke pressed on. "When I saw this adorable place, I knew it was my perfect opportunity. Why don't you give me a try?"

The old man yelled to the back: "Gladys! Did you advertise for help? I told you not to do that. I can handle the store." Then he turned his attention to Brooke. "She thinks I can't do a gall-darned thing anymore."

From behind her, an arm reached around, plunking a can of peas on the wooden counter. The proprietor glanced at the peas, avoided Brooke's eyes, and she knew the door of opportunity was slamming on her posterior. She could feel it.

Hastily she placed her own competent hand on the counter. "My brothers will vouch for me. Austen and Tyler. I'm one of the Harts," she announced. It was a line she had clung to like a good luck charm.

At the man's confused look, she chuckled at her own mis-step, hoping he wouldn't notice the shakiness in her voice. "Dr. Tyler Hart and Austen Hart. They were raised here. I believe Austen is now a very respectable member of the community. Tyler is a world-famous surgeon."

She liked knowing her oldest brother was in the medical profession. Everybody loved doctors.

The man scratched at the stubble on his cheek. "Wasn't that older boy locked up for cooking meth?"

Patiently Brooke shook her head. If the man messed up this often, she would be a boon to his establishment. "No, you must have him confused with someone else."

A discreet cough sounded from behind her, and once again the proprietor yelled to the back. "Gladys! Which one of the Hart boys ended up at the State Pen?"

Astounding. The man seemed intent on sullying her family's good reputation. Brooke rushed to correct him, but then Gladys appeared with four cartons of eggs stacked in her arms. "There's no need to yell, Henry. I'm not deaf," she said, and then gave Brooke a neighborly smile. "He thinks I'm ready to be put out to pasture." She noticed the can of peas. "This yours?"

"It's mine," interrupted the customer behind her.

Not wanting to seem pushy, Brooke smiled apologetically. Gladys placed the eggs on the counter and then peered at Brooke over silver spectacles. "What are you here for?"

"The job," Brooke announced.

"We don't need any help," Gladys replied, patting Brooke on the cheek like any grandmother would. Her hands were wrinkled, yet still soft and smelled of vanilla. "Are you looking for work?" she asked. Soft hands, soft heart.

Recognizing this was her chance, Brooke licked dry lips and then broke into her speech. "I'm Brooke Hart. I'm new in town. I don't want to be an imposition on my family. Not a free-loader. Not me. Everybody needs to carry their own weight, and by the way, I can carry a good bit of weight." She patted her own capable biceps. "Whatever you need. Flour. Produce. Milk. And I'm very careful on eggs. People never seem to respect the more fragile merchandise, don't you think?"

Gladys looked her over, the warm eyes cooling. "You look a little thin. You should be eating better."

The hand behind her shoved the peas forward, sliding the eggs close to the edge. Smartly, Brooke moved the carton out of harms way.

"I plan to eat better. It's priority number two on my list— right after I find a job. I'm really excited to be here in Tin Cup, and I want to fit in. I want to help out. Perhaps we could try something on a temporary basis." She flashed her best "I'm your girl" smile. "You won't regret it."

"You're one of the Harts?" asked the old man, still seeming confused.

"Didn't think there was a girl. Old Frank hated girls." From the look on Gladys's face, Gladys was no fan of Frank Hart, either.

"I never actually met my father," Brooke explained, not wanting people to believe she was cut from the same rapscallion cloth. "My mother and I moved when I was in utero."

"Smartest thing she ever did, leaving the rest of them," said Henry.

Brooke blinked, not exactly following all this, but she needed a job, and she sensed that Mr. Green Peas was getting impatient. "I really need a job. My brother Austen will vouch for me."

Gladys's gray brows rose to an astounding height. "Nothing but trouble, that one. Stole from Zeke..." Then she sighed. "He's doing good things now, with the railroad and all, but I don't know."

"That was a long time ago." Henry chimed in, apparently more forgiving.

"It's getting even longer," complained the man behind her.

Gladys shook her kindly head. "We're not looking to hire anybody, and you being a stranger and all. No references, except for your brother..."

"I'm new in town," Brooke repeated in a small voice, feeling the door of opportunity about to hit her in both her posterior and her face, as well. Doors of opportunity could sometimes be painful.

"I'll vouch for her."

At first, Brooke was sure she had misheard. It had happened before. But no, not this time. Brooke turned, profoundly grateful that the goodness of small-town America was not overrated. She'd lived in Atlantic City, Detroit, Chicago, Indianapolis and six freezing weeks in St. Paul. She'd dreamed of a little town with bakeries and cobblestone streets and hand-painted signs and people who smiled at you when you walked past. She'd prayed for a little town, and finally she was about to live in one. "Thank you," she told the man behind her.

He was tall, in his mid-thirties, with chestnut brown hair badly in need of a cut. There wasn't a lot of small-town goodness emanating from the rigid lines of his face. A black patch covered his left eye and he had a thin scar along his left cheek. In fact, he looked anything but friendly, but Brooke didn't believe in judging a book by its cover, so her smile was genuine and warm.

"You know her, Captain?" Gladys asked.

Mr. Green Peas nodded curtly. "It seems like forever."

"It's about time you're making some friends in town. We were worried when you moved out to the old farmstead, not knowing a soul in town and all. I'll tell Sonya, she'll be happy to hear that."

Not sure who Sonya was, but sensing that Captain's opinion counted with these two, Brooke faced the couple. "Please, give me a job," she urged. "You won't regret it."

From somewhere in the tiny grocery, Brooke could hear a relentless pounding. A rapid-fire thump that seemed oddly out of place in the sleepy locale.

Thumpa-thumpa-thumpa.

Gladys and Henry didn't hear the loud noise.

No one did.

Because, duh, it was her own heart.

She told herself it didn't matter if she didn't land this job with this homespun couple. It didn't matter if her brothers didn't welcome her with open arms. It didn't matter if the lawyer had made a mistake.

She told herself that none of it mattered.

All her life Brooke had told herself that none of it mattered, but it always did.

Her hands grasped the counter, locking on the small tin can. "What do you say?"

Gladys patted her cheek for a second time. Soft, warm... and sorrowful.

"I'm sorry, honey. We just can't."

As rejections went, it was very pleasant, but Brooke's heart still crawled somewhere below the floor. They had been so friendly, the store was so cute with its handpainted Hinkle's Grocery sign over the door. She'd been so sure. Realizing that there was nothing left for her in this place, Brooke walked out the door, opportunity slamming her in the butt.

Her first day in Tin Cup. No job, no lawyer, an uneasy brother who didn't know she was here, and—she glanced down at the can of peas still stuck in her hand—she'd just shoplifted a can of peas. Brooke fished in her jeans pocket for some cash, brought out two crumbled dollars, an old Metro Card and a lint-covered peppermint—slightly used.

Two dollars. It was her last two dollars, until she found a job, of course. All she had to do was go back inside, slap the money on the counter and leave as if she didn't care. As if they hadn't shouted down her best "Pick me!" plea.

Brooke turned away from the store with its cute homespun sign and restashed her money. Better to be branded a thief than a reject. It wasn't the most honorable decision, but Brooke had more pride than many would expect from a homeless woman that lived out of her car.

Once she was gainfully employed, she'd pay back Gladys and Henry. They'd understand.

And was that really, truly how she wanted to kick off her new life in her new home? As some light-fingered Lulu, which apparently all the Harts were supposed to be, anyway?

After taking another peek through the window, she sighed. No, she wasn't going to be a light-fingered Lulu, no matter how tempting it might be. And especially not for a can of peas.

In the distance a freckle-faced little girl on a skateboard careened down the sidewalk. Eagerly, Brooke waved her down, hoping to recruit an unwitting accomplice so that Brooke Hart wouldn't be another unflattering mug shot on the Post Office wall.

"Hello," she said, when the little girl skidded to a stop and then Brooke held out her hand. "Can you give this to Gladys? Tell her it's for the peas."

The girl examined the proffered money, then Brooke, innocent eyes alight with purpose. "You going to tip me for the delivery?"

Yes, the entrepreneurial spirit was strong in this one. Who knew that honesty was such a huge pain in the butt? And expensive, too. After jamming her hand in her pocket, Brooke pulled out her last seventeen cents. Reluctantly, she handed it to the kid, who stood there, apparently expecting more.

"Please?" asked Brooke, still wearing her non-stranger-danger smile. At last, the little girl sighed.

"Whatever," she said and kicked a foot at the end of the skateboard, flipping it up into her hand.

"That's pretty cool," Brooke told her, and the girl rolled her eyes, but her mouth curled up a bit and Brooke knew that she'd made her first friend in Tin Cup. Sure, she'd had to pay for the privilege, but still, a friend was a friend, no matter how pricey, no matter how small.

"Whatever," the girl repeated, then pulled open the screen door.

Now that Brooke's fledging reputation was somewhat restored, or about to be, her job here was done. She dashed across the street, leaping into her eyesore of a car before anyone could see. She had big plans before she showed up on Austen's doorstep, and it wasn't going to be without a job, without any money and in a car that should be condemned.

Once safely behind the wheel, she tossed the can of peas onto the backseat, the afternoon sun winking happily on the metal. It fit right in with the hodge-podge of things. A portable cooler, one beat-up gym bag, her collection of real estate magazines, the plastic water jug and now peas.

Peas.

What the heck was she supposed to do with peas?

2

THE LED WAS blinking a steady green over his front porch, the motion detector nearly hidden beneath the old wood doorframe. From inside, he could hear the sound of a dog barking.

All clear.

Not that anyone was going to break into his less than fancy house, but old habits were hard to break. There was no dog, only a pimped out robotic vacuum cleaner with two golden LEDs for eyes and a mechanical tail that wagged. Not the cutest puppy, but Jason Kincaid had invented the only canine in the world that cleaned up after itself.

While Dog wheeled around the floor, Jason put down his keys, pulled on his faded Orioles cap and went outside to work. The missing can of peas didn't concern him. Jason hated peas, but every Monday he went to the Hinkle's store to shop. He hated shopping, too, but his father had told him he needed to get out more, so every Tuesday when his dad called, he could tell the old man—with complete honesty—that he'd been out shopping only yesterday.

Outside the house, the flat terrain was exactly the same. The front yard, the backyard, the four storage sheds and even the detached one car garage were filled with lawn mowers, vacuum cleaners, small engines, large engines, lumber and scrap metal.

He'd never invited his family to visit because the house

looked too much like a junkyard, like the long neglected habitat of a man who needed to live alone.

Which it was.

Jason pulled down the socket wrench from the upright mattress springs that had been recycled into his Wall O' Tools and got to work.

The current project was a five horsepower lawnmower in desperate need of a new carburetor or a humane burial, but Jason wasn't ready to give it up for dead. Not yet.

He'd just gotten air to blow clean through the tube when the red LED on the porch began to glow. Motion detectors had been strategically placed across the ten acres of his land, wired to let him know whenever anyone decided to intrude—like now. Jason glanced toward the road and noticed the cloud of dust.

A HAV, or, in layman's terms, a car still unidentified.

Salesmen didn't come out this far. He'd never met the neighbors, which were four acres away on either side, so when people showed up at his gate, they were usually lost.

After pulling his cap down a little lower, Jason made his way to the front gate, an eight foot, black, metal monster that he'd rescued from an old sanitarium. It looked exactly like it belonged at the front entrance of a sanitarium, which was why Jason had wanted it, and why the sanitarium didn't.

From behind the iron bars, he watched the beaten-up Impala approach. The rear door was black, the driver's side door was red, and the hood was sunshine-yellow. If Henry Ford and Picasso had gone out on a bender, that car was what the hangover would have looked like.

Jason stayed steady and impassive, not angry or unfriendly, but stood and watched as a woman exited the world's worst excuse for a car.

Her.

She still had the same never-say-die smile, which, considering the state of her transport, was just flat-out stupid. Once she was at the gate, a mere two feet from him, she held up the can of peas.

"You left these." Her voice was nice, not high and birdlike, but no cigarette smoke, either. Sonya had a low, husky voice. At one point, Jason had thought it was sexy.

"You didn't have to bring them all the way out here." He probably should thank her for it, but he was distracted by the beads of sweat on her neck, and the green sweater had to be hot. Judging from the way it was clinging to her curves, the Hell-Car didn't have air-conditioning. He didn't like that she was sweating for him. He didn't like the way his one good eye kept locking on her chest, like some reconnaissance tracking system doped up on Viagra.

"I don't mind," she told him, then put the can to the bars, as if she expected the can to slip through. Nope. Jason could have told her that metal didn't work that way. It took five hundred pounds of force to dislodge metal, or eight hundred degrees of heat. Sometimes both.

However, Jason stayed silent because he had learned that people never liked to work too hard at a conversation. Eventually, they always gave up.

"Are you going to open the gate, or should I toss this sucker over the top?"

His instinctive response was to instruct her to go ahead and throw, but two things kept him from going with the default. The knowledge that he would have crossed the crazy-lonely-man line in his head, and the beat-up sedan. Frankly, that car out-crazied his crazy-line anyway, so while she might not notice, he would.

Those were his reasons. That, and he liked her breasts.

He typed in the combination on the keypad and the gate creaked open. He'd gone through a lot of trouble to get the creak exactly right. A haunted house creak. At the sound, the woman's eyes grew wide, but not in fear. *No, she liked it.*

"I bet the kids love this place at Halloween."

"People don't drive out this far for a stick of gum." People didn't drive out this far for peas, either, but he left that part out.

"If they don't, they don't know what they're missing." While she talked, her eyes surveyed the yard, the seventy-year-old house, the mountains of scrap, the piles of engines.

Before she could trespass farther, he took the can of peas. "Thank you." Then he nodded once, held the gate open and politely waited for her to leave.

Leaving didn't seem to be part of her strategy. She ducked under his arm and wandered inside, looking at one pile, then the next. "What do you do with this stuff?"

Jason shrugged, not about to explain his hobbies to her, and not sure he could. Not that anyone would understand, anyway. Hell, he didn't even know why.

His gaze followed her as she walked around, moving from one mound to the next, drawing precariously close to the house.

His pulse rate kicked up. Anxiety or lust? She was cute, short, stacked and curious. The clothes were out of place in the September heat, but he was grateful she was covered up, cause he didn't think his pulse rate could handle any more. He liked her hair though. It was long, dark silk that hung down her back.

"What is that?" she asked, pointing to a modified bicycle. "Wait, wait, don't tell me."

Not that he would have told her anyway, so he stayed quiet while her fingers traced over the twisted metal hump with the leather seat mounted on top. Crouching down, she inspected the spring-loaded frame with the four iron-spoke wheels. It'd taken him three months to find the wheels, and eventually he'd bought them on eBay. They were perfect.

"It's an animal?"

Still he waited.

She rose, studied the thing. "First, there are four legs, or wheels. Second, the elongated back is almost like a hill...or a hump..." Her finger crept to her mouth, chewing absently. She had a nice mouth. Red lips that spent most of their time open.

His mind, always running in a tangential yet somewhat practical direction, began to think of all the uses for an open mouth: eating, breathing, kissing, sucking.

Her mouth opened wider. "A camel!"

And now that twenty questions were over, Jason needed to send her on her way. As he headed to the metal gate, he thanked her for coming. There was very little sincerity in the words, but he didn't think she would notice.

Her dark eyes flickered once. Okay, she noticed. He kicked a particularly heavy cast-iron drum. The pain was solid, well deserved. His foot would recover.

"That's some car."

Back and forth she shifted, like she was embarrassed about her mode of transport, but after seeing his mode of habitat, he couldn't understand why she would care.

"I bought it in Tennessee."

"Long drive for a car," he noted, realizing he was making conversation, lingering in her company.

It was her breasts. Had to be.

Evil breasts.

His body hardened at the thought of touching her evil breasts.

"Tennessee was on the way," she responded, hopefully not tuned in to his thoughts.

"Surprised the car made it," he told her, channeling his thoughts into another more socially-acceptable direction.

Seeing her wince, he made a mental note to stop commenting on the dicey condition of her vehicle, but it was a little hard to ignore. The inside of the car appeared to be in as bad shape as the outside, with a blanket thrown over the backseat like a tarp. The tarp was most likely designed to keep out prying eyes—like his own. A gallon jug of water was sitting in the front seat, some food wrappers, a pillow, a half-open gym bag and a small sack for trash.

Her home.

As he continued to stare at her mode of habitat, a flush crept up her face, and he knew her habitat was a taboo conversation topic, too. That worked out well for him since he wanted her off his place.

All of her, including her breasts.

"You're staying with your brother?" he asked pleasantly. As parting remarks went, it wasn't the best.

"Oh, yeah," she answered quickly, moving to stand in front of her car, blocking his view.

"Good," he said, not that he believed her. Considering the state of her car, her finances, he didn't think she was related to anybody in town. If she had family, she would have gone there first.

Probably the brother thing was a lie, as well. In which case, she'd be jobless, living out of her car...

Not that he cared.

She reached for the door handle and yanked it open, the damn thing sticking so hard that her shoulder was now probably dislocated.

Jobless, dislocated shoulder, living out of her car...

Not that he cared.

"You need a job?" he asked, sounding exactly like he was offering her a job. The woman turned, her eyes swimming with hope—until it was gone.

"You know someone who's hiring?" she asked, her eyes not so hopeful, unless a man was looking.

"I need some help here," he offered, thinking quickly. "Organizing."

Not that he wanted organization, not that he wanted human companionship, especially of the female variety, especially of the homeless, jobless female variety.

Most likely, she was needy.

His old army buddies would be laughing their asses off.

Of course, if any of them saw her breasts, they would understand.

"I'm a great organizer," she said, hands clasped tight in front of her, prayer-like, and he realized how much she wanted this.

A job.

Not him.

Not that he was even thinking sex. A man who lived in a junkyard with one good eye was no prize. Nope, Sonya had made that clear, and that was long before his junkyard phase.

No, it wasn't the sex. It was the idea of this woman being out there alone. Jason might not be the biggest people-person in the world, but sometime people deserved better. Sometimes—rarely, but sometimes—Jason noticed.

"It'd be temporary," he added, in case she thought he was charitable.

"That'd be perfect. It'll give me a chance to settle in town and find a permanent position."

"Yeah. I can't afford a lot," he said, in case she thought he was loaded.

"I don't need a lot," she told him, obviously guessing he wasn't loaded.

"Good." They stood there and stared for a minute, and she didn't seem to mind his eye patch. Since she was going to be working for him, not shrinking in horror was a plus.

Finally she spoke. "I'm Brooke Hart."

"Jason Kincaid." He should have offered her his hand, but he didn't. A handshake implied a contract, a pledge. This was nothing more than one human being helping out a woman who needed a chance to get her life together.

Not that he cared.

"So, you're staying with your brother?" he asked again, in case she wanted to come clean about her living situation.

"Yeah," she answered, not coming clean. *Message received. Don't ask about the living situation, either.*

"You can start tomorrow?"

"First thing."

"Not too early. I don't get up early," he lied. Jason got up at the crack of dawn, but he thought he should straighten up his place first. Get things in order before she started...organizing.

"Not a problem. I have a lot of things to do." She paused. "With my brother."

"Sure," he agreed like an idiot. Rather than letting her notice that he actually was an idiot, he headed back toward the gate.

"I'll see you tomorrow around ten. That'll be okay?"

The smile was back in place.

Not that he cared.

Then she nodded and climbed into the Hell-Car. Once he returned to the yard, he spent the rest of the day repairing an old wheelchair. Yet every time he looked toward the porch, it was the red LED that was lit, not the green. Sometimes animals set off a false positive, but not often, and not tonight. Someone was out there, or maybe someone had never left.

When night fell, and the crickets began to chirp, Jason quit working and then walked along the fence line, a man with no particular purpose at all. When he was a kid, he had sat on the porch with his dad, watching the sky and the stars, talking baseball and trusting the world to pass by peacefully.

After thirteen years in the army, he knew better. As he walked the fence line, he spotted what he'd been searching for. The old Impala, parked at the edge of the fence line. One dim reading light glowing from the interior.

It was dark outside and she was still out there.

Obviously no brother. No place to stay, but at least she now had a job. A temporary job.

Not that he cared.

There were a lot of things to do before tomorrow. Make the house habitable for human living, do some laundry and throw out the two-month old milk in the fridge. And while he was doing that, she would be out there alone. He tried to ignore the hole in his gut. There was nothing that he could do about the Impala that was parked at the edge of the road, but every few hours, he peeked out the window, making sure there was no trouble.

Not that he cared.

BROOKE CALCULATED THAT by day three she would have enough money to buy more suitable work clothes. First, she needed a cooler shirt, because the sweater was a merino-wool blend that was causing her to wilt. In order to have money for the car, she had sold most of her clothes in Nashville. At that time, a sweater had seemed practical. Now, not so much. The Shearling boots were looking sadder by the minute and would need to be replaced, too. Brooke believed that no matter the financial hardship, it was important to look capable and confident.

Unfortunately, the work that the Captain had given her was insultingly easy, as if she wasn't capable of anything more. That morning, he'd handed her a sheet of paper and then indicated a knee-high pile of assorted mechanical whatsits, a tiny island in a yard of complete chaos.

"Here. Write down everything you see."

"That's an inventory, not an organizational system," she pointed out, and he glared at her out of his one visible eye, which he probably thought was intimidating, but she thought it was more sexy pirate. She knew he wouldn't want to hear that, so she pulled her features into some semblance of lemming-hood.

He didn't look fooled. "Inventorying this pile is step one. Once that's done, we'll talk about step two."

She nudged at a wheelless unicycle with her boot. "It's going to take me fifteen minutes to do this. Why don't you let me sort by type?" By all indications, he'd tried to do that in the areas closest to the house. Wood boards were stacked together, some kind of electric gizmos were lined up like bowling pins—wait, they were bowling pins.

He put his hands on his hips, doing that intimidating thing again. "You don't know what each item is."

Unintimidated, she picked up a springy thing attached to

a weight with a circular metal plate on the end, some piece of the Industrial Revolution that'd gotten left behind. Probably on purpose. "You really know what this is?" she asked.

At the Captain's silence, she dangled the part higher in the air.

As a rule, Brooke was usually a people-pleaser, but she had issues with someone thinking that poor people didn't have a brain in their head. It was apparent that the Captain was giving her busy-work in order to give her money because he felt sorry for her. Charlene Hart would have taken the money and ran, possibly stopping for happy hour on the way. Brooke Hart needed people to see her as something more than a charity case—someone positive, someone good.

His gaze raked over her, inventorying her clothes, but lingering on the thingamaboobs beneath. Wisely Brooke pretended not to notice. "You're not dressed for working outside," he told her, because apparently his optimal working wardrobe was a thousand-year-old pair of jeans, a white undershirt, and a denim work shirt that hung loose on his rangy shoulders. Perhaps if Brooke had discretionary funds, she might have sprung for something more functionally appropriate. But no, she decided, even if she were as rich as Trump, she still wouldn't be caught dead in clothes that were so…démodé.

Not wanting to argue about her outfit, she held the doo-dad up higher, just so that he would notice her chest. Cheap, yes, but effective. "You don't know what this is, do you? Insulting my clothes won't detract me from the truth. Exhibit one, an antiquated widget that got rusted over in the Ice Age."

He muttered under his breath. "I'll give you money. Go into town. Buy something. At least better shoes."

And now she was back to being a charity case. Brooke placed the doo-dad on the ground and pushed up her sleeves. "I'm here to work."

"You can't work in those shoes."

Seeing the stubborn set to his jaw, Brooke decided that there was no point in continuing the discussion. She walked toward the front gate, skirting one hill then another. A demonstration to the unbelieving that her boots were just fine.

Unattractive? Yes, but this was from a man who thought exterior appearances unimportant. Or at least she hoped so.

"Where are you going?" he yelled, just as she reached the gate.

"I can't work under these conditions. You're trying to micromanage everything and I'm accustomed to more responsibility. I suggest you find some able-bodied teenager who needs detailed instruction and doesn't mind a dress code."

"It isn't a dress code," he yelled back. "More a dress suggestion."

She turned, stared him down in silence until finally he shrugged.

"You win. I won't say another word about your clothes."

Still, there was disagreement in his face. Brooke stayed where she was. "I can help you with your inventory, but you have to let me do my job. Do you have a computer I can work on?"

"In the house."

"Good. I can use the computer to look up whatever I don't know, and you can work in peace. We'll get along fine, and I'll guarantee you'll be happy with the results."

At his nod of agreement, she picked a path from one pile to another, until she stood in front of him. Once again, his gaze drifted to her boots.

Brooke held up a hand in warning. "If you can't say anything nice, don't say anything at all."

Judging by his four-letter response, it was a rule he needed to work on, but Brooke was down with that.

Like she'd said, if he'd let her do her job, they'd get along fine.

BY THE TIME THE SUN was baking overhead, Brooke had sorted and inventoried fourteen small heaps of contraptions that no man in his right mind would want, which only proved her suspicions that the Captain was a standard left-brainer. As even more evidence, not that she needed it, inside the house was a veritable smorgasbord of oddly designed gizmos and wuzzits. A push-button car radio hooked up to an iPod. Bookshelves made from stacked wooden pallets, a vintage Coke machine made into a bar and a small metal box with a blinking light that made her nervous.

That, and then there was Dog. The little, rounded 'pet' scooted around the floor at different speeds, and sometimes he sang "Happy Birthday, Mr. President," in a voice that sounded just like Marilyn Monroe. Some dog, indeed.

Everything seemed to belong in an art gallery, a museum or thrift store, possibly all three, but she had to give him high marks for creativity. Brooke would've never thought of an automated pot scrubber or a self-cleaning toilet. However, now that she'd seen them, she wondered why no one had ever thought of them before.

Judging from the never-ending materials she had left to inventory, he'd be making gizmos for the next two hundred years. A long trickle of sweat dripped in her eyes, and she dreamed of moving to the coolness of the house, but there were only three more piles to sort, and then she'd be done. Better to go forth and succeed, then celebrate an honest day's work. Hopefully, air-conditioning would be involved.

Out of the corner of her eye, she could see the Captain watching her from the other side of the yard. In order to demonstrate her non-wimpiness, she hefted a ten-inch flywheel motor (thank you, Google) and placed it in a neat line with the others, before noting the type on her list. It was only after she had deposited the oily thing that she knew why he was staring. In the middle of the sweater was a supersized grease stain that no amount of artistic cover-up could disguise. Sensing the beginnings of another lecture, she waved happily, but it was too late.

The Captain advanced.

"I owe you a new sweater. That one's ruined." There was a glint in his eye as if he'd been waiting for just this moment.

Nuh-uh-uh.

Pulling at the wool, Brooke shot him her sweetest smile. "It looks like a map of Canada. I think it's just the touch it needed."

His jaw twitched.

"At least put on a cooler shirt."

Certainly there was a logic to that. He seemed to be genuinely concerned, and she considered the idea, but it was only Day One, Hour Six. He'd given her a nonsense job, and now he wanted to put her in his clothes like some vagrant. So what made her different from any other hard-luck case on the mean streets of life?

Absolutely nothing, and Brooke Hart wasn't just some other hard-luck case. No, she was going to work this off with grit and sweat, and probably a lot more grease, and the Captain would just have to deal.

Of course, she'd already put in a lot of grit and sweat. Fourteen piles were now neatly inventoried and identified. Maybe a cooler shirt was a fair trade, an old-fashioned barter sort of arrangement. Yeah, that seemed reasonable, and she was just opening her mouth to accept his offer, when he lifted a can of some unknown substance and threw it on her sweater.

Brooke's mouth snapped shut as the wool plastered to her stomach like a skin mask gone bad.

Aha.

The unknown substance was glue.

3

AS THE SUBSTANCE BEGAN to dry, Brooke glared at the Captain, trying to find some words. Although as a rule she wasn't usually a believer in violence and/or retribution, she felt here there were extenuating circumstances. Her hands fisted into small glue-encrusted WMDs.

Before she could move (flexibility was difficult when epoxified), he set the can at her feet, pushing a hand through his dark hair.

"I don't think I should touch you but...ah, hell, Brooke, I'm sorry, but we need to get you cleaned up." Oh, sure, now he looked sorry.

She plucked the sweater loose from her stomach, wincing as if she were in pain, just so he'd feel worse. "What's the plan now?" she asked. "Hose me down with turpentine?"

He paused, trying to decide if that was a joke. Comprehension dawned slowly, and his mouth twitched with humor. "I wouldn't have used a hose. Go shower before you harden and turn into yard art."

Not a big fan of his sense of humor, Brooke stalked inside. If there had been a carpet or a rug, she would've worried about dripping. Not that she had any business being worried, since this was all his doing, but still...a nice rug would have done wonders for the faded wood floors, and given the place a marvelous homey appearance.

She found the bathroom, painted in a surprisingly cheery buttercup-yellow. His quiet footfall sounded behind her—so stealthy for such a big guy.

"I imagine this will take some time. The towels are where?" she asked, happy to see his face still covered in guilt.

The Captain held up a pair of large scissors.

Brooke frowned. "That isn't a towel."

"Unless you want glue in your hair, you'll need to cut the sweater, and, uh, anything else I screwed up."

Cut? *Cut?* Was he out of his mind? Didn't he know this was high-quality apparel? "I'm not cutting this."

"It's gone. Let it go. I'll replace it." His smile didn't look so sad, and that was when she knew, when his win-at-all-costs behavior became apparent.

"You did this just so that I'd have to trash it."

He nodded. "Reason and logic weren't winning the war. Sometimes covert maneuvers work best."

And still he didn't see the problem. "Aren't you the least bit sorry?"

"Of course," he said, sounding sincere...mostly.

Her eyes narrowed. "But you'd do it again, wouldn't you?"

At her words, he wanted to lie. She could see the denial building on his face, but no, the man was damned to tell the truth.

"Probably. Although I'd have come up with something a little less drastic than accelerator glue. The smell's killer. I didn't get any in your hair, or your face?" He frowned. "Are you allergic to anything?"

"A little late to ask." She grabbed the scissors, shut the door, and got to work destroying her most favorite sweater. After two not-so-awesome tries, she could see this was going to be a problem. The wool was hard, getting harder by the second, and the glue was mucking up the scissors. Determined to avoid asking for help, she hacked on, but the scissors were getting worse, and her fingers were starting to stick, and from outside the door, she could hear him pacing.

Three more times she tried, three times she failed, and finally, Brooke sighed. The shabby girl in the mirror wasn't responsible, or plucky, or capable of surviving whatever life threw at her. Dark hair stuck out in sweat-damp clumps. Her wonderful sweater was now crusted over with a glossy sheen that looked wrong.

Her brothers would disown her...again. Maybe she didn't have much, but she had her pride, she had her self-respect and she had a body that was uncomfortably stiff. All because of him. No, the Captain was going to pay for this and pay big. Slowly she smiled, the girl in the mirror looking less shabby by the minute. Thoughts of revenge did that to a woman.

Flinging open the door, Brooke brandished the scissors like a sword. "Ruined. Do you have something better? A blowtorch maybe?"

He studied her partial sweater-ectomy. Then he scratched his jaw, where the darkened stubble was starting to show. "Nah. Glue's flammable."

"This is no time for sarcasm."

"Not sarcasm. Look it up."

She glared. He shrugged. "Give me a minute."

Less than thirty seconds later, he was back with a hunting knife capable of great destruction. The Captain's face was tense, waiting for her to take the knife, but that wasn't part of her plan, and so she spun around, giving him her back. "Make a clean cut, neck to hem," she instructed. "You didn't get any glue back there. It should go easier."

The air crackled with his fear. "You're sure about this?"

"Just do it," she whispered in a teasing, taunting voice.

Gently he pulled aside her hair and in one quick slice, the sweater hung in two loose pieces, her back bare except for the single bra strap.

"You can...uh...handle the rest?" His words were rough, hesitant...awkward.

Oh, yes, revenge was a dish best served hot.

Brooke whirled around, plucked at the sweater's remains and then pulled it off, standing before him in jeans and bra. His eye flickered, mouth tightening, but to his credit, he didn't look down. Not once. The man had the self-control of a monk.

Well, pooh. However, Brooke wasn't done. Not by a long shot.

With a sticky-fingered snap she unhooked the front fastening, tugging at the tacky material, finally ridding herself of the bra, which was a genuine la Perla and had set her back an even fifty bucks.

Still the man didn't look.

Here she was, stiff and uncomfortable, flaunting herself like some cheap tart. The least he could do was pay attention. Drastic measures were called for.

"You know, I might need mineral spirits for these babies, after all. Got some?"

This time, the eye flickered and his face flushed, the scar turning a liquid silver. One gray eye met hers, the same hot liquid-silver color as his scar. Brooke's skin bloomed hot, then cold, the remains of the glue clinging to her chest, making her damp, moist, sticky...

Nope, not just the glue.

She thought he was going to touch her, was dying for him to touch her, but instead he spun on his heel and walked away.

"One can of mineral spirits, coming right up."

4

JASON FLEW TO THE BACK shed before she spotted the tiny drop of glue on her knee and decided the jeans had to go, too.

God.

The word was a curse and a prayer, a testament to what a woman's bare breasts could do to a man's good intentions.

The shelves in front of him were filled with paint and oil and transmission fluid, and as his eyes scanned the contents, he realized that he didn't have any damn mineral spirits.

Not that she needed mineral spirits on those beauties. The dusky hue of her nipples needed nothing more than a touch, a taste. No, chemicals would be a crime against nature. His fingers flexed, itched, copping a cheap feel from a nearby paint can that did absolutely nothing to relieve his pain.

Now what the heck was he supposed to? Her little striptease was payback, teasing, a cock-busting joke for throwing glue on her.

And *who* had thought of the glue?

No, he was going to have to face her, pretend that he'd never seen her naked, pretend that all this was no big deal.

After pulling down a tin of degreaser, he glanced at the no-big-deal bulge at his fly. She wouldn't miss that. No, she'd laugh at his misery. She'd think that he deserved it.

Which he did, but he didn't want her to know that.

Only one way to take care of that problem. Efficiently, Jason unzipped his jeans, taking matters into his own hand, and five minutes later, he was back to his normal-size piston, and all it had taken was the mental image of Brooke Hart, naked with dark-fire eyes, open-mouthed invitation, taut, perky breasts and the arousing shimmer of epoxy.

Oh, he'd been alone too long.

Once again, he felt the pull in his balls, the hardening in his cock, and he groaned in sexual agony.

Another ten minutes. That'd do it.

He was sure.

Maybe.

THEY BUMPED ALONG the road in the Captain's pick-up, a tense ride because apparently the man wasn't up to having a conversation.

Maybe she'd gone too far, maybe she'd ruined the image that she'd been going for. Slutty, instead of spunky. But slutty was preferable to pity.

She peeked at his profile, the right side of his face so normal, so capable. Then she thought of his bad eye, his scar. Lots of people would pity him, and he would hate it, just like she did.

It was a short drive to the heart of Tin Cup. Her new hometown. Her first day in Tin Cup, she'd tried to find the law offices of Harris and Howell, but only located lawyer Hiram Hadley. After hammering on his door for ten minutes, the dry cleaner next door said that he was in North Dakota taking care of his father who'd been ill. Other than that, she'd had little desire to explore, since she wasn't eager to find Austen until she'd got herself in a more suitable situation. Still, she was deathly curious about this place, so she scanned the picturesque landscape, the neat clapboard homes, the rangy mesquite trees. It was so different from the places she'd been before, but the sight of the planters lining Main Street cheered her. It felt like home.

Not that she wanted to meet anyone when she was dressed

like this. The Captain had given her a large, drab olive T-shirt. Though neatly tucked into her jeans, the shirt still looked wrong. That, and she wasn't comfortable being without a bra. She crossed her arms over her chest, and he glanced at her. Then down.

Brooke smiled tightly.

"I shouldn't have ruined your sweater." This time, he sounded appropriately chastened. A no-holds-barred flash-job could do that to a man.

"No, you shouldn't have."

"Aren't you going to apologize, too?" he asked, apparently believing that she shared some blame in ruining her sweater.

"No," she told him in a cheery, blame-free voice.

The Captain blew out a breath. "You don't know me. You shouldn't take stupid risks with someone you don't know."

This time, she blew out a breath. "Life is all about risks, taking chances. It doesn't matter how safe and comfortable you want things to be. They never are."

"No," he agreed. "I'm sorry."

This time he wasn't apologizing for the sweater. He was apologizing for all the hardships in her life, which didn't make her any happier. "I don't want to be your cause du jour."

"I don't believe in causes."

She doubted that, but kept quiet.

"You don't have to sleep in your car," the Captain said, braking at the lone stoplight in town.

"Inviting me to sleep somewhere else?" she teased. She wanted to hear him say it. She wanted to hear him admit that he wanted her. Some of it was pride and ego, some of it was that she wanted to be wanted, but the most urgent part was that she wanted him.

Charlene Hart wasn't a fan of upstanding men. She liked her men footloose and flawed. And in the ten years since her death, Brooke hadn't moved in the sort of circles where softhearted men roamed.

The soft-hearted man next to her looked at her, one eye that clearly saw so much. "No invitations. You can take the couch."

She shrugged, as if it didn't matter.

Moments later he turned down Main Street, pulling to a stop in front of a tidy row of shops. The Hinkles' grocery was there, a post office, Dot's Diner and Tallyrand's. "It's not Paris, but Tallyrand's has some good shirts. And shoes."

Then he passed her a credit card. "Get what you need."

She stared at him, squared her shoulders. "I'll pay you back."

"I know."

Then she smiled, liking his confidence in her, liking the way the sun played in his hair. The Captain needed a haircut, and tomorrow, she would tell him. "Thank you."

"Your brother should take you in." He paused. "If he is your brother."

Did he have to ruin it now? "You don't ask me questions, I won't ask you any, either."

The Captain nodded. "Fair enough. Get what you need. An hour's enough time?"

"More than enough."

Two HOURS LATER, and Brooke had yet to show up at the truck. Jason considered leaving her in town, but as tempting as the idea was, it was a hot afternoon, and he couldn't bring himself to abandon her.

Her or her breasts.

Deciding that he had to find out, he made his way through the seven stores of downtown Tin Cup before finally tracking her down in the same place she'd started—Tallyrand's. Tallyrand's was a combination feed and clothing store, owned by Rita Tallyrand, who was the former Ms. Pecos Valley back in 1957. It wasn't the sort of personal detail that Jason usually remembered except that Rita reminded everybody each time they came into the store.

"Captain!" Rita called out, and Jason managed a smile, immediately spotting Brooke next to the shelves full of shirts. She was still wearing his old T-shirt. Two hours of shopping and zilch to show for it?

Jason closed his eyes, telling himself to be patient, but then Rita waylaid him and he knew escape was impossible. What was worse than a nightmare?

"Captain," she whispered, eyes fixed on Brooke. "You know her? Gladys said you knew her. Who is she? One of the Harts? There was no girl, but that's how she introduced herself. Said she was a sister. I wanted to call the Sheriff, to find out what's what, but the Sheriff was out babysitting for Mindy. Have you seen the new baby?"

It was gossip like that that kept Jason far away. "No."

Rita frowned. "No, you don't know her?"

"I know her," he volunteered, choosing not to divulge any more of the pertinent facts he knew about her, not that they were facts, exactly. More supposition, he supposed.

"She's a Hart?" Rita asked again.

Now this was where it got tricky. Jason knew that Gillian Wanamaker and Austen Hart were tight, and if he told Rita that Brooke was a Hart, and it turned out that Brooke wasn't a Hart, but part of some wild, best-forgotten weekend from Austen Hart's past, then Gillian would be crashing down Jason's door because not only did Gillian Wanamaker have a possessive streak, but she was the sheriff, and also carried a gun.

After glancing at Brooke, he laughed in a knowing way. "She's not a Hart. Not even a family friend. Seems like she read about the Hart family troubles and thought the whole thing was romantic in a Bonnie and Clyde trailer trash sort of way. Too much television in her life," he added, not wanting Rita to think that Brooke was mentally unstable or anything.

Rita still eyed Brooke suspiciously. "She's been browsing in the shirt section for two hours. Maybe Gladys is right about the girl's possible sticky fingers, although I don't see where she could hide a shirt."

"She's a good kid."

Rita shot him a curious look. "Not a kid."

Rather than confirm that Jason knew she wasn't a kid, but a healthy, well-developed woman, he chose to keep his mouth shut.

"Can you get her out of here?" Rita asked. "I want to close up and make it home before I miss the news."

There was nothing more that Jason would like than to get her out of here. As he approached her, Brooke smiled and motioned him closer.

"I can't decide between the darker blue with long sleeves, or this plain cotton tee. The long-sleeved one is better quality, but—" she glanced at Rita and pitched her voice low "—it's a little pricy."

Patiently Jason removed both shirts from her hands and gave them to Rita. "We'll get them both."

Brooke grabbed the shirts back. "No. We won't. One shirt."

Rita watched the exchange, not saying a word. Smart lady.

However, Jason knew that Brooke wasn't going to give in. Part of him understood her need to make it on her own. Part of him thought she was an idiot for being too stubborn, and part of him, a very masochistic part, wanted to see her naked again.

"One shirt," Jason agreed. That was his hard-on talking.

"Which one?" Brooke asked, holding up one shirt then the other.

"The blue one looks nice with your hair," Rita offered, now realizing that money would eventually change hands.

Brooke flipped over the price tag, chewed on her lip. "But it's so expensive."

"All cotton," Rita explained. "And look at the seams. You're not going to get that sort of stitching for a song."

And still Brooke shook her head. "I don't know."

Slowly Jason counted to ten.

"It's worth every penny."

Brooke chewed on her lip. "I don't know. Maybe if it was... oh, ten percent less. Then I wouldn't feel so extravagant."

Jason counted to twenty this time. Didn't help.

Rita considered the offer and finally nodded.

"Ten percent, but only because you're a friend of the Captain's."

"My family is from here," Brooke said, following Rita to the register. Rita turned, giving Jason a knowing wink.

"Well, sure, sweetie. Is this cash, check or charge? I'll need four forms of ID if you're writing a check."

Brooke handed her Jason's credit card. "Charge, please. I'll need the receipt."

Jason knew the instant that Rita read his name on the card.

"Credit is so fast these days," Rita murmured, folding up the shirt. "Just one quick slide and then, whoops, look what you've done."

"I don't believe in credit myself," Brooke told her, noting the frilly bookmarks displayed on the counter, studying each one carefully. "It's too easy to lose your head."

Rita looked at Jason. "Isn't it, though?"

This time Jason counted to ninety-nine in multiples of three. Still didn't help.

After Rita handed the bag to Brooke, she smiled. "You'll be staying with the Captain?"

"Oh, no," Brooke laughed, as if the idea was ludicrous. "He's my boss."

Rita raised her brows. "Really?"

Brooke laughed again, not so quickly this time. "I needed a job, and he offered me a position at his house. Inventory. I think I'd like to organize things a bit better. It's a little chaotic." She pulled the package tight to her chest. "I'm new here. I'm trying to start off right. I know I'm a stranger, but I hope you'll give me a chance."

Seeing the sincerity in Brooke's face, Rita thawed. Jason un-

derstood. "We don't get much entertainment out here, so sometimes we make up our own."

Brooke leaned in closer. "I know exactly what you mean.
Maybe sometime I could come in and chat?"

Through the window, Jason could see the setting sun and he
wanted nothing more than for this day to be through. "I think
Rita wants to close up," he told Brooke, in case she decided that
now was a good time to chat.

Rita clucked her tongue. "They are *always* impatient, aren't
they?"

Brooke laughed and Jason hurried her out the door.

ON THE DRIVE BACK, Jason watched as Brooke took out her
new shirt and laid it over her lap. Her fingers worked the buttons, and he realized that this was a woman who wasn't used
to a lot of clothes.

"I'm sorry about the sweater," he apologized again, but this
time, he felt like words weren't enough.

"I wouldn't have kept it," she told him with a forgiving smile,
as if it didn't matter, but Jason knew she would have kept that
sweater until she died. The right thing to do would be to buy
her a new sweater. Something pretty. Something nice. Something extravagant.

"I'm sorry about what Rita was thinking," he continued. Apparently, today was the day that apologies were flowing like
wine. Sonya had always hated that he never apologized.

"She thought we were having sex. It's not a big deal."
Brooke's head was down, dark hair hiding her face from view.

"It wouldn't be if it were true, but it's not, so it is a big deal."
He sounded like the world's biggest prude, but he didn't mind.
He didn't know why he didn't mind, but when Brooke smiled
up at him, he knew he'd said the right thing.

"I can cook dinner for you if you like."

Such nice words, such dangerous words. In the back of his

head, Jason knew this wasn't smart, but on the other hand, he didn't want her to starve, either.

"I have a frozen pizza, not much else." It wasn't meant to be an invitation. But it was.

"A frozen pizza and a can of peas," she reminded him with a smile that shot straight to places he'd rather not be thinking about right this second, but like a dog, he kept on thinking, anyway. He kept on panting, too, kept on remembering the sight of her perfect breasts.

A tiny voice urged him to take, but there was something in her eyes that held him back. He saw desire there, sure, but also he saw gratitude, and he felt as if he should lay out the ground rules before she did something they would both regret.

"Brooke?"

"Yes?"

Suddenly, a rabbit jumped across the road, and Jason swerved to avoid it. Brooke fell against him, her hand clutching his thigh, his engorged crotch.

Damn.

Quickly, her hand was gone, and Brooke shot to the opposite side of the bench seat. It was safer with her there.

Jason cleared his throat. "This is a very small town, and there are a lot of behaviors that are frowned upon."

She glanced at him, a provocative smile on her provocative mouth. He wanted to taste that provocative mouth.

"Are we having the sex talk?" she asked.

"It's not a sex talk," he protested, then rubbed his face where his scar was starting to throb. "It's more of an anti-sex talk. This is a dangerous situation and I know you think you're attracted to me but, hell, Brooke. I don't want a woman in my bed because I bought her a shirt."

It was the wrong thing to say because off came her shirt. Jason tried desperately not to stare at the twin mounds of taut flesh. Failed. "Can we please wear our clothes?"

She turned, offering her breasts before him like some buffet plate. "It's your shirt and you think I want to sleep with you because you gave me a shirt. Ergo, no shirt. No problem."

His mouth grew dry, his cock started to ache and his foot was pushing as hard as it could on the gas. "Put on the shirt."

She grinned and ran a hand through her hair, dark against her perfect ivory skin. "No."

"Please," he asked nicely, hearing the crack in his voice.

"No. I'm an adult, capable of following the call of my loins, and if your shirt is going to get in the way..."

Jason kept his eyes on the road, but it didn't help distract him from his desire for her. Up ahead he could see his long, gravel drive. His bed, her laying across his bed, wearing nothing but him.

"Brooke," he tried again, not looking. Damn. He was looking. The woman had the most perfect set of breasts on the planet, and apparently she wasn't shy about showing them off.

This was probably how Hart got in trouble with her. They were probably somewhere in Vegas, she pulled off her shirt and kapow. Circuits were fried, good intentions were lost and sex was had. Halfway up the drive, he slammed on the brakes because he needed clothes on her before they made it to the house. In the truck, there were rules, gearshifts. In the house, all bets were off.

"Is there a problem?" she asked, laying her arm across the back of the seat, so hot, so warm, so...

"Brooke," he repeated, pleading, since all he wanted to do was touch her, kiss her, take her. Her fingers tiptoed across the edge of his seat, flicking against his neck. It was the first time she'd ever touched him.

Jason turned, met her eyes firmly. "No."

She cocked her head. "You don't want me?" She knew he did, but he couldn't tell her. It was the last armament keeping him in check.

"I don't want you."

Her hand slid from his face to his hard-on. Softly, tortuously, she squeezed. "Liar."

"This isn't right."

Brooke slid closer, her breasts brushing against his arm, and he could smell his soap on her, his shampoo. "Kiss me. Make it right."

As she said the words, she licked her lips and that was all he could take.

Jason grabbed her, pulled her astride him, and devoured her mouth like the starving man he was. Her fingers stroked his hair, his face. So long, too long. He explored her mouth with his tongue, feeling her warm welcome. It was like drowning.

His hands grabbed her breasts, knowing exactly where to touch, and she arched into him, riding his cock like they were already there.

He wanted her already there. He wanted inside her. He wanted to feel her. All of her. With clumsy fingers he attacked her fly, feeling the metal give, sliding beneath the rough denim, finding...her.

His finger thrust inside her, and she nipped at his lip, and Jason knew he wouldn't make it to the house.

It had been so long. She felt so good. His finger pushed harder, higher, feeling the wet heat. Each time he thrust, she rode him. Hard, sure...sweet.

A woman at a vulnerable place, a woman who needed respect and patience.

Sweetness.

Some of his calm returned and he kissed her again, trying to take things gentle and slow. Her mouth tasted like peppermint and fire and her hips kept arching toward him, riding him... loving him.

Patience?

He was going to die.

"Take me here, Captain. Please."

Her hands poised over his fly, waiting.

And who was he to stay no? Resigned to his fate, Jason opened his one good eye, stared at his house, blinked twice, and then prayed that his vision was wrong.

Survival instincts kicked in, he pushed Brooke aside and fumbled for the damned shirt.

"What's wrong?" asked the topless woman who didn't think that modesty was a good thing.

Wrong? She had no idea of the trouble her breasts were about to get them into. Everything was wrong because approaching the truck in her ridiculous heels was Sonya.

Seeing the other woman, Brooke finally had the sense to cover herself. "Who's that?" she asked, and he could hear the hurt in her voice. He hated the hurt.

"I'm Sonya Kincaid. Mrs. Sonya Kincaid."

Brooke gasped, but before she could kill him Jason clarified the situation. "Ex. She's my ex."

5

OUT OF THE THREE OF THEM, Brooke was the only one completely relaxed. Inside the house, Sonya was perched on a barstool and the Captain brooded unhappily on his couch. Brooke pulled in a footstool from the porch and prepared to watch family dynamics in action. On television, families fought and then laughed, all in a thirty-minute interval punctuated with fast-food commercials. In shelters, families never fought, only stared ahead, silent and shuttered, not wanting to give anything away. Brooke suspected reality was somewhere in between.

She glanced curiously back and forth, until Sonya flushed pink.

"Could we have some privacy?" asked Jason's former wife in a snippy voice that Brooke thought was stress rather than a natural condition.

"I could go out to the car," Brooke offered cheerfully.

"She's a guest," the Captain said. "She stays."

At his words, Brooke looked at Sonya and shrugged innocently.

"Why don't you tell me why you're here?" the Captain asked his former wife. Sonya Kincaid was very pretty in a very blond way and was wearing a sleek red suit that matched her lipstick perfectly. She wasn't what Brooke would have expected of the

Captain's ex-wife. She was way too neat, but maybe that explained the divorce.

Sonya brushed at her skirt, which was immaculate like the rest of her. "Aunt Gladys called last night. I had been planning to drive out to see you anyway, so I decided it was time to stop by. She was concerned. We all are."

The Captain scowled. "You drove out here for nothing."

Sonya nodded at Brooke. "Apparently not."

Sensing the tense undercurrents in the room, Brooke felt it was time to clarify the situation. "Primitive sexual urges are completely normal. No reason to worry about that. Giving in to our animalistic nature is inevitable."

Sonya rolled her eyes. "Oh, please. You're taking advantage of Jason, and there's no one out here to put a stop to it."

The Captain stood and glared at his former wife. "Get the hell out." His voice was low, gruff, and it was the first time that Brooke felt a shiver of fear.

Quickly, Sonya gathered her purse and started for the door, but Brooke called out before she could leave.

"Wait. Don't go like this. You walked in on an awkward situation. I'm sure that seeing your ex locked in a torrid embrace with someone new was difficult, and you've got a right to be a little bitchy." Brooke winked at the Captain. "But we're all mature adults here, and I know the Captain is a big enough man to forgive you." Then she smiled at him. "Isn't that right?"

Sonya didn't seem happy, but at least her nostrils had lost that pinched look. She stared at the Captain, and Brooke waited, hoping that she'd done the right thing.

Finally the Captain waved a hand, and Sonya sat. "So why are you here?"

"Can we discuss this in private?" Sonya asked, apparently not one to learn from her mistakes.

"No. Brooke stays."

Once again, Brooke shrugged innocently and Sonya sighed. "I want to talk to you about the test well."

Test well? Now Brooke was intrigued. This was oil country, the land of black oil and undiscovered riches. *Her home.*

"No," snapped the Captain, apparently not so intrigued.

"Why?" his former wife asked, a perfectly reasonable question in Brooke's opinion.

"After the discharge, I moved out here to be by myself. The last thing I want is people hanging around here."

"You need the money," Sonya argued.

"You mean you need the money," the Captain replied. "You have the house in Killeen. I have this place. You got the better deal. Case closed."

Sonya glanced at Brooke. "Let's not have this argument in front of the girl."

Brooke grinned. "Don't mind me. I'm thinking of making popcorn."

"Jason!"

"Brooke," the Captain warned.

Brooke held up her hands to keep the peace. "No popcorn."

By now the Captain's color had returned to normal, his scar faded to the color of bone, and Brooke was happy to see the smile at the corners of his mouth. He was having a good time... just like she'd intended.

He leaned back against the couch, legs splayed, the faded jeans clinging to powerful thighs that were as hard as bricks. Remembering exactly how they felt beneath her, Brooke felt a momentary throb between her legs, a reminder of an itch that had yet to be scratched. Secretly, she checked the digital clock on the wall. Eight-seventeen. It was still early. Darn it.

"How's Tom?" the Captain asked.

Sonya crossed her legs, uncrossed her legs. "He left, and please don't lecture me. I don't want to hear it."

"I'm sorry," the Captain said, and his former wife's eyes were wide with surprise.

"Did you love Tom?" Brooke asked, which was not any

of her business, but Sonya seemed heartbroken and Brooke wanted to know exactly who had broken her heart. The Captain or this Tom?

"I thought I loved him." Sonya peeked under lashes at the Captain, apparently still fostering some hope. "I was wrong."

While the Captain watched his former wife, Brooke held her breath. If there were still feelings involved, she certainly would get out of the way. It was the honorable thing to do, but...

Brooke frowned, not nearly so intrigued anymore.

Sonya stood. "I'll leave now. I'm sorry for interrupting. Think about the well, Jason. At least then you could hire someone to haul away this junk."

Brooke kept quiet, this wasn't her concern, and after she heard the door close, she found the Captain watching her. There was no fire in his gaze, no feeling at all.

The apathy hurt, and she wished it didn't.

"There's a bunk in the shed outside," he started, and Brooke managed a smile.

"I'll sleep in my car. It's more comfortable and I bought this goose-feather duvet in Oklahoma. It's very nice." Brooke moved toward the door, but the Captain took her arm before she could leave.

"I'll take the shed. Sleep in the bed. You need the rest."

Okay, rest wasn't what she'd been thinking. The Captain noticed her look, and his hand fell away. "I knew this wasn't smart."

"You still love her?" Brooke hadn't meant to ask, but the words were out before she could stop them.

"No. A long time ago I was stationed at Ft. Hood. I met Sonya. We got married. After I was in Iraq, she met Tom. Three months later we were divorced."

And instantly Brooke understood the depths of Sonya's betrayal. Wishing she could do more, Brooke covered his hand, marveled at the strength, the competence, the heart within him.

For a moment he held on before opening the door. Brooke frowned, wondering what she had missed. "Why are you leaving?"

He touched her hair, smiled sadly. Somehow the Captain seemed worldly wise. "It's not right."

"You think I'm taking advantage of you?"

"No. I think I'm taking advantage of you."

The anger simmered slowly inside her, building, spilling over into something more dangerous. "Do I look stupid?"

The Captain took a cautious step back. "No."

"Then why have you decided that this is a bad idea? You were a happy man earlier. You seemed thrilled." She glanced at his crotch. "All of you."

The Captain flushed. "It was a mistake. You're in an uncertain situation. I'm the only person you know in Texas."

"Except for Austen," she reminded him.

The Captain's expression was alarmed. "I don't think it's a good idea for you to see him."

Brooke sighed. "Well, no, not until I get back on my feet. And I will," she added, seeing his skepticism.

"I know, but sex confuses things."

She glared. "Do I look confused?"

"No."

"Are you confused?"

"No."

Somehow the Captain could be very dense. "Then why are you still wearing clothes?"

This time, she was happy to see an appropriate level of apprehension. "You haven't eaten," he pointed out, an obvious stall tactic, and Brooke took a predatory step closer.

"If I was hungry, I would say so. I have a tongue in my head. I know how to use it."

The Captain took another step back. The door snapped shut.

"This is gratitude," he argued.

Her hands went to the hem of her T-shirt.

"Not the shirt. Not again." He swore, and Brooke realized that she needed to change her tactics, so she did.

She came to him, rose up on her toes, and laid her head on his heart. It was a good heart, a noble heart, and Brooke was pleased that Sonya had thrown him over.

Sonya was an idiot.

Ever so slowly, his arms wrapped around her, iron bands made of steel. Everything faded to silence, except for the beat of her blood. He tilted her chin, met her eyes, giving her a last chance to leave. However, he felt right, this felt right, and she reached up to trace the jagged edge of his scar with a gentle touch.

Instead of letting her touch him, the Captain bent, covered her mouth with his, kissing her urgently, with no gentleness at all. His strong hands skimmed lower, molding her hips to his, and when she felt the hard ridge honing between her legs, Brooke groaned happily.

This was what she wanted, he was what she wanted. He pulled her shirt over her head, and his mouth moved to her breast, her nipple, sucking until the flesh was taut and needy. The stubble on his jaw was rough against her skin, a friction that was both pleasure and pain.

There was something about this man that spoke to her, aroused her. Underneath the scars and the machines was a man who cared. A man who didn't want to.

Tonight, she wanted to give him what he had given her. Peace. Hope. Happiness.

Needing to feel him, she tore at the buttons on his shirt, ruining a perfectly good garment, but his mouth was making her crazy, the prodding pressure between her legs was making her crazy. Her hands explored the smooth planes of his back. With her lips she tasted the warm salt of his neck, and her fingers teased his nipples until he told her to stop. The couch was too far, the floor so convenient, and they fell there, the Captain stripping off her jeans and her panties, thrusting a finger inside her. Her eyes locked with his, the gray darkened to smoke. With each stroke, her muscles pulsed, the pressure building higher and higher.

It was like nothing she'd ever felt. The pleasure, yes. The security, no, and that was the most erotic thrill of all. Her nails dug into the wall of his shoulders, anchoring there because her body was about to explode.

She could see the sheen of sweat on him, feel the strain in his body, his arms. Total control.

Her legs flexed and she shuddered, and still his hand moved. Faster, harder...

Yes...

A low whimper broke from her and when she was ready to come, he stole his finger from her. She whapped at his back, but then his mouth trailed kisses down her breasts, her stomach. With rough hands, he parted her legs, and Brooke's heart stuttered and then threatened to stop.

She couldn't survive this. It was too much.

Head bent, he sucked at the skin of her inner thigh, playing, then tracing with his tongue. Because the Captain was an evil man, one finger traced her plump outer lips, lazy, insidious, diabolical.

Her hips arched up to meet him, to beg him, to kill him, but she could tell that he liked seeing her like this, liked her incoherent speech.

"Please," she managed, when his finger slid inside her, his mouth a whisper's breath away. Then his tongue flicked once, tempting her pulsing core, and the world started to spin.

Her fingers tangled in his hair, not teasing at all. A push, a pull, anything, anything.

This time, his tongue flicked twice.

Brooke yelped.

His hands gripped her thighs, and this time, oh, yes...this time.

His tongue moved over her, sucking her swollen lips, her

clit, sucking her soul. She was going to explode, she was going to die.

The next thing she knew, she was floating, and she could hear her name. He was saying her name.

"Brooke?"

She opened heavy eyes and seeing the Captain's worry, she smiled. "Mmm?"

"You haven't had enough to eat. You passed out."

She grabbed him by the neck, pulled him down, and gave him her best "not hungry for food" kiss. The Captain, being an astute man, kissed her back, slid his cock between her thighs, and with one powerful thrust, the world went golden again.

JASON PRAYED SHE WASN'T going to faint because he needed to come. She was so hot, so wet, so perfect. Brooke was every man's fantasy, every man's dream, but the thin smile on her face was cause for concern. Each time he thought of pulling out, her muscles pulled him in, locking him there and, oh, hell…

Over and over he thrust, his balls pulling tight. Just when he knew he was going to explode, her eyes opened and stared, taking in his face, his body, and he waited for her to look away. Instead, she smiled, the world's most beautiful smile. A man could drown in the light of her eyes, and there was nothing he wanted more. Her legs tightened around him, her muscles clenched, and the smile turned to something more carnal.

"Captain," she whispered in invitation, and that was all. His muscles froze, his back arched, and he wanted to roar. But there was only one sound, one word he could say.

"Brooke."

THREE HOURS LATER, the Captain had prepared frozen pizza, topped with peas. It wasn't gourmet, but for Brooke, it hit the spot. Her other spot. Apparently tonight the Captain was two for two. They ate on an old army trunk that the Captain had rigged up for a table. As he had pulled the heavy trunk in front of her, he apologized, saying that he wasn't used to company. Considering the man was doing his heavy lifting in the nude, Brooke had added in a lot of unnecessary directions, simply because she liked to watch him move.

His body was long and lean, with muscular thighs, powerful arms and, not that she was going to tell him, but his ass was divine. Made for a woman's hands. Like hers, for instance.

His face fascinated her, too. The scar and eyepatch were an odd counterpoint to the full lips, and there was a dimple on his chin as well. Before his accident, she suspected that he'd had a very boyish appearance. Now, he looked like a man who had shouldered the world without complaint.

Brooke finished her slice and downed her beer, and then watched as Dog wheeled the dishes to the sink.

"He's very helpful," she commented, watching as the tray was shuttled from floor to sink with the help of a pair of grips attached to a robot arm.

The Captain watched the arm extend, frowning when one fork got caught in the grip. The arm pushed, contracted, pushed, contracted, and eventually the fork fell in the sink. "I don't use it a lot," he explained, and she knew that by tomorrow morning, it would be fixed.

"Why don't you patent any of this?"

Long legs stretched out in front of him, and he shook his head, his hair still tangled by her hands. "That's too much work."

She supposed that living alone, the Captain was accustomed to being nude. Since Brooke had grown up with communal bedrooms and bathrooms, had always had a roommate, privacy was a luxury that she couldn't afford, and it was never wise to be nude when living in a car. Most of her life had been spent in pajamas. Until now.

She yawned, watched his eyes lock onto her breasts and smiled.

Yes, nudity was nice.

His cock stirred and, well, she found herself fascinated by the chain of action and reaction.

The Captain noticed. "You haven't been in a lot of relationships, have you?"

"More than enough," she answered truthfully. Although she'd had sex several times, she'd never been in a relationship. Charlene Hart had set a poor example and Brooke had met too many men who didn't understand the word *no*. She had learned very quickly and very painfully that a woman with little money, traveling alone, was a target for predatory men.

"How well do you know Austen?" he asked.

"He and Tyler were in New York last year." She winced at the memory. "The meeting didn't go over as well as I'd planned, but this time, I think I have it. A more independent, less needy approach."

He reached out, touched her hair. "Take your time. Get your house in order. Did you have enough to eat? There's some frozen dinners in there, too. I could heat one up."

"No, and next time, we'll have real food. I'll cook," she offered. It was obvious that the Captain didn't.

"No need," he said and once again his gaze tracked over her, lingering and then sliding away. The Captain stood, picked up the clothes scattered about, and pulled on his jeans.

"I'll be in the shed. Use the shower. Yell if you need anything."

And yes, they were back to the sleeping arrangements. Brooke rose, artfully stretching like a cat. "A shower would be great." She pulled up her hair, rolled her neck and then winced.

Instantly he was at her side. "Are you okay?"

"I must have some kinks to work out. You have some sort of massager gizmo, do you? I would love that—" she told him, reaching around and kneading one shoulder, then the other "—right here." She thrust her chest out, a flagrant cry for attention that a woman would have recognized immediately. Then she put her palms on her rear. "And here."

The Captain looked pained. "I don't think I have anything that can help."

There was an instant when Brooke considered abandoning her quest, but she couldn't in good conscience kick him out of his bed, and besides, she wanted him to hold her again. It was for these reasons that she launched into a series of stretching positions designed solely to make him see things from her point of view.

When she flexed her arms, he licked his lip.

At her toe touches, he actually groaned.

Yet still, the man resisted.

Finally she stalked over, put his hands firmly on her ass and sighed. "These are killing me. Can you just rub a little? And put some muscle in it, if you wouldn't mind."

The Captain removed his hands, grabbed her and pulled her toward the shower. "It's easier this way. Trust me."

THE CAPTAIN HAD BUCKETS and buckets of hot water and she was glad he had no massaging gadgets, because his hands, his mouth and his cock worked best of all.

He rubbed her muscles until she wept and then he stood behind her, entered her and made her weep again.

When she was sure there would be no more arguments about where he would sleep, he dried her off, put on his jeans, grabbed a pillow and headed for the front door.

Furious and naked, Brooke raced after him, and dragged him inside. "Do not think I have used all the weapons at my disposal."

At first, she thought she'd lost, but then the Captain tapped his chin and his mouth twisted into a magical smile. "Really?"

This time he didn't argue, and she pulled him under the covers, curled up a decent one foot away from him and waited. Eventually his arms crept around her, and Brooke fell into a deep, satisfied sleep.

JASON WOKE WITH Brooke's hair in his face, her thigh on his cock, and one full breast branding his arm. No matter how much he needed to, he couldn't move. The softness of a woman's skin, the fresh smell of her hair. It'd been a long time.

Brooke sighed in her sleep and Jason frowned. He had questions about her past, her family, all the things that he didn't understand, but he knew better than to ask. Maybe the answers would scare him, maybe the questions would send her away, or maybe the questions would bind her to him tighter.

So instead he lay there, watching her sleep, her body wrapped about his like a vine. He knew her body, he'd used her body, but it was her face that he tried to avoid. Seeing with one eye didn't make him blind. She was wary, she was innocent and she trusted him completely.

It was the Stockholm syndrome with the kidnapping part. Now what was he supposed to do with her? He had yet to tell her that Austen was living with the Sheriff, and Jason had heard rumors the two would be married soon. The last thing the Sheriff would want was her soon-to-be-husband's former-weekend-fling staying with them—even if she didn't have a place to live. Nobody could be that understanding. And since Austen wasn't an option, Jason couldn't send her away. Nor could he keep her.

She stretched, her thigh rubbing him, and her lips pressed a kiss to his shoulder.

While his brain wondered what he was supposed to do with her, her fingers closed over him and began to move.

She shifted over him, giving him a full-bodied good-morning kiss that had him instantly awake. Her body rose high, she pushed back the dark curtain of her hair, and he didn't understand why this goddess was in his bed.

Not that he was complaining.

As if they had all the time in the world, she arched in the sunrise, the light skimming her breasts, and he wanted to touch her, but his hands stayed firm at his sides.

Then she smiled at him in the way that only she could, and

he fisted his hands. She leaned over him, kissing his torso, his chest, continuing lower until her vulnerable mouth closed over him. Jason shut his one good eye because this way, he could be blind. For the moment at least, he was blind to everything but her.

THE NEXT DAY TURNED as hot as the one before, but while she worked out in the yard, Brooke was getting to like the feel of the sun on her skin. The West Texas landscape was so flat that it seemed to stretch forever. The trees were stubby and squat and, in the distance, she could see oil wells pumping steadily. It was only day two, but already she'd left her mark. The old milk crates she found were much more suitable than the small mountains the Captain had created. And more portable. He had argued that he needed the crates for another project.

"All fifty-three of them?" she asked, with only a hint of sarcasm.

One of the things she liked best about the Captain was that beneath the trappings, he was a very practical man. "Leave me three," he told her, and so she counted out his three and then moved the rest to her work area near the porch.

By late afternoon, the milk crates were filled, the parts inventoried, and her new blue shirt was cool, crisp and holding up nicely.

"You need to eat," the Captain told her just as she was putting a stack of copper tubing away.

Once inside, the Captain poured her a glass of water and pushed back her hair, looking concerned, his usual expression. "You're red. I don't have any sunscreen. I should have thought about that."

Brooke put a hand to her warm cheeks. "I'll be fine."

He shook his head. "Stay inside for a while. I need to get some things from town. I'll be back."

She scanned the room, with its lack of standard living room accoutrements and it's odd hodge-podge order. Some might have called it haphazard, but by now she had seen into the Captain's hodge-podge brain, and there was never any haphazard at all. "What am I supposed to do here?"

"Lay down. Watch television."

None of which sounded appealing, so she nodded in agreement, watched him drive away and then immediately started to clean. Oh, sure, the sink was spic and span, the stove had never been used. Instead of dishes, the cabinets were lined with jars of nuts—and not the eating kind, either. There were rows and rows of Mason jars filled with screws and wires and tiny unidentified plastic pieces that, according to Google, were transistors.

With a heavy sigh, Brooke shut the cabinet doors. This was the Captain's home, and yes, it wasn't the way she would accessorize her home, but she respected his space.

Needing to do something, she decided to tackle the bedroom next, but the white cotton covers were straightened with military precision. There were no pictures, no books, an absolutely sterile environment—except for the metal sculpture in the corner. The piece was nearly two feet high, an assortment of rounded metal spheres, with two pipes on the sides, plastic tubing streaming from the top. She studied the placement of the screws, and eventually she knew what it was.

A female.

Oh.

For a long time she held the piece, the metal cold in her hands, but these weren't her things. Carefully she put the piece back where she found it, and turned to find the Captain had returned.

"I made it for Max," he volunteered before she could ask. "He was an old army buddy. It was a birthday present. A joke." He came over, pressed a small button she had overlooked and twin light beams shot from the two rounded spheres on the top.

"Oh," was all Brooke could say.

"It's an army thing."

"Very creative."

The Captain took the sculpture and put it in a box, setting it next to the doorway. "I should have mailed it a long time ago."

His face was missing the openness of before, and she missed it. "You don't have to hide this because of me," she said, pulling the sculpture back from the box, and then pressing the button, watching the twin red lights shoot from the woman's bosom. Smiling, she pressed the button again. "Did you name her?"

"No, she really is for Max."

And yes, she believed he had made the sculpture for Max, but... "When's his birthday?"

"Last month." The Captain shrugged, completely missing the obvious. "I've been busy."

Brooke put the sculpture in the box, suspecting that the Captain would mail it off tomorrow. "He'll be the only person in town who has one."

The Captain folded the lid, putting the sculpture firmly out of sight. "Anyway."

Curious, she sat on the bed and wiped her cheeks as if she was tired. "Didn't you ever make one for you?"

"I have Dog."

Hearing his name, Dog whirred into the room. "You could get a real dog," she suggested.

Soullessly he stared at her through his one good eye. "Why?"

"I've always wanted a dog, a fluffy puppy, probably three, and lots and lots of cats."

He sat down next to her. "You didn't have any growing up?"

"No. You?"

"We had one dog for... I don't know. It seemed like forever."

"What was his name?"

"Dog."

Brooke laughed and he smiled back. Then, with an absent shake of the head he stood. "Maybe I'll get another one. When I'm ready."

Realizing the moment had passed, Brooke stood, too, following him out of the room. "You know, I've been thinking about the hardware in the kitchen. Now, before you start to argue, hear me out..."

THE NEXT MORNING, Brooke woke up alone. Outside, she could hear the Captain whistling, the intermittent sound of a drill and birdsong. For a few minutes, she allowed herself to be lazy, to twist up in the sheets and bury her head in the Captain's pillow.

Here, in his bed, the scent of him surrounded her and comforted her. This was Texas, this was home. This odd combination of dusty land and fresh-cut wood and welded metal and burned scrambled eggs.

She hugged the pillow closer, breathing deeply of the other scent, the musky smell of sex.

Once again last night he had tried to sleep in the shed. Unfortunately, her face had gotten sunburned yesterday and she needed help applying cream to the afflicted areas. When she remembered his capable hands on her, her fingers skimmed over her breasts, and while there was the standard biological response, she didn't experience the same kick. The burning heat of his skin was missing, the earnest magic of his mouth. No matter how hard she closed her eyes, the bed was cold without him.

In Brooke's experience, nothing ever lasted very long and good memories should be stored away carefully, trotted out at bus stations or all-night diners, or when your employer decided that rubbing himself against you was romantic. There weren't many good memories in Brooke's life, and being with the Captain was the most decadent memory she'd ever kept.

Men usually didn't try to be good, but the Captain sure did. Every time he fought against his attraction, she only wanted him more. The hungry way he kissed her, as if he could never have enough. The way he touched her between the legs, the way his gaze grew so heavy as he watched her come. She slipped a finger inside herself, surprised by the throb, surprised by the ache. A void.

Hidden beneath the sheets she touched herself, pleasured herself, temporarily feeling a void she never knew she had. Faster and faster she stroked, finding a mechanical rhythm without hunger and life. Eventually the bubble inside her burst and her muscles shuddered and then relaxed.

Quickly she got out of bed and straightened the sheets. After cleaning up in the bathroom, she dressed for the day, but unfortunately, the void inside her remained.

THERE WAS BREAKFAST on the table. The Captain had attempted scrambled eggs. Next to the plate was an envelope with her name on it. Curious, Brooke drew out the single sheet of paper and twenty fifty-dollar bills. They seemed to be real. Not sure what to make of this, Brooke read over the invoice. Apparently the Captain was paying her for three days work, plus an advance against her salary.

At the bottom, in neat letters, he'd handwritten *Buy New Shoes.*

Brooke laughed and folded up the invoice, wondering who bought thousand-dollar shoes. However, she wasn't going to take his advance, only the money she'd earned. After removing one fifty and folding it in her pocket, she hid the other nineteen bills in a Mason jar in his cabinets, buried somewhere between oversize eye bolts and a Russian Geiger counter. Someday he'd find his money, but not today.

As soon as she hit the front porch, he pointed to a floppy hat that was hanging on the rail. "You need to wear that today."

The hat was too big, and the camouflage pattern wasn't something she would have chosen for herself. However, until she could buy something suitable, it'd do.

While she positioned the hat on her head, the Captain watched, frowning at the way it hung low in her eyes. He scratched his jaw, and then walked to the shed, returning a few seconds later with some sort of tool.

Without a word, he took off the hat, folded a pleat in the back and with one click, he'd adjusted the size perfectly.

When he returned the hat to her, she examined his work. "What is that?"

"Staple gun," he answered, and then after that he walked away.

A MORNING BREEZE WAS blowing in from the east, cooling the air. Brooke worked silently, but she noticed that the Captain wasn't doing his usual today. Long wooden boards had been pulled from the shed. He'd dug four small holes in the yard, filled them with cement, and then anchored in four wooden posts. However, Brooke chose not to ask, instead focusing on what apparently was a collection of antique medical instruments.

After lunch, the Captain dragged out a ladder and climbed up on the roof of the house. Fascinated, Brooke watched as he connected the boards from the top of the house to the posts, making some sort of frame.

Still, the Captain hadn't volunteered any information and Brooke decided that this was none of her business, and she'd worked on until the sun was low and red, looking like a ball of fire at the end of the world. The Captain continued, unwinding some sort of dark netting and then nailing it to the frame.

At sundown, Brooke went inside, typing in her notes on the Captain's computer. Two hours later, she could hear the hammering on the roof, and she worried that it was too dark to be safe. Deciding that prudence overcame privacy, she marched outside and found him on the roof.

Finally she had to ask. "What's going on?"

He climbed down from the ladder and dusted his hands. "Weatherproofing."

She examined the netting above her head. "For what?"

"It's something I should have put up a long time ago. Keeps

off the heat. Keeps off the sun." With that, he gathered up his tools and went inside.

Brooke looked up, saw the moonlight and the stars streaming through like tiny dots of lights. All she could do was smile.

SOMETIME DURING THE DAY, the Captain had brought in an old dining-room table and chairs, or maybe he'd built them, she wasn't sure. There were frozen Salisbury steaks for dinner and Brooke made a mental note to drive into town and by food. Real food. Twenty-five dollars would go a long way toward some fruit and vegetables. When you were raised on breakfast cereal and soup, real food was very appealing.

Dog took away the dishes, and after Brooke curled up on the couch, he brought her a beer. The Captain had taken over the table, repairing a hand mixer, but Brooke decided there were questions she wanted to ask, questions she had a right to ask since they were about her family, her property and her future financial prosperity.

Although the Captain was studiously ignoring her, Brooke wasn't fooled. A person should be aware when they are the focus of attention—wanted, unwanted or otherwise. When she and her mother were living in a shelter in Cleveland, they had been robbed four times because Charlene Hart wasn't smart enough to know when she was the focus of unwanted attention. Then Brooke had taken over security, hiding their cash in her shoe, and the robberies had stopped. No, it was smart to always know.

The Captain always knew. She supposed that was the military background, which made sense because if Brooke wasn't alert, she might have been robbed—if the Captain wasn't alert, he might have been killed. Maybe someday she would ask about that, but for now, she felt like she needed to keep the conversation on more impersonal things.

"May I ask you something?"

He looked up, looked nervous, but nodded.

"I've noticed all the oil wells around here. Do you think they've found it all?"

"Probably." Apparently believing the conversation to be over, the Captain went back to his task.

"But Sonya doesn't believe that's true. Why does she think that?"

The Captain, apparently now realizing the conversation wasn't over, put down his screwdriver. "Look, I grew up in Baltimore, not Texas. I haven't lived out hre that long, but I've seen how the oil industry happens. Maybe they are doing some more work out here, but it's a crap shoot. Tin Cup is at the perimeter of some fields and every time that gasoline goes up, some greedy suits crawl out from their rock, hoping to make a buck."

He waited, hand poised over the screwdriver, and Brooke decided that she could find out her answers later.

Eventually, the Captain realized that she wasn't going to press him and returned his attention to the mixer.

Not wanting to disturb him, Brooke picked at the corner of his army trunk and thought how much nicer it would look if she painted it. Nothing very flashy, maybe a soft blue. She liked blue. After glancing at the Captain, she thought that maybe she'd ask next week.

He put down his screwdriver and looked up. She noticed that he didn't sigh. "They drill test wells, see what happens, lots of people show up, all sorts of rigs and machines, making a mess with no respect for the land."

Brooke nodded and the Captain went back to work.

A few seconds later he sighed and put down the screwdriver again. "It's not like she needs the money. She's a lawyer. I send her money. The house in Killeen is paid for. I don't get it."

He paused, apparently expecting Brooke to now take part in the conversation, which she did. "Maybe she wants it for you."

"I don't need anything."

"I know."

The Captain went back to finishing the mixer, next pulling

out a board with wires and lights and switches, but apparently he wasn't happy with that. He swore and looked up. "Why'd you ask?"

"Austen's place isn't far from here. I was thinking how cool it would be if there was oil on the Hart land. I mean, I don't care about being rich or anything, but…it'd be nice. We could build a house, maybe have a garden. Curtains. Blue curtains, I think."

The Captain stopped what he was doing and studied her, his mouth a hard line. "I should have told you this earlier because you should know that Austen's involved with another woman, and I think you should leave him alone."

6

WORDS WERE DANGEROUS THINGS, which was why Jason never used a lot of them. He would have liked to blame Brooke's red face on sunburn, but he wasn't a stupid man, and the aloe vera that he'd rubbed all over last night had really done the trick.

"Either that is the most disgusting idea that anyone has ever thought about me, or else you think I've traveled across half the continental United States on the basis of some delusional family. So, please tell me, Captain, am I an incestuous sleaze or a crazy lady? And you can only pick one."

Jason opened his mouth, thought better of it, and shut it again. She was steaming mad, which he found disgustingly arousing, but he knew that he had to man up and admit the truth.

"If Austen is really your brother, then why the hell are you broke and living in your car?"

It was another mistake. Her eyes filled with tears and Jason hated to see a woman cry, and this was Brooke, who, as he had just told her, was broke and living in her car.

She didn't answer, not that he expected her to. Instead, he watched her stomp to the door, open the door, stop, slam the door, go back to the bedroom, emerge with his pillow, open the door, stop, and then she glared at him.

"Your money's in the jar. I don't need it." The door slammed, and Brooke was gone.

Furiously, Jason swore, picked up the circuit board and threw it across the room, watching the tiny pieces scatter across the floor.

A long time ago, he would have known what to do. A long time ago, he would have been better able to think on his feet. A long time ago, he wouldn't have been so far off the mark.

A long time ago, it wouldn't have hurt so bad.

BROOKE DIDN'T LIKE feeling stupid, she didn't like feeling small. She didn't like being broke, and she didn't like living in her car.

The front seat was too cramped, she noted, bashing her knees on the steering wheel for the eighteenth time, her goose-feathered duvet smelled like French fries instead of burned scrambled eggs, but the pillow smelled exactly like the Captain.

She should have been smarter. She should have known better, but all the *shouldas* didn't help.

Furious with herself, she kicked at the door, tossing this way and that to find a more comfortable position.

The Captain tapped on the window and she ignored him.

"I'm sorry."

"Go away."

"Brooke, you can't sleep in the car."

"I belong in the car. Go away."

"You don't belong in the car."

"I don't belong in the house."

"I can't leave you out here like this."

"You don't have to take care of crazy people."

"You're not crazy. Come in the house."

"No."

"At least talk to me."

"I am."

"In the house."

"No."

She heard him try the handle, but the doors were locked. Car doors should always be locked.

After a few minutes he left, and Brooke was alone. She should be happy that she was alone. She should be happy that the Captain had given up. She was so happy, she kicked at the door. It hurt just as badly as before, but the pain in her foot was better than the pain in her head.

There was a click and then the back door creaked open, and the Captain climbed in her car.

"I don't want you in my car."

"Technically, your car is on my property."

"I can park somewhere else."

"I'm sorry, Brooke. I'm very, very sorry."

The sincerity in his voice ripped at her heart, and she knew that was the best and worst thing about the Captain. If he saw a person in a hole, he needed to pull them out, but sometimes a person needed to crawl out of the hole themselves. Brooke didn't want him to see her as a hole-dweller. She wanted him to see her as a desirable woman, and she knew that some of the time he did.

Right now, with her feelings so raw, she wanted to hear him say it, wanted him to admit that he wanted her. It wasn't very nice of her because he would never tell her that, although it meant he could be as silent and therefore as miserable as her at least.

The silence grew, filling the car until Brooke kicked at the door. "Get out."

"You can sleep in the house, or I can sleep out here. You pick."

In answer, Brooke kicked the door once again.

The morning sun hit Jason in the eyes, and he twisted his neck, a hairbrush stabbing him in the face. Three times he stretched, but the knots in his body remained.

In a lot of ways, Jason knew the situation was for the best. Brooke should have gone to her brother right away. Idiot.

From the front seat, he could hear her soft breathing and

knew she was still fast asleep. If he closed his good eye he could forget the stack of magazines under his knee, he could forget the duct-taped seat cushion and forget the hurt in her eyes.

If he closed his good eye, he could see her welcoming him in his bed, remember the way she felt in his arms.

But sex was a dangerous drug. Brooke was a dangerous drug so Jason opened his one good eye and climbed out of her car, the door creaking like an old woman's knee. Her breathing caught, and he knew she was awake, but she didn't say a word, not that he expected her to.

As he walked toward his house, he didn't look back. He heard the sound of her engine, the sound of her wheels on the drive and, soon enough, Jason's life was restored to the same place it'd been before.

BROOKE FOLLOWED the map to the Hart homestead, excitement roiling in her stomach. This was her home, the place where Charlene and Frank Hart had lived together in bitter matrimony. She'd put off this part of the journey, the last part, out of fear. She had wanted the meeting with Austen to be perfect, but since Brooke had very little experience with perfection, she now recognized the flaw in her plan.

The Captain hadn't thought she was capable. No, the Captain thought she was certifiable. Excitement changed to a hollow emptiness, and she got angry with him all over again. However, today was for new beginnings and she made herself smile at the bright, sunshiny day.

A new start with a new brother, a new home, and what did the Captain know, after all?

After she took the last turn onto Orchard Drive, she drove two long miles seeing nothing but trees and grass. When she finally spied the house, she stopped, stared. Frowned.

There was no picket fence, no charming garden, no bounding dog. Frankly, as a home, it lacked just about everything.

There was a man and a woman working on the house, actually it seemed more like demolition than renovation. Considering the condition of the place, demolition seemed optimal. Her brother, Austen Hart, was swinging a sledge hammer, destroying one of the two interior walls that still remained. A very pretty, stylish woman was using a chain saw to slice through some rusted out pipes.

Welcome home, Brooke, she thought, and then laughed at herself. She'd seen worse, she'd survived.

After she parked the old Impala, Brooke climbed out, prepared to see her brother. Hopefully he would remember who she was. "Austen! It's Brooke! Your sister," she added, mainly as a reminder.

Austen put down the hammer, the chain saw shut off, and Brooke made her way past what was left of the porch steps. The woman looked her over, and Brooke wished she'd taken the Captain's advice and sprung for new boots.

"I'm his sister. Brooke Hart." She held out a friendly hand. "Very pleased to meet you."

The woman shook her hand, and Brooke noticed her fabulous nails and tried not to be jealous. "Gillian Wanamaker."

With the back of his sleeve, Austen wiped the sweat from his brow, but didn't offer his hand until Gillian Wanamaker nudged him in the side.

Instead of shaking her hand, her brother pulled her into a hug, and it was the world's most awkward hug. Brooke knew this because she had experienced more than her fair share of awkward hugs, some wanted, some not.

"I didn't know you were coming to visit. Hell, we would've put out a welcome mat." Austen glanced toward the house and laughed. It was an awkward laugh. "What are you doing in town?"

"I came to see the house," Brooke told him. *And maybe stay forever.* Austen walked her through the remains, and she wondered what it had been like when her mother and father had lived there. When Austen and Tyler had lived there.

"Not much to see right now. It's a work in progress. The old structure was condemned and the lawyer gave me the green light to tear down the place."

Gillian pointed to a freshly poured slab in the distance. "The new house is going up over there." Then her attention returned to Brooke. "Austen didn't mention where you lived, or maybe he did, but in this whole getting-married hoo-doo, it probably slipped my mind."

"I'm from New York," Brooke answered, then nodded to the house. "It looks great."

"Have you talked to the lawyer?" asked Austen. "He was trying to track you down."

"That's why I came, but he's out of town. Do you know what he wants?" Brooke asked, trying to sound casual.

Austen began to laugh. "This is your inheritance."

Brooke swallowed. "I'm in the will? My father knew about me?"

Austen shook his head. "The state executed the will last spring because you have a legal claim and it's only right that you get your share. We're sitting on four acres, so you get one-third of that and one-third of the house.

"One-third of the house?" asked Brooke, trying to look excited.

Austen wasn't fooled and he laughed, and she liked to hear him laugh. "It doesn't work that way," he explained. "Once you sign the papers, I'll write you a check for the cash equivalent. I should warn you, it's not a lot, probably nothing more than a couple of haircuts for you."

Brooke wasn't disappointed. Much. A couple of New York haircuts went a long, long way. It'd keep her in peanut butter until she could find a new job. And maybe she could spring for a motel room.

"And one-third of the mineral rights," Gillian added, which perked Brooke up. Certainly the house wasn't what she was expecting, but still, one-third of something was infinitely preferable to one-third of nothing. She was about to ask her brother more when he noticed the Impala parked at the end of the road. "You drove from New York, or is that a rental?"

"I borrowed it from a friend," Brooke told him because she could see he didn't approve of the car's ramshackle condition.

"Must have been some friend."

"What do you do in New York?" Gillian asked, smiling at her, not nearly as awkwardly. "It must be so exciting."

"I, uh…" began Brooke, not wanting to lie, because this was her fresh start, and she wanted to make the right impression, but…

"She works for an art gallery," Austen replied.

"I quit that job," Brooke stated quickly.

"You're in art?" Gillian asked, and Brooke knew that she was going to have to give some sort of response, but her already frayed nerves were starting to go, and the sun was very hot, and this wasn't going nearly as easily as she'd planned, and Gillian was watching her with concern.

"You're looking really pale. I bet you're not used to this weather." Gillian glanced at Austen and clucked her tongue. "You don't look so good, either, sugar. You know, let's ditch this place and go somewhere hospitable to chat. I've got some chocolate cake at my place. Are you hungry? I don't mean to brag, but it's the best thing you've ever tasted."

Then Gillian Wanamaker grabbed Austen's hand, linking them together, and Brooke approved and the panic faded. "Come on, sweetie. We need to show this one how real family is done."

THE WANAMAKER HOUSE was far more in line with what Brooke considered a home. Needlework pillows covered the sofa, family pictures hung from the wall, and from the kitchen came the smell of warm chocolate cake. It was the perfect place for Brooke to get to know her brother better. And hopefully he would want to know her as well, not that she was making any progress there, judging by the closed expression on his face.

However, if ever there was a place that would make a non-family a family, the Wanamaker household was it.

Gillian's mother, Modine Wanamaker, was a plump maternal type with a flour-dusted apron and a welcoming smile.

Emmett Wanamaker was a man of few words, as apparently were most of the men in Tin Cup. He finished his cake, pushed back from the dining room table and fled for the football game in the other room. Austen appeared to want to join him, but Gillian stopped him with a look.

As Brooke finished the last crumbs of her cake, she put down her fork and smiled at her brother, who smiled warily back. "Congratulations on your engagement. I love the ring, and I imagine the wedding is going to be fabulous."

At the mention of his fiancée, some of the wariness disappeared, and Brooke mentally patted herself on the back. Apparently all the Harts were romantics.

"I'm lucky to have her," he said, taking Gillian's hand, his feelings apparent on his face.

"When's the big day?"

"Middle of November."

"Will you be living in the new house or here? This is such a nice place." Brooke ran her finger over the embroidered chair rests. She'd never learned how to create such beautiful things, and she had always wanted to, but it seemed frivolous unless she had a wall to hang it, on a sofa to throw it over or a chair to decorate. Like this one.

"Originally the new house was going to be for Gillian's parents," Austen said, "and we were going to live here, but then Gillian and I decided that a new place would be good."

"This is Gillian's house," Modine explained.

"Don't explain, Mama." Gillian smiled at Brooke. "Our housing situation has always been complicated."

Brooke nodded because she understood that. Still, this was like the best of all worlds. It had the feel of family, of home, of love. Austen must have had that at the old house, as well. "I'm sure you had some wonderful memories growing up."

"Not a single one, but all that's going to change." Austen met her eyes, and she saw the determination there. Romantic and fool-hardy. Brooke found herself liking her brother more and more.

"So tell me what you're doing now?" Brooke asked, and for the next half hour, Austen told her about his life. He talked about his job for the railroad commissioner, helping out on her campaign for governor and keeping an eye on construction of the new rail line through the town. He bragged about Gillian's contributions to the town, he talked about Tyler and his surgical advances in New York, but not a word about the house on Orchard Lane, or Frank Hart. No questions about Charlene Hart at all, which was probably for the best since Brooke didn't like to speak ill of her mother. Brooke had lied to her brother once, and she wasn't happy about the idea of lying again.

"Now that you've heard the Austen Hart saga, how about you? When I saw you in New York, you were getting married, too, weren't you?"

Sadly, Brooke shook her head. "It wasn't meant to be." True love couldn't be bought or rented for two hundred dollars an hour. "I think we were at different places in our lives. Different dreams. Different goals." Peter, her pretend fiancé had wanted her to pay for a cozy hotel suite at the Plaza. Brooke merely wanted to make a good impression on her brothers.

Gillian nodded. "I know. You can't fill out some application and get love made to order. You fall when you fall."

Her mother clucked her tongue, then began clearing away the dishes. "I knew Junior was all wrong for you."

After her mother bustled from the kitchen, Gillian looked at Brooke apologetically. "I'd love to have you bunk here, but we're overflowing as it as. Mom and Dad moved in with me a few years ago, and they have the guest room, and Austen takes the couch, and I can't ask you to sleep on the floor. Once the construction on the new house is finished, we'll move in there and let Mama and Daddy take over this place. Hopefully they won't decide to give this one away, either."

"I wasn't expecting to intrude..." Brooke started, but then Gillian interrupted.

"There's a nice little hotel just down the road. The Spotlight Inn. Tell Delores you're family, and she'll treat you right."

Brooke thought of the fifty dollars in her pocket and wondered if the family discount would be enough. Better to save her money for more important things. Like gas, or food. Not wanting to complain, she managed a smile. "The Spotlight Inn sounds lovely. I'll check in tonight."

IT WAS THIRTY MINUTES of courteous chit-chat, before Gillian found the opportunity to drag her fiancé into the living room, without seeming rude.

"Now, Austen," Gillian said, using her most patient voice. She loved this man dearly, but at some point in their relationship, he would need to start telling her things. "I know you think I'm just some dizzy-headed blonde, in spite of the fact that I'm the duly elected sheriff of this town, and have spent the last five years keeping it afloat. Not that any of that is important, mind you, because I would be a very small-minded woman if I let such thoughts wound my pride. However, during the last seven months we've been together, we've made sacred promises to each other. We are to be married in a mere forty-five days because we have created a relationship based on trust and honesty. And yes, you have explored my body more intimately than any gynecologist ever could. As such, I am deserving of the truth. A sister? Sweetie, as far as deep, dark secrets of your past, a sister is the least of your concerns. A sister is family, a blood relation, a woman who shared your mother's womb."

Austen's face squared into what Gillian termed his stubborn look. "I didn't grow up with her, Gillian. She cruised some all-

American life, and yes, we share some DNA, but she's pretty much a stranger. I don't know squat about her."

Glancing toward the closed door to the kitchen, Gillian was glad she had insisted on extra insulation for the house, but since she didn't believe in leaving anything to chance, she set her voice to a whisper. "And you won't know anything unless you talk to her."

"You're going to make me do this?"

"Don't you want a sister?"

"No. I have one brother, and it took me nearly twenty-five years to understand that one. Besides," he grabbed her hand and his eyes went all dark and moonstruck, "you're my family, Gilly. You're my heart, my soul, my blood. How am I supposed to have room in my heart for anyone else?"

Her eyes narrowed. "Romantic talk will not relieve you of your familial obligations. Why, if you gave her half a chance, you might end up liking her."

Austen glanced at the door, glanced at Gillian, then sighed. "All right, but did you see the car? She's got money, her step-father was some save-the-world preacher and, Mom—god-dammit, Mom turned into one of those mothers who makes homemade soup and wears aprons."

And then Gillian understood. On the outside, Austen was some big macho doofus, but on the inside, he was just a little boy who'd had his mother stolen away. She wrapped her arms around him, soothing wounds that would never heal. "Your mother left the best part of the Hart family behind."

"Except for Frank."

"Except for Frank, but in spite of your mother's bad deci-sion-making skills, I don't think Brooke has had such an easy time of it."

He pressed a warm kiss on her hair. "You're just saying that to make me like her."

"Did you see her boots?"

"No."

"Austen, those boots looked like something the dogs had chewed up and spit out. She needs a family. She needs a brother. She needs a home."

"You know all this because of your top-notch investigative skills?"

Gillian smiled. "Call it women's intuition."

He laughed, slid a familiar hand down her backside and squeezed. "What's your women's intuition telling you now?"

Her hips moved forward in a frankly provocative invitation, but true love would not be denied. "Sneak into my room later, and we'll discuss it in extensive detail."

Austen heaved an extravagant sigh. "Tell me that someday we'll be able to share a bed for the entire night. It's like I'm sixteen all over again."

She patted the Texas Longhorn beneath his fly and then moved away, before they were doing it on the sofa again. Having herself, her parents and Austen all living under one roof was a painful exercise in delayed sexual gratification, but Gillian knew that once they were married, these days of stolen quickies and shared showers would be behind her.

Before she could leave the living room, Austen snagged her by the waist and pulled her close for a deep kiss.

THE WEEKEND PASSED like the world's longest hangover but Jason hadn't touched a drop. Normally, he lost himself in the art of repair, or a drive to San Angelo where he would inspect the scrap yards for whatever caught his eye. Or maybe he would call his father, say hello to the old man and listen to him rail about the Orioles or his property tax bill or his most recent trip to the doc.

Not this time.

It weighed on Jason's conscience, not knowing that she was okay. He had assumed the worst about her, and he'd been wrong. Now she was back out there alone.

He was a moron.

His conscience wasn't going to shut up until he knew she was sleeping safely under somebody's roof. Somebody that wouldn't take advantage of her—like he had, he reminded himself, which only made his conscience holler more.

By Monday morning, he spurred himself to action. For Jason this meant driving into town and wandering aimlessly until he could discover some answers.

It took him thirty-seven minutes to discover that he wasn't a good aimless wanderer, and no matter how hard he tried, he couldn't do casual.

Blame it on the military.

At the Hinkle's, he picked up some eggs and milk. At Zeke's Auto Garage he ordered a new air filter. At Dot's, he bought himself a cup of coffee, and read the *Tin Cup Gazette*. After reading a four-page account of the Friday night bingo game where Father Louis banned Emmaline Herzog for cheating, Jason remembered why he didn't like the *Tin Cup Gazette*.

Once his cup of coffee was empty, he took a long, hard look at his purchases, and donated the milk and eggs to Dot. In the future, he would know that perishables were the last to be bought, not the first.

At the First National Bank and Trust, he opened another safety deposit box, walking away with a brand-new coffee maker as part of some promotional event. The library had a closed sign in the window, so he proceeded to the town hall to find out if he had any unpaid parking tickets.

For six freaking hours, Jason wandered the four streets that made up downtown Tin Cup, in the process learning several things. Brooke's brother was not getting coffee or buying groceries or cashing a check at the bank or chatting with the sheriff at the Town Hall. If Brooke's brother was going to turn unsociable, why did he have to pick this day to start?

But then, as the afternoon sun was starting to fade, Jason finally spotted the elusive Austen Hart exiting the post office.

Jason plotted his strategy, deciding that if he walked east on Main, backtracked up 17, he could probably duck into the feed store and bump into Hart on the way out.

Everything worked exactly right. Jason exited the store, taking a position in front of Hart, then halting abruptly.

"Whoa, sorry. You okay?" the man asked after he'd run into Jason, which was what Jason wanted, but he still felt like a moron. Oh, yeah, because he was.

Absently, Jason rubbed his shoulder, which didn't hurt, but at least it was something to do. "Fine." Then he scanned the streets, frowning. "You know where I could get a twelve-volt battery?"

Austen laughed. "Not here." He held out his hand, one of those good ole boy sort of shakes. "Austen Hart."

"Jason Kincaid. I don't get into town much. You live around here?"

"At my fiancée's house for the moment. I own a place that should've been condemned by the county. It's going to take some time to fix. You?"

"Five miles west on County Road 163."

"The old Hinkle place? That property runs up to mine. That's you?"

At Jason's nod, Hart continued, a lot chattier than Jason could ever be. "We're neighbors. After we get it fixed up, we'll have you over, throw some steaks on the grill."

"We?" Jason asked, taking the opening, running with it. "You have family here?"

"Gillian's my fiancée. She's the sheriff," Hart answered, which wasn't what Jason had hoped to hear.

"Nice to have connections."

"Sometimes I speed, just so she can cuff me," Hart said with a friendly laugh.

The man was easy to like, knew how to converse with anybody, but he said nothing about Brooke. Jason racked his brain for impromptu conversation, but Dog's limited vocabulary skills meant that Jason was out of practice. "Not a big town. You grew up here?"

"Me and my brother. Don't believe what you hear. Long story."

Another opening. Steer it back to the family.

"You know, I would've killed to have a brother. It was me and my little sister, and she was always tailing after me. Eventually she grew out of it, but not soon enough. Know what I mean?" The story wasn't true. Jason had five brothers and one sister, Sara, who was still in Baltimore. Sara had never followed any of the Kincaid brothers around, but creating some sort of friendly rapport was Jason's last shot at interrogation. At first he thought he'd blown it, but then Hart nodded like he agreed.

"It's good you know your sister. Mine just showed up on my doorstep this week. Up until last year, we didn't even know she existed. Now that she's here, I'm as clueless as a pig wearing a watch."

At least that was some progress. Jason shot him a sympathetic look. "Families are a true pain in the ass. That's why you're in town? Escaping all that estrogen at your fiancée's?"

Hart shook his head. "Brooke—that's my sister—isn't staying with us. The house is packed as it is, so Brooke took a room at the Spotlight. The inn's not real fancy, but at least this way she gets her own bed and doesn't have to wait in line for the shower. Mornings are killer at the Wanamaker house."

Jason smiled stupidly, but inside he was seething. He knew that Brooke wasn't at the Spotlight Inn. No, she'd be homesteading it in her car, parked on some desolate part of the highway, a target for overzealous cops or where serial killers could happen upon her.

After a fast check at his watch, Jason pretended to be rattled, not hard since he was still seeing red. "Look at that! Four o'clock. Time flies, doesn't it. Listen, it was great to meet you. I'll see you around."

With that, Jason set out on a search-and-rescue mission.

Hopefully Brooke would see things in a practical manner and come home.

Probably not. Bring the heat, bring the stupid. It was the Army way.

BROOKE DIDN'T WANT to be happy to see the Captain. She didn't want to be relieved when his truck popped into view, but she was. When she watched his long body climb out of the cab, she felt a heavy weight lift from her shoulders.

Weakness and knotted muscles, nothing more, she told herself, still mad that he'd misjudged her. It wasn't relief, but the heat of the sun making her dizzy. As he approached her car, she schooled her features into appropriate disapproval.

The Captain opened the driver's-side door and scowled. "You could have come back."

Brooke snorted. "I'm the crazy lady, remember? The flaky little nympho who chases men across the country because I looove them."

The scowl deepened. "I'm sorry."

"Your apologies would mean a lot more if you didn't keep screwing up. You should move back from the door. You're blocking my view."

"Why didn't you tell your brother you couldn't afford the hotel?"

"Would you tell your family that you couldn't afford a hotel? Would you tell your family if there was a problem? And don't even think about lying to me, because I know you better than that."

"Hart seems like a nice guy. He'd understand."

Of course he'd understand. Everyone would understand. And she would be branded as the Incapable One for life. No, thank you. Brooke lifted her chin. "Once the lawyer returns and the paperwork is signed, Austen is going to buy me out."

The Captain pulled his cap off his head, pushed it back, and she could see the frustration in his eyes. "And what are you going to do until then?"

"I'll find a job, If I can't find one here, I'll go to Houston, or Dallas. There's a job for me somewhere."

The frustration in his face faded and gentled into something that made her dizzy again. "Your brother isn't in Houston or Dallas. Your home isn't in Houston or Dallas. You already have a job here. Come back to the house."

"Why should I go with you?" she asked, wanting to hear the words. Wanting to hear him say that he wanted her, that he needed her, and it scared her how badly she ached to hear those words.

Mutely he stared. Patiently she waited.

Finally, he pointed to the old abandoned farmhouse she'd parked behind. "You can't live in your car. You could get killed."

Brooke wanted to scream. Instead, she smiled sweetly. "Your concern for my safety is touching, but unnecessary. I've been doing great in my car. That's the pleasant thing about inanimate objects. Unlike I do with human beings, I don't expect them to care." She tried to pull the door closed, but the Captain was not only animate, but immoveable. *Darn it.*

"You won't come back?" he asked, a blinding glimpse of the obvious.

"No."

He scanned the horizon, rubbed his jaw thoughtfully. "There's laws against public vagrancy. I can tell the Sheriff. Imagine how she would feel knowing that her future sister-in-law lives in a car."

No!

Brooke pounded on the steering wheel, wishing it were his head. "You wouldn't dare."

The Captain only smiled.

He would dare. He was that way.

Brooke closed her eyes, blocking out his image, blocking out the shabby inside of her car. The Impala wasn't supposed to be home. He was supposed to believe her. Austen should have welcomed her with open arms.

Brooke felt the pain deep in her soul, felt it work through her, and then let it pass. Her world had never been what it was supposed to be, and sometimes, late in the night, she worried that it never would.

Tired, sore and spent, she opened her eyes and saw the Captain waiting for his answer. There was dust on his boots, his jaw was locked and the single gray eye was the color of iron.

In answer, Brooke pulled back her hair, tightened her jaw and met his gaze evenly. "Don't think I will let you touch me." Even as she said the words, she knew it was a lie.

"I wouldn't expect you to. To be honest, it'll be a lot easier. Things won't get messed up. Take your job back. I'll sleep in the shed. The pay will be the same and, in return, I keep quiet."

And no, even when blackmailing her, he still had to be the gentleman.

"I won't let you sleep in the shed. It's wrong."

His eyes flickered toward her. The steel turned into heat. "Don't go there, Brooke."

"Take the couch," she clarified. She hated this. Hated that she could never be a guest, only a burden.

"No."

The wind kicked in, the smell of dust, dirt and defeat. "Please. This is hard enough."

"Why is that? Why is it so hard for you to accept random acts of kindness?"

Her shoulders slumped because, in the end, Brooke would never be as strong as she wanted, never be as smart as she wanted. She wiped at the final humiliation—her own tears. "Take the couch. Please."

For an endless moment, the Captain stood over her, strong and silent, but in the end, he slammed the car door and swore.

Slowly, Brooke repaired her face, shored up the cracks in her dignity and then followed the Captain's truck home.

7

THE GOLD-LETTERED SIGN OVER the doorway said "Hiram Hadley, Esquire," but it might as well have said "Brooke's Future—Enter Here." Without knowing it, Austen had given her the best present ever—hope. With the money that her brother was going to give her for her inheritance, she'd have a down payment on a place to call home. This was her chance for the Captain to see her as someone valuable, too. People very rarely saw Brooke as someone valuable.

In Detroit she gotten by on a grocery clerk's salary until the store had closed. In Minnesota she had waitressed in a bar, until the manager had kept her late one evening and explained her new job resonsibilites, which involved her mouth meeting his penis. She introduced her knee to his balls, and decided that St. Paul wasn't the place for her. Brooke had spent the last ten years moving from place to place, looking for a spot to belong, but for the first time, Brooke didn't want to leave, she wanted to stay, but on her own terms, on her own two feet.

Briskly she knocked at the door, but alas, Brooke's future was not answering.

In case Mr. Hadley had returned and was hard of hearing, Brooke knocked harder. "Hello! Is anyone in there?"

"Good golly, missy. Can you stop the hammering? Even my cat is getting anxious."

Slowly she lowered her arm and turned, finding the dry cleaner, a pudgy man with a balding, bullet-shaped head, scowling at her. However, contrary to his statement, his cat was definitely not anxious. The round animal was winding his way through Brooke's ankles, rolling on the cement steps, belly-flopping one way then the other. Brooke reached down and petted the more forgiving feline. "I'd like to speak to Mr. Hadley."

"He's in North Dakota."

"Well, yes, I know that."

"Then why are you knocking on his door?"

Brooke rose and held out her hand. "I'm Brooke Hart. You're the dry cleaner? I've heard you do very good work."

Grudgingly he shook her hand, kerosene-like fumes drifting to Brooke's nose. "Arnold Cervantes. If you need something cleaned, I'm your man. But I still don't get it. If you know Hiram's gone, then why are you here?"

His tone wasn't very nice, but Brooke reminded herself to remain friendly. If she worked with those chemicals all day, she wouldn't be a happy person, either. "Doesn't anyone else work in the office?"

"Lizzie's his secretary."

"Why isn't she answering the door?" Brooke asked, which she thought was a very logical question.

"She's in Dallas while Hiram's taking care of his dad. He gave her the time off. Seemed silly for her to sit in the office and twiddle her thumbs while he's gone. Why're you so all-fired to talk to Hiram?"

"I have some legal matters with my brother that need to be arranged. It's regarding the Hart property. Mr. Hadley called me."

"Why didn't you call him back?"

"He doesn't have an answering machine."

The man began to laugh.

"This isn't funny," Brooke told him, deciding that pretend-friendly had gone on long enough. "I drove a long way to talk to Mr. Hadley and everybody here thinks it's normal that his office is shut down."

Looking somewhat ashamed, the dry cleaner blew out a breath. "Sorry, missy. Give me your name and a phone number and I'll call his father's place."

"You could just give me the number and I'll save you the trouble," Brooke suggested, not wanting to admit that she didn't have a phone and not exactly sure that Mr. Cervantes would do it anyway.

The man picked up his unhappily mewing cat. "You know those trusting folks who believe everybody is who they say they are and want to chat all day on the phone?"

"Yes."

"Hiram's not one of them. Got to check everybody out. Probably why he went into law. Give me your name and number and I'll call him tonight. If it's an emergency, I'm sure he'd fly back and take care of matters, seeing as he's left you in a lurch and all."

An emergency? Was this an emergency? It wasn't like Brooke didn't have a roof over her head now. The Captain's roof, and yes, there were a lot of issues to be worked out between them, but Brooke fully intended to work them out, because no matter how mad he made her, he also made her feel safe and relaxed and desired. Most important of all, there had been times when she saw respect in his eyes. She'd had moments in her life when she was safe or relaxed or desired, but never respected—unless she was pretending to be someone who she wasn't, but with the Captain she didn't have to pretend.

No, this was no emergency. "I can wait until he gets back. I don't have a phone."

"I think what we have ourselves is a failure to communicate, missy," the man said, laughing again. She didn't think he was laughing at her, and she decided the Mr. Cervantes wasn't as bad as she had assumed. However, the fat cat in his arms was staring at her, not respecting her, because once again, Brooke was letting the door to her future close. No, not today.

"Wait." She wrote down her name and put the Captain's phone number after it. "This is my work number."

Mr. Cervantes adjusted the cat, freeing one hand, and then tucked the number in his pocket. "I'll pass it along and tell him it's an emergency."

"No!" she yelled, and now Mr. Cervantes was staring as well as the cat. "I mean, it's not a huge emergency. I get anxious sometimes. I should learn to relax more. It's why I moved out here. I lived in New York once."

"New York, huh? Pretty fancy place. You're going to find out we do things a lot different out here."

Brooke smiled at the man, because everything about this town was different, and that was exactly why it felt like home.

AFTER DINNER, Brooke watched Dog clear the dishes, noticing that this time, there were no glitches or flaws in the mechanical grips. Every time the Captain found something off, he had to repair it. Including her life. But she could repair her life first. If the mineral rights on the Hart land turned into real dollars... If the Captain could see her as something more than a mechanical automaton to be repaired. If only he could see her as a woman again.

If only...

From across the room, the Captain sat at the table, tinkering with a gutted radio, studiously avoiding talking to her. Not that she wanted him to, but the silence between them had changed from something companionable to a war zone, and she wished he could repair the glitches in their relationship, as well. Not happy with the status quo, Brooke stood, preferring the lonely security of his bedroom to this.

"Brooke."

She stopped, turned. "Is this work related?"

He looked at her impassively, scarred and patched, a man who had suffered a lot more than her. "Please" was all he said, but that small conversation was better than nothing at all. Brooke snagged a barstool, pulling it close to his chair. Her foolish hands itched to straighten the screwdrivers or stroke the rough stubble at his jaw. Instead she folded them tightly in her lap.

"How are things with your brother? He's nice to you?"

They were conversing formally, like an employee and boss. Whatever. Brooke met his eye, equally cool. "Austen is nice enough. I like Gillian. They invited me to dinner tomorrow evening, so you won't be burdened with my company. Feel free to roll out the keg and strippers."

"You're usually nicer than this."

"I know. I felt like being catty."

The corner of his mouth lifted and she remembered the feel of his lips on her neck, the taste of him on her tongue. Her gaze drifted to the hefty ridge beneath his fly and stayed there. He knew. The air was charged with the tension, her overheated nerves sparking, nipples on alert. When he leaned closer, Brooke held her breath, but then the mulish Captain pulled back. "You should take the money and stay at the Inn." His voice was as rough and hard as his resolve.

"I'll only take what I earn," answered Brooke, because she could be just as stubborn.

He didn't look happy, but obviously he knew better than to argue. "All right," he agreed, turning back to his work, and she told herself she didn't care.

At the dismissal, she climbed down from the stool, acting the perfect employee and the perfect guest. "We're done?"

He picked up his screwdriver, pretending to work. Brooke knew better. The Captain's twists were always properly seated, never a wasted movement, much like when he was inside her. Not liking the direction of her thoughts, she looked away. "Do you need any clothes or female things?" he asked politely.

"No, thank you."

"Did you talk to the lawyer?"

"He's out of town."

"When is he coming back?"

"I don't know," she answered, and finally he looked up.

"Nobody has a phone number for him?"

Brooke shrugged. "I'm handling the situation. You don't need to be concerned."

She was surprised when his screwdriver tapped against a metal plate. The Captain wasn't a tapper. "I can be concerned."

"Everything is fine. When he comes back, I'll collect my money, take a room at the Spotlight Inn and I'll be out of your hair forever."

"I don't mind you staying here. I like you staying here, Brooke."

"Why?"

At her question, his scowl deepened, hard grooves cutting into his face. Realizing she wasn't going to get an answer, Brooke gestured to the couch. "Do you have an extra pillow and sheet? You'll need them."

"Are you going to give me my pillow back?"

She chose to ignore the question. "If the sheets are in the bedroom, you should get them now." There was an invitation in her voice that irked her, as if all she wanted was some sign that the Captain wanted to be in her bed again. One look, anything…

But, no.

"Get some rest. I'll see you in the morning," he said.

All night she watched the clock on the bedroom wall, wishing the time would move on. The bed was big and empty without him, and to make matters worse, she could hear him restless on the couch. Her feet wanted to go to him. She wanted to curl up beside him, but that wouldn't solve anything. From the other room, she could hear him mumble and swear because the couch wasn't long enough, and his feet were hanging over the side. His head would be cramped against the armrest, which, if she returned his pillow, wouldn't be a problem.

But the pillow stayed and Brooke lay there, uncomfortable

in her own guilt. If he had come to bed, she would have melted like chocolate in the sun, but he didn't, and so Brooke pulled the pillow close and breathed in his scent.

Sadly, it wasn't enough.

THE DESIGN OF THE HOUSE didn't necessitate Jason passing by the bedroom to take a shower, but there he was, lurking in the doorway, watching her sleep. Bare shoulders poked out from under the covers, and he was grateful for the early morning chill in the air that kept her safely beneath the sheets.

In fact, as she snuggled deeper in the bed, he was feeling pretty good about the situation. There was nothing in the cloud of dark hair that would ink sexual fantasies on his brain. Nothing indecent in the graceful curve of her neck. In fact, if he wanted to, he could have stood there all day without getting turned on. Of course, then he'd officially be a stalker, which was a helluva lot creepier than just some guy with a hard-on, because 24/7, most men had hard-ons. It was the nature of the beast. Look at a cloud. See a woman's breasts surrounded by an elephant. Hard-on.

Wait for paint to dry, imagine long, stocking-encased legs hidden in the glossy swirls. Hard-on.

And yet, he thought proudly, here he was, watching her—most likely nude because she wasn't shy—and he was flaccid, limp, not even a drop of blood heading in the wrong direction.

Then she rolled over, and her arm slipped underneath the pillow. She had wonderfully sensual arms. Thin, but not toothpicks. There was muscle on Brooke Hart, more than she knew. When he had been on top of her, and her eyes were so aware, those sensual arms had locked him close. Her sleek thighs had wrapped around his hips, soldering them together...

Brooke sighed, her breathing deep and even, and Jason swore silently because his cock stood out like Pinocchio's nose, just as long, just as wooden, just as stupid.

It wasn't fair. There was absolutely nothing carnal in the way she was so innocently sleeping, except for the way the sheet was drifting lower, lower...

The morning light lingered on her body, the rose-tipped breasts that he'd touched and held, the slender curve of her hip...

Closing his eyes didn't help. Jason wanted to move, but wisely he told his feet to get a clue. One hand flexed, then the other, so Jason told his hands to grow a pair and deal. Sadly, his cock stayed where it was, miserable and alone. Deep in his heart, Jason knew he could control his feet and his hands, but his dick was being a dick, and knowing he couldn't stand there forever, Jason stalked toward the shower, a little louder than he normally would have because he wanted freaking Sleeping Beauty to wake up. He wanted Sleeping Beauty to throw back the covers, the sunrise following the curves and the shadows and...

Realizing the situation was deteriorating fast, Jason fled. Once in the shower, he set the water on ice-cube cold and waited for his hard-on to wither away. Nada. He counted to one hundred in base ten. He recited the first nineteen digits of pi and still nothing changed. With one hand braced against the tile wall, he designed a new water controller in his head. It didn't help.

Seventeen minutes later, his skin was blue, his fingers were prunes, but his brainless cock didn't care, and so for the tenth time in four days, he reached down and took himself in hand.

One-eyed Kincaid. Miserable, full-cocked, one-eyed Kincaid.

At this rate, his other eye would go blind, too.

WHILE JASON TURNED HIMSELF into an icicle, Brooke smiled to herself, letting the warm sun linger where he'd looked. Ah, it was bliss to see a man in such pain. To see his face so hard with lust. She liked it when he looked like that, so intense, so focused, so needy...for her.

It was too bad he was suffering alone in the shower, but that was the agreement, and that was what was smart, and frankly, he didn't deserve her until he admitted how much he needed a woman in his bed. Not just any woman, though. No, only her.

Still, it was a shame that he was so stubborn and wasn't there now. A crying shame, she thought, remembering the way his big body felt on top of her, feeling him push deep inside her, his hard chest rough against her breasts. In the warm sun, her nipples grew achy, and her hips arched, searching for him, wanting him. Desire flowed through her, as soft as the sun, and she could feel her body swell. From the other room, she could hear the sounds of his shower, knew the water was darkening his hair, glistening on his chest, running down his long legs...

Soon Brooke reached between her legs, imagining his hands there, his hungry mouth on her breasts. If she closed her eyes, it was his body covering her, his industrious finger pleasuring her, his burning touch that was heating her skin.

Faster she stroked, her eyes tightly closed, her hips straining to meet him. Finding nothing above her but cool air, her teeth cut into her lip, willing her hand to be longer, thicker, warmer...

But, no...

Furious with him, furious with her useless hand, Brooke swore and opened her eyes.

The Captain.

He was leaning against the doorjamb, a towel wrapped around his waist, not that it mattered because the man was huge when aroused. Brooke froze on the spot, legs splayed open, her body exposed.

If she smiled at him, if she opened her arms...

But, no. Instead she stared, melting under his white-hot gaze, willing him to take the step.

Only one.

It was humiliating to endure, her eyes pleading, her thighs

wide, and the Captain standing fast. Eventually her eyes drifted closed.

For a long, long time there was only the lonely silence, and when Brooke dared to look again, the Captain was gone.

THEY DIDN'T SPEAK for most of the afternoon—thankfully. Every time Jason happened to glance in her direction, all he could picture was the heavy invitation in her eyes, the glistening dark curls between her legs, the swollen pink flesh that begged to be filled.

His cock would never recover. Ever.

His cock's opinion notwithstanding, he knew he'd done the right thing. Brooke was too vulnerable. When she got her own place, when she told her brother that she was basically broke and Hart told her he didn't care, then she'd be glad that Jason had been the sensible one.

He noticed as she bent over a milk crate, her shirt gaping open, the line between her breasts damp with sweat. He wished that he'd never tasted her, never taken her. Best to ignore her, best to forget.

It was while studiously ignoring her non-presence that he ripped his finger on a jagged piece of metal. He swore, not loud enough that she could hear, because if she wasn't concerned about him bleeding to death, he'd be happy to die in her ignorance of that fact.

However, Brooke didn't seem concerned, picking through a collection of old vacuum radio tubes. Mumbling something unpleasant, Jason escaped inside to bandage his thumb. As he passed by the kitchen, he spotted a strange object hanging over the sink. A piece of wire, twisted into two cirlces with four dangling wires. Yellow resistors had been threaded onto the wire, and from the top circle extended a red Zener diode. It was either a hippopotamus or a... Jason cracked a smile.

A unicorn.

A note was attached to the rear leg.

"In case you forgot, I'll be joining Austen and Gillian for dinner tonight. There is chicken salad in the refrigerator. I will try and restrain myself from doing anything embarrassing.

Your eternally loyal employee."

Jason laughed. It didn't matter how bad things were in Brooke's world, it didn't register with her. A more level-headed man might have called her delusional, the way she plodded ahead, ignoring all the warning signs in front of her. But there was something fascinating about her world that made a less level-headed man want to stay and explore. Listen to the pure joy of her laugh, see the happiness she found in the ordinary, lick the sweat from the golden skin of her breasts.

Hell.

Shaking off the lust, Jason reminded himself that *platonic* was the word of the day. And platonic did much to explain why he spent the next two hours rigging up an old computer terminal display. By mounting a wireless router to it, he could send messages to the display via his phone. Best of all, the portable motion sensor would alert him when someone was skulking around. Elaborate, yes. Overkill, probably. Egotistical, definitely.

And somebody was definitely curious. He could see her spying on him as he lugged the computer into the house, where he wedged it on the kitchen counter between the vise and rotary saw. Three minimal modifications later and his first message was glowing in eerie 1970s' green.

"Sarcasm is not pretty. Thank you for the chicken salad. Is that dill or arsenic?

Your extraordinarily patient boss."

He stood back and admired his own genius, then returned outside. Brooke stood underneath the shade netting, clipboard in hand, unmoved by his genius or pretending to be unmoved.

However, it was a mere twenty minutes later that the motion sensor triggered the alarm on his phone. Not so unmoved after all, he thought, aware that she was no longer nearby.

Patiently he waited until she returned to the yard, then he pocketed the gasket he'd been meaning to attach to the faucet and went to investigate what she'd done. Inside he found a new note hanging from the unicorn.

"Since sarcasm is not pretty, I thought you would be more likely to appreciate it. Your bandage is turning red. Please make sure the bleeding stops. If you need assistance with a tourniquet, I'm very good at knots.
Your medically talented employee."

Quickly he changed his bandage, and escaped to the privacy of one of his sheds before he texted his response.

"I am touched by your charity but, no, I don't need medical attention. There is a fifty on the table. We need milk. And you could buy shoes. See, that is how charity works.
Your even-tempered and generous boss."

Shortly after that, Brooke changed her clothes, skipping down the porch steps with a pink scarf tied around her neck. She had stolen some of his white light-emitting diodes, using them as a light-up hair ornament. Mutely she glided toward him, nodded once, and then he watched as she drove off in her wreck of a car. Exactly forty-seven minutes passed before he allowed himself to read her response.

"I took the fifty. You owe me for today's work. I don't need shoes. My boots are awesome. Maybe I'll buy a vibrator instead. Don't wait up.
Your self-sufficient employee."

Jason tilted his head back and laughed.

THE CAPTAIN WAS WAITING up for her when she got home, and at first, she pretended as if she didn't see him sitting in the kitchen, a half-gutted cylindrical gadget laying out on the table. Not that it was really a kitchen with the piles of tools, the clunky air compressor, and the neatly organized rows of milk crates along the wall. She liked that he was at peace amongst the chaos. It never flustered him or frustrated him. No, the Captain was a very passive man for a soldier.

"How was dinner?" he asked casually.

"Good," she answered, equally causally, leisurely strolling across the room, clutching the brown paper bag to her chest. It was empty, there was no vibrator, but he was intrigued yet trying not to look intrigued and Brooke mentally patted herself on the back.

The Captain inspected the bag, met her eyes and then buried himself back in his task. Okay, not so successful after all.

"How was your brother?"

"Good," she replied.

"Did you tell him?" he asked, still not looking at her.

Brooke stopped, aware of the knot in her stomach. It wasn't a fun, sexual tension knot, but the less fun, truthiness knot. "Tell him what?"

"Tell him where you're staying."

"No."

"Is he nice to you?"

She knew the words were an effort for him. The Captain wasn't a man for light conversation, but at least he was giving it a try. "I think he's warming. Given time, I'm sure we can establish a solid foundation, and at that point, I'll explain my situation."

At that, his scar silvered in the fluorescent lights. "Can I ask you a question?"

Another surprise.

"Are you sure you want to?"

"Yes."

She leaned against the sofa, the very place where he was going to sleep tonight—alone—and sniffed. All across America, men were sleeping on couches because their women had kicked them out of the bed. Trust the Captain to be the exception. "You should understand that asking questions implies something more than a traditional employer-employee relationship, and I'm not sure that it's covered in our agreement."

The Captain stayed silent, which told her much about his opinion of her snarky remark.

"I'm sorry." Charlene Hart had been snarky when she drank, and although Brooke knew she had picked up some of Charlene's less than admirable habits, that didn't mean she had to like it.

"It's about time somebody besides me gets to apologize."

"I try not to screw up," she told him, and she did. Lately, she seemed to be doing it less. Apparently his meticulous nature was starting to rub off on her, which was a good thing. Details had never been her strong point. "I think I'm doing a better job at not screwing up than you," she added, only because it wasn't very often she could feel superior. It felt nice to flaunt it.

"Can we get back to the question?"

"Talking about your mistakes is a lot more fun," she answered, neatly dodging the question.

"Brooke," he said, frustration in his voice.

"Captain," she answered, with a pointed glance at the tiny sofa, equally frustrated.

"What happened?"

As probing questions went, it was pretty much the worst. She didn't like the abnormalities in her life. She didn't like feeling like a freak, someone who never belonged anywhere, but out of all the people she'd ever met, it was the Captain who would probably understand best. She suspected he'd had his share of abnormalities as well, and he didn't seem to care. Brooke dropped the useless sack on the couch, her fingers locked on the hard back for support, and then took a long breath.

"My mother was a very nice woman with what she called a joyous spirit, which meant she loved her spirits a little too much—usually vodka because it doesn't smell. She had very little education and very few skills, and since she wasn't very fond of the drudgery of the workplace, she usually avoided working and would hook up with whatever kind stranger wanted to take her and her daughter in."

Just as she'd expected, he didn't look surprised or disapproving. No matter the way the wind blew, the Captain stood tall. "Where did the two of you live?"

"A lot of places. The road was our home."

"When did she die?"

"January 1, 2002. Cirrhosis of the liver, although there was no confirmed diagnosis. I just assumed."

"You've been alone since then?"

"Yes."

"Working?"

"Some. I lived in Rhode Island for some time, a receptionist for a chiropractor, Dr. Morgan Downey Knox, the third. He was very particular about the way I answered the phone, but I was able to improve my vocabulary. While I was working in the doctor's office, I looked up Tyler, and arranged the meeting in New York. My mother didn't like to talk about my brothers, or my father, or Texas, but I knew a little and I wanted to know more. I thought creating this great life in New York would convince them that I was normal, but it took a large pile of cash, pretty much everything I had."

"You are normal."

"No one's normal," she said, smiling at the one-eyed man surrounded by left-behind parts.

"There's a point. So why do you want to be normal?"

"Don't you?" she asked, but she knew the answer. She just wanted to understand why.

He shook his head, not giving her the answer she wanted. The Captain was a tricky man, particular about his secrets and not wanting people to know he was tricky. Being particular about her secrets as well, Brooke understood.

"Can I ask you a question?" she finally asked, because this was important.

The Captain considered it and then nodded. "Seems fair."

"Why do you do all this? Why all the repairing and the fixing and the creating?" As probing questions went, it was pretty much the worst, but she figured the tricky man owed her.

"Because nobody else does."

"You like to be different?"

"Different?" He frowned at her choice of words, scratched at the brown stubble of his jaw. "It's not different. It just is."

"What's the best thing you ever created?"

His uncovered eye narrowed, not so impassive, not so comfortable now. He liked living in chaos, but the worst sort of chaos was the chaos inside. That sort of chaos wasn't so easy to fix. Brooke understood that, too.

"That's question number two."

"You can have a question number two if you'd like," she countered. It was only fair.

At first she didn't think he would answer, but eventually he did, because in the end, the Captain was a fair man, too.

"I was a maintenance officer in Iraq. The *muj's* were blowing up all sorts of shit, soldiers, too. Standard issue wasn't working for the trucks, so we had to get creative. They needed metal plating, shields to protect from the blast. So, me and Mad Max, we started scrounging whatever we could get our hands on, and we hobbled together some of the butt-ugliest transports ever. It worked. The *muj* still tried to blow up shit, but after that, men came home. Finally the beltway clerks pulled their head out and got wise to the problem, and then the Humvees rolled off fully loaded with one thousand pounds of ballistic-resistant American steel. But for a while, me and Max, we did some good work."

The Captain smiled at her then, and Brooke smiled back. Good work, indeed. Brave, resourceful, matter-of-fact. Most of the world would never know, which was too bad because the rest of the world could learn much from Jason Kincaid. "Why did you enlist?"

He shrugged. "Seemed like the right thing to do at the time."

"Why did you leave?"

"That's question number four," he reminded her.

"I'll give you four questions," she offered generously, because she liked this cautious give and take, and if he was willing, then Brooke believed she should be willing, too.

"I stopped being useful, and didn't want to sit behind a desk." After he finished, he waited, watching her expectantly. Give and take.

"Your turn."

"After your mother died, why'd you stay on the road?"

Why? "Nowhere was home. I kept trying to find it."

"Is this home?" he asked, a deceptively simple question. This small town—where she'd never lived before—felt like more of a home than anywhere else, but it wasn't because of her brother, or the Hart land, or the chatty dinners at the Wanamaker house. If she told him the truth, would he put up one thousand pounds of ballistic-resistant American steel? She glanced down at the couch and smiled to herself. When she looked up, maybe there was more in her eyes than she wanted, but hopefully a man with fifty-percent vision would only see half as much. "It's a start. What about you? Is this home?"

His one good eye looked at her, looked through her, and Brooke's fingers gripped the cushions a little harder.

"I don't need a home."

"Everybody needs a home," she insisted. Everyone, including the Captain. Especially the Captain, who was normally a very intelligent man. But there were some things that the Captain pretended not to see, and she believed it was time someone pointed them out. Nicely, of course.

He shrugged again, brushing off her words. She longed to shake him, wake him up to the world, but the Captain was a tricky man, surrounding himself with Dog, the tools, the half-gutted cylindrical doo-hickey…

Then Brooke began to feel whole, a little wiser. He'd made a home, he just never knew it. With that, she walked over, kissed him once on the cheek, a silent invitation in her eyes, not so hidden this time. However, the Captain was a hard man who believed that the world didn't need him, and he stared impassively.

Completely unfooled, Brooke retrieved her empty paper bag from the couch. The empty paper bag containing her imaginary vibrator, which she fondled as if it were a man. The Captain turned pale. "Knock, next time," she instructed, and then strolled away, satisfied with his quiet moan. Wisely, she hid her grin.

Two DAYS LATER, when Brooke awoke, she pulled her money from her boot, counted it out and beamed. More than enough for shoes. The Captain was already outside, taking apart some large metal tank, and Brooke approached with a spring in her step, because finally…finally, the world's ugliest boots were going into the trash.

"I need to go to town."

He pulled off his cap, put down the drill in his hand. "Shoes?"

She didn't care for his judgmental assumption, even if it was the truth. Her right boot had a hole on top, and the West Texas dust had turned both shoes an unfashionable pasty gray. "Possibly. If I'm so inclined."

Then he smiled at her and she decided she didn't mind his assumption quite so much. "Good. Tallyrand's has the best selection. Or, if you want, we can drive into Austin. There's a great scrap yard on the east side of town."

Normally she would have agreed, but when funds were limited, shopping was a blood sport best done alone. "Tallyrand's will be fine. Maybe Rita will have time for a chat."

"Rita always has time for a chat." He paused, tugged at the bill of his cap. "What are you going to tell her?"

"Does it matter?"

"I should know, in case anyone asks."

"You're my boss. That's the truth."

He nodded. "The truth is always the easiest. No open toes."

"Excuse me?"

He pointed at her feet. "No sandals."

"Does this workplace now have a dress code?"

"Do you want to rip your toe off?"

Well, when he put it like that. "No. However, in deference to your somewhat overwrought, safety-first attitude, I'll find something practical, yet still cute."

He smiled again, a quicksilver tilt to his mouth. "Good luck with that."

Boldly, because Brooke was never safety-first, she rose up and pressed a kiss to that quicksilver mouth. Automatically he pressed back, and for a few precious seconds, they were joined. Before he could move away, she stepped back and was rewarded with a quick flash of disappointment in his eye. Then the normally passive gray gaze returned and "Humph" was all he said before picking up his drill.

It was a good thing he couldn't see her grin.

THE TOWN OF TIN CUP came alive early on weekdays, the streets full of pickup trucks, delivery trucks, shopkeepers opening their stores. Yes, everyone was opening except Mr. Hadley's law offices. Apparently, Mr. Cervantes wasn't as diligent as she had hoped. Brooke shoved a note through the mail slot in the door, and then dropped in to Hinkle's grocery to restore some of the long-lost Hart honor. Gladys, still remembering the shoplifted can of peas, treated Brooke suspiciously until Brooke complained about the weather, just like she'd seen Gillian do. Weather complaints seemed to be the quickest way to mend fences, and then Gladys complained about her gall stones, and by the time Brooke left the store, she knew she'd won the older woman over.

Down the street, Tallyrand's was full, farmers picking up their weekly feed supplies. The line was curled halfway around the store, and one barrel-jawed old man wasn't happy, complaining in a loud voice. Rita ignored him, and the old man's voice grew louder before Brooke stepped in, asking about the weather, asking about his crops, until finally the old man lightened up, blushing under all the attention. Rita noticed, just as Brooke had hoped, and shot her a grateful smile.

A person could never collect too many friends. Having friends was the first step to belonging.

Once the line was cleared, Brooke found the shoes and now Rita was definitely ready to chat. Today, the former beauty queen was dressed in tight-fitting jeans tucked into ornate boots, and a burnt orange and white glitter vest.

"How long have you known the Captain?" Rita asked.

"Two weeks. When I first arrived in town, I was searching for a job. He needed help, and I applied."

"I didn't know the Captain was hiring."

"Oh, yes. He stays very busy."

"Doing what?" Rita pretended to dust off her glass display shelves, but Brooke wasn't fooled. This conversation would be relayed in its entirety to pretty much anybody as soon as Brooke was out the door. No, Rita was an excellent way to upgrade the Captain's reputation in the community.

"The Captain fixes things. He owns a thriving repair business."

"Business? He doesn't take any money for that. The widow Kenley called him about her broken washing machine that up and died, and he told her not to worry about it. He'd take care of everything."

"And he does a little art work on the side," Brooke told her, not wanting Rita to think that the Captain was some mere Maytag repairman.

"Art?" Rita raised a beautifully penciled brow. "The Captain? He's an artist?"

After glancing around, pretending to check for lurking ears, Brooke motioned for Rita to move closer and spoke in a hushed whisper. "He's a very talented artist. You should see some of the things that he's done."

"Paintings?" Rita whispered back.

Brooke picked up a set of cowbell windchimes and listened to the hollow clanging sound, deciding that cowbells were not the best choice in making windchimes.

Next to the wind chimes was a shelf full of cactus, the prickly pear kind, guaranteed to thrive in all climates or your money back, at least that was what the sign claimed. Brooke picked up the small plant, tested the sharp prickles and promptly put it back.

"Not paintings exactly," Brooke explained. "I think his stuff defies the structure of most artistic genres, but you know how the art world is. Always wanting to put things into a box. When you stare into the soul of one of the Captain's pieces, it's like techno-art crossed with steampunk crossed with a very efficient environmental message. I simply call it 'the Kincaid.'"

"Really? I had no idea. I never could figure out why he would want to move to Tin Cup after he left the service. Didn't know anybody but Sonya's aunt and uncle, Gladys and Henry, and they weren't that close. We always thought he was traumatized by the war. PTSD."

"Oh, no. He's very, very normal. Eccentric, but normal."

"You seem to know him very well."

"I understand his work."

"Do you have an art background?"

If one counted the year's worth of auction house catalogs she'd picked up in New York, then sure. "I dabble."

"How's your brother?"

"I had dinner with him and his fiancée last night, as a matter of fact. Love the ring."

At that, Rita frowned. "You saw it?"

"Well, yes, she's not very shy about it. But it's sweet, seeing them together. He seems to have done a lot of really great things for the town."

"I know, I know. He seems to have gotten his act together, sure, but we all know he's got some no-good mischief in his past, and those memories don't get washed away so easily."

This was the second time that people were accusing the Hart family of criminal acts. However, Brooke liked Rita, she wanted a discount on the smart pair of leather ankle boots that were sitting on the side table, and she wasn't going to argue. "It seems like he's really turned things around."

"It's the Sheriff's doing."

"Maybe Austen had something to do with it, as well," Brooke added, needing to defend her brother in some way. "The Hart family is very civic-minded."

"I suppose."

"Can we talk about some shoes? There's one pair here, but there's a scratch on the leather."

Rita picked up the shoe, bright red lips pursed until they disappeared. "I have another pair somewhere. Let me get them for you."

Brooke pulled the woman back. "You know, I like these. I like the scratch, and I like you, Rita. Let me take these off your hands. Say, twenty-five percent off. I think that's fair for damaged merchandise."

"They're very good shoes, and twenty-five percent... Well, Brooke, honey, I'm just a struggling storeowner, and in these lean times..."

Right then the shop-bell rang, and a well-to-do lady came through the door. With perfect timing, Brooke held the shoe out in front of her, just as the new customer passed. "It's a very large scratch. Almost a hole. And who wants a pair of shoes that already have a hole."

"There's no hole," Rita insisted, finally starting to look nervous.

Brooke smiled nicely. "Let me ask the lady what she thinks. I bet she thinks there's a hole."

Now genuinely alarmed, Rita grabbed the shoes, and pitched her voice low. "I'll go twenty-five," she said, wising up to the fact that Brooke was no amateur shopper.

Brooke nodded, followed her to the register, noticed the hand-made sale signs and then felt a pang of conscience. Rita wasn't some billionaire shopkeeper rolling in the dough. This was her community, her family, and the Harts were supposed to be very civic-minded. "What you said earlier...if it's a problem, I could do twenty."

Rita gaped for a second, and then started to chuckle, as if surprised that generous thoughtfulness might come from a customer...or maybe it was only the Harts. "You're a cool customer, Brooke Hart, but I like you. For that, I'll go twenty percent and not a percentage point more."

"And the cactus, but I'll pay full price for that," Brooke told her, picking up one of the small plants, being careful not to get stuck. The Captain could use a few more living things around the house, and Brooke thought a cactus was the living thing most likely to survive under his care.

Satisfied with their agreement, Brooke counted out her cash and then took a quick peek at the new pair of shoes in her bag. Practical and still cute. The Captain should never have doubted her.

WHEN BROOKE CAME HOME, the first thing she did was to show off her purchase.

The Captain watched and made primordial *humph* sounds as she twisted her foot one way, then the other. "You could have found something more solid."

"They're leather. The soles are some specially designed long-lasting rubber. And they look great with jeans."

He made another *humph* sound, took another look at her shoes, took a long look at Brooke and then walked away.

This time, it was Brooke who made the primordial *humph* sound. This hands-off, safety-first attitude was getting old. She had forgiven him his earlier missteps, mainly because he was too nice of a man for her to be angry with. The Captain cared. She'd been careful not to be too slutty this time, better to ease him back into her bed. Thinking strategically wasn't something that came naturally to her. Charlene Hart didn't have a strategic bone in her body, and she'd been the sole role model in Brooke's life, so Brooke didn't fault herself for not having developed that quality yet, but she noticed that the Captain was very strategic. He could spend long minutes staring at an engine or part, prodding it gently, turning it over in his hands like a clump of clay. Everything the Captain did involved forethought and planning and patience.

Later that afternoon, she investigated the far side of the house, where a line of tarp-covered piles dotted the ground like tents. Under the first tarp, she discovered a treasure trove of old sinks, basins, faucets and one extralarge claw-foot tub. It was a beauty, with generous sides and an elegantly sloped back that rose higher than the front. Down the side of each leg was a raised design of some sort, and kneeling on the ground, she wiped at the grime, delighted to discover that it was a dainty mix of hearts and lilies entwined.

"You want to put something in that? It's a little heavy to haul things in, but I could put some wheels on it..." the Captain said, coming to stand beside her.

"It's perfect," she announced, picturing how it would look, gleaming white, overflowing with bubbles. Completely impractical and yet...

"Not without wheels. How do you move it?"

"It's not a container, it's a bathtub." For once, amid all the mechanical doodads and gizmos, little Brooke Hart could educate the Captain.

"Yes, I can see that," he answered, completely deflating her mood.

"You don't move bathtubs. You put them in one place, run water into them, and then bathe."

It was rather fascinating to watch the Captain experience a lightbulb moment. His forehead furrowed as the wheels turned, and then when everything clicked into place, his head tilted slightly to the left, and then he would nod once, mainly to himself, as if the universe was aligned again. "Do you want a bathtub?" he asked, and Brooke giggled.

"It was a serious question," he added, looking a little hurt.

"It won't fit in my car," Brooke explained, wondering why he hadn't grasped the impracticality of the situation.

"What about here? My place."

Her heart missed a beat.

"Here?" she probed carefully, aware of the many subtleties in the one small word, but of course, the Captain wouldn't be aware of such nuances in his question.

"Here. For now. At some point in time, you'll have a place of your own, but for now...here."

And then she realized he was serious and she was surprised at how much the idea hurt. Not the owning a bathtub part, but the idea of leaving one behind. Brooke had a lot of experience in leaving things behind. Usually it didn't hurt, but that was probably because she'd never had anything worth keeping before.

Brooke rose to her feet, and wiped her palms on her jeans. "That's too much trouble. And it wouldn't fit in the bathroom. Besides, I love showers. Much more efficient, and quick. Who knows when the hot water's going to go. No, showers are a lot smarter."

"Haven't had a lot of bathtubs, have you?"

"Some," she admitted. Fourteen was the exact number, not that anyone was counting.

"I could..." he started.

She held up her hand before he did something that made it even harder for her to leave. "No."

His mouth tightened, but he didn't argue.

"I'll use it to put the do-me-hootchers in," she rambled on. "I was looking for something extra-large."

"Do-me-hootchers?"

"Those," she explained, picking up a small, elongated...do-me-hootcher.

The Captain met her eyes, but Brooke was a little smarter now and kept her own eyes carefully blank. "Those are Geiger counters from the second world war."

"Geiger counters," she repeated, storing it away in her head. "Then the tub will fit the bill nicely."

"I'll put the wheels on it tomorrow," he promised.

THE NEXT MORNING, the bathtub disappeared and she told herself it didn't matter. Someday when she had a fine bathroom, she would buy a heart-stopping tub. Something big, modern, with jets because who needed old fashioned frills? Completely impractical, and until then, showers were great. They were hearty and invigorating and...

Once more she glanced toward the empty spot and sighed. It had been pretty, with the curly-cue legs and the back designed to ease well-worn muscles. *Oh, well. Things to do, abandoned gadgets to sort.*

To keep herself busy, she took the tiny cactus and placed it on the window-sill in the kitchen, right next to some sort of meter. What the meter measured, she didn't know, but it set off her cactus nicely. After cleaning the dust from her hands, she went back outside, wondering how long it would take the Captain to notice the plant.

Not like she was noticing him. Earlier he had abandoned his work shirt for a cooler tank top, and sweat poured lovingly down his back. Every time he lifted a heavy tool, the sturdy muscles in his arms bunched. He had a steady, powerful rhythm, pulverizing the hapless metal into a quivering mass of pliable goo. Her mouth felt dry and her thighs began to quiver, and she put a hand on the porch railing for support.

Yes, there were lots of things to do, the Captain among them, but she was learning to be patient, as well.

IT TOOK TWO DAYS FOR Brooke to make the perfect batch of brownies. The first night, the Captain had watched her silently. The next night, he abandoned his latest project and offered to help.

"You know how to make brownies?" she asked, curious because up to this point, the Captain had demonstrated no culinary abilities at all.

"I can follow instructions," he said, coming to stand next to her, peering over her shoulder into the bowl.

"So can I," she told him, in case he thought she needed assistance.

"I should learn," he admitted, and grudgingly, too. It made her happy to know this wasn't about lack of faith in her abilities, but a lack of faith in his own.

"How to make brownies? They're very easy," Brooke told him, efficiently cracking two eggs in the bowl, dropping in one small shell in the process. Quickly she fished it out with her finger. "You're supposed to use a spoon, but sometimes I cheat—to make sure it tastes okay."

Brooke licked at her finger, noticed the Captain watching and made a long production of taste-testing, curious to see exactly how much self-control the Captain acutally had.

His gray eyes darkened to black, and she could feel his growing erection brushing against her thigh. Her pulse quickened and, deciding on bold action, she offered up her chocolate-covered finger.

The Captain took a cautious step back. "I should learn to do more in the kitchen."

Patience and strategy, she reminded herself.

"Did Sonya do all the cooking?" Brooke asked, not sure he would answer, but tonight, to her surprise, he did.

"I was away most of the time."

"What about your mother?"

"Mom always cooked. Great stuff—meat loaf, crab cakes. She made a Thanksgiving turkey that would knock your socks off."

"You miss her?"

A shadow of loneliness crossed her face, and she felt the ache cut through her heart. "Yeah."

"What about the rest of your family?"

At her question the loneliness was gone, as if it never existed. "I thought you wanted to make brownies."

"Families are important," she told him, because loneliness could be hidden, but it never disappeared. This she knew well.

The Captain laughed. "Says the woman who's dodging her brother until she reaches some arbitrary number in her bank account."

"The brownies are for Austen. I'm going to see him tomorrow."

"Good," he said, and his hand reached out, touched her mouth. Brooke forgot to breathe.

Gently he brushed at her mouth, her cheek, and the ache in his eyes made her dizzy. "Chocolate."

"Of...course," she said, stumbling over the simple words.

His touch disappeared, her breathing resumed and the intimate moment was gone, as if it never existed. Brooke poured in the last of the flour, still warm from his touch, because tenderness could be hidden but it never disappeared, either. The Captain possessed more tenderness than he knew.

Carefully she added the salt and baking powder, measuring each amount precisely. The Captain's close presence made precision difficult, but she thought she managed beautifully.

"You're going to see him, talk to him, show him what a great person you are? Or are you going to make something else up?"

The confident way he said it made her want to believe him. Made her want to think that Austen would welcome her as a sister. But the few times she'd seen her brother, welcoming wasn't even close.

She beat at the better until her hand began to hurt. Without a word, the Captain took over. "I'm bringing brownies," she told him, stilling his hand when the mixture was glossy and rich.

"You don't need the brownies, Brooke. He'll like you. I swear."

She saw the faith in his one good eye and it made her want to believe, but a lifetime of disappointment was hard to shake. Once the brownies were in the oven, she smiled at him and dusted the flour from her hands. "A little insurance never hurt."

THERE WAS SOMETHING very satisfying about tearing into a wall with a sledge hammer. The plaster kicked up a god-awful amount of dust, but Austen coughed happily, watching the destruction of his old home. He'd never felt right about putting a new house over the old one, however, this piece of the land would make a kick-ass garage where he could work on the Mustang. Or maybe he could find a sweet GT-40 for Gillian. He pulled back the hammer, ready to do some more damage when he saw the twin beams cutting through the dark.

There were headlights flickering up the drive. Not Gilian's high-powered halogens. These were different. Older.

Impala older.

Instantly, he knew. It was Brooke. His sister.

Austen tossed down the hammer, wiped the dust from his face and conjured up a smile that was worthy of greeting long-lost relatives. Even the ones that made your stomach tighten in knots.

As she picked her way through the debris, Austen shook his head apologetically. "I wasn't going to stay out her very long. Gillian's expecting me at the house for dinner, and I try to keep her happy."

"I could help you," she offered, looking so eager that he almost agreed.

"Nah. I've got it covered," he said. She seemed disappointed, and he reminded himself to be nicer to her.

"I can't stay very long anyway. I just wanted to give you

these," she said, holding out a plate of brownies. Brownies. His sister had made him brownies.

"Wow. That's really nice and all. Are they homemade?"

"They are."

Austen stared at the paper plate, and the plastic-wrap covering, and realized what was wrong with this picture. "Brownies. How'd you make brownies at the Inn?" As soon as he saw the horror in her eyes, he wanted to kick himself for saying the wrong thing. Of course they weren't homemade, but she'd gone out of her way to make them look homemade and now he'd gone and embarrassed her.

However, to her credit, she recovered quickly. "I borrowed the kitchen."

"You went to a lot of trouble for me. Thank you."

"You're my brother. I don't mind."

There was a long silence, and Austen winced, trying to think up casual conversation. Making casual conversation was a necessary requirement in the field of politics, but somehow, with Brooke, his mind always went blank. Desperate, he blurted out the first thing that popped into his head. "How are you getting along in town? People treating you okay?"

"Everyone has been very nice," she told him, sounding as if she meant it.

"Wasn't expecting that, but miracles happen all the time."

The silence dragged on, and he could see some of the light fading from her eyes. "I should go," she said, and began to walk away. Like a jerk, he nearly let her.

"Brooke!"

"Yeah?"

"Have you talked to Hadley?"

"No. He hasn't called. I left a message with Mr. Cervantes and put a couple of notes in the door, but nothing yet."

"I don't know the number at Hadley's father's place, but Gillian could get it. I could call."

"There's no rush," she said. "I've liked staying here and wandering aorund the town. Seeing where you all lived. What was it like living here?"

At first, he thought about lying. Making up some story that would fit her fairy-tale theory, but this time, when he looked at her, he noticed soething different. A sturdiness and a strength. And she was his sister, after all.

"We didn't have a good time of it. Frank was mean. See that tree?" Austen pointed to the oak in the front yard. "Those holes? Frank like to take his Winchester and shoot at the tree. Stupidest thing you ever saw, but that was our father, Frank Hart. Drunk and stupid. Sometimes I would make up conversations with Mom. Have these long talks wither her in my head."

It was hard to keep the bitterness out of his voice, and unfortunately, Brooke had noticed.

"I should go," she said, and he watched her leave, holding the plate of brownies like a fool.

"Listen, these are great," he called after her. "We'll do dinner again, real soon."

WHEN BROOKE RETURNED HOME, the Captain was waiting on the porch. He'd hauled up a red leather bench seat and was sitting on it, like a swing.

"How'd it go?" he asked, and she sat down beside him, running a hand over the glossy material. It was one more overlooked item that the Captain had restored, making it shiny and useful again.

"He liked the brownies."

"You okay?"

"Yeah." She traced the lines of the seat, not really wanting to talk about Austen. If she had made great progess, if she had restored their relationship to something shiny and useful, maybe she would have felt better. "I like this. What's it from?"

"Ninteen sixty-seven Cadillac DeVille."

She didn't say much, and the Captain must have known something was wrong. He reached out and took her hand and stayed with her, watching the night.

It was so peaceful here. The dark sky stretched beyond forever, but she didn't feel alone. The Captain was the quietest man she'd ever met, the hard security of his hand invited her to confide. "It's not a quick process, is it? Getting someone to like you."

"I don't think you'll have too many problems. You're easy to like."

"Thank you. You are, too."

"You're not very picky. You like everybody."

"Almost everybody," she corrected. "But I still don't have a lot of friends."

"I don't, either. I've learned not to lose sleep over it."

Off in the distance, she could see the lights of town, a cheery beacon in the night, but she wouldn't have traded anything for this.

"What happened with Max?"

"What do you mean?"

"The status is still in the box, and you don't forget. So I'm assuming there's a reason you haven't mailed it."

Next to her, she could feel the tension run through him and she realized her mistake. "I didn't mean to pry. I'm sorry. You've been very good about not prying."

He didn't say anything for a long time, but then he kicked his boots out in front of him and leaned his head against the seat's back. A very relaxed pose, certainly, but the tension still hummed through him like a live wire.

"IED in Afghanistan. The medics got him halfway to Landstuhl before he died. It was last year. Christmas."

Oh. She wanted to comfort him, but she knew she was many months too late. Instead she squeezed his hand, wishing she could absorb all the tension inside him. All the tears that he would ever shed. "I'm sorry."

"Everybody dies."

He said it so easily, as if he had no feelings, as if he were as lifeless as the machines that he worked on. "Yes, and if you care, it always hurts," Brooke said softly.

He turned and stared at her, eyes as dark and mysterious as the night. "Did you hurt when your mother died?"

"Yes. I still loved her, even with the way she was. She was my mother. But I was more afraid than anything. She was all I had."

With his free hand, he reached out and stroked her hair, one touch, before his hand fell away. "I wish I'd been there."

"I wish I'd been here when Max died."

"Me, too."

There were so close, so perfectly aligned, and Brooke felt the stutter in her heart. "Captain?"

Abruptly, he stood. "I'm going inside. You should get some sleep."

After he left her, she stayed a few moments, watching the orange moon burn high on the horizon. But soon, the air blew cooler, the dark felt gloomier and the magic of the night had gone.

THE NEXT WEEK PASSED slowly, with the Captain maintaining a determinedly distant presence.

Brooke had little experience with seduction. The few times in her past that she'd actually desired sex with a man, they had been more than willing, and after she'd taken her pleasure, she had sent them on their way. No muss, no fuss. All was simple and straightforward, with little effort at all, but not with the Captain. No, he had ignored her subtle invitations and long come-hither glances. By the time Wednesday had rolled around, Brooke decided to abandon attempts at nuance. Previously, the obvious had worked successfully, so tonight the obvious seemed the way to go again.

After dinner was over, when the Captain had assumed his customary place, turning the kitchen table into a work table,

Brooke seized the opportunity to unbutton her shirt. Three buttons were free before he noticed.

His gaze was locked on her hands, the tic was back in his jaw, and the screwdriver was digging into the table's surface, but she didn't think he realized all that. "What are you doing?" he asked. A silly question.

"I'm getting comfortable. You're so busy I didn't think you would mind." Her fingers parted the shirt, pulled it off her shoulders, leaving her best sheer bra underneath. "Does this bother you?" she asked, an innocent smile on her face.

"Brooke."

She liked the way he said her name, low and graveled. The rough sound rolled down her spine and she shivered, not cold at all. Still smiling, she unbuttoned the fly on her jeans. "Is there a problem?"

"Yes."

Deciding there was no point in revisiting the argument, she pulled at the zip, easing the denim over her hips, enjoying the raw pain on his face. There was so little he ever exposed, hiding behind his patch and his scar.

Tonight, the gloves came off.

As would her bra.

Defiantly she unhooked the front clasp. "Ignore me. No problem." The clasp came loose. The Captain swallowed.

After easing the bra from her shoulders, Brooke dangled it over the couch.

The Captain didn't move.

If she had known he was going to be this difficult, she would have dressed in more layers. However, Brooke was accustomed to making do with the resources at hand, and she slid her thumbs in the wispy material of her panties, easing them down her legs.

The Captain still didn't move.

Undeterred, she sat on the couch, kicked her feet out on the coffee table in front of her, and turned the television on. Two could play the ignorant game.

It actually felt rather liberating, sitting in the nude, feeling his tortured gaze on her, and doing nothing at all. She leaned back, letting the warm night air drift over her, electric current dancing on her skin, her nipples peaked with the thrill.

The Captain stood and she held her breath, waiting. Slowly he approached, casting a glowering shadow over the couch, and she could feel every inch where he stared. She raised her head, met his eyes and felt her heart twist at the pain in his uninjured eye.

"Why are you doing this?"

Didn't he get it? "You are the best man I've ever known."

Patiently she waited for his response, because he would be the one. This time, he couldn't hide.

"That's not a good reason for sex."

Well, no, it spoke to things a lot more powerful than sex, but okay, if that's the way they were going to play it, then she was more than prepared to list all the good reasons for sex. "I watch you during the day, and I want to pull off your shirt and run my hands over your shoulders, feeling them tense where I touch. You have such strong, capable shoulders. Sometimes in my mind, I lay my head there, and I feel revived. I remember your mouth on my breasts, hard and hungry, and my nipples ache to be tasted again. And then I remember how you felt between my legs, filling me, loving me. I get so wet and lonely and I hurt. I don't want to hurt anymore. When I'm with you, when you hold me… I'm home."

There it was, the last of her secrets, and she had nothing else to give. She longed to look away, but she didn't. No, there wouldn't be two cowards in the room. His fingers gripped the edge of the couch, inching closer to her, but not close enough. "This isn't your home. I can never be what you want."

His words were designed to hurt her, she knew that, but it was *his* knuckles that were white against the brown cushions, not hers. Desire strained on his face, not hers. Quietly she rose, coming to stand in front of him, so close, but not close enough.

"Stop fighting me, Captain. Stop fighting this." She kept her voice low and gentle. "Was it so bad with me?"

"No."

"Do you remember? Do you lay awake, feeling my mouth on you, my skin under your hands?"

The Captain nodded once, but made no move to touch her.

"Kiss me," she urged, praying for him to move.

He stared at her lips. "I love your mouth. So soft, so generous, so open."

Her lips parted at the pretty words, but in the end, they were only words. "Take it. Take me."

"I won't stop. I can't." His voice was harsh, not nearly so pretty this time.

"I know," she said, moving a whisper closer. All he had to do was reach out...

His fingers lifted to her hair, stroked the long length, traveling down her shoulder, resting possessively on the rise of her breast. One rough thumb rolled her nipple almost absently. Each stolen touch brought an answering pull between her legs, but this time Brooke stayed still, watching the heat in his eyes, the tightness to his mouth. "They're perfect. Like something in a dream."

The easy glide of his movements were hypnotizing, seductive, and she sighed as he explored her, memorized her. Gently he traced the curve of her hip, his hands calloused, but, oh, so careful. Those same hard hands moved behind her, cupping her cheeks, sliding lower, slipping lower.

Brooke's eyes flickered close, heavy with pleasure when he parted her thighs. Such marvelously efficient hands. A Captain's hands.

His fingers stroked her back and forth, and she could hear the rasp of his breathing, feel her body swell with desire. "So soft, so generous, so wet."

It was like something in a dream. A warm, liquid dream. When his fingers slipped inside her, Brooke's knees dipped, but the Captain was quick, and strong arms lifted her, laying her on the couch. Breathlessly she waited for him to cover her, but he knelt beside her, his hand returning between her thighs, and then the dream was back.

The steady touch of his fingers was like a melody, pleasure lapping over her. So easy, so quiet, so soft. Brooke gave herself over to him, her body rising and falling in time with his hand.

Then the melody disappeared and a moan of protest escaped from her mouth, but then she felt his mouth on her aching flesh. The quiet waves of pleasure disappeared, turning dark, dangerous.

His mouth was not nearly as safe as his hand, sucking on her flesh, pulling hard and insistent, and the exquisite pressure was too much. Her hands fisted into the cushion, pulling the material, helplessly fighting against it. She wanted the dream, the safe, gentle dream.

"Do you want me to stop?" he asked, and she knew what he was doing. Testing her, thinking that she would walk away. Brooke opened her heavy eyes, and glared. "No."

His smile was hard, and once again he lowered his head. At first, she was prepared for the pressure, her body riding the waves, and she smiled to herself, but then his mouth found her sensitive nub, the friction of his tongue making her mutter, then swear, then finally scream. Colors flooded her mind, a frenzied kaleidoscope spinning faster and faster until she felt the world tremble around her.

The pressure disappeared, and her heart started to beat again. "Do you want me to stop?" he asked, his voice hard, his breathing ragged.

Her body felt limp, her eyes were too heavy to open, but the spirit would not be denied. *Did he really believe she was that weak?* Brooke waved a "continue" hand.

Then his finger pushed inside her, opening her, killing her, and then his hungry mouth moved again until it was more than she could take. She could feel the orgasm growing, mounting, before the orgasm crashed over her, ripping her in pieces. Her mouth opened to scream, to breathe, to damn the man to hell, but he was too quick, his mouth covering hers, his body blanketing hers. This time his tongue swept into her mouth, so gentle, so easy, but she wasn't fooled. Not this time.

Brooke tore at his shirt, declared war on his jeans until at last she could touch him, torture him as he had done her. Her fingers stroked his shaft, and she watched the pleasure flare in his eyes.

"I like the feel of you in my hands," she whispered to him.

"It's just a dick," he told her, inhaling sharply when she rolled the condom over his velvet skin.

"Not just," she answered, eyeing the part in question with respectful consideration.

When she looked up again, he was watching her, waiting, and in answer, she tilted her hips, feeling the head of his shaft against her.

"Take me, Captain. Please."

8

IT WAS THE ANSWER Jason needed, and he pushed inside her, feeling the give, feeling her stretch to accommodate him. Dark desirous eyes widened, locked on his face, her mouth open and wet. Quickly he covered her open mouth, blocked out her gaze, inching in farther, letting her slick heat block out everything but this.

Her body shifted to accommodate him, and with one powerful shove on his ass, Brooke embedded his thankless cock inside her.

His breathing stopped. His body frozen until he felt the soft stroke of her tongue in his mouth, across his lips. Then she opened drowsy eyes, the open-hearted gaze inspecting his face, his patch, his scar. At long last, she whispered, "Take me, Captain."

God help him, he did. Over and over he used her, trying to remember her pleasure, too, but she made him forget. So many things she made him forget.

Her generous mouth kissed his lips, the roughened skin of his scar and the marked blade of his shoulder. Her selfless fingers were never still, gliding over him like he was some damned sculpture. Brooke Hart was a foolish, foolish woman giving herself to him on the couch, on the floor. Each time his gut would cramp up in guilt, she would flutter her lashes, expecting him to fall for her cheap tricks again—as if he could be easily conned. And then she would press her perfect breasts against him, not shy at all, until his simple-minded hands reached for her, and then no surprise there—his cock was rooting between her legs, wanting her once more.

By the time the sun was yawning outside, they'd made it to the bed, and she rose over him, flaunting that Hollywood body, murmuring with her pillow-top mouth, staring at him with adoring eyes that could make a man change his mind.

No, that Brooke Hart was trouble, he thought, letting her seduce him all over again.

THE PHONE RANG at precisely 9:17 a.m. Brooke was still in bed, rolled up in blankets and pillows, but Jason hadn't slept at all. He took the call outside the bedroom, keeping his voice low.

"Kincaid."

"I'm looking for Brooke Hart. She left this number. This is Hiram Hadley from the law offices of Harris and Howell."

The lawyer. Thoughtless jerk calling so early, he thought, glancing toward the bedroom. At the moment, Brooke was suffering from a serious lack of sleep, all due to Jason's conscienceless cock, and it didn't seem right to wake her. "She's not available now, but I know she's expecting your call. Could I get your number and I'll have her get back to you?"

Hadley sighed into the phone and if Jason had been a more accommodating man, he would have taken the hint and rolled Brooke out of bed. Not in this lifetime. "I'm still in North Dakota," Hadley said, "and don't have access to my papers, but I'm returning to Tin Cup next Wednesday and I can set up a meeting with her then. Do you know if she has a birth certificate?"

The suspicious tone wasn't winning the lawyer any friends, not that Jason had ever been fond of lawyers. Birth certificate? "I don't have a clue. Why don't you look it up?"

"There's no record of a Brooke Hart being born in Texas," the man explained patiently.

Jason didn't care. "I don't think she was born here. I bet you're going to have to check all the other states."

The lawyer sighed again, even louder. The old geezer was probably unhappy with the idea of extra work. Yeah, sometimes life sucked that way. "Do you know where Miss Hart was born?" he asked.

"Not a clue," Jason answered cheerfully.

"You'll tell her I'll be in on Wednesday? And if she could provide her birth cert—"

Jason hung up.

HE HAD FOUR OPPORTUNITIES to tell her, five if he counted lunch, but oddly enough, the words never came. Jason kept telling himself that since Hadley wasn't going to be around until the following week, what did it matter? It's not like Brooke could call him, instantly receive one-third of the Hart property—which wasn't worth squat—and then her life would be magically transformed.

Except for the mineral rights...

No, that was the kicker, the fly in the ointment, the shrapnel in the eye, because Jason Kincaid also knew there was an 86.3 percent probability of oil underneath the Hart land, mainly because there was a 100 percent probability of oil under his land. He'd known since they had finished running the tests last year. The suit that had delivered the results had eyed the acreage to the west—Hart land—and then explained in full, glorious detail how the formations below the surface worked.

Of course, Jason probably should have told his ex-wife, although legally Sonya didn't have any claim to it. At the time she'd been happily married to Tom, and money muddled people's vision. It dressed things up, made the previously unsightly sightly. Attractive. Appealing.

All smoke and mirrors, designed to cover the truth.

Usually a big fan of the truth, Jason was also a firm believer in the status quo, which was the probable reason that he didn't say a word to Brooke. To give himself credit, he didn't cop a feel when she asked him what a planer was. In fact, he was purposefully cool because last night had been a world-class lapse in judgment, especially since she'd be leaving him right after she talked to the lawyer. His conscience didn't ease up, especially watching her try to haul a lead water pump across the yard. Jason shook his head, picked up the thing himself, and lined it up with eight other pumps that he would most likely never use.

"Thank you, but I could have done it myself."

Then she blinked up at him, big, trusting eyes, and it was the perfect time to tell her about Hadley's call, but she was wearing a blue diode in her hair, and the freckles were starting to pop on her skin, and Jason's brain shut down. Before he knew it, the perfect time was gone.

AFTER EXTENDED HOURS of sexual congress, Brooke expected a little more intimacy from the Captain today. A familiar touch or an occasional kiss, anything to signify a change, but no. Certainly there were times during the day when she caught him watching her with an overheated gaze, but when their glances would lock, his always shifted away.

A woman like Gillian would know how to approach the situation, but Brooke wasn't ready to divulge her feelings about the Captain to Gillian because then Brooke would have to explain why she was working for the Captain and she expected that a woman as sophisticated as Gillian wouldn't appreciate the personal satisfaction in heavy manual labor. Second, Brooke suspected that Gillian wouldn't approve of having sex with the man who was providing both a roof and paycheck. Last, and most important, Brooke knew that although the Captain had many feelings for her, he never said anything that implied a romantic relationship. Other than the long, deep kisses, or the way he made her ache between her legs, all of which were not things that Brooke felt comfortable divulging to anyone, much less her future sister-in-law who was mostly a stranger and engaged to Brooke's brother, who was even more of a stranger. No, the situation needed patience and strategy, and Brooke, who had previously been unable to strategize her way out of a paper bag, was starting to learn.

That afternoon, she sorted rubber gaskets and devised a plan to move their relationship to a higher level. The Captain had his truck parked near the black metal gate, unloading the widow Kenley's broken washing machine. Mouth dry, she admired his broad build, the firm thighs. However, this was about moving their relationship beyond the sex.

After she cleared the fog from her eyes, she went over and planted herself at the foot of the truck. "I need your advice," she began, trying to sound earnest and composed and not remotely aroused. "Rita likes me," she continued. "The Hinkles have forgiven me since I helped Henry haul a case of milk to the refrigerator in the back. I'm making good progress at creating a bond with these people."

"Then there's no problem. You don't need my advice."

"Sure I do. Gillian invited me to the chili cook-off on Friday. She said I should go and make some new friends. I think it's a good idea."

The Captain climbed down from the back of his truck and dusted his palms on his jeans. "I don't know any chili recipes."

Usually the Captain was much more cooperative when she came to him for help. Usually he was more than ready to offer advice, even when she didn't want to hear it, but today he'd been unusually distant. Acknowledging that this was going to be more difficult than she assumed, she approached the situation from a different angle. "It's Austen."

This time he frowned. "Is he giving you problems?"

Brooke shrugged helplessly. "He's not acting brotherly. It's like he's scared of me. Gillian doesn't seem scared of me. I don't understand why Austen is."

Now that he knew neither chili nor social niceties were involved, the Captain pulled off his cap, pushed his fingers through his hair, messing it up even more. Brooke longed to touch the thick strands, fix it for him, but relationship novice or not, she knew this wasn't the time.

"Why should he be scared of you? You don't look that tough. He'd take you down in one."

"Be serious," she scoffed, sliding into an easy camaraderie, a casual banter.

"I was," he said, slapping the cap on his head. Before he could go back to work, she jumped up on the lowered tailgate and sat. At first, he looked ready to cut her off again. Brooke fixed him with her earnest face, which wasn't threatening at all.

"Do you have any brothers or sisters?" she asked.

His mouth quirked at the corners, almost a smile. "There's seven of us."

Seven? Good heavens. "Where are they?"

"George is a chemist in Rockville. David is in California, somewhere outside L.A. Sara teaches kindergarten in Baltimore. John's a bartender in Miami. Robert's still in the army and, to be honest, I don't know where the hell Charlie is living now. He does consulting for some company with a lot of initials and I lost track."

"What about your father?"

"My dad lives with Sara. He likes to help out, so he does some of her repairs, and helps her with her kids."

"Do you see him often?"

"No."

"Why?"

The Captain shrugged, as if this was normal.

"Do you not get along?"

"We get along great. We talk almost every week. It's just…"

"What?"

He shrugged again. "I don't know."

"What about your brothers?"

"I see them some. Four years ago I flew up to Maryland for the holidays."

"Impressive," she murmured.

"We get along great," he repeated, more defensively this time.

"Excellent. Then you must know how brothers are supposed to act."

The Captain glanced at the washing machine, then back at Brooke. Resigned to the conversation, he climbed up on the tailgate and sat next to her, their thighs almost touching, but not quite. Definite progress. "There's not a manual."

Brooke sighed because it wasn't that she expected the Captain to be a fount of family how-to knowledge, but still... He was very smart.

"Why is he scared of me?" she asked, looking away. She didn't want him to think that people might not like her. However, he must have heard the unhappiness in her voice, because he took her hand as if he liked her. For the Captain, hand-holding was way beyond easy camaraderie. It was right up there with poetry writing and mix-tapes.

"I don't think he's scared."

"What do you think it is?" she asked, meeting his eyes, not so worried about hiding her uncertainty. This was all unchartered territory for Brooke. Family. A respectful relationship with a man. Home. She'd spent her whole life dreaming of something like this, and now it was within her grasp, unless she fumbled it all away. Charlene Hart was a world-class fumbler.

Seeing the frown on her face, the Captain squeezed her hand. "I don't know what his problem is. I barely know the guy and it's not like I've seen the two of you together."

"Come to the cook-off," she pressed. "Tell me what I'm doing wrong."

"I'm not going to a chili cook-off," he muttered, and while he didn't look thrilled at the idea, he didn't look stubborn, either. Brooke allowed herself a tiny squeeze on his hand, as well.

"Please? I don't know how to do this, and I don't want to mess it up." Yes, she was talking about more than her brother, and she suspected he knew. Once again, he didn't look thrilled at the idea, but he didn't look stubborn, either.

"I'll go," he agreed.

Progress. Definitely.

THE TIN CUP CHILI-PALOOZA was scheduled for the Friday of homecoming weekend. The week before, the town hung a banner across Main Street that read, Go Lions, Maul Midland, as if the Tin Cup high school football team was not going to get eaten alive by the state's powerhouse.

However, Brooke seemed excited, and the night of the hell-a-palooza she changed outfits four times, all the more telling since Jason knew she only had three to begin with. Not wanting to disappoint her, Jason told her that the red sundress was the best. He neglected to mention that her legs were starting to get a mouth-watering tan, that the modified-transistors hanging from her ears looked cute next to the slender curve of her neck, and then there was the way she wasn't wearing a bra.

Three weeks ago, when Brooke had first come to town, the idea of Brooke not wearing a bra was sexy, but not so irresistible that he wanted to jump her. Jason told himself that the fact that he *had* jumped her was due to his own long months of monk-like celibacy, which had killed whatever restraint he normally possessed. Tonight, his restraint was threatening to bust his jeans, since now that she had put on a little weight, the hollows in her cheeks were gone, and apparently when Brooke gained weight, it went to her breasts.

He closed his good eye—didn't work. When he opened it again, they were still going, and Brooke was bouncy, cheery, nipples pebbling against the flimsy material.

During the daylight hours he worked very hard to keep from touching her, but right now, all he wanted to do was push the dress aside, put his mouth to her, pull up her skirt, while the long, tan legs wrapped around...

"What do you think?" she asked, twirling in front of him, the skirt floating dangerously high.

Jason reached for the tools on his kitchen table, found a screwdriver, and jammed the metal head into his palm. *Better.* "It's okay."

At his half-hearted comment, Brooke stopped her twirling abruptly. "Okay? That's all?"

Realizing that, yes, he'd disappointed her again, Jason tried to make amends, while not sounding like a man with a raging hard-on that didn't give a damn about a dress. "Pretty," he told her.

Instantly her smile bloomed, and once again she twirled like a kid, her red high-heels clicking on the old floors. "Thank you," she said, and planted a kiss on his cheek.

The cheek kisses were becoming standard. He wasn't sure whether they were supposed to be sexual or paternal. In his mind, little girls kissed their grandparents on the cheek, but when Brooke kissed him, her lips stayed on his skin one second longer than seemed proper, her mouth a little more slack than what Jason thought paternal entailed. It was a lot easier to blame her kissing skills for the steel in his cock, rather than this own dirty mind, but no matter how hard he tried to erase the image, his mind always came back to one naked Brooke Hart.

Her chest brushed against him.

"You look pretty, too," she said, eyes lingering on his face.

Jason laughed, glad to not think about one naked Brooke Hart. "I'm not pretty."

Her fingers brushed at his unruly hair, traced the line of his freshly shaven, thankfully un-nicked jaw. "You are to me," she said, her voice soft and floaty, and he didn't want to justify her foolishness with a smile. It would only encourage the foolishness, but he smiled anyway.

"We'll take two cars tonight. You're trying to be respectable and people will talk if I drive you home."

"You think they might guess that we're doing the nasty?"

she teased, and he didn't want to be teased. Not while he kept picturing her skirt around her waist.

"Can we not talk about this?" he said, putting his screwdriver away, forcing his good eye off her legs.

"I'd like to talk about it," she said, and his good eye wandered back to her legs, up over her cherry nipples.

"Where are your car keys?" he asked, his voice polite and sensible.

"I hid them." She tilted her head, long hair falling around her shoulders. "Want to know where?"

"No."

"Then we'll have to take your truck. I can sit close if you'd like and you can slip your hand up my skirt."

Jason swallowed, feeling his jeans start to cut off his blood flow, only a good thing. He didn't like this flirty, butterfly Brooke. He didn't like to think about slipping his hand up her skirt. "Have you been drinking?"

"Nope. Not a lick." Her mouth curved up, and tonight it was extra red, extra glossy, extra wet. *Hell.* Jason took a step back.

"You can't do this at the cook-off. If you want Austen to like you, you can't be picking up strange men and having sex with them."

"You're not a strange man. You're very normal." She took a step forward, her hand sliding over his fly. Jason bit through his tongue. "Wonderfully normal."

Regrettably, he removed her hand. "Brooke."

She moved an inch closer. "Captain."

Sweat pooled at the back of his neck. "We need to leave."

"Why?" she asked, so close that he could feel the burn of her breasts.

"You don't want to be late," he explained, very logical, very rational, all while some odd perfume was seducing his nose.

"Better to be late than early." Not content with nose-seduction, she unbuttoned the top button on his shirt, pressing a possessive kiss to his chest. When she raised her head, there was a bright red lipstick mark on his chest. Definitely not a grand-father kiss.

His hands reached out to grasp her hips and move her away, but accidentally landed underneath her skirt, discovering nothing but hot skin and a tiny thong.

"Captain," she whispered, her voice shocked and shameless, exactly like in every porn movie ever made. "What are you doing?"

"Looking for your car keys."

She raised a brow and wiggled beneath his clumsy hands. "Very clever. Do you think they'll guess?"

Of course they would guess. They would see the lust in his eyes, they would see the way his fingers were always reaching in her direction. They would see the world's most obvious hard-on in his jeans. "You're going to hate yourself if you ruin your chances with Austen." Even while he was warning her, his thumb was stroking the slit between her legs, feeling the swollen skin already damp with desire.

She closed her eyes, and he heard a pleased hum in her throat. When she opened them again, the longing there shocked him. "I like seeing you like this, crisp white shirt, no ballcap to hide your hair. You have great hair, like old copper, but soft, touchable." Her fingers tangled there. "You should get dressed up more often."

The wistful comment only cemented his belief that Brooke, much like every other woman, wanted a traditional man with a traditional job in a traditional house, but his cementlike beliefs didn't stop his hands from staying between her legs, finding her slick, swollen and traditionally aroused.

When his finger slid inside her, she gasped, small crooked teeth clutching her lower lip. He knew just how that lower lip felt. "We're going to be late," he warned, feeling his restraint slip away. "You might mess up your dress. And think of all the time you spent getting it just right."

"Save the dress," she ordered with a laugh.

Not giving her a chance to change her mind, Jason fisted the material in his hand, raised the dress higher, until he could see the bare legs, the strapping red heels, and the tiny red scrap of silk.

No, there wasn't a woman alive who was hotter, livelier, more giving than Brooke Hart, and although he knew her infatuation wasn't going to last, he still wanted this. Part of him knew he had to be careful with her dress and he turned her around, bent her over the back of the couch, her dark hair falling low down the slender curve of her back. His hungry gaze traced over the ripe curves of her ass, and she was completely relaxed, completely trusting that he wouldn't hurt her at all. Quickly he unzipped his fly, sheathed himself and then slid between her cheeks, pushing higher, watching her body arch in response.

"I'll be careful," he promised, his voice tough as nails, and he leaned over her, sliding loose one shoulder of her dress, baring her breast. She took his calloused palm, cupped it over the flawless skin, sighing as his thumb rolled back and forth over those cheery nipples that had mocked him earlier.

Slowly, ever so carefully he filled her, listening to her quiet sighs of pleasure, feeling her heart race under his hand.

Dog rolled closer, the red eyes unblinking, unseeing, but still accusing, and Jason swore.

Brooke turned her head, met his eyes and laughed. It was a great laugh, filled with life and joy, and Jason didn't want to laugh back, but he did.

She leaned lower, hips tilted higher, and Jason wanted to swear again because this was not gentle and careful. He closed his good eye, but he could feel the clench of her muscles around him. He could smell her sex, and he moved faster, plunging deeper inside her, fingers pulling at the fragile material of her dress.

Her head lolled, her breathing as hard and as fast as his cock. Her hand squeezed his, pressing hard into the soft tissue of her breast. His ham-fisted fingers tightened and twisted on her skin, her dress, and he drove her even faster, not gentle, not careful. He could hear her words, nonsense, and her hips moved with him, making this too easy, too good. Wanting to feel her come around him, his free hand slid between the front of her thighs, stroking her where they were joined. *Temporary,* he reminded himself. *Only sex.*

"Please," she gasped, and his finger pressed hard against her clit, telling himself it was only sex. Instantly she froze, smooth legs locked against him. Long shudders racked her body, and unable to resist, he pushed aside her hair and pressed one small kiss on her neck. Her skin smelled like perfume, rich and exotic. Perfume mixed with sex. Rich, exotic sex.

The kind of sex that was never enough. Jason thrust one last time, nothing rich, nothing exotic. As he spilled himself into the condom, his fingers clenched, and the fragile material of her dress split into pieces.

There was a second afterward when he didn't want to leave her, when his hand refused to release the soft skin of her breast, but it was that quiet ripping sound that jerked him back to reality. That and the stiffening of her shoulder, the way she didn't meet his eyes.

Quickly he withdrew, pushed the ruined fabric down over the dream of her hips and cleaned himself up.

She turned, examined the torn dress, and then looked at him as if nothing was wrong.

"I'm sorry," he apologized, but she waved it off.

"It doesn't matter. I liked the jeans and shirt better. Let me change, find my keys, and after that we can go. And look, not too late after all."

9

THERE WERE CERTAIN indignities that a man wasn't supposed to endure, namely any TV show with Housewives in the title, bubble baths or competing for an apron that said "Kiss the Cook."

Tables lined the high school parking lot, covered with sterno pans and red-checkered cloths. The air was filled with the scent of peppers because everybody knew that if the late afternoon sun wasn't hot enough to kill you, then the food should. Jason arrived a good fifteen minutes behind Brooke, not that it mattered since he picked her out of the crowd right away.

Even in jeans and a yellow button-down she was gorgeous, dark hair waving around her face, dreamy eyes that saw life better than it was. No, in Brooke's world, jeans were just as nice as a ripped sundress.

For a man who had seen a lot of bad, a ripped sundress shouldn't be eating at his gut. Jason told himself not to dwell on ripped sundresses or past mistakes. No, for tonight, all he would do was buy himself a beer, find an unoccupied lawn chair, and pretend that he could dissolve into the ground.

After he'd found an isolated spot, Austen Hart dragged a chair over and clinked his bottle. Obviously Jason was failing at pretty much everything today.

"Howdy, neighbor! Gotta say you look like you're having a hell of a time. Got some chili in the competition?"

Jason stared with his one good eye. "Do I look like I wear an apron?"

"Didn't think so. Me, neither. I'm just here for the free beer because the bartender likes me." Austen waved at the older woman who was pulling beer from the cooler in the back of her truck, who promptly waved back. "Gillian warned me not to get liquored up, but I'm thinking that several cold beers is the only way to escape judging this event."

"Got that right," Jason agreed, and then realized if he acted too miserable, Brooke's older brother was going to wonder why Jason even bothered to come at all. Because he was a sap. That was why he bothered to come.

He had come to help her. That was why he was here. Once he'd pulled his face into some semblance of cheerfulness, he waded into the conversation that he thought would help Brooke. "How's it going with your relative? Who'd you say was visiting? Your brother, your sister? Ah, hell, I don't remember. Who's the relative?"

"Little sis. That's her over there." Austen pointed his bottle in the direction of the woman who only minutes ago Jason had bent over his couch. Oh, not the time to think about sex. Really, really not the time. Discreetly Jason moved his bottle lower in his lap.

"She looks like a nice kid," he commented innocently.

Austen shook his head sadly. "I think that's the problem."

"Why?"

"She looks so normal, so ordinary, so average. My old man, well, let's just say things were very not normal, and... I don't know."

"What?" prompted Jason, now curious.

"You really care?"

Quickly Jason backtracked because he didn't want to care and most of all, he didn't want Brooke or Austen to know that he did. "It's either listening to you or taste-testing chili and pos-

sibly revisiting the experience for the next five days. I think
your family history sounds fascinating."

"I like you, Jackson," Austen told him, taking another swallow of beer.

"It's Jason."

Austen clicked his tongue. "Oh, yeah. The Captain. Were
you a captain in the service?"

"Staff sergeant."

Brooke's brother threw back his head and laughed, and
Jason noticed Brooke looking curiously in their direction. Jason
looked away.

"And how did that turn into captain?" Austen asked, and it
seemed only fair to give the guy the truth.

"My ex didn't like being married to a staff sergeant, so she
told her aunt and uncle that I was a captain, and it stuck."

"It's better than Sarge."

"True," he acknowledged, and then steered the conversation
away from himself. He was here to help Brooke. Help her establish a relationship with her brother, help her find a better place
to stay. Yeah, he was here to help her, absolutely nothing more.

Jason took a sip of beer, then kicked back in his chair, looking as thoughtful and wise as a one-eyed man could be. "I have
a lot of brothers and sisters, and we were never that close, but
family is important. I mean, I have one brother, Richard, and
he's a total ass, but he's family and I have to stick by him. You
need to stick by your sister, too." It wasn't the truth, but the lie
was for the greater good. Lately, he'd been justifying a lot by
the greater good, which smacked of bullshit, but what the hell.

"I'll stick by her as long as she's in town."

Austen talked as if Brooke Hart was temporary. "Maybe
she'll want to settle here."

"I don't think so. She's a city girl, used to neon lights, high-
dollar shopping and spa treatments involving mud."

Was Austen really that blind? Hell, Jason was at fifty percent vision, and even he knew that was wrong. "She doesn't look like a city girl to me."

"Appearances can be deceiving. Besides, every woman is a high-dollar shopper."

"Including the future missus?"

Austen laughed again. "Gillian just wants people to think that. Although she does pay more for a haircut than I pay for a suit."

"She seems nice, your future missus—for an officer of the law."

"Thanks." Austen studied Jason and the laid-back expression was gone, his eyes a little sharper than before. "You were married to one of the Hinkles?"

"Sonya."

"Oh, yeah. She was a cheerleader when I was a freshman." Jason held up his hand. "Don't tell me any more."

"I was only going to say that she seemed nice."

"She's okay."

"The bloom's off the rose?"

"I was never a rose. I think she wanted a rose." Jason took a long drink of cold beer, realizing that what she'd done didn't bother him so much anymore.

"Sucks."

"Nah. I don't think it would have lasted anyway. We spent more time apart than together."

Austen considered that for a second. "Don't you get lonely out there?"

Jason's first instinct was to lie, but he liked Brooke's brother, and so he settled on the truth. "Maybe."

"You should get out more. Go to Smitty's and get a beer. I'll tell Ernestine that you're a friend and she'll set you up with a free drink. You know, the town's not too bad. Not that there's a lot of women in Tin Cup, but there's some. I could ask Gillian to ask around. She knows everybody."

Jason coughed suddenly. "Not in the market."

"Probably smart. If you change your mind..."

Across the parking lot, Gillian Wanamaker strode onto the stage and Jason noticed the way Austen stopped talking and drinking to stare. Then the mayor shuffled up the stairs and stood next to her, and Austen resumed the conversation again. "You ever watch football?"

"The Redskins. Not a popular choice in Texas."

"Did you grow up in D.C.?"

"Maryland, around Baltimore."

"All right, I'll let it slide, but don't tell anybody, will you? Trust me, people in this town don't ever forget."

On the stage, Gillian raised a longneck high. "Ladies and gentleman, children of all ages, it's finally happened! Mark your calendars because three weeks from now, a mere ten days before my wedding, the mayor will be breaking ground on the new train station, and I want all y'all to come out and watch the future of Tin Cup begin to unfold. As you know, none of this would have been possible without Austen Hart, and I'd like everyone to raise a glass, because the Hart name means something to this town, not just to me. To Austen."

Bottles clinked. There were a few cheers and just as many boos, but Austen laughed good-naturedly and looked at Jason. "Like I said, they got a long memory in this town, and if they know you're a Redskins fan, you're dead."

It wasn't his football loyalties that bothered Jason the most. Although she was pretending not to look, Jason could see Brooke staring at her brother, so much loneliness in her face. "I bet she'd like it if you spoke to her. You know, like a brother. She seems a little lost."

"Brooke?"

Jason tried to sound astoundingly innocent. "Oh, is that her name?"

"Yeah. Brooke Hart."

"Then you should go over and talk." Jason sipped his beer and then nodded wisely. "It's family. It's what you do."

LATER THAT NIGHT, the crickets were out and somewhere a coyote was howling at the moon. An ordinary Texas night, except for the bubbling chatter of the woman sitting next to Jason on the porch.

"I think he's coming around. He didn't act too nervous, and even asked which chili I thought was the best."

"None of the chili was the best. What happened to hot-dog eating, or pie eating or even turkey legs? Chili is just a recipe for disaster."

"You're making a funny, aren't you?"

"Bad chili is nothing to joke about."

"Did you have a good time?"

"Sucked," he told her, but he smiled and she knew he was lying, and he didn't mind.

Repeating her brother's words, she told him, "You should do more. Get out more."

He leaned back on the seat, stretched his legs in front of him. "Why? If there's one place in the world that God meant for man to be alone, it's here." In complete contradiction to that statement, Jason moved his foot to press the tiny button at the base of the swing. Instantly, the canopy netting was full of twinkling lights like a thousand fireflies brightening up the night.

Jason watched, fascinated with the excited glow in her eyes, the bubble of laughter in her throat. For Brooke, everything was new and wonderful. He was going to miss this. He was going to miss her. She pressed her lips to his cheek, to his mouth, and he felt his body stir.

In the scarred remains of his heart, he knew that she wanted more. He knew she wanted the life that she'd never had. He knew that not encouraging her infatuation was the right thing to do, the honorable thing to do, but it didn't stop his hands from tangling in her hair, from him feeding on her mouth, from pulling her into his lap with a thousand fireflies twinkling behind her in the sky.

The right thing wasn't supposed to hurt. The right thing had never hurt before. Hardly anything had ever hurt before. It was a helluva bad time to start getting sensitive now.

And that was what he told himself when she undressed under the lonely Texas moon, when she impaled herself on his cock and he watched her dark eyes as he moved inside her, and no matter the bright watts burning overhead, it was only her that he could see.

WHEN IT CAME TO FAMILY, Gillian Wanamaker followed strict Emily Post protocols, and no matter how fast Austen wanted to run away from his sister, Gillian believed that in the end, Brooke's wistful smile and brand-new boots were bound to win him over. After all, not that he would ever admit it, but Austen Hart was a soft-touch.

And in the interim, when Austen didn't conform to Gillian's ideals of hospitable behavior, Gillian would fill the void with a visit and some snicker-doodles and mini-pies.

Since she was on a mission, and wanted to be casual, she dragged her best friend, Mindy, along.

"Now remember, she's family and doesn't know a soul, so be nice."

Mindy folded her arms over her post-baby stomach. "I'm always nice, Gillian Wanamaker. The post-partum hormones might have taken over my body, but they can't steal the mind."

"I'm rambling. I'm nervous."

"And why in Sam Hill are you nervous? Don't make me call you silly Gilly again. Once in a lifetime is enough."

Gillian slid her sheriff's cruiser into the inn's parking lot and scanned the scene. Then swore.

"What?"

"She's not here," Gillian deduced, then glanced over her shoulder, looking at the cute autumnal baskets stacked neatly in front of her shotgun and Kevlar vest. "Let's go ahead and taken them in. The chocolate is going to die in the heat, and what sort of sister-in-law gives out melted chocolate?"

"Delores will eat those suckers up if you leave them at the front desk with her."

Good point. Gillian considered it for a minute. "Unless I pick up the hotel phone and leave a voice message in Brooke's room saying that the basket is at the front desk, and making sure that Delores can hear."

"She could delete the message."

"She's not that smart."

Mindy met her eyes. "You're right. Hormones again."

Sure enough, inside the Spotlight Inn, Delores was working the desk.

"Girl, look at you," Gillian gushed. "I swear, you get prettier all the time. You've lost weight, haven't you?"

Delores smoothed the blouse over her definitely trimmer stomach. "Weight Watchers. Down nine pounds in four months."

Gillian pumped her fist in the air. "You go, girl."

Right then, Delores noticed the basket. "That sure is kind of you, but sweets are taboo."

Gillian laughed, one of those "I'm such a ditz" laughs. "Actually, I brought it in for Austen's sister, Brooke. Cute little thing. Walks around like she's a bit lost. I didn't see her car in the lot, but you tell me which room she's in and I can plop this on her bed. Maybe add a little note."

"Who?" Delores looked at her blankly, and although the desk clerk had many faults, she *always* knew her paying customers.

Mindy started to talk, but Gillian nudged her in the side. "Did she not check in yet? I could've sworn that Austen said she was staying here."

Delores shook her head. "No reservation. All we got is four dentists from Abilene and the railroad surveying crew from Austin. That one foreman is kinda hot. Too bad you're taken."

Gillian flashed her ring, which she was in a habit of doing, which her mama always told her was ostentatious, but Gillian believed that a newly engaged woman should be a little ostentatious, unless she wasn't in true love, which Gillian most definitely was. "Listen, if you see Brooke, don't tell her I stopped by. I want this to be a surprise."

"Do you want me to call you when she checks in?"

"Do you mind? I want to make sure she feels right at home."

Delores saluted. "On the case, Sheriff."

Once they were outside, Mindy started in. "What's going on?"

For a moment, Gillian pondered this new dilemma. "I sent her here, but I don't know that's where she landed."

"Where else could she go?"

"Nowhere."

"Call her," Mindy suggested. "Tell her you have a surprise. Trap her in a lie."

"Now calm down, Mindy. There's been no lying. She's family and besides that, she doesn't have a cell."

"Who doesn't have a cell?"

"My great-aunt Cora doesn't have a cell."

"She's nearly eighty."

"Doesn't matter. It's not that strange."

"It's strange," Mindy pronounced, and privately Gillian agreed, but right now she needed to look unconcerned.

"I'll drop you back at your house, then I need to make an appearance at the courthouse."

Mindy looked at her, disappointed. "I thought this was a mission."

"Doesn't Brandon have a two o'clock feeding? You're going to let that poor baby starve?"

Mindy sighed. "It's very difficult being a mother."

"Tell it to the hand, sweetie. Tell it to the hand."

TWO HOURS LATER, Gillian was still combing the town for a beat-up Impala that should have stood out like not only a sore but bruised, beaten and banged-up thumb.

But there was no Impala to be found. At that point, Gillian grabbed her radio, prepared to issue an APB for the missing vehicle, but official sheriff directives meant official paperwork, and official records. Gillian's gut told her that official records were never a good idea where family was concerned. So, she drove down Main, turned at Pecos, past the drive-in, across the interstate and even wandered across the county line. Still no Impala.

Actually, in a fine twist of fate and logic, it wasn't until she'd abandoned her search that she found it. As she was heading over to Austen's house, she happened to glance at the old Hinkle place, and lo and behold, there among the sheds and tires and tubs and two-by-fours sat an Impala as if it belonged there.

Gillian knew her town and she knew who lived there. Sonya Hinkle's ex, Jason Kincaid. Sonya had been an over-achiever in high school, two years older than Gillian, with that Hollywood platinum hair that Gillian had secretly coveted until she found out that Sonya was driving into Austin to get her hair colored every two months.

According to official records, Jason was thirty-four years old. Staff sergeant with the U.S. Army, honorably discharged when he lost his left eye. He was a loner, who liked to pick up scrap metal and parts. Suspected in the gifting of a lawn mower for the Strickland landscaping company, an industrial strength dryer for the homeless shelter at the church and a large wooden pirate ship for the elementary school. All allegations were unproven and since he went to so much trouble to keep his good deeds quiet, Gillian chose not to reveal that the set of prints on the dryer came back a ten-point match.

So, why was Brooke parked at the house? Maybe she knew him from New York, Iraq...*here?*

Gillian drummed her fingers on the steering wheel, sizing up the situation, knowing that it required some discreet snooping around, of which she was something of a professional.

Her mouth pulled into a thoughtful frown, and she shifted the car into Reverse. She'd get her facts in a row, and when she did, she'd tell Austen, but she'd have to craft the moment exactly right.

First, a little moonlight Hart-house demolition to lift his mood. Next, a long bout of Austen Hart loving. Then, when he was lying next to her, sated, happy and full of the intangible wonderment of their emotional connection, she'd tell him that his little sister had hooked up with the Captain.

Who woulda thunk it? Little sister worked fast.

10

BROOKE WAS LEAVING Hinkle's grocery when Gillian rushed toward her, pulling her into a big hug. Brooke froze, then quickly returned the hug before Gillian thought something was wrong.

"Hey, sis! What are you doing?" Gillian took Brooke's sack of food in her arms, then led her down Main, past Dot's diner, past the What in Carnation flower shop, past the fence in front of the Presbyterian church until they were standing at the park located next to the base of the courthouse steps, Lady Liberty watching Brooke skeptically.

Brooke managed a smile. "I should get my food back to the hotel before it goes bad."

Gillian pushed her down on a wooden bench and then plopped down next to her, her sheriff's badge blinding in its glare. Brooke wasn't used to seeing Gillian in uniform and to tell the truth, the badge and the gun made her nervous. Still, this was Gillian, one of the nicest, friendliest people Brooke had ever met. There was no reason to be nervous.

Lady Liberty glared. Brooke gulped.

"You don't have any perishables in there, do you?" Gillian asked, watching Brooke with those clear blue eyes that saw all. "I know there's none of those mini-fridges at the Inn. I love those things. Don't you love those things, with those little candied almonds, but gah-ah-ly, can you believe what the big cities charge for them? Being from New York, you know all about those mini-fridges, don't you?"

Oh, God. She knew. Brooke tried an innocent expression and knew she'd failed. She'd never been very good at the art of deception, folding under pressure like a cheap suit. "I was planning on telling you and Austen the truth."

Gillian cocked her head, giving her an understanding smile. "Did you think we would care? Now, I know that some people stand in judgment in this tiny pill of a town, but, sweetie, we're family, and you don't have to keep secrets from Austen and me."

Brooke's shoulders slumped from the relief of it. "All I wanted was for him to like me."

Gillian frowned. "That's so sweet. Of course he likes you—doesn't he?"

Brooke frowned. "Don't you know?"

Gillian's clear blue eyes narrowed. Now she looked like a cop. "What are we talking about?"

"What are you talking about?"

"You and Jason, carrying on. Gotta say, you don't let any grass grow under your feet. But if that's not what we're discussing, then what are we discussing?"

Brooke blinked, trying for guileless. "The Captain, of course."

Gillian leaned back on the bench, and laid an arm across Brooke's shoulders. It should have been comforting. It was a trap. "Brooke, first of all, I think you're cute as a button with those darling little puppy-dog eyes, but not only am I a trained law enforcement professional, I love Austen Hart, and don't think I would hesitate to break your face into little puppy dog pieces if there's anything that you're hiding from him that would hurt him. Unless he's not your brother?"

Gillian smiled with even white teeth. It was a beautiful smile. Brooke wasn't fooled.

The other woman was breathing fire, overly protective, fiercely loyal, just like families were supposed to be. Something Charlene Hart had never learned, and something Brooke desperately needed. Maybe it was time to tell the truth. Maybe all that over-protective loyalty would cover sins of poverty and omission, as well.

"I did what I did because I wanted Tyler and Austen to like me. They don't know me, and I don't think they like me."

"You took Austen's mother away from him and his brother. She left them and traded in for a better life in New York. You got a great stepfather, they got Frank Hart. Sweetheart, it doesn't matter if you were sitting in your mama's stomach when she left. You could be the most perfect sister ever and he'd still have issues. Now what are you not telling me?"

Brooke took a deep breath. "I don't have a stepfather."

"You lied?"

"Yes."

"If that wasn't your stepfather's house in New York when the boys visited, then whose was it? Your mother's?"

"I don't know who it belonged to. There was an open house. I bribed a Realtor to let me use it for a couple of hours."

"Where was your real home?" asked Gillian, looking not so threatening, not so judgmental.

"I didn't have one."

Gillian's mouth curved into an indulgent smile. "Of course you did. Maybe it wasn't some hoity-toity mansion in New York, but everybody has a home."

Carefully Brooke met her eyes. "Not everyone."

It took Gillian only a few seconds to comprehend, and pity flashed in her eyes. "I'm sorry. It must have been very hard on you and your mother."

Gillian was inviting her to tell some hugely sorrowful tales about life on the streets, just like most people did when confronted with a homeless person. Charlene Hart had thrived on her hard-luck stories, but not so much Brooke. "Austen and Tyler didn't miss very much when they were growing up without their mother."

"A family isn't about money or a house. It's not like they were rolling in it, either. They wouldn't have cared if Charlene Hart was poor or not."

"They might care if she had substance abuse problems."

Gillian's mouth drew into a little "oh" of enlightenment. "You should know your father Frank was a drunk, a vile SOB with a mouth as bitter as his black heart. Sounds like your mother was no prize, but that's all on Frank and Charlene, not you, not Austen, not Tyler. I've never known three people more determined to pretend that everything's fine. It's not, but now you three have each other, so the secrets have got to stop. You have to tell Austen. I'll keep quiet for a couple of days because it needs to come from you, but I won't keep it forever. Lies have a way of coming out, and people get hurt. I won't let him get hurt. His father has already hurt him enough."

Easy words from a woman who had lived a normal life, but there was a certainty in Gillian's face that inspired Brooke and made her want to believe Gillian. There would be a remarkable freedom in knowing that the pretense was over. All her life she'd pretended, but maybe Gillian was right.

Eventually Brooke nodded. "I'll do it."

Gillian patted her on the shoulder, as if everything would be okay. Brooke liked that about her future sister-in-law. Her confidence in the future. Of course, people who had a home usually did have that confidence. And now Brooke had a home, too. Or at least part of one. Slowly she smiled.

"And since we're family now, tell me all about Jason," Gillian prodded. "How the heck did that happen?"

"He gave me a job."

At the words, Gillian's eyes widened with shock. "What sort of job?" Then she held up a hand. "Nope. If there's illegal shenanigans going on, I don't want to know." She paused. "No, no, that's not right. As your future sister-in-law, I have to know if you have a life in crime."

Brooke laughed. "There's no crime. He's paying me to organize his parts."

Gillian's cop-look was back. "Parts?"

"You've seen his land. He has a lot of parts. He doesn't know what he owns. I'm grouping things together and writing it down."

"But you're living there."

Sometimes people missed the obvious. "I couldn't afford the motel."

"Oh." Gillian nodded. "Oh. I thought you were…you know."

Brooke felt a hot flush on her cheeks, but hopefully Gillian wouldn't notice. "He's very nice, but I don't think he sees me that way." It was a modified version of the truth. A version that would meet with the Captain's approval.

"You like him?"

Brooke nodded.

Gillian rolled her eyes. "Well, then I don't know what's wrong with the man."

Brooke liked the sympathy, the unwavering support. Family. It was nice. "It's all right. I've got enough on my mind right now."

"You come stay with us," Gillian offered, because of course Gillian would offer Brooke a place to stay. It was the next logical step, and Brooke wanted to whack her head against the bench for not thinking ahead.

"You don't have enough room in your house. You have Austen. Your parents. I'm perfectly comfortable where I am." It was a good answer, the one that made Brooke's situation seem reasonable, however, Gillian was not to be dissuaded.

"We have a sleeper sofa and a blow-up…" She stopped, swore. "Stupid me. We'll get you a room at the Spotlight. You don't have to stay with Jason. Austen and I will pick up the tab. That way you can have some privacy and a place of your own. It'll be temporary until the lawyer gets back and the papers are signed, but I bet you'll love it."

"That's very kind," started Brooke, "but—"

Gillian gave her arm a friendly squeeze. "No buts, sweetie. You're family."

HAVING DIFFICULT conversations was not one of Brooke's strengths, and because any conversation with the Captain was a difficult conversation, having this particular difficult conversation was not something she knew how to do.

Leaving here would be like cutting off an arm, or a leg, or a heart.... She wiped at her tears, because the last thing she wanted was to bust out bawling in front of him before the conversation even started. Every time she looked around the house, she could feel the sting in her heart.

Outside was even worse. Such a beautiful place, and no one would ever see it the way she did. The practical shade netting was like a twinkling night sky. The swinging bench seat on the porch was the literal Cadillac of porch swings, perfect for watching the sun wake to the world. The cactus she'd placed in the window was sturdy and immoveable, not only decorative, but able to survive and thrive. All of these little things were home.

Most of all, the Captain felt like home, which was why Brooke was avoiding the conversation like the plague. Eventually, it was late afternoon, and if Brooke wasn't at the hotel by dark, Gillian would know there was a problem and the Captain would realize that Brooke hadn't told him she was leaving, and then the Captain would wonder why she hadn't told him that she was leaving, surmising that Brooke didn't want to leave and hadn't planned on telling him—which was exactly the reason.

This sort of strategic, long-term thinking was smart and needed to be done, but that didn't mean it hurt any less. There was no way that the Captain would invite her to stay if she had other options and now Brooke had other options. More than anything, she wanted more time, but since it was now three o'clock and she had piddled away another seven minutes by thinking, time wasn't a luxury that Brooke could afford.

After changing into her favorite white tank top, she made her face look presentable. She brushed her hair until it shone because she knew the Captain loved her hair. When ready, she appeared outside where the Captain was rolling the widow Kenley's washing machine into the bed of his truck and slamming the tailgate closed. Determined to get this over with, Brooke swung open the passenger door of the truck and planted herself on the seat.

After he got behind the wheel, the Captain, to his credit, didn't tell her to get out, but instead shifted to face her, giving her the full-on pirate stare—a feeble attempt at intimidation. "Why are you here?"

"You can't lift the washing machine out by yourself," Brooke pointed out.

"Sure, I can. How do you think I got it here? Little elves?"

Trying another tactic, she rolled down the window, propped her elbow on the door, feeling the sun warm on her arm. "It's a great day. I'd love to go for a drive."

She could feel the touch of his gaze skimming over her chest, her mouth, and she knew what lay behind that look, but yes, this was the Captain. "You'll get sunburned."

"Are you ashamed to be seen with me?" It was a cheap shot, worthy of Charlene Hart, but Brooke had tried logic and seduction, and if pity was all she had left, well, so be it.

The Captain muttered something obscene. "It's not you. You're beautiful and smart and you make people want to be around you. No man in his right mind would be ashamed to be seen with you."

It was the most extravagant thing he'd ever said. He thought she was beautiful, a word she hadn't been sure was in his vocabulary. "Really? You're not just saying that to be nice?"

"I don't say anything just to be nice."

"Yes, you do," she corrected. "You don't like anybody to know that you do, but you do."

"Why are you here? I know there's a reason. What it is, I don't know, but I know it's going to scare me."

If it had been left up to Brooke, she would have squandered away a few more minutes, but the Captain was a master of efficiency, and she resigned herself to telling the truth. "We need to have a discussion."

"We don't have to drive into town to have a discussion. We can discuss at the house."

No, they couldn't have this discussion at the house. The house was her home, and not having a lot of places to call home, she didn't want to ruin the memory of the first one she'd ever had. "Start the truck," she instructed, waiting patiently until the low rumble of the motor filled the cab.

The big black gates swung open, soon they were moving, the caliche gravel crunching under the tires.

"Did you talk to the lawyer?" he asked and there was worry in his voice. It pleased her that he might not be happy to say goodbye.

"No. But I talked to Gillian. I confessed the truth."

He glanced sideways, because the Captain was more cagey than Gillian, or perhaps he knew Brooke better than Gillian. "What truth did you tell her?"

For a man who valued honesty, he seemed tense, and maybe she should have spit things out more clearly, but that involved levels of personal growth that she had yet to obtain. "The one and only truth."

"You've got a lot of secrets up in the air, Brooke. Sometimes I have a hard time keeping track."

"Sarcasm is not necessary."

"What truth?" he asked.

Brooke gazed out the window, watching the oil wells that dotted the landscape as they passed. "I told her I couldn't afford the Inn, and I told her that Charlene Hart was a drinker and that I was working for you in order to generate income."

"Did you tell her anything else?" he asked.

She turned to study his profile this time, the quiet strength that she admired and envied, and the same quiet strength that made her want to cry. She wanted him to need her the way he needed air.

"You mean, did I tell her that I know you in the Biblical sense?" she said, some of her anger creeping into her voice.

He nodded. "That's the one."

"No."

"Smart."

"Gillian assumed things, though. However, in order to preserve your reputation, I denied it and told her that you were the perfect gentleman."

"I am the perfect gentleman."

"Who likes the sex."

"All men like the sex."

"Anyway, you're off the hook," she told him casually, because she didn't want him to invite her to stay out of a sense of responsibility or a guilty conscience. She wanted him to invite her to stay because he wanted her until he ached.

"What hook?"

Brooke smiled at him, as if it was the best sort of news. "Gillian and Austen are springing for a room at the Inn. Now I have a place to stay. I don't have to impose on you anymore."

MOST TIMES, Jason believed that the trips into town were too far and too long, but this time, the trip to Mrs. Kenley's house wasn't far or long enough.

He locked his hands on the wheel, shifted the gear into Park and concentrated on the one hundred and fifty pounds of metal in the bed of the truck instead of the forty kilotons of nuclear fission that just exploded in his gut.

Brooke looked at him, expected a response or, more precisely, an invitation, but Jason wasn't that guy and he escaped the suffocating cab, hopping up into the truck bed, focusing on what needed to be done.

Apparently it was a no-brainer for Brooke to believe that he wasn't that guy, she was already standing at the foot of the bed, laying the two-by-fours in place, waiting for him to slide the washing machine down the makeshift ramp. When had she gotten so efficient, when had she figured it all out? Uncomfortable with the idea that Brooke didn't need him anymore, Jason tugged at the bill of his cap, but the cap, the patch over his eye, not even the big fireball of the westerly sun wasn't enough to block her from his sight.

She met his eyes, and he could see so much there. All her dreams, all her pain, and there was a voice in his head that said, *Take her home, keep her forever.* But then she smiled at him, sad, smart and forgiving, and the voice in his head shut up.

"You need to train Dog to do this, Captain," she teased, smartly moving past the tension. "Otherwise he'll get fat and lazy."

Jason laughed, a hollow, rusty sound, and Mrs. Kenley waved from her front porch. Together, he and Brooke moved the washing machine up the porch and into the old laundry room on the back of the house.

"I appreciate the work, Captain. You always do such nice work." The woman laid a familiar hand on her machine and Jason understood. People bonded with their machines because machines were dependable and infallible. A machine could never disappoint.

Then she beamed at Brooke because people were always smiling at Brooke.

"I don't think we've met, honey. You're not Sonya unless you shrank about half a foot and dyed your hair." The old woman peered closer. "You're not Sonya, are you?"

Brooke chuckled, pushed at her hair and Jason could imagine the silk in his hands, until he jammed them in his pockets and he couldn't remember anything at all.

"No, I'm Brooke Hart. Yes, one of those Harts and, no, I don't have a criminal record."

"I like this one," Mrs. Kenley said to Jason. "You should keep her."

"This one? I thought I was the only one." Brooke looked at him again, half teasing, mostly not, and his gaze shifted away.

"Should I make her jealous, Jason, or tell her the truth?"

No, he didn't want anyone to tell Brooke the truth. That was what he loved about her, that ability to not want to know the truth. Jason picked up the boards and the rollers and made for the door.

"Stump Tinkham said his afternoon soaps were breaking up, and he thought the antenna on the roof had gone wonky. I didn't say anything to him because you're always so busy, so I'm not going to say anything to you, either."

"I appreciate that, Mrs. Kenley. I won't stop by his house."

On the way home, Brooke was quiet until the big black gates yawned open to welcome him home. "You make these repair trips into town often?"

He managed a smile. "Nah. Not at all."

THEIR LAST DINNER TOGETHER was a quiet affair. More quiet than usual.

After Dog cleaned up, Brooke waited for the Captain to bury his head in some board or transistor or engine, but instead he brought out a large cardboard box.

"There are some things that you'll need, and some things I thought I would replace."

He deposited the package on the coffee table in front of her and took the chair opposite, waiting for her to open it.

Charlene Hart didn't believe in presents or surprises, at least not the good kind, so Brooke prepared herself to be disappointed. With shaky fingers, Brooke lifted the lid and then her breath caught.

Not disappointed here.

On top was a forest-green cashmere sweater. Not so practical in the Texas sun, but the wool was softer than anything she'd ever touched before. "It's lovely," she told him, lifting it out and holding it against her.

"Since I ruined the first one—"

Quickly she cut him off.

"This one is a lot nicer." She didn't know what a green cashmere sweater meant and she didn't want to think it meant anything, but the heart was a very hopeful thing. "Captain…"

Quickly he cut her off. "Go on. There's more," he said, and she focused her attention on the box. He was right, there was more.

A red sundress, complete with a matching red necklace. A new pair of shearling boots. Three pairs of jeans, a pencil skirt in charcoal gray and coordinating blouse in taupe. She'd never owned a pencil skirt before, and this one looked classy and sophisticated, and she thought she was going to love it. After that, her fingers dug through the box a little faster. Next was an old-fashioned cotton nightgown, with tiny flowers and delicate lace on the front.

It wasn't elegant and sophisticated. It was the most beautiful thing she'd ever owned. She met his eyes, dazed by the treasures in front of her. "This is too much."

"No. I ruined a lot of things for you. You're going to need all this. There's more."

More? Not sure what more entailed, she dug into the tissue paper, wondering if more meant a house key, a card, or a permanent toothbrush on the sink.

Instead, she pulled out a mobile phone and an envelope of cash. More truly sucked.

"You need a phone and the money's to get you started. Consider it an advance on your salary."

Salary. Oh, yes, that other thing she hadn't wanted to tell him. "Gillian found me a job at the court house. Filing."

"Filing is good. You'll be a good filer." He looked at her, not sad at all, because in the end, the Captain was a practical person and Gillian had provided a practical solution, but Brooke was tired of being practical and strategic. Strategic thinking hadn't yielded the thing she wanted most of all.

"Captain," she started then his mouth was on hers and she couldn't breathe. His hands tangled in her hair, not practical, not sensible. No, this was perfect. The sort of impossible perfection that is so perfect that it hurts. Tears stung at her eyes, and the Captain lifted his head and swore. Gently, he wiped the moisture away, as if he didn't want to hurt her, but the tenderness was like a nail to her heart.

"I'm sorry," he apologized, as if a green cashmere sweater was a poor replacement for his heart, because it was. "I'll take the couch." Small words, painful words, and then he was pulling away. Her last night and he was robbing her of that, as well.

Brooke put a hand to his arm, asking for the last time. "Please?"

11

JASON FISTED HIS HAND in her hair and locked his mouth to hers. He closed his eyes, closed out the house, the world, ignoring everything but this. But her.

Strong hands dug into his shoulders, his neck. Not the timid hands that she'd used before. She stroked his hair, his scar, and the gentle touch hurt more than the IED ever had.

Needing to stop the pain, he lifted her in his arms, carrying her to bed. There was no moon, no stars. Here a man could hide himself in peace. With unsteady hands he undressed her, so careful not to rip, not to tear, not to ruin anything else. Brooke didn't know how fragile she was, but Jason did. He buried his face in the tangled silk of her hair, memorizing the feel of it against his cheek. His mouth whispered against her neck, lips moving with words he would never say. Blindly he found the sensitive spot beneath her right ear, felt her shiver in his arms, and he pulled her closer, wanting to make love to her in the way she deserved, but then her knee was sliding between his legs, rubbing his greedy cock and tortured balls, and he nearly...

No. Tonight was all about her.

"Captain," she whispered to him and he wished that he was. He wished that he was everything that she saw.

In the dark he filled her, completed her, adored her, and

sometime before the dawn, when the night sky was done with black, she slipped from his bed and dressed.

THE SKY WAS GRAY, a tired, drizzling rain falling on the ground. Brooke stood on the front porch, her hands locked to the wooden railing until she made herself release it.

She had a new life waiting for her. The one she'd always wanted. A home. A family. Not perfect, but very, very real. Belonging. It felt good to belong. Comfortable, peaceful, safe.

Once she picked up the bag and box of her belongings, her feet descended the steps. One, two, three, four. The front walk was clear now, a tidy brick pathway that had been obscured from sight. She'd cleared a path to his doorway because...

No. The drops of rain fell in loud plops on the bricks, on her face, but the cool dampness suited her mood.

The entire yard was a lot neater now. Five sheds, newly painted and organized. A clipboard containing each inventory hung from a nail on the inside wall. He wouldn't lose things again. Yellow wildflowers poked up here and there among the grass. The Captain would call them weeds...

Her lips twitched into a sad semblance of a smile and this time when she scanned the yard, she noticed a sheet of plywood leaning against the side of the house. The rain would ruin the wood and make it unusable. She knew that now, and she grasped the rough edges, intending to move it out of the rain. It was a big one, six-by-six, she thought to herself, because she knew that now, too.

As she pulled, the wood revealed what had been hidden behind it.

Her fingers tightened on the plywood sheet because her knees had gone wobbly. There was the tub. Glistening ivory, with curly-cue legs and an elegant back. The rusted spots had been sand-blasted away, the fresh enamel was a smooth, pearly white. Now that the tub was exposed to the elements, the rain slid down the sides like a foolish girl's tears.

While she stood there, the rain picked up, turning into a stinging lash that whipped at her face, hitting the tub metal hard, but she couldn't move.

No one had ever done something like this for her...except the Captain.

One sob escaped her throat, only one because she had a new life waiting for her. A home. A job. A family.

A family. The Captain wasn't her family. He didn't want that.

No, this part of her life was done. With remarkably steady hands, she took the plywood and put it neatly back in place, and there was nothing left to prevent her from leaving. Brooke took one purposeful step with a new and improved mood and found the second step easier than the first. The lines and the curves of the path guided her, and then the steps came faster, because she knew she needed to do this fast, put him behind her before she stomped her self-respect into the mud.

The rain was falling in solid sheets now, her vision blurred completely, but she knew the way out. She had practiced this walk in her head, but she hadn't expected that her heart would weigh her down.

One last time she turned, and through the blur she could see the Captain on the porch, watching her go. Ruddy stubble lined his jaw, but there was no reason for him to shave now. His bare chest was riddled with puckered, silvery scars, long healed, long hardened. A pair of unfastened jeans clung to strong, capable thighs. But his bare feet weren't moving. His hands weren't beckoning her to stay because the Captain was strategic. One naked eye watched her, as stormy gray as the sky, and because Brooke's scars were fresh and raw, she stood frozen, waiting for the impossible.

The Captain stood tall, immovable. Brooked lifted her face to the rain.

This time she was smarter and stronger, and she wasn't so eager to fail. Outside those monstrous black gates was a life. *A future.* After keying in the combination, she waited impatiently for the gates to open and then loaded her things in the car. Before she drove away, she checked the mirror, safety first after all, and she could see the Captain still standing, locked away behind his black gates. She flipped on the windshield wipers, the rhythmic swish-swish like a knife slicing through her heart.

After the house disappeared from view, Brooke stopped the car at the side of the road. She cried and sobbed and swore, and by the time the rain had eased, she'd dried her eyes, repaired her makeup and was off to start her new life, leaving her heart and her tears behind her.

BROOKE SPENT MOST of Tuesday in the courthouse, learning the ins and outs of Sheriff Wanamaker's organizational system, of which there were none. Eventually, she shooed Gillian away, explaining that she needed to find her own method. Gillian seemed to understand. Promptly at five o'clock, Gillian appeared.

"You're ready for tomorrow?"

Tomorrow was the meeting with the lawyer. Gillian's face was drawn into a Mother Teresa look of concern and compassion, but Brooke wasn't fooled. This was about Austen, the man she planned to marry. "I tried to call Austen yesterday, but he was tied up at the Capitol."

"He'll be at the old house in the morning. Meet him there."

Brooke looked into Gillian's eyes and knew this was it. No more stalling, no more avoidance. She could do this. The Captain believed in her, and it was time that Brooke did, as well.

"I'll be there."

"If you don't tell him, I will."

Brooke smiled. "You won't have to. I swear."

THE NEXT MORNING, she drove to the old house, and found her brother there, pulling down the last remains of the house and piling it in a long roll-off container. In the few short weeks since she'd lived in Tin Cup, she'd seen a different world than the one Charlene Hart had ever given her. Here, people did whatever needed to be done, fixed what was broken, and didn't whine about the process. Practical and simple. Brooke approved.

As she approached him, he was throwing in the last boards, and she jammed her hands in her jean pockets, waiting until Austen was done. "Thank you for what you're doing. For transferring over a part of the estate. You don't know what it means to me."

"It's the right thing to do. Legally, you're entitled. Before I sign the papers for the transfer, I wanted to talk to you. I wanted to get some things out in the open."

"Go ahead."

"I heard you were in charge of the ground-breaking ceremony for the train station?"

He winced. "That's something of an overstatement. I wrote a press release, and got JC here to speak. "

"Who's JC? What do you do for him?"

"Her."

"Oh."

He almost smiled. "Yeah. We get that a lot. She's running for governor next year, and I do her public relations, mainly. A lot of organizing events for the Masons and the PTA. A lot of writing, involving words like *leadership, growth* and *vision*. You want a bumper sticker?"

Brooke shot a sad glance at the Impala. "That wreck of a car might cost her the election."

He walked over, raised the hood and inspected the engine. "She's not too bad. A little body work. I could do a bit of tinkering under the hood. You'd be surprised with the difference. This car could be a thing of beauty with the proper amount of TLC."

"You're offering to fix it?" she asked.

He considered her for a moment. "Yeah. I could."

The generous offer was making it harder to confess her actual financial situation. "I might have misstated some things, and you might not like it."

"Don't know until you spit it out," he told her, pulling out a rag and wiping the grease from his hands.

"She wasn't very nice."

"Who?"

"Our mother."

"Sorry, sis. I wouldn't know."

She heard the sarcasm in his voice, and she spoke quickly before she lost her courage. "I photoshopped all those pictures on the wall in New York. The house wasn't even mine."

This time she had his full attention. "Go on."

"She liked to drink."

"No wonder she married Frank. It explains a lot." He laughed, but his eyes were shrewd. "Bet that really tweaked the preacher man, didn't it?"

Brooke stared at the ground. "I never had a preacher for a stepfather. I never had a stepfather."

"That was a lie, too? And the fiancé? Peter?"

"An acting student. I picked him up in a bar and paid him six hundred for the night."

For a long while Austen was quiet, and when he spoke, his voice wasn't nearly as mad as she had expected it would be. "Why didn't you just tell the truth?"

She looked at her car, looked out on the horizon, then looked at her brother with a sad smile. "I thought if I told you and Tyler that I was homeless, you two would get weird about it, but you both were weird about it anyway."

"We're not the family kind."

"I am."

"Sorry, sis."

She didn't believe his words. A man who was building a house for his bride? That was family. "I like Gillian. She's the family kind."

"Yeah."

"Do you want me to leave town? I can pack up my car and be on my way." Hopefully the car would make it.

"Is that what you want?"

She met his eyes. "No."

He waved a hand as if he didn't care. "Then don't."

"Are you ever going to stop being weird around me?"

Her brother shrugged.

"I need to belong somewhere," she said, by way of an explanation.

"And this is the place? There are a lot more glamorous locales."

"The people are nice."

"Except for Boolie Suggs at the *Tin Cup Gazette.* Don't cross her."

"Is that why the article said that Tyler was at the state pen?"

"Boolie likes to make things up. Now that I think of it, you might want to apply there. You two would really get along."

The words stung, and Brooke swallowed hard. "I should go." As she walked toward the car, Austen caught up with her.

"Brooke. Wait. I'm sorry. I figure once the wedding is over and this place is built, I won't be as irritable. Stay if you want, although to tell you the truth, if I didn't have something to keep me here, I'd be long gone. For the life of me, I just can't figure out why you'd want to stay here." He was staring at her ruefully. "Building a house in this little helltown isn't the smartest move I've made, but I'm here, too, which you could consider says something about both our smarts. I guess Tyler struck the motherlode when it comes to Hart brains."

"I bet you're really smart."

"Why do you think that?"

"Because Gillian is smart and I don't think she'd be marrying you otherwise."

He reached out and tweaked her nose, and no one had ever tweaked her nose before. It was a very brotherly thing to do and she found herself smiling. "Very perceptive, little sister. Maybe you inherited some brains, too. You're coming to the wedding?"

"My future sister-in-law would kill me if I didn't."

Austen laughed. "She's registered at Tallyrand's. I asked her, what's wrong with registering at Victoria's Secret, but no."

All the wariness was gone from her brother's eyes, and it occurred to Brooke that she should have told the truth a long time ago. The Captain was very smart that way. Sometimes the truth wasn't so bad after all. "I think I'm going to like you."

"Buy her a black teddy for the wedding shower and I'll forgive you anything. And listen, before we talk to the lawyer, you should know something. There's some serious money on the table if we lease the mineral rights on the property. They're doing some seismic tests next week. It's not, oh-praise-jeezus-I'll-never-work-again money, but it'll keep you comfortable for a while."

Her brother had no idea how long Brooke could exist on very little funds. One man's comfortable is another woman's champagne dreams. "I like comfortable," she told him easily, as if her insides weren't screaming for joy. "You're going to the lawyer's?" she asked.

"Is it time?"

She held out her arm to her brother and smiled. "It's time."

THE LAWYER'S OFFICE was just as stuffy as Austen remembered, a dark, two-room place with a monstrous wooden desk, three leather chairs and four diplomas hanging from the wall. Six months ago he'd been here, walking away the not-so-proud owner of one half of the Hart house, appraised value of $837, one half of the Hart land, appraised at $7000 and one half of the mineral rights, value unknown. Little did he realize how such a small financial transaction could turn into an emotional goldmine.

Because of that one short trip back home, he'd found a new job and, best of all, found Gillian again. Today he was here to make things right for his sister. To pay her for her fair share of the inheritance and to sign over to her a third of the mineral rights.

"I prepared the paperwork, Austen. I think we have everything we need. You'll write a check to Miss Hart here for the financial value of the messuage." The lawyer paused, chuckling to himself. "Love that word. Just rolls off the tongue. That's lawyer-talk for house and land. Then we transfer one third of the mineral rights."

"Tyler signed his part, already? I tried to call yesterday but Edie—that's his girlfriend—said he was in surgery."

"I didn't need his signature. Tyler signed over his parcel to you already, Austen."

And they thought the lawyers knew it all? Ha. "I think you've made a mistake there, Hiram. He didn't say anything to me. Maybe you've got your last will and testaments confused."

The old lawyer pulled out a sheet of paper and slid it across the desk. "No mistake. All signed, sealed and delivered."

Austen studied the document, double-checked the signature and, God knows, it looked like that same illegible doctor's scrawl that Tyler used, but it couldn't be. He pushed the paper away.

"He would have told me," Austin insisted. Nobody knew his brother like he did. It wasn't that Tyler wasn't generous. It's just that he never thought of things like that. And since Austen didn't, either, it worked.

"He wanted to surprise you. A wedding present," the lawyer explained.

"Tyler doesn't like surprises."

"I bet Edie does," Brooke added in a quiet voice.

"If she made him do it..."

"Austen..." his sister began, smiling at him as if he were being a little slow. Now, normally Austen didn't mind that, but considering Brooke's recent disclosures, he didn't think that people in glass houses needed to be hurling stones. "She didn't make him do it."

"You know that for a fact?" he shot back, because he would feel more comfortable if duress had been involved.

"No, but call him. Ask him about Edie if it will make you feel better, but I think it's meant as a gift."

The lawyer coughed discreetly. "Dr. Hart was very insistent. I don't think there's any coercion here." He pulled out a business card and handed it to Brooke. "I believe Clayton Oakes is handling lease for the mineral rights. Nice fellow, does honest work, but watch the royalty rates. You can always negotiate a few points higher. I have his number written down, but call me if you think he's trying to low-ball you."

It was at that point that Austen stopped listening and waited for the world to resume it's normal, less dizzying rotation.

"Are you okay?" Brooke asked, sounding like a sister.

Austen slowly shook his head. "This isn't Tyler. Y'all don't know him. You know, the Harts, we're sort of 'all for no one' and 'no one for all.'"

Brooke laughed, a disbelieving laugh, as if they were a family. "Maybe you don't know him as well as you think. Maybe all for no one sucks. Why don't you call him? You should and, while you're gone, I'll have a chat with Hiram." Brooke looked happy, cheerful, as if this were a good thing.

Austen frowned, stared at the paper and then rose from the chair. "Yeah. Maybe I'll call."

Once outside, Austen pulled out his phone and tapped Tyler's number on the touch screen, and then quit. What was he supposed to say to his brother? Thanks? What the hell are you doing?

A wedding present? Sure, he expected his brother to give him something. A silver tankard with the date engraved on it. Maybe some fancy plates or crystal. But this?

There were lines here that weren't usually crossed. On Tyler's birthday, Austen sent a card and a gift certificate to a nice restaurant, usually a steak house, because they'd never had a lot of expensive meat growing up. At Christmas, Tyler called and told him "Merry Christmas," and then sent him a sweater. Always cashmere. Usually blue.

As for Thanksgiving, that was a holiday usually spent solo. There were strict rules in the Hart family, and here went Tyler, breaking a rule—and Tyler was not, as a rule, a rule-breaker.

Austen sat on the curb and stared down the main street of Tin Cup, noticing the friendly waves in his direction and the way it all felt so...*good.*

So when had this hell turned into home? Was it when Dot started sliding him extra bacon with his breakfast at the diner? Or when Gillian's parents had told him and Gillian to take the Hart land and build a new and better house on it, something for Austen and Gillian, and the grandkids when they came?

So many bad memoires of Tin Cup, Texas, but not anymore. Now, the memories were coming up good—Brooke Hart included. Still contemplating this new, contented sort of feeling, Austen hit Tyler's number on the phone and waited, waited.

Finally, it was no surprise when he reached his brother's voice mail.

"Ty? It's Austen. Your brother. The lawyer told me what you did. Thanks. Say, Edie didn't put a gun to your head, did she? Nah, I'm sure she didn't, but it's nice what you did. You didn't have to. I mean, I know you're not suffering for cash or anything, but, dude...it's nice. Thanks."

After that, he hung up, laughed at his own foolishness, and then called Tyler's number again, waiting patiently for the beep.

"And one more thing. I know you're going to be here for the wedding, but could you and Edie stay on through Thanksgiving? We should do that, don't you think? We'll get some turkey and beer...and watch football. Gillian will love it. What do you think? I'd like to have you down here, bro. It'd be nice. We're family."

Austen hung up and smiled.

Family, what a concept.

Then he called his brother's voice mail again.

"I promise this is the last message, but I talked to Brooke this morning. Lots of crazy shit to tell you, bro. You wouldn't believe it. She was lying her ass off about the stepdad, the house, getting married and Charlene taking her on all those trips." He laughed, and it was a good laugh. "Yeah, she's definitely one of us. I think I'm going to like her."

THE LAWYER SHUFFLED his papers, coughing in that way people have when they're annoyed, but don't want the world to know they're annoyed, but of course, the world knows anyway. "I'm sorry I missed you last week. If I had known you had your birth certificate, I would have let Austen proceed with the paperwork. You can't be too cautious these days. I hope you understand."

Brooke understood only too well. "How is your father?"

"Better, thank you for asking. He's not a good patient, and likes to have someone to listen to his complaints. I'm sorry that it took longer than I thought. Did Mr. Kincaid give you my message?"

Brooke lifted her head. "No, he didn't say a word."

"I called the number you left for me."

"The Captain is a very busy man. I'm sure it slipped his mind," she assured Mr. Hadley, knowing very well it hadn't slipped the Captain's mind.

"Not that it matters," the lawyer droned on. "Mr. Oakes will need your signature on the mineral rights lease, assuming the signing bonus and royalty rates are agreeable. Remember what I said, don't let Clayton low-ball you. It's a tidy sum, and I bet a little extra revenue will come in handy. First, the train station, now some new oil and gas work. The times, they are a-changing, don't you agree?"

Brooke blinked, recognized the man was waiting for an answer and nodded stupidly. Why hadn't the Captain said something? She told herself not to read anything into it. Most likely he'd forgotten, or he hadn't thought it was important, or maybe there were a million other reasons that meant nothing at all.

Still, after transfer of the mineral rights was done and Austen's check was folded neatly in her pocket, Brooke sprang from her seat with an extra happy bounce.

No, she didn't want to read anything into it, but maybe the times were a-changing after all.

JASON WAS OUTSIDE, removing nails from some old railroad ties, when he heard a ringing noise coming from the house. The phone.

Jason's first thought was that Brooke was calling, that her car had broken down, that she'd lost her job, that she needed something. Him. But then he lifted his head, checked the desolate landscape and realized that mirages existed not only in the desert, but also in brain-dead men's imaginations, too.

However, he laid down the nail puller and headed for the house, his stride a little faster than it should be for a man who didn't believe in the power of his imagination.

"Kincaid," he answered, keeping his voice curt and not regretful at all.

"Jason, it's George."

As Jason listened to his brother, a chunk of bile rose in his throat. He tasted scrambled eggs and felt the hot sun grow cold. Quiet and alone, he sank down to the couch and stared until the vision in his one good eye grew blessedly dim.

THERE WAS A MINDLESS COMFORT in copying and filing that Brooke needed at the moment. Leaving the Captain had left an emptiness inside her just as she was starting to learn exactly what *together* could mean. Sometimes when she walked along the friendly streets of town, she felt so very alone, looking at a world that she'd always wanted to be a part of, and yet feeling as if she'd never belong.

Maybe some people were born with the ability to blend in, whatever their surroundings, but not Brooke. Not yet, but hopefully she could learn.

She suspected that Gillian had dug up some busy-work for her that had been ignored, and it seemed that all around her, people were going out of their way to help Brooke get on her feet. Hiram had told her about a small apartment that would be vacant before the end of the year, and the rent was cheap, even by Brooke's standards. Gillian's mother had been bringing small casseroles by the Spotlight Inn so that Brooke wouldn't have to go into town to eat if she didn't feel like it. And best of all was Austen. He'd changed the oil and transmission fluid on the Impala. Helped her pick out a new rear tire—apparently the old one was on its last treads. He was starting to feel like an older brother.

Next door in Gillian's office, Brooke could hear her arguing on the phone in that butter-melts-in-her-mouth fashion that Gillian had. In the end, Gillian usually got what she wanted, but apparently not this time.

The normally coolheaded woman flung open her office door and screamed.

Politely Brooke laid the files on the floor. "Is there a problem?"

"This wedding is going to kill me. It's supposed to be the happiest day of my life, but do you think anybody gives a rat's patootie? Heck, no. It's just, 'I don't think we can get lilacs in November, Gillian.' Can you believe it? This is America. They can get whatever the heck they want, and who cares if it's November? Ask me if I care if it's a free-range lilac or a genetically pure lilac. I just want my lilac. Do you think I'm crazy?"

Brooke decided it wouldn't be the best time to laugh. "You're not being crazy. Maybe I can help."

Gillian raised a brow. "You can get lilacs for me?"

"No, but I bet I can get the florist to work a little harder."

Gillian looked doubtful and, yes, Brooke couldn't blame her for that, but frankly, people needed to stop underestimating what Brooke was capable of, and the best route to do that was for Brooke to step up to the plate and throw a touchdown, or something like that.

"You don't mind?" She crossed her eyes and still looked gorgeous. "I'd be soooo grateful."

"Not a problem. Let me give it a shot." Brooke stood, rolled her shoulders and prepared for battle. "I'll get you the lilacs. I swear."

WHAT IN CARNATION was a tiny shop full of flowers and stuffed teddy bears, and one very busy florist, Luna Chavez, who bustled back and forth, but had a calming, zen sort of smile.

"I'm acting for Gillian Wanamaker. She doesn't know I'm here, but when I left the courthouse, she was in tears, and I had to do something."

"Tears?" Luna put down her scissors, concern in her eyes.

Brooke hesitated, then nodded. "You think a strong woman like that would never cry, don't you?"

"I felt so bad, but there is nothing I can do," Luna explained, holding her hands up innocently.

"No way to get the lilacs in?"

"I tried very hard, but they're not in season, and the plants will not grow whenever we want. It is nature's way."

Brooke exhaled, deeply, sadly. "It's too bad that nature has to be so cruel. First her mother... Now this." Slowly, head down, Brooke moved toward the door.

"Her mother?"

Brooke turned and shrugged as if the weight of the world was a heavy, heavy thing. "Don't worry. I'm sure she'll be fine."

Now Luna was clearly alarmed. "Wait! Is there something wrong with Modine?"

"Maybe I shouldn't say anything, maybe I'm butting in where I shouldn't, but I love Gillian like she's my own sister, and she's just too proud to tell people what's really going on. The Wanamakers are very proud people, but of course, I'm not telling you anything that you don't know."

"Has Modine seen a doctor?"

"It's all very hush-hush. I'm sure it's nothing. But the waiting is awful. It would mean so much to Gillian if she could make everything as easy as possible. Austen would be here to handle a lot of these details, but he's at the Capitol today, planning for that breaking-ground ceremony for the new rail line, and Gillian was just ready to give up, and she never gives up, which tells you how bad it is...."

"I didn't know."

Brooke shot her a calming, very zen smile. "I know. Don't worry about it. It's nature's way."

This time, Luna was not so accepting of the adage. Give these people a crisis and who knew what they could do? "I could call my wholesalers in Houston, but it's a long way, and they'll charge an arm and a leg for delivery."

"I'm sure that Gillian will pay whatever is necessary," Brooke assured the woman, not that it was going to come to that. She poked at the nearest teddy bear and managed a sad smile. "Not that she's having an easy time of it, you understand, having to support her mother and father, God bless them. I can't believe that in this day and age, folks can be so generous around here...." Brooke laughed. "But of course you know that."

"I would never charge her the full price for the delivery. Miss Gillian is very nice."

"Of course not. I can see how much her family means to you, and you've got such a sweet, kind-hearted face..." Brooke hugged the teddy bear to her chest and smiled.

"Let me get the wholesaler on the phone. Dan is the manager and he likes me. They shipped me a lot of limp roses last month, and he offered to give me a break on another delivery. It's time I took him up on that offer."

Brooke nodded politely. "I'll wait."

Yes, whenever there was a crisis afoot, people could work miracles. She'd have to remember that in the future.

While Luna disappeared, Brooke picked through the cards on display, eyeing the brightly colored planters, and sighing at the rose bouquet in the window. The roses were plastic, since real flowers would never last, but even plastic flowers were better than none.

Behind the glass counter, there was a trio of plants and flowers sitting in a box, waiting to be delivered, and Brooke decided that nobody would care if she poked through them to see who was getting what. Out of the corner of her eye she checked to make sure that the coast was clear and bent to look at the arrangements. Henry Hinkle was sending a bouquet of daisies to his wife for their anniversary. Brooke smiled and made a note to herself to stop by the grocery later and wish them well.

Apparently the librarian was in the hospital—Brooke would have to ask Gillian about that—although it probably wasn't serious because the pot of delicate flowers was topped with smiley-faced balloons, and who sent balloons if it was serious? No, serious was the somber little plant in the corner with the maroon satin bow. The wooden container was square and plain. Square and plain meant serious. One Valentine's Day, Brooke was temping at a florist's, mainly to get bus fare out of Cleveland, and she knew a little. No, the little plant didn't bode well for someone.

Carefully she opened the card.

Jason, I'm very sorry for your loss. Your Father was a very special man. Love, Sonya.

Jason? The Captain?
No....
Suddenly not caring so much about balloons and blooms, Brooke grabbed the delivery sheet and checked the last name to see if there was more than one Jason in Tin Cup, Texas, population two thousand one hundred and forty-seven.
Jason Kincaid.

Oh, God.

Brooke peeked into the back of the shop, but Luna was still on the phone.

The lilacs would have to wait.

12

JASON OPENED THE DOOR and found Brooke on his doorstep, sympathy in her eyes.

"I'm sorry."

"I'm fine," he answered, not inviting her in because he didn't need sympathy.

"Can I come in?"

"No. I'm not very good company."

"You were never good company." Then Ms. Brooke Hart, who only got pushy at the worst possible times, brushed past him to make her way inside.

Once there, she scanned the room, noting the stack of dishes in the sink, Dog unplugged in the corner, and the half finished bottle of Jack Daniels sitting next to a computer terminal. He didn't want her to see this, didn't want her to see him like this, but he wasn't completely blind, and unfortunately, neither was she.

Tired and hung over, he rubbed at his face, the stubble like a wire brush scratching his hands. He frowned, trying to remember when he'd last shaved.

Brooke came to stand in front of him, put a hand on his arm. "Captain."

"I was a Staff Sergeant. Not a captain."

Instead of arguing, she took his arm and led him out to the porch, the midmorning sun bright in his eyes.

"You look like hell," she stated, no sympathy in her voice at all. With more force than he deserved, she pushed him down on the polished red leather bench seat.

"I've missed you, too," he said, wishing for sunglasses, anything to block out the light, because his head felt as if it had been detonated—never a good sign.

"Do you have a headache?" she yelled, speaking louder than necessary.

"I'm not deaf."

"Do you need aspirin?" she bellowed into his ear.

He started to tell her to go away, but although Jason might be knuckle-headed about some things, he'd never been a liar. "Yes."

"Do you have aspirin?" she asked in a more humane voice now that she had broken his will.

"In the cabinet," he answered, and once again Brooke was leaving. When she returned, she held out two pills and a glass of water.

Not wanting to look too eager, Jason swallowed the pills and the water. Brooke sat next to him on the swing and waited quietly for the hammering in his head to stop.

Fifteen minutes had passed when Brooke reached for his hand, taking advantage of his weakened state. He let her.

Slowly the explosions in his head began to ease and the sun rose higher, losing its laser sights on him.

"Thank you," he told her.

"You could have called me."

No, he couldn't. Calling her implied that he needed her. Calling her implied that he had lain awake with a hole in his gut. No, calling her was out.

Cowardly avoiding that conversation, Jason stayed silent.

"Tell me about him," she asked.

"Not much to tell," he answered, because he didn't know how to talk about that, either.

"I never knew my father, and I'm not complaining because

I think it's a good thing I never met Frank Hart, but I like the idea of a father. Tell me about yours."

Her quiet words made him feel like an ass. On the life scale of bad things to happen to people, Brooke outranked him, but very few people would ever guess that. It was a humbling experience to be outmanned by a girl.

To make her happy he began to talk. He told her about the furniture that his father had built, the set of pirate-ship bunkbeds that he'd given Jason on his seventh birthday. Jason told her about his first car, a 1947 army jeep that he and his father had rebuilt. There were so many things to tell her, and the words tumbled out. About the three-bedroom house in Maryland, and the arguments he'd had when Sara hogged the bathroom. He told her about the model rockets he'd built with his father, specifically the Little John missile, the most powerful rocket ever engineered for hobby purposes, especially with the retrofitted nitrous-oxide boosters. Everything had been great until it scared the neighbor's cat and Mrs. Chapman threatened to call the police. Jason's father promised to patch the cracks in her dilapidated sidewalk if she wouldn't.

For a long time he talked and Brooke listened, soaking up his life like a sponge. It was late in the afternoon, when the sun was shimmering on the grass and the air was starting to cool, that his voice grew rusty from use.

"When's the funeral?" she asked.

"Day after tomorrow. They delayed it until the weekend so that David could fly in from California."

"You're not going, are you?"

He didn't like the way she said it, like there was something wrong with his decision.

"What's the point of a funeral? People are dead, they're dead."

"Did you ever think your family might need you?"

"No."

"You're making some very poor decisions that you're going

to regret for the rest of your life. You're too smart to be so stupid." Then she slipped her hand from his and stood. "I have to go. Gillian needs lilacs and the florist is going to close soon. You should fly to Maryland, Captain."

She'd never looked at him like that before, clear-eyed, not missing a thing.

Then she turned and left him again, and he noticed that she didn't hesitate this time and it hurt. Wanting to make her turn around, he called after her.

"I'm a Staff Sergeant, not a captain."

Brooke didn't turn around, didn't look at him. Instead she lifted her hand in an unladylike gesture that was beneath her.

It was nothing less than he deserved.

HIS BROTHER GREETED HIM on the doorstep, looking older, the coppery-brown hair thinned near the top. "I'm glad you came."

"It's family," Jason told him. "It's what you do."

Then his brother clasped him on the shoulder. "Sara's not taking this very well," he said, and Jason heard the crack in his voice because George had always been the soft one.

Jason nodded once, and George pulled him into a hug, and when Jason smelled the ghost of his father's aftershave, his eyes filled with tears, and silently the two brothers stood in the doorway and wept.

THE GROUND BREAKING for the train station was the third Thursday in October, and Jason hadn't meant to go, but he ended up doing his grocery shopping that day, and maybe he'd dressed a little nicer than usual to go grocery shopping, but he thought that as a citizen of the community, it made sense to show some civic pride.

The land had already been cleared, red construction flags tagging the perimeter. Off to the left side, two rows of chairs were set aside for dignitaries, and the Tin Cup High School band was playing Dr. Who.

Idly he scanned the crowd, looking for familiar faces until he found Brooke's. She was standing next to her brother, in the chic-chic skirt and blouse that he'd bought for her, and she looked exactly like he knew she would. The crowd was filled with overalls and jeans, but Brooke stood apart from the others, poised and polished, her dark hair twisted up in a bun. Finally she had come into her own, dumped the little-lost-Brooke look, because it was obvious even to a one-eyed man that she'd found her home at last.

The old mayor hobbled out first, rambling about cattle drives and whorehouses until Gillian interrupted his speech and brought JC Travis up to the stage. It was a smart move for the woman who had rescued the town, kicking off her campaign for governor here. She spoke of the future she envisioned, how they needed to look forward and be ready for a new town, a new state, a new world. Her words were full of inspiration and hope, and the crowd stayed stone-cold silent, lapping it up, because a small town needed to believe in itself. Then she and the mayor picked up their shovels and dug into the dirt. As actual work went, it didn't amount to much, but all around Jason, people whistled and cheered.

It was then that Brooke noticed him. She nodded warily and he nodded back, waiting for her to come to his side. Ten long minutes passed before he figured out that she wasn't going to come to him, and he told himself he should ditch the whole thing and go home. Then she met his eyes and his head started swimming, and he found himself walking over—just to say hello and to see how she was. It was a matter of civic pride.

"How are you?" she asked, poised and untouchable, even her freckles were hidden underneath her makeup, and Jason felt an irrational urge to wipe it all away.

But, no.

"I'm good," he answered, completely rational. "I went to the funeral," he added, surprised that he was telling her, but pleased with her smile.

"I'm glad."

"You were right," he added, because he owed her that.

"I know."

"How's things with your brother?"

She smiled up at Jason, looking not so untouchable, and he jammed his hands into his pockets. "He's a goofball. I didn't know that."

"A lot of men are. Don't hold it against him."

She giggled, an unrestrained gurgle of laughter and he realized how much he missed that sound.

"Are you still at the Inn?"

"For now. At the end of the year, I'm renting a room from Doc Emerson."

Jason frowned because she belonged in a real house, a real home. "The Doc's got a bad track record on maintenance. I overhauled his AC unit two years ago, and it was a wreck. You should have your own home."

"I'm saving up for my own place. Something small, and close to Austen and Gillian's new place. With room for a garden. I've always wanted a garden. And now I have a nest egg. I've never had a nest egg before. And maybe I'll have a bigger nest egg, we're not sure."

She was talking fast and when she caught on to what she was doing, he saw the flush on her face. Something sharp and painful squeezed in his chest because even in pencil skirt and heels, she was still the woman he loved.

"Why are you not sure?"

"We're leasing the mineral rights on the property, and the signing check is awfully sweet, but Austen negotiated an extra deal. He said the oil companies are all a bunch of sharks, and you have to be careful. So if the seismic tests go well, and it looks like we have oil underground, they'll kick in a bonus."

Once again something sharp and painful squeezed in his chest because she was going to get her nest egg. She was going to get her house. Her garden. Her life. And that was his signal to leave. Jason managed a tight smile. "Don't worry. I've got a good feeling about that. I bet you get everything you want."

TWO WEEKS LATER, Brooke's life had settled into a regular routine. Her days were spent at the courthouse, at night she went over to help Gillian with the wedding preparations, and then finally, when exhaustion set in, she would drive to the Inn and fall into bed, hoping for a long, peaceful sleep.

The sleep was long in coming, and sometimes it was peaceful with the most marvelous dreams where the Captain was dreaming next to her. On those mornings, she woke up with a smile on her face—until she realized she was alone. It was at that moment that she plastered a smile on her face, opened the curtains, took a hot shower and told herself that everything would be fine.

When she walked into the courthouse, Mindy and Gillian were waiting for her. Mindy had her car keys in hand, sunglasses on her head, and Gillian was holding up *People* magazine and waving an envelope.

"I'm pleased to report that no longer will they say that your check is in the mail. Mr. Hadley dropped this off a half hour ago."

"What is this?"

"Bonus check. Gotta love the oil business."

Slowly Brooke pulled the check out of the envelope and gazed in awe, counting and recounting the zeroes in case there had been a mistake. No mistake.

"Come on. We're headed to the Canyon Lake spa for a little R&R. We deserve it. And as you can now afford it, and as my almost-sister, you get to come along and listen to me fret. They serve wine with the mud baths, so that'll dull the sound of my whining. I promise."

"I have to work," Brooke began, because she had heard of these things called spas, but she'd never seen one, been at one, and… She glanced down at the check in her hands.

"Darling, one thing you have got to learn if you want to fit in here—and you do want to fit in, don't you?"

Mindy bobbed her head. "Of course she does."

Gillian took Brooke's arm and began leading her out the door. "You have to learn to relax and have fun, let down your hair a little."

"Speaking of hair, can I get a cut? Junior's started pulling mine, and that kid has got some power in his grip. Takes after his daddy, I think."

Gillian looked at Brooke, pushed her sunglasses low on her nose. "What do you say?"

Once again Brooke looked at the check. This was real. "Oh, my God. I'm in."

BROOKE HAD NEVER BEEN wrapped in mud before. She'd never worn cucumbers on her eyes. She'd never had her hair blown out and, most of all, she'd never looked so gorgeous...and the Captain would never see.

They were riding in Mindy's car, hitting the interstate and heading for home. Mindy and Gillian were in the front seat chattering about the wedding until Gillian noticed that Brooke wasn't saying much at all. "For a woman who's just been manicured and fluffed, you're looking mighty sad. If you're going to be sad, I have failed in my duty as a positive influence."

Mindy snickered. "You are no one's positive influence, Gillian. You just like to think that."

"Hush up, former BFF. Don't disillusion the girl before she's gotten a chance to love my good side."

"It's been a lot of fun," Brooke said, because it had been fun, until it hadn't.

"Then why are we not smiling?"

"I don't know."

"She's just got a case of the sads, Gillian. Let her be."

"Is that all?" Gillian asked, lifting her sunglasses and studying Brooke's face.

Brooke nodded, but Gillian didn't seem convinced. "Things will get better. I promise. Make some new friends. Hey, you show up at Smitty's looking like that and it'll start a riot."

"That would be nice," Brooke told her, with absolutely no enthusiasm.

"You've got some hurts that need healing?"

Brooke shook her head because Gillian had enough to worry about.

Gillian reached over to the backseat and patted her knee, an encouraging smile on her face. "Don't worry, honey. It'll go away."

"You're sure?" asked Brooke.

"Depends on how bad you got it," Mindy added, glancing over her shoulder. "A woman can crush on a guy or lust for a guy, and that sort of hurt, that goes away. Sure, it smacks on the ego, but eventually it disappears."

Brooke wasn't sure that it would disappear. There wasn't another man in the world with a heart like the Captain's, and there was no other heart that she wanted more.

Noticing Brooke's doubtful expression, Gillian's perky smiled faded. "It's the real stuff that hangs on and stings like a mother. Shopping and wine, they'll make you feel better, but then the ship sinks and you're floating alone on a piece of ice in the ocean, and all around you, everybody else has found a lifeboat, but not you, no, you're in the water, freezing and dying, and somewhere in the distance, Celine Dion starts to sing. That, my friend, is the misery of love."

IT WAS DARK WHEN Mindy's car whizzed passed the Welcome to Tin Cup, Texas, sign and Brooke felt as warm and well pampered as a hand-rolled limp noodle. Her skin had never glowed like a pearl, her hair had never been so glossy and thick and the sleek black designer dress that she'd bought made her look like a million dollars. She'd never paid that much money for a dress before, but Gillian had told her that she needed to splurge every now and then, and Brooke had talked the price down another twenty percent because the prices were highway robbery. In the end, Brooke had waltzed out of the store, turning heads as she passed.

This was a new experience, feeling as if she'd been reborn. Brooke didn't usually like inviting male attention because it never ended well, but this was her new life, her new future, Gillian and Mindy encouraging her every high-heeled step of the way. All evening Brooke had watched and learned, and by the time the dinner at the fancy Austin restaurant was done, the waiter was eating out of Brooke's hand, too.

It was a shame to waste all that effort on Delores at the Spotlight Inn, so after Gillian dropped her off, Brooke climbed into the beat-up Impala. For a second she hesitated, until she examined her own reflection in the mirror, the confident smile, the million-dollar hair. She shook out her expensive do and decided that there was no better time to show up at the Captain's door and show him who Brooke Hart really was.

He greeted her at the door, and she was pleased to see the flash of heat in his gaze. "You look nice."

"Thank you. Gillian and Mindy took me to Austin for a day of beauty, and I wanted to show off. Can I come in?"

The heat dimmed, but he nodded and stepped aside.

The front room looked a lot better this time. The dishes were put away, Dog was idling in the corner, and there was a bowl of fruit on the kitchen table.

"I like the hair."

She made a great show of swishing it around, just like in the shampoo commercials. "It's great. They put a special treatment on it, I thought it felt like grease, but it smelled a whole lot better. And here," she said, stepping close and holding up a strand. "You should feel."

The Captain took the strand, and dropped it as if it burned. "Nice."

"Do you mind if I sit down?" she asked, and before he could

answer, she seated herself on the couch, legs crossed oh-so-se-ductively so that he could notice that the skin of her legs was as smooth and buffed as the rest of her.

His good eye rested on her legs and then rose up to her face and, sadly, he knew exactly what she was doing. Brooke crossed her arms over her chest, not defensively, not at all.

"Make yourself at home," he offered, taking the chair opposite her and she studied him, noticing the changes. He was shaving, a tiny nick under his scar, and his hair had been cut. Some of the scruffiness was gone, and she realized that she wasn't the only one who had gotten some polish.

"What are you working on now?" she asked, a poor attempt at conversation because, despite her newfound confidence, her man-handling skills weren't nearly as good as she needed them to be.

"Automatic garage-door monitor for Ernestine Landry. She forgets and leaves the door up at night. I put up a signal in her bedroom. Green is shut. Red is up."

"I'm glad you're getting out more."

"Not that much."

"Still." She picked up the decorative throw pillow on the sofa and smiled. "It's nice. The place looks…friendlier."

"Thank you."

She sat there for a few more minutes, acknowledging that her man-handling skills were crap, and finally she rose and smoothed the dress's tight skirt over her thighs. "I should go."

He didn't argue with her and showed her to the door, but then Brooke faced him because she'd never felt so mouth-wateringly gorgeous, so ready to live a grand life. He wasn't supposed to be able to ignore her. Not the Captain.

Like always, she reached up and pressed a kiss on his cheek, and then his arms were around her, and he was kissing her urgently. With a laugh, she tangled her hands in his hair, hearing a low hungry growl in this throat. His hands slid under her dress, tugging the material up because it had been too long, and tonight she wanted him to fill her.

Like always, her legs parted, and she didn't think he noticed that she was smooth and buffed. Like always, his hands gripped her, cupping her to him and she smiled against his lips, her thighs cradling his heavy cock, feeling a surge of desire filling her sex, a surge of emotion filling her heart. For Brooke, this was home. He was the only home she had.

She raised her head, opened her eyes, and her fingers moved to the buttons down the front of her dress. "I want to do this for you."

The Captain stepped back, his breathing ragged, his erection straining against his jeans, his face flushed with everything he wouldn't admit, but it was the steady look in his eye that defeated her. It didn't matter how pretty she was, or how buffed she was, or how much he wanted her. For the Captain, it would never be enough.

"Brooke," he began and quickly she shook her head.

"No. This is no more than what was always between us," she promised. She slid the top buttons open, revealing the satin bra beneath. "I bought it for you. I wanted to see your face when I showed it to you."

It wasn't lust on his face, but caution.

"Don't do this," he warned, but she didn't listen, because she didn't want to listen. She wanted the sparks and the fire and all those things that normal people were supposed to have. She wanted his mouth on hers, she wanted to feel him hard between her thighs. What the hell was wrong with that?

She made a move to slide off her bra, but he stopped her with strong hands, unshakable hands.

"Stop. You have no idea how beautiful you are. How perfect you look in silk and pearls."

She could hear the pain in his voice, but it didn't matter. Not when he was throwing her away. Not when he was throwing them away. "I did it for you," she pleaded.

"No. You did this for you. You need to know who you are, what you're capable of. You have a shot, Brooke. Don't waste it on me."

"Waste it?" she said, her voice loud in the quiet room. "This is right. We are right. I love you, Captain."

"Jason. My name is Jason. You should learn it. You should use it."

Why couldn't he see? "You don't understand. You will always be a captain to me. My Captain."

Sadly he shook his head. "You just started getting your training wheels, Brooke. You're finally where you want to be. Live that life. You deserve that life."

"I deserve more. The bravest. The most noble, the most honorable. The best of them all."

"Then go find him."

They weren't the words that she'd dreamed of, and in that instant she hated the expensive bra and the smooth, buffed skin and everything that she had done. She wanted to hurt him, wanted to throw the words back in his face, but instead she pulled down her black skirt, buttoned up the luxurious silk of her dress and turned to him because she would not lie. No more lies. He'd taught her that. He thought she needed to search for the best and the bravest?

She looked at him, eyes filled with tears, her voice filled with anger.

"He's already here."

JASON STOOD IN THE DOORWAY for a long, long time thinking that she'd come back, but eventually the darkness swallowed her up and he could hear the fading sound of the rattling cylinders of her engine and he knew she wasn't coming back.

He closed the door, turned out the lights, and Dog whirled next to him, bright LED eyes that never saw, never felt, never loved. It was the cold comfort that he'd always craved.

For the first time, though, cold comfort wasn't enough.

13

FORTUNATELY FOR BROOKE, the days before the wedding passed quickly. During the days, she would work at the courthouse, and at night she stayed at Gillian's house until late, doing whatever was necessary to make sure that her future sister-in-law stayed sane. Brooke had never imagined the stress involved in planning a wedding, and each day she watched Gillian decline into what Austen termed "Bridezilla."

Sometimes Austen and Gillian would go for a drive, and Brooke would stay behind with Gillian's parents, doing what she could to help, and puzzling over the odd dynamics of this family thing.

It wasn't exactly what she expected. There were arguments and times that she'd rush off to her room at the Inn, soaking in the tiny bathtub, crying at the late-night movies on TV. Sometimes it didn't matter if the movie was sad or not. Sometimes she just cried.

She didn't see the Captain in town, not that she thought she would, but sometimes she would sit in Dot's diner for breakfast and hear someone mention his name.

On the Tuesday before the wedding, Tyler and Edie arrived. Tyler was quiet and somber, choosing to sit back and listen, letting Austen or Edie dominate the conversation. Sometimes he would peer at Brooke curiously, and she wasn't sure if he approved of her or not.

Friday night, before he and Austen took off for a bachelor party, which Gillian insisted that she didn't want to know anything about, Brooke gathered her courage and decided to approach Tyler just like a sister would, which basically meant cornering him in the kitchen before he could run.

"You look like her," she told him. "You have her nose."

He stared impassively. "I never noticed."

"She was passed out a lot. I studied her a lot."

"I'm sorry."

"Don't be," she told him. In many ways it had been worse for them. Sometimes unconscious and passed out was better. "I like Austen."

"He's easy to like," Tyler stated, his voice flat and calm. Maybe it was the doctor thing, or maybe he just didn't like her.

Brooke tried again. "The day in the lawyer's office. You really got to him. He wasn't expecting that."

At last, success. Tyler's mouth slowly drew up in a smile. "Good."

"I haven't had a lot of practice with this."

"What?"

"Families. I might say something weird, or do the wrong thing, but it's only because I don't know exactly what to do. I might make a lot of mistakes, but don't give up on me. You and Austen are all I have."

He looked surprised and almost pleased, but before he could say anything, Austen grabbed him by the arm, pushing a cowboy hat on Tyler's head. "There. Now you look like a fake Texan. People will buy you extra shots, just for the hat alone."

Tyler was eyeing his brother, but Brooke knew that his words were for her. "I'm in for the long haul, whatever it takes."

IT WAS FIVE DAYS BEFORE the wedding, past 1:00 a.m., and Gillian was in her living room, stuffing candy hearts into red velvet pouches.

"Candy hearts?'" asked Austen, coming to sit next to her, and thankfully, not snickering too loud.

"I saw it in *Modern Bride*," she explained, which she liked as an answer because people only nodded, as if no more words were required.

"You can't sleep?" asked her future husband, guessing correctly because he saw more than most.

She shoved the piles of pouches aside and threw herself into his arms. "Nerves. Sexual frustration. I think I've had too much caffeine."

"I can solve one of those problems."

She drew back, drawing strength from the easy confidence in his eyes. "I want it to be perfect."

"I thought it was always perfect," he teased.

"The wedding, not the sex."

"Okay. I can live with that."

She glared at him, signaling that this was important.

"The wedding's going to be perfect," he assured her.

She picked up a candy heart and popped it in her mouth, until she remembered that she hadn't run today and she couldn't afford the calories. "I'm worried."

"We could always elope," he said as he pulled her into his arms, squeezing tight, and she stayed there a moment, temporarily considering the idea. "It's going to be great," he promised.

"It's Jason."

"Kincaid? Why are we talking about Jason Kincaid?" he asked, his hand gently stroking her hair.

"He has to be at the wedding. She loves him. He loves her, but he's being very stubborn."

His hand stilled. "Who loves him?"

"Your sister. Can't you tell?"

"Most likely you're just so much in love that you're seeing it everywhere."

"Don't be a tool," she warned, because after four cups of coffee, teasing would not be tolerated.

"Only your tool, darling. Only yours."

She lifted her head, giving him the full force of the Gillian Wanamaker gaze. "You'll get him there?"

"I'm no miracle worker." He looked doubtful, and it tugged at her heart that he still didn't know how many miracles he'd performed.

Gently she kissed him, feeling the same jump in her pulse as though she were sixteen all over again. "You keep telling me that like I'm supposed to believe it. Stop being silly, sweetheart, and make me forget all this."

He pushed her down on the couch, quiet, so as not to wake anyone else, and he kissed her like they were sixteen all over again and nothing else existed.

"Soon, Gillian Wanamaker. Very soon, and then you're all mine," he whispered.

"Stop being silly, sweetheart. I was yours all along."

BROOKE HAD BEEN TO exactly two weddings in her life. Jessica Price's, who had been Dr. Knox's cleaning lady at the chiropractic office, and there was the New Year's Eve in Chicago when she had been paid thirty dollars to be part of the well-wishers at a civil ceremony. Yet, in spite of her less than ideal experiences, Brooke still possessed those girly dreams of huge bouquets of flowers and pink-pearled ribbons and long white dresses. It was completely unsurprising that Gillian had those same girly dreams, as well.

The morning of Gillian and Austen's wedding, the chapel had been transformed into the culmination of Gillian's dreams. The room smelled of lilacs and magic and happily-ever-afters. For one quiet minute, Brooke stood alone in the church, waiting for the magic to seep into her soul. There were always dreams to be found, but now she knew that sometimes dreams lurked in unexpected places. Sometimes magic could be found locked behind black metal gates, hidden among old lumber and engines. Sometimes dreams could be buried behind a black eyepatch and a scarred profile, because those places—the places where hearts feared to tread—hid the most fragile of dreams.

She wrapped her arms around herself, holding those fragile dreams inside her. Gillian would have her magical day, and Brooke was happy for her, and today, of all days, she was going to laugh and sigh and be the perfect wedding guest because this was her family now. This was her life.

Back in the bridal room, Modine Wanamaker was fussing with Gillian's hair, and Mindy had her camera, recording the day for posterity. In the corner stood the flower girl, Carmelita Ruiz's daughter, who was sucking her thumb, eyes large with wonder, because all girls dreamed of huge bouquets of flowers and pink-pearled ribbons.

As for the bride, Gillian looked panicked, and Brooke knew just what to say. "The pianist is already here, all the music is accounted for. The flowers are set up—including the lilacs—the cakes and the food are being put out in the reception hall. The photographer has been here for three hours. Austen and Tyler are in the back, fully dressed, but the groom looks appropriately pale. The preacher isn't here yet, but he had his hospital visits this afternoon, so he's not expected for another half-hour, and you look like a dream."

The panic on Gillian's face disappeared, replaced by the normal resolve. "Wow. I didn't realize how close I was to actually throwing up. This is better. This is good." She flashed Brooke a grateful smile. "You know, I'm glad that Austen had a long-lost sister instead of a long-lost brother, because right now, I need all the support I can get."

Impulsively Brooke hugged her, and then Gillian whispered in her ear. "Someday we'll do this for you, little sister. Just you wait."

JASON PLANTED HIMSELF in a secluded corner outside the church, pacing back and forth, watching the people enter through the wooden doors, people who had no strong fears of entering a church or dressing in a suit or mingling among the masses. Max would be laughing at him now, telling him that a soldier feared nothing. Since Max had feared nothing and gotten blown up in the process, it probably wasn't the best advice.

However, Brooke Hart was inside that church, and if Jason wanted her, if he wanted a real life, it was time to give up the fears, and hopefully not get blown up in the process.

He could hear the ghost of Max's laughter, he could see the familiar face of his father, and Jason looked up to the blue, blue sky, felt the warmth of the sun on his skin and then put a hand on the door, wincing at the loud, creaking sound.

Bring the heat, bring the stupid. It was the Army way.

BROOKE KNEW THE SECOND he walked in the church. From her spot in the second pew, she couldn't see him, but she heard the creak of the door. All eyes were on the bride and groom, who were exchanging their vows.

All eyes except for one. Her skin tingled with awareness, and the air crackled with the magic that had been missing before. Brooke's mouth curved into a contented smile because in a world of love songs and poetic vows, Brooke believed that it was the smallest steps that meant the most.

THE RECEPTION HALL was filled with people dancing, along the walls buffet tables were laden with food and Brooke waited patiently for the Captain to appear.

It didn't take long. He presented himself in front of her, handsome in a black suit which made his eye patch and scar seem dashing.

"May I have this dance?" he asked, waiting until she nodded, before sweeping her into his arms. A smaltzy love song played over the speakers, but Brooke thought it was perfect.

"I like your suit. Is it new?"

"I bought it for you." Such simple words, but the look in his gaze was anything but. She told herself not to get carried away though his words and the dance were all too much, so she burrowed her head on his shoulder, admitting it was a lot nicer than his pillow, which she'd accidentally stolen.

"It was a lovely ceremony. I cried at the end." She unburrowed her head, and looked up at him. "Why didn't you tell me the lawyer called? Mr. Hadley said he spoke to you."

The Captain murmured something uncomplimentary about Mr. Hadley. "I didn't want you to leave. I knew you would, but I didn't want it."

"I would have stayed if you had asked."

"I know, but it wouldn't have been right. You depended on me too much, and I wasn't comfortable with that."

"I will always depend on you. I'm sorry."

"I love you."

"I know." She looked around, and noticed the attention they were getting. For once she didn't mind. "They're staring."

"It's a good thing I'm half blind," he told her, his mouth in a nervous smile, then turning down in a frown. "Brooke, they're staring because I'm the Boo Radley of this town. All my own doing, I fully admit that, but you can't do this. I'm the guy who scavenges the junkyards and the scrap yard, picking up the things that everyone threw out."

She reached up to sooth the frown, and made a silent vow to make him happy because he deserved to be happy. Every day he thought nothing of all the things that he did, all the people that he helped, but in this, Brooke knew that the world depended on the Captain, just as she did.

"I spent my life living in the trash, but you were the first person who ever pulled me out and dusted me off and treated me with respect. I never understood how important that is. Loving me for me. It's not something I'm ever going to forget, and it's why I love you, and why I will always love you. No one else in the world can ever do that for me."

Right then, the song changed and Celine Dion came on, and the dancing slowed and Brooke locked her arms around his neck and kissed him. It was a long and forever kind of kiss, a floating-on-the-ice kiss, and she knew that everyone was staring and she didn't care.

Finally, at long last, Brooke Hart was home.

Epilogue

IT WAS BROOKE'S first Thanksgiving with her family. Gillian and her mother had been baking for three solid days, and there was enough food to feed the masses, but even with all that, Thanksgiving morning had Gillian going on about the giblets, making everyone nervous in the process.

Edie and Tyler had flown down, and Edie was debating with Gillian's mother about the proper way to mash potatoes. Brooke offered to help, but in the end, it was easier to stand alongside the counter and watch everyone yell and argue with a dreamy look on her face. This.

This.

Jason came to stand next to her, a Washington Redskins cap in his hand. "You look like it's Christmas in November."

"It's great, isn't it?"

"It is."

She reached up and touched his scar, then his mouth, watching the warm gray gaze grow hot. She felt the heat slide down her spine, contentment settling firmly in her heart.

"What are my brothers doing?" She used the words a lot. My brother this. My brother that, and Jason never laughed at her, which she appreciated.

"Don't make me break a promise," he warned.

At that point, Gillian looked up from her stirring, spied Jason, and flashed him an angelic smile. "Jason, darling, can you go find Austen and drag him in here? There's some placemats in the buffet with needlepoint turkeys, and I've got my hands full with the giblets right now."

Brooke smirked. "You're going to have to break that promise."

ALARMED, JASON LOOKED at his one true love and mouthed, "Needlepoint turkeys?" But she only smiled.

Sadly realizing he had no choice in the matter, Jason approached the living room, which he had privately termed the DMZ. Austen and Tyler were gone, as was Emmett Wanamaker, and at that point, Jason considered his task complete. But then he sighed because Brooke had high expectations for this family dinner, and while he thought turkey placemats were slightly demeaning, he knew that Brooke was loving it all, and it made all the hell worth it.

Almost all the hell worth it.

Hell, yeah, it was worth it.

He found them outside, four folding chairs huddled around a tiny black and white TV, watching football. Cowboys and Redskins.

Now that was Thanksgiving.

"Who's winning?" Jason asked, watching as the Cowboy quarterback threw an interception right into the arms of the Skins receiver.

"Skins up by seven," Austen answered.

Jason shrugged innocently. "Don't blame me because your boys are playing like girls."

Emmett Wanamaker glared, but Jason glared back, and frankly, very few people could outglare a one-eyed man. Naturally, Emmett caved. "Gillian wants you to find placemats," he told Austen, doing what he'd promised. "They're in the buffet. Somewhere."

Austen looked at his father-in-law for help. "What placemats?"

Emmett's eyes were fixed on the screen, watching as the Redskins lined up on the Cowboys' seven. "Damned needle-point turkeys. They're going to be accidentally destroyed in a fire someday, mark my words."

"Talk to Austen then," Tyler said with a laugh. "He's great at accidentally setting fires."

Austen shoved his brother in the ribs, and then the Redskins scored and Jason let out an all-American hoo-yah. He could just imagine his own family celebrating the same moment.

It was twenty minutes later when Brooke found him there, having pulled up another chair, as she leaned over his back she pressed a small kiss against his ear.

"Happy Thanksgiving," she whispered.

Jason smiled at her, counting her freckles, counting his blessings, and decided that this family thing was a fine thing after all.

* * * * *

Keep reading for an excerpt of
It Started With A Royal Kiss
by Jennifer Faye.
Find it in the
Greek Paradise Escape anthology,
out now!

CHAPTER ONE

A PRINCE.

A genuine, sexy-as-all-get-out royal prince.

Indigo Castellanos swallowed hard. She couldn't believe she'd come face-to-face with Prince Istvan of Rydiania. She didn't want to be impressed—not at all—but she couldn't deny being a little bit awed by his mesmerizing blue eyes and tanned face. Just the memory of his shirtless body sent her traitorous heart racing.

She never in a million years thought they'd actually meet. When she'd taken this artist position at the Ludus Resort, she'd known the prince had ties to the private island. Still, it was a large resort—big enough to avoid certain people. Sure, the royal regatta was going on, but she'd mistakenly thought the prince would be too busy to attend. And if he did make an appearance, he wouldn't meander around the resort like some commoner.

And then, when she did meet him, she hadn't said a word. If staring into his bottomless eyes hadn't been bad enough, she'd been stunned into silence by his muscled chest and trim waist.

She gave herself a mental shake. None of that mattered. Not at all.

Nothing changed the fact that the prince came from the same family that had cast her father out of his homeland. But she didn't have time to think of that now. Besides, she didn't expect to see the prince again.

She perched on a stool beneath a great big red umbrella. Her bare, painted toes wiggled in the warm sand. She was so thankful for this job. It helped her care for her ailing mother. And she would do anything for her mother.

"Is she sitting in the right position?"

The woman's voice drew Indigo from her thoughts. She focused on the mother and young daughter in front of her. The girl was seated on a stool. "Um, yes. Why?"

"Because you were frowning." The mother didn't look happy.

"So sorry. Your daughter is just perfect." Indigo forced a reassuring smile to her lips. "The glare off the water is making it hard to see."

Indigo shifted her position on the stool. She couldn't afford to have her clients think she wasn't happy or they wouldn't continue to bring their children and family members to have her draw caricatures of them. And without the clients there would be no job—without a job, she wouldn't be able to pay the mounting medical bills.

She forced herself to concentrate on her work. Her art was what had gotten her through the tough times in her life, from her father's sudden death to her mother's collapse. Whereas some people lived charmed lives—Prince Istvan's handsome image came to mind—other people were not so fortunate. She didn't let the challenges stop her from striving for something better—from believing if she just kept trying, good things were awaiting her.

Minutes later, she finished the young girl's caricature and gently unclipped the paper from her easel. She handed it over to the mother, who didn't smile as she examined Indigo's work. She then held it out to her nine-year-old daughter and asked her opinion. The girl's eyes widened as a big smile puffed up her cheeks. And that was all Indigo needed to make her day. After all, it was as her father used to say: *it's the small things in life where you find the greatest reward.*

"Wait until I show my friends."

"Now what do you say?" the mother prompted.

The girl turned her attention to Indigo. "Thank you."

"You're welcome." In that moment, it didn't matter that Indigo was doing fun sketches instead of grand works of art. The only thing that mattered was that she'd brought some happiness to this girl's life.

"May I see it?" a male voice asked.

Indigo turned her head, and once again, she was caught off guard by the handsome prince. Her heart started to pitter-patter as she stared at him. What were the chances of them accidentally running into each other again?

"Oh." The mother's hand flew to her chest. "Your Highness." The woman did a deep curtsy.

The young girl's eyes filled with confusion as her gaze moved between her mother and Prince Istvan. Then her mother gestured for her to do the same thing. While the girl did a semi curtsy, Indigo sat by and took in the scene.

Was the prince here to see the mother? Did they have some sort of business together? Because there was absolutely no way he was there to see her. Not a chance. The royals and the Castellanos no longer intermingled—by royal decree. The reminder set Indigo's back teeth grinding together.

The prince turned in her direction. His eyes widened in surprise. Was it because he wasn't expecting to run into her again so soon? Or was it that she wasn't falling all over herself in front of him doing a curtsy? She refused to bow to him.

She should say something, but her mouth had gone dry. Words lodged in the back of her throat. And her heart was beating out of control. What was wrong with her?

The prince turned his attention back to the drawing. "It's fabulous. And who would the pretty young woman in the drawing be?"

"That's me," the girl said proudly.

The prince made a big deal of holding the sketch up next to the young girl, and then his dark brows drew together as his gaze moved between her and the drawing. "So it is. You're lucky to have such a lovely sketch." He returned the paper to the girl. "Enjoy your day."

The mother and daughter curtsied again. Then the mother reached in her bright orange-and-white beach bag. She withdrew her phone. With the consent of the prince, she took a selfie with him. Though the prince smiled for the picture, Indigo noticed how the smile did not go the whole way to his blue eyes.

After the woman repeatedly thanked him, she turned to Indigo. "How much do I owe you?"

"Nothing," Indigo said. "It's a courtesy of the resort."

"Oh." She dropped her phone in her bag. "Thank you." And then her attention returned to the prince. She curtsied again.

Indigo wondered if she'd looked that ridiculous the other day when she'd first met the prince. She hoped not. But she had been totally caught off guard.

She expected him to move on, but he didn't. His attention turned to her. "And so we meet again."

She swallowed hard. "Your Highness."

Quite honestly, she didn't know what to say to him. He certainly didn't want to hear anything she had to say about him or his family—about how they were cold and uncaring about whom they hurt in the name of the crown. No, it was best not to go there. She didn't think her boss would approve of her vocalizing her true feelings about the prince's family.

She glanced down at the blank page in front of her. She could feel the prince's gaze upon her. What was he thinking? Did he recognize her?

Impossible. She'd only been a very young child when her family had fled Rydiania. Back then she'd been scared and confused. She'd had no idea why they were leaving their home and everything they'd ever known to move to Greece—a land that she'd never visited, filled with people she did not know.

"Shall I sit here?" The prince's deep voice drew her from her troubled thoughts.

"If you like." In an effort not to stare at his tanned chest, she barely glanced at him. Though it was a huge temptation. Very tempting indeed. Instead she fussed over the blank sheet of paper on her easel, pretending to straighten it.

What did he want? Surely he wasn't going to take the time to flirt with her when she had no standing in his regal world. So if he wasn't there to flirt with her, why was he lingering?

Curiosity got the best of her. "Is there something I can do for you?"

He smiled at her, but the happiness didn't show in his eyes. It was though there was something nagging at him that he didn't want to share with her. She wondered what could weigh so heavily on a prince's mind.

"I would like you to draw me."

Her gaze lifted just in time to witness him crossing his arms over that perfectly sculpted chest. *Oh, my!* The breath stilled in her chest as she continued to drink in the sight of his tanned and toned body. She wondered if he spent all his free time in the gym. Because there was no way anyone looked as good as him without working at it.

Her attention slipped down over the corded muscles of his arms and landed on his six-pack abs. It wasn't until her gaze reached the waistband of his blue-and-white board shorts that she realized she shouldn't be staring.

"Will that be a problem?" His voice drew her attention back to his face.

This time when she stared into his eyes, she noticed a hint of amusement twinkling in his eyes. She'd been totally busted staring at him. Heat started in her chest and worked its way up her neck. What was she doing, checking out the enemy?

Just keep it together. You need to keep this job.

Her little pep talk calmed her down just a bit. She drew in a deep breath and slowly released it. "Surely you have better things to do—erm, more important things than to have me sketch you."

She couldn't believe she was brushing off an opportunity to sketch a prince. If her friends could see her now they'd probably rush her to the hospital, certain she'd lost her grip on reality. But Istvan wasn't just any prince.

"I'm right where I want to be. Go ahead. Draw me."

Indigo hesitated. If he was anyone else but a member of the Rydianian royal family, she'd have jumped at the opportunity.

She'd grown up hearing stories of how the royal family wasn't to be trusted—that they put the crown above all else, including love of family. Her father was never the same after the former king, Georgios, and those in service to him were cast out of the kingdom. How could they do something so heartless?

"Is there a problem?" The prince's gaze studied her.

Unless she wanted to reveal the truth and put her new position at the Ludus Resort in jeopardy, she'd best get on with her job. She just had to pretend he was like any other guest at the resort, but she feared she wasn't that good of an actress.

She swallowed hard. "I don't think my sketch would do you justice."

He arched a brow. "Are you refusing to draw me?"

She thought about it. How many times had this prince been denied something he wanted? She doubted it ever happened. Oh, how she'd like to be the first to do it. But even she wasn't that reckless.

"No." She grabbed her black brush pen. Then her gaze rose to meet his. "I just want you to understand that it won't be a conservative, traditional portrait."

"I understand. And I don't want it to be. Just pretend I'm any other patron." He settled himself on the stool while his security staff fanned out around him.

He was most definitely not just any other person—not even

close. And yet he didn't have a clue who she was or how his family had destroyed hers. She thought of telling him, but what would that accomplish?

As she lifted her hand to the page, she noticed its slight tremor. She told herself she could do this. After all, the sooner she finished the sketch, the sooner the prince would move on. And so she pressed the brush pen to the paper and set to work.

It was impossible to do her job without looking at him. Her fingers tingled with the temptation to reach out to the dark, loose curls scattered over the top of his head. The sides and back of his head were clipped short. His tanned face had an aristocratic look, with a straight nose that wasn't too big nor too small. Dark brows highlighted his intense blue eyes with dark lashes. And a close-trimmed mustache and goatee framed his kissable lips.

In order to do her job, she had to take in every tiny detail of the person in front of her and translate them onto paper. And normally that wasn't hard for her. But sketching the prince was going to be the biggest challenge of her career as her heart raced and her fingers refused to cooperate.

She glanced around at the finely dressed men with hulking biceps and dark sunglasses. They were facing away from Istvan and Indigo, as though they were giving them some privacy while protecting them from the rest of the world.

"Don't worry about them," Prince Istvan said as though he could read her thoughts. "They're here to make sure there are no unwanted disturbances."

Indigo kept moving the black brush pen over the page. On second thought, the prince was really a pleasure to sketch with his strong jawline and firm chin. And then there was the dimple in his left cheek. Under any other circumstances, she'd readily admit that he was the most handsome man she'd ever sketched. But she refused to acknowledge such a thing—not about a member of the Rydianian royal family.

Prince Istvan might not have had anything to do with her

father's dismissal from his lifelong service to the royal family or his subsequent banishment from the country, but that didn't mean Istvan wasn't one of them—raised to be like the uncaring, unfeeling royals who had destroyed her family.

"Does it take you long to do a sketch?" His smooth, rich voice interrupted her thoughts.

"No."

"How long does it usually take?"

She wasn't sure what to make of him going out of his way to make small talk. "Five to ten minutes. It all depends on how much detail work I do."

"That's amazing. It would take me twice as long to draw a stick figure." He sent her a friendly smile that made his baby blues twinkle.

She ignored the way her stomach dipped as she returned her focus to the drawing. Why did he have to be the prince from Rydiania? Why couldn't he just be a random guest at the resort?

She smothered a sigh and focused on her work. She took pleasure in the fact that she didn't have to do a true sketch of the prince. Her job was to exaggerate certain characteristics. She chose to elongate his chin and emphasize his perfectly straight white front teeth. His hair was perfectly styled, as though not a strand would dare defy the prince. She would fix that by drawing his hair a bit longer and messier. And then she took some creative liberty and added a crown that was falling off to the side of his head. A little smile pulled at the corner of her lips. It definitely wasn't the image of a proper prince.

The man on the page was more approachable. He didn't take himself too seriously. And this prince wouldn't endorse the demise of innocent and loyal subjects. If only fiction was reality.

With the outline complete, she started to fill in the sketch with a bit of color. When she first took this job at the resort, she'd considered just doing black-and-white sketches, but she was partial to colors. And it didn't take her much more time.

When she focused on the prince's blue eyes, she had a problem combining the blues to get that intense color. Maybe she should have just done a plain light blue color like she would have done for any other person. But it was though his eyes held a challenge for her. How could she resist?

When she glanced at him, it was though he could see straight through her. She wondered what he thought when he looked at her. But then again, he was a royal, so he probably didn't even see her—not really. He most likely saw nothing more than someone who was there to serve him.

Indigo switched up color after color. Her hand moved rapidly over the paper. He became distracted with his phone. With his attention elsewhere, it was easier for her to finish her task.

"I see you've decided to get a caricature done," a female voice said.

Indigo paused to glance over her shoulder to find her boss approaching them. Hermione wore a warm smile. Indigo wondered if Hermione had a secret crush on the prince. It wouldn't be hard to imagine her with him.

But then again, Hermione was now sporting a large, sparkly diamond ring. And her fiancé was almost as handsome as the prince. Hermione and the prince made chitchat while Indigo continued to add more details to the sketch. At one point, she leaned back to take in the partial image. Her discerning gaze swept down over the page. She surprised herself. There wasn't one negative aspect of the sketch. How could that be?

No imperfection that had been exaggerated. No big front teeth sticking out. No bulbous nose. No pointy chin. Nothing but his hotness exaggerated on the page into a cute caricature. And the crown she'd added to make him look like a carefree prince—well, even that didn't look like a negative. In fact, it just upped his cute factor.

As Hermione moved on, Indigo was still puzzling over the image that lacked any of her normal exaggerations. Was this really how she saw him? Like some fun, easygoing and kind royal?

Obviously not. He was heir to the throne. He would do things just as they had been done before—stepping on loved ones and family for the good of the crown.